> "But grand conspiracies *do* happen, don't they?
> They're not *never* true . . ."

When her daughter, Lotte, was born, Dani had welcomed the chance to be a stay-at-home mother. To be good at something, for once. But now Dani can't stop thinking about her seemingly healthy husband, Clark, dropping dead. Not because she hates him (not right now, anyway) but because it's become abundantly clear to Dani that if he dies, she and Lotte will be left destitute.

And then Dani discovers The Temple. Ostensibly a yoga center, The Temple and its guardian, Renata, are committed to helping people reach their full potential. And if that sometimes requires sex work, so be it. Finally, Dani has found something she could be good at, even great at: meaningful work that will protect her and Lotte from poverty and provide true economic independence from Clark. Just as Dani is preparing to embrace this opportunity, Renata disappears. And Dani discovers there might be something else she's good at: detective work.

Darkly comic and razor sharp, *Normal Women* explores how we value female labor—and how we don't.

Also by Ainslie Hogarth

*Motherthing*

# Normal Women

# *Normal Women*

## Ainslie Hogarth

STRANGE
LIGHT

Strange Light is a registered trademark of
Penguin Random House Canada Limited.

Published simultaneously in the United States of America by Vintage Books, a division of Penguin Random House LLC, New York.

**Library and Archives Canada Cataloguing in Publication**

Title: Normal women : a novel / Ainslie Hogarth.
Names: Hogarth, Ainslie, author.
Identifiers: Canadiana (print) 20230141153 | Canadiana (ebook) 20230482953 |
ISBN 9780771000645 (softcover) | ISBN 9780771000652 (ebook)
Classification: LCC PS8615.O3735 N67 2023 | DDC C813/.6—dc23

This is a work of fiction. Names, characters, places, and incidents either are the product of the author's imagination or are used fictitiously. Any resemblance to actual persons, living or dead, events, or locales is entirely coincidental.

Book design by Christopher M. Zucker
Cover design by Mark Abrams
Cover illustrations: CSA-Printstock / DigitalVision Vectors / Getty Images
Printed in the United States of America

Published by Strange Light,
an imprint of Penguin Random House Canada Limited,
a Penguin Random House Company
www.penguinrandomhouse.ca

10 9 8 7 6 5 4 3 2 1

Penguin
Random House
Canada

*For J and W*

*Normal Women*

# 1

THEY'D ENDED UP slicing her open, which was great. She was sort of hoping for a C-section. The stories Anya's friends had shared about their incontinence, their prolapses—one of the women, Ellen, describing the way a hunk of her bladder or vaginal wall (*who knows!*) would slip down throughout the course of the day. *Bulge.* She'd framed it as a minor irritation, easy enough to poke back in, no different from enduring the day with a sock that keeps slipping beneath your heel. Except it was every day. And it was body parts. Very inside ones. Creeping out like some activated fungus. Which was why pretty soon, Ellen explained, casually, hooking an invisible hair from her mouth and tucking it behind her ear, she'd be looking into some sort of scaffolding. A mesh—interlocking her fingers, miming weight—that would hold it up for her. *Like basketballs*, piped in Dawn, another one of Anya's friends who Dani had recently met, *in a high school gym equipment room, remember??* Laughing, nodding. Though Ellen, Dawn, and Anya had all gone to different high schools, the equipment rooms, with their suspended basketballs and oily, low-frequency stench, were very much the same.

And Ellen, Dawn, and Anya had all heard of the mesh too. Because they all knew someone, a woman, secretly held together by it. Dani wrapped her mouth gracelessly around a blast of corn chips and wondered why the fuck no one had told her about the mesh *before* she got pregnant.

"Well, Elaine had a fourth-degree tear," Anya revealed, thumbing a wayward gob of guacamole back onto her chip. Anya, in many ways the worst of them, Dani's oldest friend, who she loved like a sister but also found unkind, judgmental, manipulative, competitive, and actually a bit racist in ways she seemed to perceive as simply good sense: "Immigrants are driving up the cost of living in the top cities, I'm sorry, but it's true. If you come here from somewhere else you should have to start in, I don't know, some middle-of-nowhere town that needs the economic push, you know? It's only fair. And it's good for *everyone*."

Anya had experienced both, a C-section and a vaginal birth, and though the vaginal birth had been *amazing, oh my god*, it'd also left her with chronic incontinence (*Do you know that I piss myself? A little bit? Every goddamn day?*) as well as what the doctor referred to as *sexual dysfunction*, which was so severe her husband, Bill, had taken up yoga. His back, once a densely knit tapestry of chronic pain, was now limber as a river reed. *We should have stopped fucking years ago*, he joked, and Anya nodded readily— *honestly, though*, a hand on Dani's arm, her tone edged with a conspirator's sincerity, *he's like a different person*.

By almost every metric Anya was a very Normal Woman. At the very least she engaged with the material trappings of their sex in a way that Dani had never been able to—Anya exercised regularly, or at least complained regularly about not exercising enough; she had defined triceps, lean thighs; she monitored her protein intake, and knew the difference between soluble and insoluble fiber. Anya spent time outside, her chest and shoulders tanned to a fine, freckled hide. Nails always buffed, cuticles repressed, hair a multifaceted illusion of fresh blonds. Her leggings were expensive, their crotches fortified, and she'd always, since high school, had her bikini area waxed professionally, sugared when that was the trend. Eyebrows too. Threaded now. By a woman in the mall who apparently Anya would have preferred to start her life in the prairies. Dani imagined a small farming community with perfect eyebrows, in stark contrast to the shaggy and wild wheat they sowed.

Basically, Anya was the portrait of *self-care*, a pursuit the mothers in the online mom forums held sacred, and another maternal obligation for all but the lucky few to fail at spectacularly.

Dani wasn't exactly sure how she and Anya had managed to remain friends for so long other than they both liked drinking too much and had once known, intimately, the versions of one another they hated most: the raw, cruel, earnest material of their youth they'd both taken great pains to pasteurize and recast into forms more consciously selected. When Dani and Anya were alone with one another, they allowed these former selves to unfurl languorously from their facades, accessing big, true laughs and rare peace, despite having, technically, nothing in common.

"What's a fourth-degree tear?" Dani had asked at that lunch with the *mom friends*, the last lunch, she didn't realize at the time, before she would go into labor. She leaned back in her chair as though distance from the explanation might inoculate her from it. She folded both hands over her moon of living belly, protecting the little person inside too. Nine months pregnant. Almost there.

"A bad rip," said Ellen, still chewing, clearing away nacho debris with a long pull of margarita. "Poo hole to goo hole." She raised her eyebrows.

And maybe that's why the C-section happened. Because Dani had just wanted it so very badly: sweating, panicked, coiled help-lessly around every contraction, incapable of just letting go, of *breathing*, her mind's eye yoked to Ellen's salted lips, tight around the vowels: "p*ooooo* hole to g*ooooo* hole." And the body is just such a mysterious thing, especially as it pertains to childbirth. In fact, after reading book after book about the connection between fear and pain, the orgasmic, ecstatic, *rapturous* birth experience, the power of visualizations—*I am petals unfurling, I am huge, I am opening wide as a cave, exactly as I should, for my baby to spill without pain*—one might even come to the conclusion that the body is *only* mysterious as it pertains to childbirth. That other-wise it's actually pretty predictable: a system of sphincters and pipes and cables that harmonize chaos like the warming of an orchestra pit, ins and outs and organs thumping, processing fuel, petals unfurling, becoming huge, ejecting waste and sometimes life, and that was Lotte, Dani's precious baby, who mercifully bypassed her vagina, cried only when she really meant it, and completed a truly sublime figure eight when she pressed her face into Dani's breast to eat.

Wide awake in the hospital that first night, Dani's facade warmed, then thinned, to accommodate her new identity, this new *love*. And not just for Lotte either. She loved everyone now, every human being, because they'd all been babies once. And she cried from exhaustion but also because everyone was actually so good inside.

To love something this profoundly.

It was no wonder some people were destroyed by it.

Dani spent the first two days of Lotte's life gathering information from the nurses. What if she's constipated? *(Rub her belly, this way.)* What if she stops latching? *(Just keep trying, this way.)* What's the difference between spit-up and vomit? *(There's no retch to spit-up, no effort, you'll know.)* Look at her hips—are her hips too small? *(I'm not sure what you mean.)*

These women who answered all of Dani's questions, who cleaned the blood that gushed from Dani's numb nethers, who grabbed her breast and pressed it into Lotte's face as if it were some mess the infant had left on the carpet, they somehow erased the decades of shame Dani had tattooed all over her body: flat, runny breasts and nipples too big; trunk-like thighs, coarse, forever razor-burned, even in places she never shaved! Being treated this way, like a piece of machinery designed to keep this baby alive, was the freest Dani had felt in maybe her whole life.

Clark sat in a grubby vinyl chair in the corner of the private hospital room, watching curiously as she was manhandled, ready to jump for whatever Dani or Lotte might need. Thick and dark around the eyes, maybe as exhausted as Dani but certainly less severed in half. He made a little performance of reacting to Dani's relentless questions, hands up, head shaking, *my wife, my crazy wife!* But after the nurses left, he huddled up with Dani, going over the answers, greedy for more, and with new questions of his own, which, of course, Dani didn't have the answers to, but she would soon enough, whether she found them online or through another shameless session with the next unsuspecting nurse.

They acted this way in front of people, settled into these public roles without ever really discussing it: Clark, the laid-back one, easygoing, a golden retriever of a man; Dani, the neurotic, a shih tzu or chihuahua or some other quivering abomination of nature. It was important to Clark, Dani knew, to project this particular image of masculinity: A man is calm; a man is rational. A man doesn't *fret*. And Dani didn't care if people thought she was neurotic. She *was* neurotic. They both were; in their truest private they were both that way, simmering with dread for the moment they had to leave the hospital room, cross the parking lot, all alone in the car with their maybe abnormally small-hipped daughter. Clark's road rage intensified by exhaustion, by their brand-new, precious cargo. Dani hunched over the car seat, screaming at him from the backseat: *Would you just fucking relax, for fuck's sake?!*

And now here they were! At home! Everyone alive and well, and Lotte about to give Dani another intoxicating shit to mark in the poop chart! Dani loved—*loved*—to watch Lotte take shits. The real hard work of it, when a body was this small. Tense, as though a string had been drawn tight through her face and fists and feet. Dani sat down low, legs crossed, leaned in close to Lotte, secured in her bouncer chair, offering help, rubbing Lotte's stomach, four firm fingers clockwise along the intestine's curve just like the nurse had shown her.

And then Lotte would embody the kinetic still of a raindrop caught in a window screen, lock in to Dani's eyes as though she were about to upload every secret she'd borne from the womb, Dani teary-eyed—*I'm listening, sweet angel, I can hear your perfect voice*—and then Lotte would release a long, shockingly robust fart alongside an ooze of odorless gold. Lotte's mouth tuning into the shape of her own tiny asshole, a cinched, roving O until it was all over. And Dani shrieked like a hysterical disciple, kissed Lotte's feet, her hands, her head—*Amazing baby! Amazing girl! You're so strong! You're so good!*—and Lotte would accept the kisses as a dog does: intrigued, unthreatened, but not entirely *sure*.

This, *finally*, was work that Dani enjoyed. Work she was actually *good* at. Each day brought with it some new victory: a warm, fresh roll of fat, evidence of the hard work of breastfeeding; a smile at just the right time, proof that she'd grown a good and standard baby. When Lotte transitioned out of her newborn clothes and into her 0-3-month wardrobe, Dani felt it like a promotion, beaming with pride. For a moment she understood the thrill the witch must have felt in "Hansel and Gretel" when she'd sufficiently fattened up those naughty children for roasting.

Ten pounds, then eleven. Twelve! Which seems like nothing until it's a squirming, bouncing, *fragile* twelve pounds, mass that wriggles and twists and buckles at the hinges.

Dani and Lotte, they were moving on up, into the next pay grade, where the stretches of sleep were longer, the feedings less frequent, the need less intense. And the returns—smiles and giggles and chatter and sustained eye contact—rich beyond her wildest dreams. They were becoming real humans together, for Dani a return, though, in her opinion, as an *improved* version of her former self, and for Lotte a whole new form.

And there was nothing better than this. Not the perilous exhaustion, of course. Not the purgatorial boredom. And certainly not the intense pressure to make everything perfect for this brand-new creature you created, the world reminding you, with what felt like renewed wrath, of what a shithole it is. But rather *this*—this wholesome and complete sense of meaning. It was warm, thought Dani, actually warm, places she'd been cool inside now honestly and truly warm. Finally she could stop thinking about herself, about what she had or hadn't accomplished with her life. It didn't matter anymore if Dani was special. Because *she* didn't matter anymore. Lotte had obliterated her, released her from that suffering.

And despite being more stressed than ever at work, helming

the flagship project of a brand-new office in a brand-new town, late nights, sometimes weekends, emails all the time, Clark was the most incredible dad—eager to take Lotte whenever he could, endless endurance for peekaboo and patty-cake and head-to-toe raspberries. He leaped for every diaper, scarfed his dinner so he could take her off Dani's hands. "My mind is so calm around her," he said one night while they watched Lotte asleep in her crib, wrapped tight as a cigar in a bamboo swaddling blanket, a gift from Anya.

This wasn't true, of course. Clark was as troubled as ever, maybe even more so. Tricked by love. Confusing it for peace. To see him fooled this way filled Dani with the urge to kiss him. So she did. In a way she never had before. Like their intimacy *mattered* now. And this kiss triggered a hunger within them both, more mouth, more skin, but also more *love* between them. Less fighting. They *loved* each other, didn't they? How could they have ever fought so much before? And was it a lot? Or was it actually just the normal amount of fighting that two humans in love must do in order to not subsume one another, actively keeping parts of themselves too prickly to be absorbed.

It was healthy to fight this much, Dani decided. Despite what the moms in the mom forums said. They were all lying anyway. Women like that were incapable of acknowledging unhappiness in their marriage, for the same reason a soldier might find it difficult to acknowledge shortcomings in the country he'd killed for.

Clark and Dani were parents now. A *family*. Something more sacred about the way they engaged with and treated one another. Their lovemaking a solemn act that produced little angels like Lotte, who would be looking to them as models for her future relationships. From now on there would be a terrible punishment for failing to love each other properly: having to watch their most precious treasure lock herself into the same miserable patterns that they had. Neither of them could take that, they both knew. So they agreed, tenderly, without words: *We'll never be careless with each other again.*

Everything was perfect. Everything *seemed* perfect. It should be perfect. Dani had a beautiful baby who filled her poo charts like an absolute prodigy. She had a renewed love for her husband, even *enjoyed* having sex with him again, despite the warning from the forum mothers, and Anya, that a husband's touch might trigger blind rage for a while after baby. And most of all, she'd been annihilated, blissfully, finally, by true meaning in her heart.

But of course, over the long days and the longer nights, all that began to fade. Dani's positive connection with her body severed, her perception of it drifting back to its familiar patterns of shame and disgust—Lotte was still perfect and beautiful, but sex with Clark again became the chore it'd been before they'd started trying to conceive (*TTC* in the mom forums). Purpose-driven sex was a real turn-on to the women in the forums, Dani included, it turned out. The trick *after* baby, they said, assuming you weren't facing the additional challenge of having been fortified with mesh, was to find a new purpose. Maintaining a happy marriage. Creating a devoted husband. *Could you possibly want that as much as you'd wanted a baby?* asked one of the forum moms. *Try it, try it, and you may.* A quote, they all knew, from *Green Eggs and Ham.* So they commented their LOLs. Dani lolled too, but she would never have posted it.

Many nights, sitting awake in the rocking chair, enjoying the hydraulics of Lotte's feeding, always feeding, somehow always, endlessly *feeding*, Dani would scroll through the mom forums, seeking advice and reassurance from women who chronically misspelled *aww* as *awe* and called each other *hon*, which didn't seem right to Dani—shouldn't it be *hun*? And she could never not read it as a dig, even though she knew that many of them didn't mean it that way.

> *How much Vaseline are you using, hon? Sorry hon, we chose not to mutilate our son's genitals so I'm not sure what to do about an infected circumcision.*

> *Well hon, why did you post at all? If you have nothing to say? Mamas please be more intentional about how you post, I'm sorry, it's just a pet peeve of mine, all this digital clutter.*

There was one particular woman, a beast called MUM2GABBY, whose posts were usually all-caps gripes about other mothers. Subjects like *YOUR BABY WANTS TO LOOK AT YOU NOT THE BACK OF YOUR PHONE!* And then a long rant about having spotted a mother who dared to be reading on her phone while nursing her child at the park. Other things poor Gabby's horrible mother hated: working mothers (*You HAVE a job, you're a MOTHER NOW!*), daycare before the age of three (*Why even HAVE KIDS if you're not going to RAISE THEM!*), the actress Kristen Bell (*DO NOT GET ME STARTED!*).

Often these forums presented themselves because they contained some extremely specific phrase Dani had typed into the search bar, usually a query about one of the many infinitesimal defects that present in every human body, minor deviations

introduced over three hundred thousand years of reproduction
and not a big deal at all. Things like:

> *four or five purple veins along newborn's temple*
> *slightly dark cuticles newborn*
> *purple beneath eye newborn??*

Dani searched through galleries of rashes and skin conditions.
Galleries of healthy stools. Unhealthy stools. Diarrhea. Spit-up.

> *spit-up slightly clear???*
> *signs of pyloric stenosis*
> *small white bump on roof of baby's mouth*
> *are Epstein pearls painful??*

Galleries of gingival cysts.

> *newborn one eye a bit wonky when first waking up*
> *breaths per minute awake baby*
> *breaths per minute sleeping baby*
> *breaths per minute sleeping baby SIDS???*

Galleries of cyanotic newborns.

> *baby won't sleep*
> *baby won't sleep in crib*
> *baby won't sleep in crib SIDS*
> *baby only sleeps when dead*—she blinked—*when held*

Baby only sleeps when *held*.
Baby only sleeps *when held*.

Dani's chest tightened around her racing heart. Eyes over-whelmed with tears. She shoved her phone beneath her thigh. Bit her lips to keep from sobbing out loud.

And Lotte's chin bounced and bounced and bounced, rhythm undisturbed.

*Lotte, I'm sorry, I would never, I would never ever, ever, my love, my sweet angel baby. I don't know why I saw that, I certainly didn't type that. I didn't type that. I would never, ever type that.*

Feeding, feeding. Eyelids slowing. Sealing.

Content. Oblivious. No sense yet that she'd been born to a monster.

# 2

THEY'D BEEN LIVING in the city when they found out Dani was pregnant. A condo: one bedroom, plus a pitiful, windowless den, and a whole closet taken up by a washing machine and a dryer. They looked at a few houses in their neighborhood and beyond, almost all of them near dangerously run-down, hastily disguised with fresh paint and pot lights and still well out of their price range. They decided to revisit the matter of their inadequate housing *after* the baby was born. Maybe it wouldn't be so bad having an infant in a seven-hundred-square-foot sock drawer, sixty feet in the air.

"We'll make it work!" Clark declared, with suspicious optimism. Almost as though he'd already known about the promotion he announced six months later. The real estate development company he worked for was opening a new office. In Metcalf, of all places. Dani's hometown. An area positively *booming* thanks to the grand reopening of the Silver Waste Management Corporation (now known as the Silver Waste Management *Campus*, or

SWMC around town), where innovative approaches to managing garbage had attracted a haughty crowd of environmental consultancies, AI think tanks, and tech start-ups, which, all together, began to resemble what people like Clark called a *hub*.

Naturally, the coffee shops appeared first. With a hermit crab's entitlement, they began occupying the criminally small cubbyholes that developers like Clark carved from crumbling strips of brick storefront. They sold cortados in short brown cups and hot new literary fiction and austere notebooks and expensive espresso machines that would collect dust on the counters of hectic businessmen, checking their teeth for sesame seeds in the chrome dash before zipping out the door to grab a cortado before work.

And then there were the taco joints with takeout windows and vegan carnitas, where you could buy a jar of homemade salsa for $10, queso for $12.

And that pizza place with the graffiti walls and COWA-BUNGA signature pie to appeal to the nostalgic millennials, the former Teenage Mutant Ninja Turtles fans spending a fortune on real estate and nacho dips.

It was Dani's father who'd started the original Silver Waste Management Corporation. Daniel "DJ" Silver, the Garbage King of Metcalf, even back then a sizeable kingdom of waste-processing innovation. At one time he employed almost the entire town, made more money than any single man could know what to do with or spend in his life. He sponsored Little League teams and bought decadent dinners for the soup kitchen every holiday; he supplied public schools with sports equipment, bought a trampoline for the musty downtown Y. There was a fountain named after him, his portrait above a plaque in city hall, and tales of his famously humble beginnings nurtured false hope in underprivileged children all over the county.

For a long time Dani didn't know they were rich. She grew up in the same drafty old farmhouse her father had, where her mother still lived: a basement besieged by warm-blooded vermin, cold air gushing between warped bones. No one with money would have lived that way. But they did. Thirty years ago this unnecessary suffering signaled proof of DJ's fine character; today locals thought Dani's mother should feel ashamed to still be there—the woman who'd squandered his fortune, carrying on, unpunished, in his beloved family home.

Metcalf.

Dani squished her eyes shut.

*Metcalf.*

Clark sensed her reluctance, feelers sharpened by his trade. He leaned forward, slid his fingers between hers. "I know," he said, forcing his way into her eye line. "Trust me, I *know*. But Dani, you're not *failing* by *going home*. Quite the opposite. Honestly, that the idea of going back home has somehow been warped into failure, that's got to be, I mean, I don't know, you're the philosopher, but that's got to be by capitalist design, no?" Dani raised an eyebrow; he pressed harder. "Unmooring us from ourselves, our roots, making us wary of such easy and *inexpensive* peace. Boosting the illusion of this endless journey, endless *growth*, all so we can buy our idea of home instead. Create the void, then fill the void, right? You know, all that stuff. Look, the fact is, this is a huge promotion. And a fuck ton of money. The signing bonus alone is basically our down payment on a house. And you won't have to work again at all if you don't want to. You could just be with the baby." He drew a long, meaningful look at her stomach. She rolled her eyes and shook an offended whinny from her snout as she tipped big, jiggling curds of scrambled egg onto their plates. "Except I don't *want* to just stay home with the baby," she said, setting the pan on the table and docking herself in her seat. At almost seven months pregnant, Dani's belly was no longer even remotely adorable. She was a big, sweaty spectacle. Ample. Enormous. A reluctant god: Crowds parted for her on the sidewalk; bus seats materialized out of thin air. She accepted these grand genuflections hurriedly, without eye contact, hating every second of it but not wanting to seem *ungrateful*. She snatched a bite from her toast and left the crumbs where they landed.

Clark sat down across from her. He picked up his fork, speared a cherry tomato, glittering with salt, and pointed at her with it. "You *know* I didn't mean it like that." He slid the tomato off his fork with his teeth.

Clark didn't know what he was talking about. He had no idea how he was supposed to mean it or how he wasn't supposed to mean it. He knew he didn't want to *seem* like a man who would prefer his wife to stay home with his child. He knew that.

And Dani didn't really know what she wanted. She should feel proud to be a stay-at-home mother. She should feel *lucky*. It's the hardest job in the world, that's what everyone always said, and though Dani was sure the work itself was indeed very difficult— extremely difficult, possibly much more than she could even handle—she suspected that what made the job even harder was the utter lack of respect a person got for doing it, from assholes like her.

It wasn't completely preposterous for Clark to have made this suggestion either. On the advice of the forum mothers, she'd put their unborn daughter's name on all the daycare lists within reasonable walking distance from their condo—*Six months pregnant? Girl, you're already too late!*—and then cried on and off all night picturing some aromatic administrator pulling her baby screaming from her arms, fists full of Dani's jacket, refusing to let go, cortisol boiling scars into her as yet unmarred brain, all so Dani could, what, return to another pathetic office job? Some insignificant little company, disseminating worthless digital content for very little money, where the only thing she did with any care at all was ensure she was out the door at exactly five o'clock. Maybe if Dani were a human rights lawyer, performing good work for those who needed it; a dentist, securing a sound financial future for her family. Even if she simply *enjoyed* her work, at all, it might be different. But none of those things was the case. Despite identifying strongly as a feminist, Dani didn't have a career. And while maybe she could technically be a feminist without financial independence, having to ask Clark for money certainly didn't feel in the spirit of the thing.

"I just . . ." She prodded her scrambled eggs with her fork, struggling to come up with a reason they couldn't move to Metcalf, but everything she thought of withered against the argument of more money, cheaper housing, her mother nearby. Anya. Her oldest friend. Probably still her *best* friend, really. "I've just got a bad feeling, Clark, about moving to Metcalf, I've got this"—she swallowed. "I've got this"—she swallowed again—"gulp-resistant lump in my throat. Honestly, it's not going away." She gulped, audibly, putting her neck and shoulders into it, making it hurt this time. She raised her fingers to her throat, pressed gently, feeling for the sea urchin that must surely be lodged there.

And Clark, a good person at the moment (sometimes he was a bad person), honored her nebulous dread; he raised the fingers not currently occupied by cutlery, a calming gesture, and cooed, "I understand. I really do. It's different for you, to go back home, you've got your . . . *legacy*." Dani winced. Embarrassed. It was fine for her to *secretly* believe she had any kind of legacy in

Metcalf, but she didn't want anyone else, even Clark, to know that she felt that way. If she did have any *legacy,* her continued absence was all that sustained it. A generation of Metcalfians who once knew her, paused from time to time to wonder whatever happened to that Danielle Silver. Where did she get away to? And the possibilities were endless. Because she'd been royalty, the Princess of Trash, vanished without a trace: A kind of Anastasia Romanov. A garbage Anastasia Romanov. If she returned now, they'd know exactly what happened to her: *Whatever happened to that Danielle Silver? Oh, I just ran into her in the mall, actually, she was in line at Kernels, yes, just waiting her turn to purchase a small bit of popcorn, yes, a little treat for herself, yes, she deserves a little treat. That Danielle Silver? She lives in one of the cozy pre-wars near the creek. She got married, yes, had a baby, yes,* just the one, *yes, and now stays at home to raise her just like the rest of us. Yes. She stays at home. With* just the one. *That's right,* just the one. *Just like Bunny. More like Bunny, it turns out, than DJ. Away from us, we hadn't known. Away from us she might have been anyone. But back home we see, we all see. Her mother's daughter, through and through. Too bad. Really too bad. We could have used another DJ Silver. Remember the feasts DJ Silver put on at the soup kitchens? Remember the graphing calculators he bought the remedial school? And my god, remember that* trampoline? *I don't know any kid in this town who didn't just come* alive *on DJ's trampoline.*

Dani closed her eyes. Listened to the gentle ruckus of Clark's utensils against his plate. Toast shattering between his teeth. "Nothing's happening yet"—his voice muffled by food. "It's just an offer for now, something to think about. And if I don't take it, we can figure something else out. The condo's not so bad for now." He swallowed. "We'll make it work!"

Dani nodded, closed her eyes, rested a hand over her belly.

"Are you okay?"

"Yes." She exhaled. "Just kicking." The baby pounded her legs, dragged against the fleshy upholstery of her uterine perimeter, the slow, exploratory pace that Dani already understood to be part of her personality.

*Metcalf.*

Moving to Metcalf.

Because Dani didn't really have a choice, did she? Clark was acting like she did, because of course, once again, he knew he didn't want to *seem* like the kind of man who allowed his salary to influence the power dynamic of his marriage. But of course it did. And they both knew it. The money had made a decision. And Dani would go where the money went. So she opened her eyes, found Clark innocently wiping yolk from his plate with his last scrap of toast, awaiting her approval *like* a very good man, *like* a man who would have halted his career based on the vague anxieties of his chihuahua wife. At least this way she could feel as though she had some control too. Better this way, wasn't it? She shuddered, fighting off a hazy picture of the alternative: how it would look to do away with the performance altogether. Dani swallowed the sea urchin with wincing effort. And agreed to move back to Metcalf.


That night Dani sweat through the bedsheets, Lotte thrashing inside her like she never had before. A protest. A warning. The Princess of Trash returning to her kingdom. The king dead. The queen insane. And Lotte the trigger to some hellish prophecy that would destroy them all.

If Lotte could have known Dani's thoughts that night, the way she'd be able to in thirteen years or so, with all her *teenage powers*, she would have read her mother with the precision of a surgeon, hormone-mad, sociopathy laser-focused on the pathetic host she'd shed like snakeskin. The way it ought to be. The way it had been since mothers started having daughters. *Wow, Mom, do you really think you're that special? That you've been in anyone's thoughts at all? A* hellish prophecy, *for god's sake? It must be exhausting, honestly, to be so fucking bored.* And even Clark, accustomed by now to Lotte's casual cruelties, would wince at that one, barely exhaling the word *daaaaaaaamn* as Lotte turned and left. Leveled up. Mother eviscerated. Eviscerated, but also, secretly, *sickeningly* delighted. Because finally Dani knew, once and for all, a gift from her daughter, exactly who the fuck she was.

# 3

TWELVE MONTHS went by in Metcalf without incident.

Not a single trace of a single hellish prophecy.

Twelve months in the cozy Dutch colonial they'd purchased in Corkton, an area recently christened by real estate agents and young newcomers. Young newcomers like their neighborhoods to have names; they like a coffee shop they can walk to—extra points for a tasteful graffiti mural showcasing the neighborhood's new name. Newcomers like a bus route, even if they never use it, and a library, and a decent park. And though Dani wasn't technically a newcomer to Metcalf, she also very much was, so they'd paid a premium for their little spot in Corkton, with its fluorescent patch of yard and charmingly uneven brick driveway.

There were four bedrooms, in case of more babies. Two bathrooms, in case of simultaneous food poisoning. One good-sized garage, equipped with bike racks and plywood cupboards and a pegboard for the tools they'd eventually need to acquire. For *maintenance*—an annoying little word, halted by consonants, and intimidating to them both. People their age couldn't be too choosy about homes, though—not enough inventory, low interest rates. It's *basic supply and demand*, their real estate agent parroted when they had to go slightly outside their budget for this place. But it was homey, and *you can't beat Corkton*, so they'd both been very happy to get it.

Twelve months tripping on the driveway's treacherously dilapidated brick.

Twelve months developing their eyes for weeds, yanking them up by the roots from the lawn, the garden, the walkway, clutching them as they quivered dirt, all the way to the leaking, bloated yard-waste bag in the backyard, which one of them, probably Dani, would have to deal with somehow, and soon.

Twelve months populating the garage with other things too, like a pruning saw, a weed whacker, a multi-bit screwdriver and a stud finder and a *wheelbarrow*, which Dani had genuinely thought didn't exist anymore, a relic, like a butter churn, but it sure came in handy when Clark had tripped in the driveway for the last motherfucking time and insisted on etching up the bricks and lugging heaps of gravel back and forth from the garage in an effort to even it out. It didn't work exactly, but it was much improved, and a few times Dani caught Clark glancing at his handiwork with pride. Sometimes she found his pride quite sweet: traces of some hale stock, bolstering his marrow. Other times she found it quite obnoxious: evidence of his unseemly appetite for praise. As though moving a few wheelbarrows full of gravel was *such an incredible feat*; as though he should be *honored* for his hard work by way of braised meats and blow jobs and quiet, unconscious gestures of respect. The way dogs do it: Clark going through doors first, getting the prime spot on the couch, the bigger piece of meat, all because he'd ever so slightly evened out the driveway. Not even all the way. She still tripped sometimes, a fact that she'd sharpened to a point and hurled at Clark to great effect in the deepest dark of their most recent argument. And how he looked at her, the fucking baby, as though denying his well-earned fanfare were the apex of cruelty, emblematic of everything that was wrong with her.

There were twelve months of centipedes.

They ate the ants.

Twelve months of humidity.

It fed the mold.

Which was easy to keep on top of, not a dangerous mold, according to the internet, but it needed fairly regular attention and would eventually have to be addressed by adding an expensive dehumidifying apparatus to the heating and cooling system, a dangerously warm factory hidden in an unsightly part of the basement, bings and borps and grinds and whirrs that made Dani and Clark uneasy. Clark once referred to it as *the reactor*, and so now that's what they always called it—a thud issuing from the basement after the heat kicked on, a shared glance, "Just *the reactor*," he'd say, then laugh nervously, return his attention to whatever they'd put on the TV that night. Usually some television show Clark's colleagues were talking about, something based on a British novel about a woman accused of murdering her husband or her child or her mother, or sometimes she's solving the murder and discovering that *she* was the murderer the whole *time* because she has a *drinking problem* and *blackouts* and all signs point to her, but then it was the husband after all, who you thought it was in the beginning but then it seemed too obvious but then of course it's obvious because it's always the husband. Because even though sometimes you think they're the best people in the world, you must never forget they're actually the worst.

And this house was where they'd brought Lotte home from the hospital; where Dani had rocked and bounced and breastfed till her back muscles melted and fused. She watched a thousand movies with the sound low so as not to rouse Lotte, closed-captioning describing the 20th Century Fox intro—(*dramatic percussion*) + (*brass fanfare*)—Dani had found that funny. She told Clark and he'd found it funny too. And now sometimes, when either of them was about to do something quite unimpressive, like, say, yank up a small weed with a dainty claw of easily bested roots, they'd say "Dramatic percussion, brass fanfare!" as the other marched it sheepishly to the bag.

In this house Dani had coached Lotte through her first word, *Mama!* Had watched her cut bright white teeth so suddenly that Dani shrieked when she saw them, like something elves had delivered in the night. This house was where Lotte had learned to crawl, learned to eat, learned to *sleep*, because apparently babies couldn't do that right either. *Sleep-training.* The hardest thing Dani'd ever done, listening to Lotte cry all alone in her bedroom, wailing for someone to pick her up and rock her out of her misery. Clark had held Dani close, almost unsettlingly stoic, while she sobbed in bed, clutching Lotte's flashing monitor, vibrating with her every scream like some poor attempt at immersive theater. "She's fine," Clark assured her, as if he could possibly know. "She's just tired. She *wants* to sleep. This is how she'll learn." He stroked Dani's head. *Oh, my silly little dependent. Always fretting. Never calm.*

*Baby only sleeps when dead.*

That had happened in this house too.

In Metcalf.

Where every little thing was both much, much better and much, much worse.


And then one night Clark came home from work and told her that a coworker of his, someone she'd never met before and Clark barely knew, had been diagnosed with colon cancer.

Dani held a slice of roasted chicken between a large fork and a carving knife, like a woman who'd committed to a very specific way of life when she chose her prosthetics.

"What?" she said, not because she hadn't heard him, but because she needed a moment to process the sudden shift in the room's shadows, as though a bulb somewhere had fritzed. She blinked, glanced at the fixture above the table to be sure, scanned the dining room, which a moment ago had been the warm embodiment of her family's lovable chaos, but now, in this new light, felt artificial and silly. Impermanent. A room drawn onto the interior walls of a shoebox.

"Eddie, the controller, he's got colon cancer. Aggressive too. He hasn't said as much exactly, but speaking with him today, I don't know. I don't think the prognosis is good." Clark had washed his hands in the kitchen before entering the dining room; they were cool when he touched Dani's arm, activating a patch of goose bumps. He leaned over and kissed her cheek, activating a patch of goose bumps there too.

"Is he going to keep working?"

Clark shrugged. "Probably." Then he fixed his eyes on Lotte, already in her high chair, smiling at him, saying, "Da, da, da, da, da, da, da." She reached up with both hands to touch him, then pulled back quickly and squealed with delight when he got close enough to kiss her too.

"You tease," said Clark, sitting down next to Lotte. Dani bristled at the word and sat down in front of her plate. Roasted chicken, mashed potatoes, steamed broccoli, something she'd flung together in the moments she was able to steal from Lotte's fervent needs. Clark had no idea what a feat it'd been, but that's fine. It's fine. He ate it, of course, without comment, as though she'd pressed a button and it appeared, but that's fine.

Lotte flung a spear of chicken from her tray in an act of gleeful rebellion; she toyed with a bucking, buttered egg noodle like prey; accepted a few peach slices into her mouth from Dani's hands; and every few minutes dropped everything to eagerly slurp spinach-and-pear puree from a bag, iron-fortified, high in fiber. These bags were the real MVPs, Dani hated to admit, when it came to Lotte's transition to solids. MUM2GABBY, she'd warned about the bags. And Lotte's eyebrows were crusted over with some combination of it all, making her look angry and bewildered, but still smiling, like a dementia patient.

"Colon cancer, my god," said Dani, scooping a few more noodles onto Lotte's tray. "That's really awful, Clark. How old is he?"

"Thirty-three." Clark shook his head. "Two kids. Divorced, I think."

Dani lowered her head, wanting to honor the tragedy the way a good person would, by sitting for a moment, in the moment, with this awful, heartbreaking thing that'd brushed against their lives, but she was finding it very difficult to be still and present and grateful for her family's health, too distracted by the fact that Clark honestly *still* hadn't mentioned the meal, at all, sitting there like a clueless fucking boy-king, lovely meals as much a fact of his existence as morning erections. No *idea* what an absolute *feat* it was to execute a beautiful spread like this while chasing after a one-year-old dementia patient all day long. All he had to do was say *thank you*. He didn't have to comment on the flavor or the cook or anything—both perfect, by the way. But just say *thank you*, just *acknowledge* that Dani had once again *done it all*, as she did every day, without complaint, far, *far* more impressive than answering emails, attending meetings, signing off on other people's hard work. For this Clark got money, independence, and respect; he got to feel genuinely productive and connected to other human beings in the world. Meanwhile Dani was all alone, as always, a shameful necessity, tucked away, like the bulky wad of cords that kept their television working. Juggling, among many other things, carrots and lemon and onion and poultry seasoning, all while protecting Lotte from toddling into disaster.

Dani would never fish for a compliment, though, the way that Clark did about the goddamn driveway. The way a child would. She would be passive-aggressive instead, like a fucking adult.

Though she supposed she could also just *tell* him how much work it'd been, how much work it always was, to make sure dinner was on the table when he got home, which he'd technically never *asked* her to do, but that was the genius of it, wasn't it? He didn't have to ask her. The agreement they'd fallen into had existed long before they did: termless, conditionless, completely unvetted. His role clear and well-defined: go to work, make the money, *provide*. Hers fluid and shifting: duties tethered to the whims of a child, the fancies of a husband. Accepting duties outside the contract was for her an expectation; for him above and beyond, further proof (as though he needed any!) that he was a good, *good* man.

But she couldn't bring that up now. Not right after he mentioned the coworker, a man he knew a little, a man a year *younger* than he was, about to most likely die of arguably the worst kind of cancer, not just extremely deadly but also extremely undignified: colonoscopies, fecal tests, enemas, an assault on one of the body's most guarded holes—a shared hole, existing across all bodies, bearing probably the most signifiers of any hole. Certainly the most signification.

Maybe Dani was just exhausted.

Or, she very suddenly realized—*baby only sleeps when dead*— a little depressed.

For a while now.

Twelve months, even.

She excused herself and went to the bathroom and cried, briefly but violently, then chased the red from her face with a cool towel.

# 4

THAT NIGHT DANI ROTATED her shoulders against the mattress, pulled her hair out from behind her neck. Still not comfortable. She sat up, assaulted her pillow. Lay down. Still bad.

Fucking colon cancer.

If detected early, colon cancer was highly curable. Screening, early detection, that was crucial. She remembered something from a job she had once, copyediting long-form advertising content for a group of media brands aimed at senior citizens—a colorectal polyp can take up to fifteen years to develop into cancer. Fifteen years with a time bomb ticking away quietly in your bowels; fifteen whole years to deactivate it! Healthy young men dying before their time, just because they'd been too proud to have their only hole probed, too scared to discover what secrets might lurk there.

Dani propped up on an elbow and leaned over so she could see Clark's face, furrowed at his phone as he thumbed through barbecues. "Do you think we need a side burner?" he asked, without looking at her. "For, like, corn on the cob? It might be nice, but I also feel like they're just—they get so filled with spiders, don't they?"

"Do you know when Eddie's last colorectal screening was?"

Clark closed his phone, set it facedown in his lap, and turned to her. "What do you think?"

"Well, do you at least know what Eddie usually ate for lunch?" *Please god, corned beef. Please god, potato chips and burgers and processed cheese. And beer. He'd drink at work? Oh, yeah, every day, beers all day. Sometimes meth. Meth! My god. Oh, yeah, loved meth. Couldn't get enough of meth. I guess that's the problem isn't it. And meth causes colon cancer? Well, I'm sure it doesn't help! No, I'm sure you're right!*

"I don't know, I never noticed. Usual stuff, I think. Leftovers. Sandwiches. I don't know." He picked up his phone again. "I'm not going to go for the side burner. We have too many spiders as is."

"But he wasn't a vegetarian, right?"

"I don't *know*, Dani."

"He probably wasn't. You'd know if he was, I'm sure." She looked away, lowered her voice—"They love to let you know"— visualizing Wanda, her mother's best friend and most loyal defender, always dressed for gentle, joint-friendly exercise, yak-king in Bunny's kitchen between snaps off a pepperoni stick about how even though the doctor had insisted she reintroduce meat into her diet, she was still a vegetarian. "In the way that really *counts*, you know?" Bunny had nodded emphatically, and Dani, to dodge the grip of visible scorn, had drained her face so thoroughly of expression that she nearly slipped into another realm. Wanda then transitioned to her next favorite topic: the retired service dogs she fostered—their urinary crystals and hip dysplasia and unusually loud stomach gurgling, which she referred to, with the inexplicable smugness of a dickhead ordering a French dessert, as *borborygmi*. Dani didn't know how Bunny could stand it.

"Did he smoke?"

"I don't think so."

"Did he drink too much?"

"Well, not at work! Dani, come *on*." Clark slid his phone onto the nightstand, rolled over to look up at her. "I barely knew the guy."

"Well, this shouldn't be too hard to talk about then!" She threw herself back onto her pillow, arms crossed over her chest like a child. She felt agitated. Embarrassed. Which of course made her double down on the reaction. She turned away from him, clicked off her bedside light, waited for Clark to tap her cold shoulder, initiate its thaw with his gentle conflict-resolution voice: *What is troubling you, my silly little dependent?* But she refused to engage. Because she didn't actually *know* why she was so angry. Not yet, anyway.

It wasn't until a few hours later, still wide awake, too hot and clenching her jaw, that she realized she was actually worried about *Clark* getting colon cancer.

About Clark dying.

And not because of how much she loved Clark (though she did, she really did love Clark, who she knew, without question, was extremely grateful for all her hard work with Lotte, couldn't have assembled a chicken and watched their demented child at the same time if he tried, a very, very good man, no question, that was Clark) but rather because, now that Lotte was here, it'd become painfully apparent to Dani that she was, by the real world's standards, quite useless, having never developed any of the regular skills other women her age had. Even mesh-fortified Ellen had an MSW, for Christ's sake.

Dani, on the other hand, had completed an undergraduate degree in philosophy, which led to a succession of random office jobs that paid only marginally better than minimum wage, plotted far from the curve of any recognizable career trajectory, or at least one recognizable to her. She'd copyedited ads for collectible coin sets, vacuum erection devices, compression socks; she'd served as the volunteer coordinator for an affordable artist studio, data entry for a search engine optimization firm, customer service for a web hosting company, weekend admin at a music school—jobs that, with geographic distance from her hometown, the cachet of being *in the city*, she could make sound reasonably impressive to Anya and Bunny. Enough that Bunny could spin them into something even more impressive to Wanda, when she could get a word in at all, that is.

And before Lotte, these jobs really *had* been fine. Because Dani was special. A creative. Maybe. *Had* to be. Uniquely talented in some way she simply hadn't uncovered yet. Because it wasn't possible for a regular person to loathe work as much as she did, to be so profoundly bad at it. To be this smart and this stupid at once.

She was always well-liked in the office, and that had to mean something. She made her coworkers laugh, she made them happy, she made the whole place brighter, and that wasn't even a delusion; that was the truth. She was good at small talk. At making people like her. Observant in ways that made people feel special. But over the years it became evident that she was merely a jester, making her coworkers chuckle a bit throughout the day, rallying a good shit-talking session about one of their more loathsome bosses. Then they would go home at night and not think about her; they would go home at night and prepare documents for promotions and raises and leave Dani in their dust. And Dani had no clue how to even go about preparing a document like that. No idea if she even wanted to be promoted anyway. And was certainly too proud to admit *not* knowing how to do it, too proud to admit to *wanting* something, *really wanting something*, in any capacity to anyone *ever*. Which was why Clark couldn't die. Because she didn't know how she could possibly support Lotte adequately, make the *real* money that a person needs for nice clothes so no one would tease her, glasses and braces and college, oh god, *college*.

She was good at being a mother too.

A jester and a mother. Hadn't these been valued professions once?

Colon cancer. A car accident. Any day Clark could be flattened by a semi on the expressway.

Aneurysms. Heart attacks. Strokes. Disease. Slippery showers. That uneven fucking driveway, the toe of his boot catching brick, head splitting like a rind.

Almost morning, her cerebrospinal fluid practically frothing now, the image of some displaced psychopath breaking into the office, the boardroom, spraying the suits who'd evicted him with lead, their bodies, some sitting, some standing, blasted into grotesque jigs that make the shooter howl like a wolf behind his machine gun.

It could fucking *happen*. It *did* happen. Not often, but it did, and why wouldn't it happen to Clark? He was a terrible person sometimes. Sometimes he deserved it. And at work he definitely deserved it. Land development. Real estate. *A parasite. A monster. A bad, bad man.*

# 5

THE NEXT MORNING Dani woke up spun and fragile as a torch of cotton candy. She unfastened her molars. Mouth sore. Sandy. Throbbing.

Clark was already awake, downstairs with Lotte. He always let Dani sleep in on the weekends because he was the type of man who knew that mothers were tired.

He stood at the stove, stirred a pot of oatmeal absently, absorbed by a podcast in which a man with a heavy accent, a doctor, she assumed, explained the difficulties of reconstructing a human ear. Lotte sat close to Clark's feet, hunched pudge, banging a plastic ladle against her thigh. Dani snuck in behind them both, snatched Lotte up from the floor, maneuvered her body to deliver an ambush of kisses—her neck, her belly, her thighs, her feet—and startled Clark from the doctor's hypnotically gruesome descriptions.

"Are you hearing this?" he asked.

"Not really," said Dani, grabbing one of Lotte's bare feet. "She needs socks."

Clark hit pause and switched over to one of Lotte's unhinged playlists. "Apparently kidnappings happen all the time in São Paulo, it's a whole industry, kidnap a rich person, cut off their ear or their finger, send it to the family, get your money, boom. It's tidy. No one dies. So this plastic surgeon, because he's constantly doing these ear, nose, finger reconstructions, he's become the world's expert on reconstructive surgery. He's developed all these new techniques, discovered all these things. So now people from all over the world go to him. Dog bites, freak accidents. And the areas near the hospitals are flourishing because of it—hotels, restaurants, all for people and families traveling for surgery. Like a tourist attraction."

Dani squeezed Lotte's chilly feet. "You know this isn't a podcast about identifying development opportunities, though, right? The takeaway isn't that you should cut people's ears off to trigger a real estate boom."

"How would you know?" He divided the pot of oatmeal between three bowls. "You weren't even listening to it."

"That's true," said Dani, and stepped out of Clark's way so he could place the pot in the sink without rinsing it.

"I wonder if the people who get kidnapped are even scared anymore, or just, you know, annoyed." He opened the fridge, eyes scanning for the milk as he spoke.

She tucked behind him, Lotte on her hip, and filled the dirty pot with water. "Probably still scary to have your ear cut off."

"But you know you're not going to die."

"Look at the tough guy here, checking his watch while he's getting his ear cut off."

"I'm not saying I'd *like* it, I'm just saying I think I'd be more mad than scared." A splash of milk in each bowl. A dash of cinnamon. Both left on the counter.

"And I'm just saying"—she eyeballed the milk and cinnamon as obviously as she possibly could, the pinched focus of a novice telekinetic—"that I think what *you're* saying is ridiculous. Someone is approaching you with a gleaming machete, about to cut your ear off, and instead of screaming and begging them to stop, you're lecturing them for inconveniencing you. Clark, this is simply not true. You'd be pissing your pants."

"It just wouldn't be logical, in that context, to be scared. I'm just pointing out an interesting *cultural* difference."

"A *cultural* difference?"

"It would make more sense if you'd listened to the podcast."

"I don't know about that." Dani turned around and lugged Lotte, ladle flailing, to the dining room, buckled her into her sticky high chair. She bent into the hamper to retrieve a pair of lightly sullied socks to slip over Lotte's kicking feet. Lotte banged the ladle on the tray a few times, stunned when Dani took it away. "Too loud, sweetie." Dani covered her ears and Lotte pouted angrily, released a rough little scream, like no sound she'd ever made in her short life. Dani realized then that Lotte might be absorbing her dark energies. And vicious, hopeless guilt piled on top of her anxiety. The kind of guilt people like MUM2GABBY thrive on: *Just get a job, you lazy, useless bitch! You stupid fucking leech! What kind of role model will you be to Lotte, dependent on a man, your whole existence resting not just on his continued breathing, but his continued interest in you. You think it's fun for him to carry an able-bodied dependent? You think he was born knowing how to succeed? Sure, it's easier for men, sure, the game is rigged to their strengths, to their continued dominance, but what, you're just*

*gonna cry about it? You have a daughter to think about. You've got to
make something of yourself, otherwise she'll grow up to be a loser too.
Just like her mother. Just like your mother. You can't do absolutely
nothing and just expect Lotte to be better, you actually have to DO
SOMETHING, you cocksucking slime. Get off your fucking ass and
DO SOMETHING.*

After breakfast the three of them went to the park. Lotte didn't
want to leave the bucket swing. They had to pry her fingers from
the chains and fight her back into her stroller. There was nothing
quite like the strength of a baby, for whom every battle was life
and death, clinging to whatever she wanted without any idea that
her fingers could easily be snapped right off.

Lotte napped well, all that fresh air and fighting.

Clark initiated sex with Dani during Lotte's nap, part of her
penance for being moody, and Dani, after some quick calcula-
tions in her head, figured they were probably due anyway. She
wrapped her legs around him, gripped his back till her hinges
were white; she filled her mouth with the fat of his hand, his
fingers—how he loved, she knew, to imagine her stifled screams.
On top she affected the posture of a figurehead erupting from
the bow of a ship. Just the sight of her this way made up for any
potential weaknesses in her performance, not that there were
any. She dragged her moans through gravel, pressed her breasts
together with her biceps, Clark's insatiable hands devouring every
part of her body, his body, his *wife*, the mother of his child, the
keeper of his home.

And afterward they both felt better, Clark from having
orgasmed and, in his own mind, delivered another stunning
series of orgasms to Dani. And Dani enjoying these postcoital

moments as she did following any burst of productivity. She might have felt the same way after cleaning both bathrooms.

"You want coffee?" she asked, launching herself out of bed and back quickly into her clothes.

Clark rolled onto his stomach and looked up at her. "We need a new coffeemaker."

"Oh, we do not."

"Dani, every cup is so grainy, it's like drinking from a tide pool."

"Well, I wasn't offering to *make* it. I was offering to go out and get us some."

"Do you want me to go?"

"Why would I want you to go? I just offered."

"I don't know. I'm just asking. There's that spot on Barton Street, with the affogatos, have you heard of it?"

"What's an affogato?"

"I'm not sure exactly. It's got ice cream."

"Do you want one of those? An affogato?"

"No. Just a coffee."

Dani was resisting the urge to ask why, if he didn't want one, he'd mentioned the affogato at all, when something else about what he'd said registered. "Sorry, that café, did you say it's on *Barton* Street?"

A look of terror swept over Clark's face; he struck out his lips with a single finger, brought Lotte's monitor to his ear. They both held their breath, praying the noise had been a one-off. After a few seconds of silence Clark smiled. "False alarm," he whispered. They exhaled. "Anyway, yeah, it's on Barton Street. Why do you ask like that?"

"Just, Barton Street used to be a real dump." More than that. Barton Street had been dangerous. There were drugs on Barton

Street. *Ladies of the night*—one of her mother's preferred terms, making sex workers sound like something that lived under your bed and waited for your sleeping fingers to dangle from the edge. She and Anya had driven there a few times in high school, just to see. A run-down strip of scrubby, unloved bars with names that didn't matter, awnings spattered in decades of street grime, dilapidated patios stacked with white lawn chairs, choked in desperate weeds, cracking through patio stone and sucking it into the ground. Back then each establishment, pressed uncomfortably close to its neighbor, had all the charm of a blood clinic, the sort of place that exists without competition, providing a service to a community. In this case these bars kept a certain type of person, a certain *element*, as Dani's mother would have put it, geographically contained. "Are you guys considering Barton Street for the condo?"

"Among other places, yeah. It's actually a nice area now. I bet you'll be surprised."

And Dani was surprised. Barton Street, at least in the warm light of day, was positively thriving: a few new bars; a restaurant with glass garage doors that Dani assumed some petite waitress would use every muscle in her body to heave up when the place opened, inviting sunshine and little birds to hop in and snatch fries from the floor. There was a café with a clever name and vintage school chairs out front. A secondhand clothing store with headless mannequins in the window, cozy cropped sweaters, high-waisted shorts, brightly patterned socks with Mary Janes. There were good bikes chained to crooked saplings the city had planted in little squares of protected dirt along the sidewalk. A gluten-free bakery. *Bottomless mimosas.*

She'd had a hard time finding parking. And the lineup in the cleverly named café was confusing. She felt judged by a young woman in an uncircumcised beanie, bent in to her computer, peering up. When Dani asked for two large coffees, the barista, who had a dark tattoo crawling up her wrist onto her thumb, politely informed her that they only served Americanos.

"Is that okay?" the barista asked, biting her lip, as though Dani, the customer, had the power to smite her.

"Yes, of course," said Dani. "Americanos are fine." Slightly offended to be taken for one of *those* customers. Ellen or Dawn or Anya might have been put off, *challenged* by yet another *pointless* deviation from the norm, but not Dani.

"And we don't have larges. There's only one size," said the barista, eyebrows raised. "Is *that* okay?"

And for some reason, to this, Dani said "Oh!" Like some scandalized puritan, rattled to her axis by the practices of this outrageous establishment. Exactly the asshole this fashionable young barista thought she was.

The barista apologized more. Dani begged her to stop, glancing back at the young woman in the floppy beanie. The barista smiled and got to work on Dani's order. Dani focused on her dark hand tattoo—a thickly lined vine of ivy—as she tamped the espresso, jerked it into the machine.

Tumbling from the café into the heat, Dani was hungry. She should have gotten a bagel or a muffin, but she couldn't possibly have asked that barista for a carb.

Back in the van she put the keys in the ignition and cranked the A/C. Sipping her bitter Americano. A moment's peace. Taking in the wholesome activity on Barton Street, skeptical now that it had ever been a *stroll* at all. That is, until she noticed The

Temple—cursive signage, a single tube of bright red neon above the door. The building itself a crumbling chunk of brown brick storefront, still standing despite everything just south of it having been demolished for nearly half a block. Like a ruin, or the last living member of a once famous rock band, forced, despite the mockery of their decrepitude, to serve as an emblem of ancient grandeur.

The Temple had an oversized patio, stamped out on the site of those former storefronts, currently bustling with—Dani blinked, squinted as she pressed forward in her seat—*strikingly* gorgeous women. One woman, wearing a long white skirt and a boxy cropped tank top, sat leaned back in a white plastic chair, clutching its arms, a tan leg, long and slender, propped in a second woman's lap. The second woman was bent over the first woman's boot, digging, unsuccessfully it seemed, at a zipper that ran up the side. The second woman wore a linen romper, beaded necklaces of varying lengths and styles, and a fascinating straw bowler. She looked up, peered across the patio, searching for someone, a third woman, who she located, finally, behind her shoulder: pleasant curves in tight workout gear, texting with both thumbs in the corner. The third woman slid her phone into a bright pink belt bag with a chunky black zipper and approached the two seated women. She leaned over and examined the boot herself and, after a few moments, twisted to paw through her belt bag. She produced something small: a bobby pin. The seated cobbler snatched the bobby pin excitedly. With great concentration she hooked the bobby pin to the uncooperative zipper and used it to successfully pull it to the top. The woman with the repaired boot clapped her palms together lightly, keeping her fingers, two of them now holding a lit cigarette, far away from each other.

She stood up, performed a little jig, handed the rest of her cigarette to the cobbler in thanks, and then disappeared through The
Temple's front door.

These women were sex workers, Dani realized, not exactly sure
how she knew, but certain all the same. *Ladies of the night*—and
incidentally the early afternoon too, so insatiable apparently were
the men of Metcalf. And they looked nothing like how she'd
expected them to. No animal prints or pleather thigh-highs or
bronzed-over black eyes. They looked like, well, *her*. Or, rather,
if she were being honest, how she would *like* to look one day—
expensive highlights in beach-wavey hair; good denim, the Lycra
well concealed; long cotton skirts and, Dani squinted, unable
to tell precisely, but what looked like, yes, real leather boots. So
actually these women were more than *fine*; they were, Dani had
to conclude based on their footwear, the smiles on their faces, the
healthy connections they clearly had with other women, doing
*better* than Dani.

*Prostitution.* The most basic supply and demand system baked
into just about every human body on the planet: the intense male
drive to, not procreate, but ejaculate—a distinction that must be
noted, that men want to fuck whether fertilization is possible or
not—and women, lucky women, have the greatest number of
holes to supply this demand. Trade built right into her biology,
pure profit for the penetrated, capitalism at work! Or at the very
least the exchange of goods and services, a function of women's
very bodies!

Dani huffed the steam issuing from her Americano, hitting
the sweet spot at the very bottom of her lungs for the first time
in twelve months. Dani would always have a coveted resource,
*breathing, breathing*, her brain slowing down, cooling off. She
was the private owner of one of the most coveted resources in the

world. And sure, there were a lot of other people in the world with the coveted resource, everyone had this resource in one way or another, but that didn't matter for now. For now all that mattered was that, like slicing open her veins, like chasing a bottle of Tylenol with a bottle of vodka, Dani had *options*. If some routine scope revealed a veritable pumpkin patch of cancerous growths in Clark's colon, she and Lotte could actually be *better off than they were now*.

*Look at this village*. Dani smiled. *We could be a part of it*.

It wouldn't come to that, of course. Clark wasn't going to die. She always *knew* that Clark wasn't going to die, or at least, that it was very unlikely. But it couldn't hurt to be prepared. To know what the options actually were for a talented motherjester in this day and age. She would come back to Barton Street. Tomorrow night. She would watch these villagers confidently leading men to wherever it was they went—someplace deep in the decomposing Temple itself, or the nearby trucker motel, or the rigs of their transport trucks, and then anywhere from thirty (not bad) to sixty (dear god) minutes later, she'd watch those women emerge from open doors or dark shadows, or dangle from the passenger-side doors of truck cabs, tight skirts inching up as their fancy footwear sniffed for solid ground, shuffling back to the patio with a wad of cash tucked away somewhere private and safe. So tidy. So fair. Expectations and limits communicated clearly, delivered to the customer's satisfaction. Everything friendly. Everything reasonable. The fair contract of an industry that's been fine-tuning itself since 2400 BCE.

# 6

THE NEXT NIGHT, after she'd put Lotte down, Dani pulled on her least tattered leggings and her sportiest-looking nursing tank top and told a lie to Clark. He'd just finished rinsing the dinner dishes, making a tower of them *next* to the sink, like a little boy with blocks, instead of filing them away in the dishwasher, where surely to god he knew they'd end up eventually. But it was *fine*, because here she was about to lie to him, and this way he a little bit deserved it.

Without a word between them she took over in the kitchen, and he exited into the connecting dining room. She listened as he spread papers across the table, cleared his throat, snapped his glasses case. When she walked in, he was scowling over his frames at an open manila folder.

"I'm taking a yoga class with Anya," she said.

He looked up and let the folder fall to the table. "Oh." He pulled off the glasses, tossed them on the table. "Right now?"

"Sorry," she said, fists clenched, nails searing crescents into her palms. For the first time in twelve months she was leaving the house after seven p.m., twelve months she'd spent hidden away from the moon, which really mattered to some women. Like Dawn, who claimed that strategic moon exposure helped her conceive her second son. "I guess I forgot to mention."

"No," he sighed. "It's fine. I just—what if she wakes up?"

"Well, then I guess we'll all die, Clark."

He pushed himself back in his chair. "I really don't have the energy for sarcasm right now." And he gestured, without actually gesturing, to the papers smeared all over the table, suggesting, without actually saying, that he had far more important things to do than quibble with his silly little dependent, who, in his opinion, was trying to shirk her responsibilities onto him, a man doing *his part*, fulfilling his end of the termless, conditionless, completely unvetted agreement they'd entered into after Lotte was born.

"That's nice, Clark."

"What?" he exhaled.

"It's fine, I'll stay home. Just in case the baby wakes up, her mother should be here, right?"

"Dani," Clark exhaled. "You *know* that's not what I meant."

Dani knew she'd struck a nerve here. Because Clark was the type of man who, in his own mind, wasn't *like* other men. Of course he'd never had a colorectal screening, or called his brothers, or cried unless he was shit-faced, but he *did* support the mother of his child in her endless pursuit of self-care. He knew to correct friends who referred to time spent with their kids as babysitting. He wouldn't dream of retreating to a pathetic man cave at night. He wore fine socks and had an adequately warm winter coat. He was *reasonable*. He was *rational*. A man of science, despite the fact that he hadn't taken a science class since tenth grade, or ever read a book on the subject. He knew, though, that scientific truth was absolute. Dani would remind him that only religious people believed in absolutes, and Clark was, of *course*, just like many *other men*, a vocal atheist! Proof of his rationality, his *intelligence*. His character! No one had to *tell* Clark to be good. He simply *was* good. He bought ethically sourced coffee. He donated a dollar when prompted by cashiers. He never took a sick day and doggedly pursued promotions and took on extra projects and stayed late and mentored his juniors. Clark did everything correctly, and all he asked for in return was everything.

"Well then, what *are* you saying, Clark? Do you want me to stay home or not? If it's what you want, then just fucking say so."

"I don't—" He slumped forward, exhaled. "I *don't* want you to stay home. I want you to go. I want you to have fun. What time will you be home?"

Something about how easily he accepted her very sudden interest in regular exercise was extremely annoying to her. Dani wasn't a *yoga person*—she never had been. But *moms* were. At least every fourth profile picture in the mom forums was a badly bowing downward dog or tilted tree pose, executed in front of some noteworthy landscape, or, if the mom was a bit cheeky, she would hold her pose in the center of a shockingly messy playroom: *Namastay in the moment today, mamas!* Gentle, nonstrenuous exercise, a finite length of time, usually an hour, serving as almost a pill of "me time," which all of them were supposed to take, if not daily, then at *least* once a week. Together, moms had fought to normalize yoga pants in public—finally a socially acceptable *and* comfortable garment for women, the first of its kind. It hadn't been easy. Many were mocked. But now we had them, thanks to yoga.

"Class is an hour"—flatly, irritated.

"It really is fine," he exhaled, oblivious to her tone. "I'm just tired." He leaned back in the chair. The light above the table highlighted the truth of this statement. Dani softened to the same texture of the flesh beneath his eyes. He *had* been working very hard. The flagship project of the Metcalf office, *his* new office, was a high-end condo development called The Ellison—bold, he called it. *Luxurious.* He often bandied about the term *functional opulence* when describing the materials, the floor plans, how the building would do more than simply respect the streetscape upon which it was built but actually help it flourish. Clark wanted to focus on community-based development, which pleased the suits from a marketing perspective. Things like this mattered to the monied environmentalists who were turning the town around; they wanted to be able to explain to their friends that they weren't part of the mass plundering of a working-class town, but rather were integrating themselves, as gently as possible, into the history of the town's *progress.* Painful now perhaps, as growth so often is, but ultimately for the greater good. The Ellison would boast exemplary thermal mass, which would help the building retain heat and reduce energy consumption. It would create the blue-print for large-scale organic waste disposal, to be implemented in residential and commercial buildings across the city and beyond. The Ellison would be made with the most sustainable materials on the market, from the frames to the carpets, lights, and fix-tures. A community garden and a gym and a vast rooftop patio. Thoughtful design. Bragging rights. Clark knew that it would draw more newcomers to the city. But finding a spot to break ground was proving difficult—bested by archaic bylaws, battled by renters, blasted by small business owners in public land tribunal meetings. Ultimately, Clark said, things would swing his way, the momentum at this point unstoppable, but those noisy citizens would certainly inflict the few injuries they could.

Dani lifted one of the brochures from the table: tall 1920s font; faceless ciphers haunting art deco mock-ups of a lobby, a gym. He'd agonized over these brochures. Late nights on the phone with the graphic designer, two Saturday afternoons at the printer, checking the colors, testing different card stock. "These look great, Clark," said Dani.

"Thanks." He smiled, replaced his glasses, returned to the hunched position she'd found him in.

She held the monitor in her hand, digitized roar of Lotte's noise machine subdued by her palm. "I'll leave this here, then?" she said, releasing the speaker and setting it down on the table. He nodded and hummed approval without looking up.

And it was that easy. She was out the door. She was in the car. She was driving to the north end of Barton Street, parking just across the street from The Temple. And with the engine very suddenly off and all the space its roaring and clicking and whirring once occupied now empty, Dani felt genuinely exhilarated in a way she hadn't since those two little lines on the pregnancy test announced Lotte's growing cellular significance. She sank low in the driver's seat, chin to chest, light hair packed itchy beneath a navy bucket hat. A few strands levitating before her face, held aloft by her breathing, hot and low and loud and steady, what Bill, Anya's contentedly celibate yoga enthusiast husband, might eagerly point out as *ujjayi* breathing, an important tool of his practice.

She tracked the activities of a few women in the street, though with these new bars and cafés, she couldn't be sure who was *working* and who wasn't. No one seemed to look like they were supposed to anymore. She thought she might have spotted the barista with the hand tattoo, trotting toward a car full of similarly alternative beauties. Or maybe they weren't even beauties. Maybe they were just young. At thirty-five, Dani had wobbled over a tipping point she hadn't seen coming: youth no longer a fact of someone's biography, but an essence, something a mystical hag might bottle and huff for energy. So now, to her haggy eyes, everyone young was a bit beautiful. Which meant that she'd once been beautiful too. She just wished she'd known.

And then the car full of stylishly dilapidated beauties lurched into drive and growled out of its spot, revealing another woman behind it, heading toward the Pleasant Stay Inn, a midsize motel into which Barton Street terminated, and The Temple's only immediate neighbor. Two stacked L-shaped floors, pink stucco, freshly power-washed, with potted plants between the thin white doors. Ornate white metal parapets along the second floor and down the stairs. The woman crossed the inn's large grassy lot confidently, long, strong legs slicing through the buoyant front flaps of a sheer duster, dark green with delicate embroidery around the chest and shoulders, a pair of shredded denim shorts and a white tank top underneath. Her curly brown hair razored into one of the big, bouncing shags Dani screenshotted almost daily but would never have the nerve to try. The woman marched up the stairs, a door on the second floor. She fiddled for a moment at the handle, executing the tried-and-true remedies for a finicky key card, once in the slot, twice; then she rubbed the magnetized strip against her duster. Finally it worked, the handle turned, and she stepped into the dark opening. In that exact instant, two more women emerged from doors on either side of hers, like a cuckoo clock. They too were dressed in the kinds of clothes Dani would only screenshot—one in a short black T-shirt dress, floral combat boots; the other in a pair of perfect straight-leg jeans, a sleeveless mock-neck crop top. The two women caught eyes, linked arms, then skittered together like shards of metal down the steps, across the parking lot, to The Temple's magnetic patio, filled once again with gorgeous women smoking cigarettes, holding light beers by their necks, and chatting in the easy way Dani's mom used to, when she worked for a brief time with Wanda at the Paradise Bingo. Just after DJ died, before everyone hated her for blowing the fortune they'd helped him earn. At the bingo, all of them had been in it together. No one better off than anyone else, sharing the indignities of their labor, like any other job, so it didn't collect in their corners and corrode their souls.

It made Dani think of a time when she worked for the only Blockbuster in town as it was going out of business. Corporate swiftly invalidated all coupons and forwarded complicated repricing guidelines, squeezing as much money as possible from the dwindling inventory. Smug looks from delinquent customers, fees now expunged, walking the aisles without shame. Regulars rightfully furious that their Blue Pass Entertainment Booklets had been stripped of all value. Dani and her coworkers had to sticker, then re-sticker, then re-sticker again the store's increasingly pillaged merchandise. Men with toothpicks wedged in the corners of their mouths wanted to know how much for the fixtures. A man and woman with matching neck tattoos tried to sell back a stack of stolen movies. Dani felt like some sort of cursed guardian, tasked with protecting this blue-and-yellow corpse from the mites and maggots drooling at the door.

Those had been the worst couple months of her life, and she'd endured them for less than $8 an hour.

She still thought of the coworkers in those trenches with

unparalleled warmth, wishing that Cam, the assistant manager, were sitting with her right now, the two of them making jokes about the asshole in calf-height white socks and orthopedic walking sneakers, renting *Barb Wire* again, "for his son," as though that lie weren't more horrifying than the truth. Or the woman with too much white around her irises who tried to get a refund for renting *Brokeback Mountain*. Dani and Cam would tape the *Back in Five Minutes* sign to the locked front door to take twenty minutes grabbing Slurpees from the 7-Eleven. They would make heaps of Blockbuster-brand popcorn and watch non-corporate-approved movies on the *big* television. But also they cleaned diligently and never failed to perform their shrinkage counts; they pushed new releases and remembered the names and preferences of their regulars—they'd both warned the wild-eyed woman about *Brokeback Mountain*, that not all Jake Gyllenhaal movies were like *October Sky*!

And that meant that *this*, with what she understood from serial killer documentaries about the levels of suffering in the sex industry, could actually be *nice*. Like how Blockbuster was, in retrospect, quite nice. How the bonds she built with Cam and the others had been so ferociously *real*.

And in that moment it began to rain on Barton Street. A friendly spritz, searing the edges off the heat. It made the patio's rough terrain look vibrant, grabbing light from a canopy of strung yellow bulbs into its slickened surfaces. Dani noticed stacked and cracked terra-cotta pots now. Battered baby dolls seated along the edge of the building, a few headless, growing vines from their threaded necks. Succulents. Fuzzy cacti. Flowering lavender. A vintage vacuum canister filled with umbrellas. Folding lawn chairs someone's grandmother would never notice missing. All set against a chain-link wall of matted ivy that ran the length of the patio to the threshold of a densely spray-painted alleyway marking The Temple's boundary.

The rain picked up steam and the villagers reacted, one welcoming it on her skin, pulling out a rickety lawn chair, hiking up her skirt, and letting it fall on her outstretched legs. Head back, hair a long golden comet's tail, grazing the concrete. Dani wished she could take a photograph, but it wouldn't do the reality justice. Maybe a professional could. A momfluencer with the right lights and camera.

Some of the other women scurried through the dark doors of The Temple; a few others, no less dazzling, stopped to finish their cigarettes beneath the rusted awnings, flicked glowing orange butts like the pesky residue of a spell from their fingers.

And then Dani spotted her, a startlingly incongruous brunette, operating a lighter with miraculous success despite the rain, permitting the eager flame to lap at a nub of black eyeliner.

It was hard for Dani to put her finger on the way in which this woman stood out. She wasn't the oldest villager or the most beautiful; in fact, it wasn't anything about *her* at all, but rather the way the other women *moved* around her. And didn't. How all of them were so conscious of her gaze, of her approval, but not, it was somehow clear, because she *withheld* her approval. In fact, it was the opposite. It was her generosity, Dani realized, which was somehow visible with the naked eye, from all the way across the street, through her rain-speckled windshield. This woman was a bottomless feeder bar, an endless supply of treats for the spirit, and the other women hopped around her like a flock of highly intelligent birds.

This visibly generous woman approached one of The Temple's windows, which Dani noticed now were deeply tinted, reflective, and pulled one eye tight to apply her newly softened eye-liner, a perfect wing. And in the way dusk both encroaches and ambushes, Dani realized with horror that the visibly generous woman was looking at her in the reflection, through the pulled-tight, heavily winged eye, her red lips pressed into a suspicious line.

Dani panicked, sat up, pulled off the bucket hat she'd idiotically assumed brought her not just anonymity but *invisibility* apparently, fucking *idiot*, and flung it to the backseat. She couldn't just drive away, not now, not now that she'd been spotted. She squeezed the wheel with both hands, knuckles about to split through her skin. *How* had this woman noticed her? How had she possibly known, with all the activity on Barton Street, that Dani was here quite specifically to look at *her*, or, rather, her village? There must have been something about the way Dani was parked, the way she looked, or perhaps this woman, after so many years on the job, simply *knew* things about people, operated at a level of human understanding that Dani couldn't possibly fathom.

Or *maybe*, Dani thought, head tilted, face pinched with grim wonder, this sort of thing happened often—women who looked just like Dani, who drove sensible vans caulked in yogurt and cracker crumbs, came to scope out the *situation*, trying to see if they could handle it. Because they too had left themselves vulnerable to poverty, not on purpose, but because that's just how it went. Evolution favors the path of least resistance. No animal in the world survived by working twice as hard for half the resources. Evolution takes the easy way. Evolution is only as good as it has to be. Like how the world works for men.

And then of course there are the babies. And the prohibitively expensive childcare. And the studies about daycare and aggres-

sion. Daycare and developmental delays. Daycare and attach-
ment disorders. Was *any* job worth that? It just made more *sense*,
didn't it? To stay home and raise them yourself?

WE WEREN'T BUILT TO OUTSOURCE OUR BABIES,
screamed MUM2GABBY.

The visibly generous woman had now turned around, still
staring at Dani. She capped her eyeliner, handed it off to another
villager, who took her place in the reflective surface, tucked in
close to embellish her own bare eyelids.

*Oh my GOD*, thought Dani, *wait, NO*. She sipped a sharp,
unsatisfying breath. Did the visibly generous woman think Dani
was a potential *client*? Dani's heartbeat gathered a sickening force,
rippling the blood in her veins. The visibly generous woman,
still staring at Dani, left the patio, stood at the curb. Her black
wedges glistening from the rain. She let a cab pass, the sear of tire
on wet concrete, then trotted out just behind it, raised a hand,
said something Dani couldn't hear through the seal of the car.

"What was that?" Dani warbled to the inside of the car, then
shook her head, embarrassed, fumbled to crack the window.
"What was that?" she repeated, sloppily concealing her nerves
with volume. But the woman went to the passenger-side door,
knocked on the window, made the undeniable *let me in* gestures.

She was older than Dani by maybe a decade, maybe more.
The pretty face of a low-maintenance brunette but with the deep,
intensely dark eyes of a dove. Mesmerized by them, coerced,
Dani reached over to unlock the door, hesitated with her fingers
hooked over the handle. She examined the rest of the woman's
face: The swollen bow of her upper lip. Her sturdy, slope-less
nose. That thick eyeliner, freshly applied, flourish aimed with
remarkable symmetry toward the tail of each manicured brow.

That generosity, her *presence*, was palpable even through the door. An important part of the village. A mother. If she couldn't let this village mother in the car, how could she continue to comfort herself with the illusion of an *option*: working among them, chatting with them on the patio, drinking, letting them into her and Lotte's life, closer than friends, than sisters even. If she couldn't unlock the door and let this woman into her car, then the only source of relief that Dani had would be completely undermined. If she couldn't open the door and let this woman in the car, then she'd be right back to grinding her teeth all night, picturing Lotte attacked by the other kids for her Reebak sneakers and Levy jeans, forced to attend community college because Dani couldn't afford to send her to the Ivy League schools she would have gotten into, perfect little genius that she was.

Dani yanked the handle and pushed open the door.

The woman brought the smell of rain and warm asphalt and cigarette smoke in with her like a veil. She put her half-empty beer bottle in the cupholder and ran her fingers along her scalp and through to the tips of her hair, then allowed a shiver to run wild through her body and whinny out her mouth. Finally settled, she turned to Dani. "Well, hello!" she said, eyebrows raised.

*Oh god*, thought Dani, *she really does think I'm a john. A jane?* "I'm not, I'm not looking for, I'm not a *jane*, I—"

The woman burst out laughing, not a cruel laugh, just a few round, good-natured spasms that made Dani laugh too, in spite of her nerves. "A *jane*! Oh, I'll have to remember that one. Honey, no," she said, winding down, "no, no, no." Four cool fingers quickly grazed Dani's arm, then stopped, squeezed. Short, strong fingernails. "I didn't think you were."

"Oh, good! Okay, good." Still smiling, bending her own

nutrient-sapped nails with her thumb. "Not that there's anything wrong with being a jane, I just, I'm not one, so. God, I'm
sorry, I—"

"No, no need to apologize. No need for anything, really, I just
noticed you there, from across the street. And I wanted to know
what the fuck it is you're doing here." Her face very suddenly
shed its friendliness. Destabilizing Dani with the depthless dark
of her dove eyes. A ghoul. A vampire. Who she'd *invited* into
the car.

Dani looked down into her lap, where her hands had found
each other, rubbing together. "I just, I was passing by, and—"

"Come on now," she said, and Dani looked up, compelled.
Just as she'd been *compelled* to open up the door. Something she
had to do. Something she was meant to do. *Hellish prophecy.* "We
both know that's not true. What's your name?"

"Dani," she said, then cleared her throat and said it louder.
"My name is Dani."

"Pleased to meet you, Dani. My name is Renata. Let me tell
you something about me, all right? This is true now. I'm a human
lie detector. I really am. No one has ever been able to lie to me.
You might have noticed just now actually, when you tried to. You
felt it, right? That block in your mind. It's my gift, all right? So
don't waste my time. Just go ahead and tell me the truth. What
the fuck are you doing here?"

And somehow this question was presented without hostility,
with actual, genuine curiosity instead. Dani would learn that this
was just how Renata spoke, the word *fuck* almost never used in
anger, instead a benign and colorful modifier, part of her thrilling
and unusual way of making a person feel completely and totally
comfortable and unjudged.

*I'm here because I'm the Trash Princess of Metcalf. I'm here to fulfill a hellish prophecy. I'm here because I'm worthless. Incapable of functioning in the straight world. I'm here because I'm both weak and indestructible. And different from everybody else. The center of everyone's universe in my own mind, except my own universe, where I am a second-class citizen. I'm here because I need money, because I want my body to be useful again . . . I . . . I . . . I . . .*

But instead Dani could only stutter, "I—I don't know. I, I, I—"

"Just spit it out, girl, I'm not mad, I'm just curious. Start at the beginning. You left your house tonight, right?" She walked her fingers along her leg. "Got into your car." She put her hands on an imaginary wheel. "Got into your little fucking uniform." She mimed putting on a bucket hat—Dani spread her fingers over her face, smiled sheepishly. "And drove here, right? What made you do all that?"

"To watch you," Dani blurted, this truth spilling easily from her mouth; it was true, Renata's essence shorting some crucial, ego-preserving synapse in her brain. And such a malfunction should be existentially terrifying, but it wasn't. Not at all. Not with Renata.

"Well, I'm flattered," Renata replied in a deadpan impression of a Southern belle.

"Not you specifically."

Renata feigned shock, pouted and crossed her arms.

"I just mean *all* of you," Dani clarified, and gestured at The Temple's patio, made only slightly sparser by the developing rain, droplets amassing on the wide shoulders of vintage denim jackets as the women waited for cabs or finished off smokes. "I might— I was curious about, th-the job."

"And what job is that?" asked Renata. She eased a cigarette out of a full pack and offered it to Dani, who accepted without thinking. The last time she'd smoked was at a house party when Anya came to visit her in college. She loved it so much she knew she could never do it again.

"I guess, well, sex work. Is that what you do here? If I've got the wrong idea, please feel free to shoot me in the face."

"No, no, not the wrong idea. But not exactly right either, I'm sure." Renata produced a lighter, the one she'd borrowed from the villager for her eyeliner. Dani rolled down their windows, set the cigarette in her lips then leaned into the flame. Spasms of guilt—Lotte watching her die of lung cancer, alone in the world without a mother. Voices from the forum, burrowing into the guilt-weakened cavities of her brain:

> *MUM2GABBY: parents may think that not smoking around their children is enough, but it is NOT, thirdhand smoke is the tobacco residue that sticks to clothing, furniture, walls, bodies, CAR SEATS, after people smoke, and it is JUST AS BAD as secondhand smoke! Little one's lungs are still developing! Children exposed to thirdhand smoke are FOUR TIMES as likely to visit the emergency room within the first few years of life.*

> *ANITABREAK: SOURCES PLEASE! @ MUM2GABBY, and the rest of you ladies, please source your comments if you're going to make a claim like that—I'm not saying thirdhand smoke isn't bad but is it really worth keeping your child away from her grandparents who smoke?? Hmmmmmmm I don't know about that.*

*ROLYPOLYLOVINIT: Um, her grandparents should be respecting her wishes if they want to see there grandchild!!!!!!!!!!!!!! It's not up to everyone else to suffer just because there stubborn!!!!!!!!!!!!!! I'm sorry but that's ridiculus!!!!!!!!!!!!!!*

*MAMAMILKBAGS: My baby spent three days w grandparents both smoked and when she came home her pupe was yellow! Its gets in their mouths okay they are inside and stick their hands in their moutsh and it smakes pupe yellow!*

Renata, quite possibly reading Dani's mind, nodded back at the car seat. "How old?" she asked.

"Almost a year." Dani held the smoke in her lungs for too long, suppressed a cough with an awkward moan when she exhaled as pointedly as possible from the open window.

Renata graciously ignored the sound. "Must be a good sleeper," she said. "If you're out here tonight." She held her cigarette out the window, stretched her neck through to drag.

"She is now, thank god."

"Your husband is at home?"

"He is."

"He has a job?"

"He does."

"Makes enough money for you to have this car"—gesturing with what Dani noticed again was a truly handsome and capable hand—"that fancy car seat"—short, clean, durable fingernails. The type of hands that remind you that these things are, in fact, tools fashioned from flesh and bone. For survival: the univer-

sal trade. Dani tried not to think about how Renata might put
her hands to use each night at The Temple. She glanced at her
own hands. The crescents that had earlier marred her palms.
She'd have to trim her nails. Depending on what a client might—
where she might be expected to—she shook the thought from
her mind, tried to stay focused on what Renata was saying instead
of where her hands had been. "I'll bet," said Renata, leaning in,
recapturing her gaze, "you even own a *home*."

A mirthless laugh, "Well, just barely," a reaction practiced
among other people her age, a way of apologizing for having
snuck into the housing market against all odds. "Actually, I don't
know why I said that," she surprised herself by saying. "I have
no idea how stretched we are with the mortgage. We might not
even be stretched at all." It felt good to admit this, to Renata, but
more so to herself. "I really wouldn't know."

Renata nodded, understanding what this meant, how useless
Dani had allowed herself to become. "Well, you're going to have
to explain it to me, then. Why are you so curious about the job?"

"Because . . ." Dani's heart began to wallop in her chest; she
couldn't look Renata in the eyes, articulating this paranoia, how
insane and pathetic she would sound, how ridiculous and naive
and spoiled a person must be to want to pick up this life instead
of, say, a community college info kit. To think that she *could*
pick up this life, with no training, no real experience, like it was
nothing, like there was no skill at all in compelling bodies to
produce orgasms. She did all right with *Clark*, sure, but there
was no possible way she was giving the most optimal blow jobs.
Often her jaw would hurt; she had no real sense of what to do
with her hands, the male body something she often just *beat* to
climax, vigorously, without enough tenderness or finesse, she was
sure. Dani couldn't speak. She bit her lips together, looked into

her lap. "Because . . ." she said again. And someone other than Renata might have saved her from this palpable discomfort, dove into it and yanked the plug by changing the subject. But Dani quickly understood that Renata wouldn't do that. Instead she let the uncomfortable silence fill the car like carbon monoxide, a dreamy billowing that lulled Dani's frantic heart, helped her open her eyes wider and declare more truth. "Because I'm worried my husband is going to die and I won't be able to support my baby."

"Why couldn't you get a job like your husband?"

And Dani lowered her head, stared up at Renata darkly. "I can't."

"Why not?"

"I'm not . . . good at this world," she said, and her voice broke at the end, eyes filling with tears.

Renata understood this completely too. "It's not a good world."

Dani tamped down the tears with a sniff. "No." And she had to laugh at the understatement. "It's really not."

"Your husband, is he sick or something?"

"Not at all. Healthy as can be." She knocked on her head, a superstitious impulse she hadn't acted on in years. Renata knocked on her own head too, in solidarity. "I just—"

"You've got a bad feeling."

Dani nodded. "A very bad feeling." The tears threatened again. Dani held them in her chest, sealed her lips against them. She looked out the window, closed one eye, held her cigarette so its glowing end eclipsed part of the Pleasant Stay Inn's massive fluorescent sign. *Stay Inn*, the sign was telling her, a message from MUM2GABBY. *Stay Inn and be with your baby, you piece of shit.* She brought the cigarette back to her mouth, dragged quickly, a shaky exhale. *Don't cry. Don't cry.*

"It's okay, honey," said Renata. She reached over, squeezed Dani's arm again, as she had when she first entered the car, and the gesture acted as a release valve, the tears spilled down Dani's cheeks like condensation, a fact of the atmosphere. "Let it out," she said. "I'll tell you whatever you want to know."

"Is this—" Dani moved her arms around, waving at the street, the bar, the patio. "I mean, I don't want to be an asshole, but is this . . . okay?" She shook her head in apology. "You don't have to answer that. I don't even know what I'm doing here." She flicked her cigarette out the window and pulled a dried stiff wet wipe from the cupholder, folded it against the fresh tears collecting at the bridge of her nose, the stale ones down her cheeks.

"Look," said Renata, pointing at The Temple. "This? This is my place, right here. This is *my* place. I own it. I bought it with the money I made *helping* people. And that's what we do here, all right? We help people. I'm sure you've got some ideas about—"

"Oh, no, I don't—"

"Don't be silly. Of course you do." Her dove eyes flickered, absorbing light, reminding Dani not to bother with lying. "You're thinking about cracked-out streetwalkers in highly flammable dresses, beaten to a pulp, strangled, murdered, right? Broken, bruised, tracked-up bodies abandoned in alleys. Which does happen. And it's fucking horrible. It's the worst thing in the world, women having to work in the shadows, no protection from the cops, no respect for their work, work they're good at, you know, everyone who works in society should be respected, doesn't matter what kind of work. But we're not there yet, unfortunately. We're getting there, but we're not there yet."

"That doesn't happen here?"

"Not at The Temple it doesn't. There are a few on Barton Street who still go it alone, of course. They don't see things the way I do, and that's fair. In many ways it's a privilege to be able to see men the way we do at The Temple, not victims exactly but . . . creatures with pain."

Dani raised an eyebrow at Renata. "Creatures with pain," she repeated slowly, as though she'd missed a step, and then a small commotion on The Temple's patio caught her eye, a tall man warmly welcomed, absorbed by the crowd. Good posture and broad shoulders in a simple cotton T-shirt, the kind folded by robots and sealed into a bag, hung ten deep from long pegs at supercenters. Though it fit him like something much finer, tailored, expensive, his the original frame for which T-shirts had been created, the platonic ideal, his body a higher truth. Clean-shaven with a tidy haircut as innocuous as his clothing, but his smile was big and sloppy and easy, his eyes pressed too deep into exhaustion-softened darkness, a sweet face that belied a troubled past, a sad secret, a lonesome life. Dani's pulse quickened. She held her neck to steady it, but also, irrationally, to quiet it. Renata heard, though, of course, uniquely attuned to the various throbbings of a human body.

"That's Brandon," said Renata. "He's a regular."

Dani realized her mouth was open. She closed it. Squeezed her thighs together. "Huh" was all she could say.

Renata chuckled. "Not what you were expecting, is he."

Dani shook her head without taking her eyes off Brandon.

"Do you like yoga?"

Dani, jostled by the coincidence of Renata asking her about yoga. "What?"

"Do you like yoga?"

"I mean, sure, yeah. I birthed a small child, didn't I?"

Renata sucked a final drag from her cigarette and flicked it directly into a puddle out the window, nodding as she exhaled.

"We teach yoga here too," she said, blowing the last bits of smoke from her lungs, waving it away from the car. "During the day usually. Sometimes at night. Mostly Kundalini. Have you ever practiced Kundalini?"

"Maybe? I think so, actually. A few classes here and there with, I don't know, people who are too hot to waitress, but not hot enough to model."

Renata laughed. "That's very mean," she said.

"I'm a very mean person." Then Dani raised her chest with a deep breath, relieved by another admission. "Oof," she laughed a bit, lighter, "that actually felt good to say." Then she laughed harder. Renata joined her. "I'm mean!" Dani wheezed. "A meanie!" Both of them on their way to fits of near hysterics, concluding, finally, in a breathless howl, a wiped tear. "Ooooooh, so fucking mean." Sniffing. "Not a nice person at all, I'm serious."

"You should come by sometime"—Renata, still catching her breath. "For a yoga class. If you want."

"And by yoga, you mean—what? Why are you making that face?"

Renata's expression had shifted into the sort of friendly grin reserved for benign errors, sweet misunderstandings. "You've really never heard of us, have you."

"Us?"

"The Temple. You've really never heard of The Temple before tonight."

"No."

"I thought you said you were from here, didn't you?"

"Did I? I mean, I am, but—"

"Why don't you come inside now." Renata patted the side of the car twice, like a horse, and reached for the handle. "I can introduce you to some of the girls. To Brandon."

"Oh, I don't—" Dani raised her hands, surprised somehow to find another lit cigarette wedged between her fingers, flung it out the window. "Maybe another night, I—"

"Okay, tomorrow then. Come by tomorrow. Okay?"

Suddenly presented with the actual prospect of entering Renata's not-exactly-brothel, her sexy yoga studio or whatever it was they did in there, Dani felt intimidated. *Nauseated?* Her bluff called. Maybe she'd never had any intention of going inside. Maybe this was all a great, pathetic moan for attention. Maybe she could never return again, not here, not even to Barton Street.

Her phone buzzed in the center console. She glanced down at the glowing screen. Clark.

"Thank you," Dani said, reaching for her phone, peeking at the text: *What time are you home?* "Tomorrow, I'll come back tomorrow." She set the phone back, facedown, smiled distractedly, both hands returned to the wheel now to indicate her readiness to depart.

Renata reached over, took one of Dani's hands in both of hers, formed a shell around it, precious, alive. Protected. Renata held her gaze. "You should, Dani. You really, *really* should come back tomorrow, okay?" And as Dani nodded, she felt the breath in her lungs evaporate.

When Renata turned and left and closed the door behind her, Dani had to inhale so quickly and deeply that it triggered a coughing fit. "No more cigarettes," she announced nervously to the empty car, as though MUM2GABBY were in the backseat, arms crossed, shaking her tight-lipped head.

# 7

WHEN SHE GOT HOME, the front door only opened halfway before banging into something big. Heavy. She shouldered it the rest of the way, against the weight of the object, so it slid along the floor. She looked down. A cardboard box. The padded foot of a blue fleece onesie flopped from the rectangular opening at the top.

"Fuck," she whispered, remembering too late, of course, that Anya had said she'd be dropping off a box of clothes tonight, for Lotte.

*I'll just bring them all over and you can take a look. Something tells me our ideas of gender-neutral are very different*—and Anya had laughed, like Dani was some pitiable radical who'd one day grow up and realize that resistance is futile.

Anya had fucked her with this box. Not on purpose, of course, she couldn't be mad, but truly she'd fucked her. Dani had no idea how she was going to explain this to Clark, who assumed she'd been *with* Anya at a yoga class, and who surely, upon opening the door and seeing Anya there, had felt quite understandably confused. Betrayed. *What time are you home?* he'd asked innocuously, attempting to lure her deeper into the lie. And deeper she'd tumbled: *Soon! Anya's just picking up a monthly pass.*

She nudged the box farther into the hallway, sat on the bench next to the door, unlaced her shoes. Dread and shame swarmed and stripped each fruiting branch in her lungs, making it difficult to breathe. Upstairs Clark's weight tortured the floorboards— bathroom to bedroom and back again. Waiting for her. A liar.

There was really no good excuse for this. She couldn't possibly tell him where she'd actually been, smoking cigarettes with a prostitute right in the fucking *van*. Inquiring about *the job. I'm not going to* do it, *Clark, I just need to know that I* can. But he would never understand. He'd worry about her. He'd force her to see a psychiatrist. He might involve *Bunny. Anya.* Everyone who loved her the most, the very last people in the world she could ever tell the truth to.

A class, though. Maybe a class. To improve her *skills*. He would believe she'd hide a class: continuing education, night classes, the practical embodiment of having given up on your specialness. And he did believe it.

"Orientation! You're going to take a *class*? Why would you hide that from me?" he asked, so gently, *my silly little dependent*, touching her face, kissing her cheek, because he knew the answer. Knew *her*.

"I don't know, Clark," she said. And he nodded, full of sympathy, the most supportive frown, a good, good person. "It's embarrassing. Human resource management? Like, I don't know, is this who I am? Dani from human resources, happy Friday from the paid narc!"

"No, no, it's not like that. I think you'll be *amazing* in human resources—you're a great listener, problem solver, communica-

tor. Everyone loves you! And they'll all come to you for help and
you'll actually be able to help them. Plus, there's always work,
especially these days, you know? Hiring is such a different ball
game now. It's not just about having the technical skills anymore,
right? It's about the soft skills, and really knowing how to build
a *team*. The *right* team. It's not just payroll and expenses, Dani,
there's software for that now. It's about understanding people,
psychology, organizational behavior. I just, I think this is a really
smart move." A spark in his eye—finally she was talking about
something he actually gave a shit about.

"Sure, right," she said, barely understanding what he was saying. She slumped, walked toward him with her arms straight
down, and fell forward into his chest. "Are you mad at me for
lying?"

He hugged her tight. "No, not at all. I think this is great."
He rubbed her back. "It's really great." She stared into the wall,
a warm clay color, sort of deliberately ruddy, textured, and
nice to look at. She stared into it. Breathed in the smell of his
clothes. His chest. And changed her mind. Clark was definitely
a good person. Supportive. Loved her. He thought she'd be great
in human resources, and why wouldn't she be? Didn't human
resources require all the skills of a motherjester? *A great listener,
problem solver, communicator.* The ability to put a person at ease.
To make a person laugh. *Observant in ways that made people
feel special.* Making people feel special, wasn't that essentially
employee retention? An important focus of HR, especially in
*this* market, according to Clark. And wasn't that the job of a
jester, of a mother, to make the *right* people feel special? Maybe
HR is where all the great motherjesters finally land. Maybe if
she took a class, even just one class, she could make a village of
the other motherjesters she found there. Maybe this was it. HR.

Her secret skill finally unlocked. Hidden from her by her own arrogance all these years. Her false sense of superiority. The Trash Princess of Metcalf.

A sex worker. Ha! Who the fuck was she kidding? Who the fuck did she think she was? She couldn't produce an original line of dirty talk if she tried; literally took an annual hiatus from her suboptimal blow jobs through allergy season. She was pretty sure she had a sensitive cervix. Weak wrists. A tendency to bladder infections. The *work*. Had she really thought about *the work*? Having sex in exchange for money? She had, of course. Of course she had. In much the same way she'd previously thought about rape or childbirth: a thing out there that could very well happen to her. An event that would remove her from her body, divide her into two. Women had to live with the possibility of these things. These *occurrences*. These great, harrowing *splits*. Had to imagine them. Had to *prepare*.

But that didn't mean she'd be any good at it.

So human resources, then. Why not? HR would never challenge her cervix. It would never give her a bladder infection or an STI. And at least she'd still get to know a few dirty secrets.

# 8

THE NEXT MORNING Dani felt groggy, disoriented, as though she'd been drugged. Had Renata's cigarette been laced with something? Was this how a woman was turned out these days? Hardly sporting. Definitely some shame in that game. The thought had barely materialized before it was gone again. Because even though she'd only just met her last night, Dani knew with absolute certainty that Renata would never do a thing like that, and secondly that no such substance, such *lady-of-the-night accelerator*, existed. Most likely it was a small sort of hangover from the single cigarette, which seemed unjust, but was actually par for the course for mothers who dared brush elbows too soon with autonomy of any kind. These mothers, she knew firsthand, were swiftly and cruelly punished by the postpartum body. She recalled her first bout of mastitis, just a couple of weeks after Lotte was born, a breast infection that occurs when you go too long between feedings, punishment for trying to take some small scrap of yourself back too quickly. In Dani's case it'd been delaying Lotte's regularly scheduled feeding by an hour in favor of a little extra sleep for them both. This resulted in hours of flu-like aching, shivering, nausea, a swift and harsh retaliation courtesy of the hormones left behind by master Lotte, the master she loved, my god, how she loved her, loved her more when she relieved the suffering, her warm body on Dani's sore breast, draining the infection for her with the merciful maw of her powerful little jaw, thank you, master, oh god, thank you, thank you, good girl. The punishments would continue as she got older, of course, but transformed. Dani would have to watch as her own errors and failings as a mother, her uncorrected habits, her untethered dysfunction, caused Lotte pain. And she would suffer again, only worse this time, Lotte incapable of simply applying the heat of her body, draining the infection from their lives with her little mouth.

Unless Dani could fix herself. Build her own independent life. Unburden Lotte of all Dani had pinned to her, inadvertently, unintentionally, but a weight on her all the same. Dani would derive self-worth from her *work*, instead. Something *normal. Realistic.* Like HR, goddammit. She opened the browser on her phone and looked up Human Resources Management. A couple of summer classes still open for enrollment. Talent Acquisition. Labor Relations. *A really smart move*, Clark had said. Dani created an account. Signed up for Intro to Human Resources Management. Fell backward onto her bed and pressed the air-conditioned fat of her upper arm into her eye sockets.

It was a pale, watery morning. Dani and Lotte went to the park after breakfast. Lotte sat on the grass, at the edge of a sea of wood chips, scraping rivets with her heels into the soil beneath. Dani sat next to her, a Rorschach of cool mud seeping through her shorts, warmed instantly against her skin. Her creases. Brandon, moving easily among the women on the patio. A *creature with pain*. She stood up quickly. Brushed herself off. Lotte looked up at her, squinting beneath the wide brim of a polka-dot sun hat.

The next day their daily outing was to a coffee shop, then a few errands at the mall.

The day after that they took their daily outing at Anya's house, her backyard, for lemonade.

The day after that they had their daily outing at the decrepit splash pad in the city's central park: ancient, sun-bleached spray fixtures, clogged jets, cracked drains. Every MUM2GABBY in Metcalf had taken to the city's social media to complain about it. Dani watched water dribble from rusty nozzles and thought of Ellen. Of her mesh. Of a type of medication she'd once been tasked to write about, to reduce urinary incontinence in men: *alpha-blockers*. An unnecessarily cruel prescription to ask an incontinent man to hand to a possibly beautiful pharmacist. Lotte held her palm beneath the leaking mouth of a large orange fish, moved it to her mouth for a taste, squeezed out a perfunctory whine when Dani told her *no*.

Daily outings were a practice the moms in the forums insisted upon: jeans once a day so you didn't become complacent about your weight gain, fresh air for baby, sensory stimulation to encourage naps, but also visibility for you, because being seen was important, mothers being seen, a human being seen. It was amazing how swiftly the shadows could destroy you.

And the moms in the forums knew this to be true because they heard it from the momfluencers—the women on social media whose job it was to perform motherhood's most perfectly imperfect forms. The momfluencers juggled their shrieking broods to orchards and petting zoos and colorful cafés. They hiked to waterfalls, swam beneath them, emerged into the peace they concealed. All the children shirtless, coiled wet hair to their tailbones. On rainy days the brood crafted, deep in concentration, tongues clipped to their lips, their momfluencer mother meditating on the sound of the rain, how it harmonized with the trickles obscuring her window, making her feel like her family was the whole entire world. And on some days the momfluencers even cried. Yes, *cried*! *Real tears! Just like you!* A deliberate crack in their perfect image: cheeks and lips dewy, swollen. Because being a mom is *hard, you guys*! When it's not rewarding and meaningful and thrilling and intense, it's grueling and relentless and cruel and infuriating. *We all have these moments, mama,* says the text below their perfect sorrow, *but remember,* every moment *with your child,* every moment as a mama, *is a rare and precious jewel, part of a priceless treasure chest of chaos and mess and rage and fear and* transformation. You can get your body back, your friends, your life, your *brunches,* but this *time,* these fleeting jewels of *time,* you *won't* get back. And these momfluencers, in their astral-white peasant dresses, from fields of wildflowers, surrounded by six or seven of their outrageously blond and gorgeous children, assured the forum moms, the real-life moms, that they were *blessed goddesses,* capable of anything, bestowed with the greatest power, the greatest privilege, on earth. *You got this, mama!* From the influencers to the forums to Dani when she packed Lotte into her stroller for walks, or sometimes a trip in the car, a drive-thru for ice cream, Dani's jeans unbuttoned beneath her shirt. *You got this, mama!*

The mall, unfortunately, was Lotte's favorite place to go. Where Dani would be most likely to run into someone she knew. And had, of course—people from high school who shrieked when they saw her, demanded the CliffsNotes of her last ten years, right there, on the spot.

Worshippers of her father. Enemies of her mother, who'd shriveled beyond recognition.

Wanda, of course, always everywhere somehow, in Velcro sandals and noisy shorts. This week Wanda had hijacked almost twenty of Dani and Lotte's *precious* minutes talking about her new house—*something bigger, much bigger, for the dogs*—and asking whether Bunny had relayed any stories about all of Wanda's *bathroom drama*. Dani lied and said that Bunny had, then used Lotte as an excuse to leave: *Sorry, Wanda, looks like we've got our own bathroom drama to tend to!* Dani showed her bottom teeth, embarrassment, apology, and Wanda threw her tough dog-lover's hands up. *Of course! I'll see you at Bunny's soon!* Then she resumed her high-elbow power walk toward the essential oils store. *Gotta get lavender*, she'd screamed back over her shoulder, *for the skunks!*

In the food court Dani and Lotte watched popcorn spew from a large metal pot, filling a glass display case like a living spectacle.

They watched a young woman with braces and a flat-ironed ponytail folded into a hairnet as she crammed raw cinnamon buns into a baking tray. Her plastic gloves were too big and kept getting stuck to the dough.

They saw men's pale legs. Frail as roots. Buried all winter. Exposed now, too soon. Cold. Tortured. Standing in line for fast food. Bringing their trays to small tables, tucking into the attached chairs, alone, knees pointing in opposite directions. Too much thigh. Unsettling tendons. Dry knees. Leg hair. White socks. Sneakers. Dislocating their jaws to accommodate towers of beef patties; fries drawn up in limp, uncooperative bushels, gobbled like a chore. *Creatures with pain.*

Dani and Lotte stood in front of the As Seen on TV store, where a person could buy, or at least see in real life, all of the unusual products hawked to people like Bunny in the dark between days. Lotte in her stroller, facing out, fresh synapses firing tests into her restless feet. And Dani, forearms teetering on the stroller handle behind her, listened to the buckles on Lotte's sandals rattle. They watched the rows of activated massage chairs, motorized fists beneath faux leather skin roving in perfect, rhythmic circles as though they were breathing. Whole minutes passed this way, she and Lotte hypnotized, breathing deeply with the chairs: fake buttered popcorn, faint cinnamon, sad beef patties, every once in a while a thrilling gust of fresh packaging. *Here you go, Lotte, my love. This is life. Be stimulated. Sleep well. And Mother shall inhale your skin, rest her eyes upon your bobbing chest, planted in this place of gratitude, living fully in this treasure trove of time.*

And Bunny's house sometimes too, where she'd recently begun to allow Bunny to change Lotte's diaper. And after careful inspection of the box, the expiration date, even allowed Bunny to feed Lotte a few unsalted crackers. Bunny's house wasn't normal inside. Bunny, not a hoarder exactly, but certainly on the fringe of something a bit obsessive and unclean. Evicted, room by room, by a vast collection of artifacts, procured from infomercials, catalogues, even this very mall. Some of the artifacts, the oldest ones, came from both the finest shops in the county and the local dump. These days Bunny mostly just occupied the kitchen and the living room, where she slept on the couch. An end table crowded with water glasses, hairpins, a cloudy mouth guard on a saucer. And Bunny, bonneted by a thin quilt, pinched tight beneath her chin, watching infomercials well into the deep dark every night. The television's light erratic. Pupils throbbing in the pale void of her face.

Yesterday afternoon the three of them sat on Bunny's porch, which, with the help of regular kibble and milk, had become a haunt for the neighborhood cats. Pouncing at weeds, stalking Bunny's warm-blooded vermin. A few cats curled up together on the lawn, roasting in a sunbeam. These cats were a sort of village too. Bunny their mother. Dani's sisters. One of the cats levitated to the porch railing, where it lifted its leg, long and straight as a geometry compass, and made a noisy, jubilant feast of its asshole. Bunny covered Lotte's eyes and Dani laughed.

"She better watch she doesn't fall in!" said Bunny, and Dani laughed more. Then she asked her mother if she had any cheese to go with the crackers. And Bunny smiled. "No," she said. "But I can buy some for next time." And Dani said that'd be nice. That Lotte liked marble. And they enjoyed a comfortable silence together, all of them staring at the cat, knowing the enormous gesture it was for Dani to allow Bunny's cheese into Lotte's mouth.

A Normal Woman. Who took night classes. Who'd soon be starting a career in human resources. Who left the house at least once a day. And was so kind to her mother.

# 9

BRUNCH WITH THE *mom friends*. There'd been twelve months of this too, meeting up with the *mom friends*, who were actually just Anya's regular friends, like how in France they must just call them *fries*.

The restaurant this week, coincidentally, was on Barton Street. *South* Barton, though, Ellen had been quick to clarify in the group text. Dani drove past The Temple several times, in half-hearted pursuit of a parking spot, mostly peering into the flock of beautiful villagers, looking for Renata.

Anya, Ellen, and Dawn were already at the restaurant when Dani dashed in, seated at a lightly distressed picnic table near the big open windows up front. A bucket of beer bottles glittered on ice at the center of the table.

"You guys didn't waste any time," said Dani, sliding in next to Anya, who greeted her with a bump to the arm, then pulled a bottle from the bucket, passed it to her with a little plate of limes. She tightened her lips into a deep, perverse smile, which

Dani returned and the two of them held for an excessive length of time before breaking into a laugh.

Ellen chuckled uncomfortably. Dawn wrinkled her nose. "You guys are weird," she said. Anya winched the nasty smile back into her cheeks and stared at Dawn until Dawn threw a lime wedge at her, which landed on the table between them. Anya looked at it, then looked up at Dawn, who knew as well as Ellen and Dani that if she'd actually struck Anya with the lime wedge, there would have been hell to pay. Anya was incapable of suffering even minor slights. Proudly vengeful. And this, Dani knew, went for anyone who slighted Dani too.

Dani picked up the lime that Dawn had thrown and wrapped it in a napkin. She could tell that Dawn was starting to get a bit annoyed by her and Anya's jokes. The Anya they'd known before Dani arrived didn't contort her face or spew nonsense or lick her lips purposefully, to the point of making others feel sick. And even though Dani did *like* Ellen and Dawn, she also enjoyed making them aware of the distinction between what she had with Anya, and what they had. She and Anya, they were the *friend* friends here. Friends forever, whether they liked it or not. The same grade school, the same high school.

Ellen had gone to one of Metcalf's Catholic schools, where, as soon as the bell rang, the girls modified their uniforms with habitual ease—waists folded, hems raised, tops untucked and knotted between the ribs. In the year that Dani had known her, Ellen's mesh had been successfully installed, and she now kept a timer on her phone that reminded her to do her Kegel exercises. She could easily carry on a conversation and clench her pelvic floor at the same time, but it took Dani some practice to ignore the vacant expression that seized her face when she did so. Recently, with the fancy camera she'd barely used since her kids were born, Ellen had started a momfluencer account. Her handle was @mymonkeys, and it was populated with the highly curated antics of the creatures who'd annihilated her saddle. Ellen was petite but durable. She had the kind of big, charming smile that forced her cheeks up into her eyes; thick, expressive eyebrows, microbladed, Dani had learned; and a narrow, unintimidating nose. She took exceptional care of her hair—a flouncing mane of chocolate brown, rich and dense and shiny. She wanted all of the mom friends to be a little bit in love with her husband, Travis, supply chain manager for every Kiki's restaurant in the county. Sometimes she brought them unlabeled jars of sauce and salad dressing they were market testing—*don't thank me, thank Travis!*—and once, a couple summers ago, several flavors of Bellini powder, which led to a near full-blown bacchanal in Anya's backyard, an event, before Dani's time, that the Normal Women referenced often. Ellen gushed about how sweet Travis was with the boys. He'd even agreed to make a few cameos on @mymonkeys, she cooed with pride. As though his presence confirmed its moneymaking potential.

Dawn had gone to the art high school, where she'd made a minor splash drawing extremely realistic portraits of a stunningly symmetrical African woman—a long, slender neck; sleepy, irisless eyes. After she graduated, it became evident she wouldn't be able to put this very specific skill to use, so she instead cultivated a perfectly fine personality around having grown a large, thriving SCOBY, which she treasured like some repulsive pet, a hairless cat or a lizard, something to stroke while plotting. Dani learned that there was no way to feign interest in someone's kombucha hobby without ultimately having to accept a burping hunk of living matter in a mason jar. Dani had felt a bit guilty when she'd flushed it down the toilet, praying that it wouldn't come into contact with any radioactive goo.

Dawn had bleach-blond hair cut straight along her jawline and the round, nervous eyes of something nocturnal. She wore expensive activewear all the time, vivid patterns painted to her body. She'd just had a baby, her second, a three-month-old named Victor—Vic—who joined them at brunch a few times, sleeping like an angel in his car seat from beginning to end. Hers had been a glorious, natural birth, an ecstatic celebration of life with minimal tearing. Dani was fairly certain that these births only happened to those who truly believed in them, like the rapturous, out-of-body worship of Pentecostal Christians. In other words, complete bullshit. Dawn still doodled the astoundingly symmetrical African woman from time to time, when she found herself idle with a pen in hand, a compulsion of her mystical body, like the involuntary prayers of zealots.

Dawn, Ellen, and Anya had connected when they'd been the only moms to bring prepackaged goods to the school bake sale. Dawn quickly pointed out that hers had been vegan donuts from a popular shop run by a woman with lavender hair. "We *know*, Dawn," Anya had groaned. "And I spent $75 on cake pops from Starbucks, we're all amazing mothers."

As easy as Dani found it to mark her claim on Anya, with inside jokes and lewd faces, she could find herself on the outside too. Sometimes when she sat down for brunch, the three Normal Women were already talking about Normal Things, like microblading and leakproof underwear. Today, for example, when Dani sat down, the three of them had been in the middle of discussing the sordid labors of family photo prep. Ellen had been in the middle of complaining about her eldest son, Declan: "I'm going to have to bribe him into getting this haircut," she continued, pinching a corpuscle of lime from the lip of her bottle and slipping it into her mouth. "With money. Straight up money. I'm going to have to pay him money. Is that not insane? Should he not just cut his hair for me for free? I honestly don't even know anymore. It's *his body* after all."

Dawn and Anya scoffed. The Normal Women had a streak of skepticism about the autonomy of human children.

"Isn't that part of what makes pictures fun, though?" Dani already regretted chiming in. "They're a little record of how everyone was at that time."

"That's what these pictures are for," said Ellen, lifting her phone. "The portraits are *mine*." The last word hissed, involuntarily, a harried warrior locked in some ancient battle.

"It's like, every once in a while you just want to see the whole family at their maximum potential," said Dawn. "You *deserve* to see it."

"Exactly," said Ellen.

Dawn, it turned out, had been laying the groundwork for a minor plot to temporarily reduce her husband's caloric intake leading up to their fall session—a potato chip shortage, she told him, affecting the area grocery stores; a price dispute with local distributors, a supply chain problem impacting a material in the bags, something like that.

And Anya had ordered matching outfits from a fast fashion retailer that covered the boys in an angry blistering rash which she kept referring to as the China Syndrome until Dani, chest tight, jaw clenched, couldn't take it anymore. "*Je*-sus, Anya, do you honestly not realize how racist that is? Plus, it's not even a good joke, the China Syndrome isn't a disease."

"Christ, what's gotten into *you*?"

"Nothing. I just, I'm tired of hearing you say this racist, unfunny thing, all right?"

"It is funny. Just because it's a movie and not a disease, it's still funny."

"It's not just a movie, Anya, it's a theory about a possible nuclear outcome. And you haven't even seen the movie. You hate Michael Douglas."

Anya smiled. "Aw, honey." She tilted her head. "You remembered."

"The actors you hate are tattooed in my mind. Now, just, enough with that China Syndrome. Please. It's awful, you don't even—"

"Oh, stop." Dawn waved her hands in Dani's face, dismissing her, as the Normal Women always did about things like this. Childish. Unrealistic. *Radical* in the way of teenagers, not yet accustomed to how things really are. "I can't listen to this anymore. Dani, come on, the Chinese don't care about anyone but themselves. And why should they? Why should we have been the only country who got to cut corners? I don't begrudge China making hay while the sun's shining, but the fact is they sell us $12 gingham dress shirts made of powdered glass and now Anya's kids look like minced pork."

Ellen and Anya both laughed, in absolute agreement with Dawn. And it made Dani feel like something feral. An alien who'd crash-landed in Anya's backyard. A sweet extraterrestrial idiot from an '80s movie, needing to be hidden, protected, snuck out for brunch, and the Normal Women thought it was adorable how she didn't know anything. But also like the aliens from '80s movies, she had wisdom beyond their wildest dreams. Otherworldly abilities. A perspective on their planet, their species, they couldn't even begin to imagine.

Dani sipped her beer quietly and listened to the Normal Women rationalize their toxicity, their racism, as simply good common sense! Then laud the non-medical professionals they trusted to slice into the meat of their eyebrows, and describe, in disturbing detail, the ways in which they manipulated the bodies that entered and exited their own.

But despite their appalling faults, Dani really *did* like the Normal Women. She really, really did. Usually. Sometimes, anyway. And maybe, eventually, she could persuade the Normal Women to not be dicks; show the Normal Women, at the very least, that all the best-looking people held the same views that Dani did.

Honestly, her fluctuating feelings toward them probably had much more to do with Anya, how swiftly Dani began to crave Anya's exalting attention; how Anya had a way of making it seem like a limited resource, and Dani responded, had always responded, like a puppy, claiming her share with growls and bared teeth, taking all she could, when she could, the rest of the litter be damned.

And back in Anya's fold, Dani quickly forgot the things she hadn't liked about Anya. Or not forgot exactly, but rather she decided that they didn't make her a bad person. And maybe too Anya had gotten a bit better. She wasn't as competitive as she used to be, guarding her flaws like the hound of Hades. She'd been open about her sexual dysfunction, for example, about how Bill's easy acceptance of it, his seamless transition to yoga, had actually sort of *hurt*. Dani had never known Anya to admit to any pain before, and certainly not the pain of *rejection*.

But of course she wasn't as judgmental either. My god, how judgmental she used to be. Dani thought of how heavily Anya had factored into Dani's own decision to give her first blow job in tenth grade: How would Anya react? Would she think less of her? Would she think tenth grade was too young? Would she *look at her* differently? Could they still share food? Anya had worked hard, whether consciously or not, to stifle the sexuality of the girls in their small circle, as though sex too were a limited resource, its scarcity necessary for her own reproductive success.

And all of them, Anya, Dawn, and Ellen, held near-professional specialties in various subjects. Ellen, basically a pelvic floor phys-iotherapist since her mesh. She could draw a perfect diagram of the pelvic basket, a cornucopia of big juicy muscles, hearty ten-dons, a fine, plump bladder. Dawn could regulate your bowels, boost your libido, improve your memory, and help you sleep, all with what she referred to as her *liquid therapies*—teas and serums and tinctures and, of course, the drippings of her pre-cious SCOBY. Anya could convincingly imitate a dermatologist if she needed to: solutions to hormonal acne, causes of dry skin. She knew the exact percentage of chemical exfoliant you could safely use while breastfeeding; she could tell, just from reading the ingredients, how comedogenic a moisturizer was, confident enough in her abilities that she used a calendula-oil diaper cream on her own face. Dani was using it now too, and her cheeks had never been more supple.

A second bucket of beer landed on the table. Dani struggled to force a fat lime down the neck of her bottle, nearly squirt-ing juice in her eyes. Anya laughed, took the bottle, fingered it down with a thunk. "I'm fucking starving," she announced, slid-ing Dani's beer back at her and twisting in her chair to search for their waitress. She nudged Dani's elbow with hers, cast a silent burp from the opposite side of her mouth. "I can't remember, is that our girl?" Anya nodded at a hustle-flushed waitress bounc-ing between tables, erratic inertia baffling her poor battered top knot. She was in her early twenties probably, thin hoops in her ears and one in her nose, thighs sprayed with a fine, shimmering down that made Dani want to hug her. Then, staring at her in a head-cocked daze, Dani was struck by how much better off this young waitress would be working at The Temple instead.

# 10

*Every organization, large or small, uses a variety of capital to make the business work. Capital is cash, valuables, or goods, anything used to generate income. Registers and inventory are capital for a retail store. Proprietary software and office space are capital for a consulting firm. And all companies, no matter the industry, have one type of capital in common: humans. It is the function of Human Resources Management to achieve organizational effectiveness through the use of people's skills and abilities. Many of the strongest and most successful companies in the world are structured around a single tenet: Humans are the most valuable resource.*

Dani closed the Intro to Human Resources Management PDF. Imagine, she thought, being a *resource*. A resource and not a drain. *Private owner of one of the most coveted resources in the world.*

She looked up the word *resource*: *A stock or supply of money, materials, staff, and other assets that can be drawn on by a person or organization in order to function effectively. "Resource" refers to all the materials available in our environment which are technologically accessible, economically feasible and culturally sustainable and help us to satisfy our needs and wants.*

A human resource.

What was Renata's *capital*, Dani wondered, pulling her jeans halfway up her thighs. She dropped to the foot of the bed, slumped shoulders squeezing post-Lotte softness into a stack of warm loaves. She inched the denim up from the ankles, sprouted from the holes of a loose T-shirt, then shook it away from her body. Standing in the full-length mirror, leaned up against the wall. Bodies, for one. Human bodies. Liquor. Condoms. Lube. The Temple itself, chunked brick and cracked patio. Yoga space. Rooms at the Pleasant Stay Inn. Could privacy be capital? She might ask tonight in class. Probably not covered in the rest of the PDF, which she wouldn't be able to finish in time. Already behind. But Clark thought it was a great idea. Thought she'd be great in human resources. And who knew, maybe he was right.

Downstairs Dani found Clark on the couch, content, well rested, eating a bowl of ice cream, captivated by a program about Brazilian jiu-jitsu. He clocked her from the corner of his eye, dropped the bowl on the coffee table, spoon rattling. "Hi," he said and cleared his throat, wiped both corners of his mouth with the thumb and forefinger of one hand. Clark held the belief that grown men shouldn't be seen eating ice cream, that it was lurid, unseemly.

"Oh, Clark, everyone does it."

He cracked a sarcastic smile. A memory passed through her mind like a cloud: Clark at his nephew's birthday party two summers ago, sun spiking off his beer can, nudging a clumsy water balloon with his foot across the lawn. His face almost entirely devoid of expression, as though he were testing himself with this small bit of merriment; that to crack a smile, bend over and pick up the water balloon, heave it at one of his brothers, would kick-start a veritable Rumspringa of dangerous revelry. And last summer, somehow, she'd found this joylessness *funny*.

She leaned over the table, looked into the bowl. "Whipped cream too? Jeeeeeeeeeeesus."

"Stop it!" He swept the bowl up with one hand and hurried it to the sink to hide the evidence. She often wondered where exactly, in the version of manhood uploaded into Clark's circuitry, this aversion to visible pleasure had stemmed from. Was it too childlike? Too feminine? What happened to joy centers in the brains of men like Clark? Did they shrivel up and harden? Dropped from the rest of the soft living tissue like Lotte's belly button stump? She wondered then, as she had from time to time over the years, about the porn Clark might watch, an oiled man delivering orgasm after orgasm to some screaming blonde, collecting points from her body like a trained fighter. A Brazilian jiu-jitsu fighter. Ugh, Clark. Truly the worst person. But also, just maybe, *a creature filled with pain.*

"Did you know Brazilian jiu-jitsu is a cult?" he asked as he rinsed his bowl.

"Doesn't Rory do Brazilian jiu-jitsu?" Rory, Clark's older brother, a podiatrist who co-owned an orthopedic shoe store with his wife. When they all drank too much, Clark and the middle brother, Owen, would accuse Rory of having committed breathtaking acts of violence as a child—slamming their heads off the hoods of cars, clutching their throats till they passed out. Rory would deny it at first, playfully, then become sullen and threatening when they wouldn't relent.

Dani leaned against the kitchen door frame, watched Clark put the bowl in the dishwasher, a chore he was capable of apparently when it was in the service of hiding his pleasures.

"Well, it's not a bad cult. Just something to do." He whipped the dishrag off the oven handle and wiped a mysterious archipelago of liquid from the counter. "But apparently it uses a lot of the same techniques that cults do to get you to keep coming back to the *academy*. That's what they call their gyms. There's lots of special language like that. Same as with cults."

"Nothing like joining a cult to pass the time."

"This documentary I'm watching says everything is a cult—brands, exercise, diets—because behavioral change is necessary for capitalism to keep thriving. Getting you engaged with a brand or an idea, and keeping you engaged, they do that by working on your brain the way a cult does, with the promise of being part of something *bigger*—community, purpose, self-improvement, whatever. Anyway, that plastic surgeon I was telling you about, from Brazil, he got his start working on famous Brazilian jiu-jitsu fighters' ears. You know how they get those puffy ears?"

Dani shook her head. Clark took out his phone, leaned next to her in the doorway as he typed, then shoved a photo in her face: an ear, or what was left of it, thickened beyond recognition, interior whorls swollen, lumpy, a diseased mollusk.

"Jesus!" Dani shrieked and covered her eyes. "What the fuck is that?"

"It's called cauliflower ear, can you believe that? It's from all the grappling and holds." He moved to grab her, and she flinched, scowled at him. He smiled and looked at the picture, shaking his head, in awe of some aspect of the injury—its repulsiveness perhaps, or how some of the fighters thought of them as a badge of honor. "Manson put *X*'s on those girls' heads. And that other guy, who branded all those women, remember? This is like that. Maybe I *should* tell Rory about this documentary."

"Don't do that. He loves it. And it's not hurting him, is it? Doesn't something have to be harmful to be a cult?"

"Not necessarily. That's what I'm *saying*."

"Well, anyway, don't tell Rory. It's hard to find good ways to pass the time. Speaking of which, I'm running late." She turned from the doorway. He followed her.

"Oh my god, your first class!"

"All right, take it easy, it's not like I brought you home a dandelion or anything."

"I'm not, no, I'm not being patronizing, I'm just really excited for you." He had the dish towel with him, wiping his hands. "Will you be late?"

"Shouldn't be."

He stepped closer to her, kissed her. His lips were sweet from the ice cream. "Go get 'em," he said, and slapped her haunches like she was a horse.

"I hate you." She marched to the foyer, slipped a pair of plain white sneakers over tiny socks, slung a tote bag over her shoulder, and stood waiting for Clark, who she knew would be following her to say goodbye at the front door. "I really do," she said when he appeared. And he smiled broadly as he inched the door closed behind her.

## 11

FROM A PARKING SPOT across from The Temple, Dani watched the minutes on the car's digital clock nip into Intro to HR's start time. One minute. Two minutes. Five. Seventeen. Missing class. She was now missing class. But it was a night class, for god's sake, for working professionals. Busy people. Who couldn't possibly be expected to attend *every* week. The course was designed to be missed. That's why the notes would be posted in the online portal. She would go next week. It would be fine. Plus, she would still be learning something, probably more than she could ever pick up in the classroom. Humans were Renata's *only* resource. Another night with her would be as good as ten classes at the college. Studying with Renata, it could be her *EDGE*, the latest in jargon, Dani knew, aimed at women determined to succeed in male-dominated industries, turning that which subjugates you into your *EDGE*.

But what if Renata was angry with her for not showing up last week? Just another pathetic tourist ogling her village from the comfort of a minivan, glamourizing what she understood from daytime television to be the most degrading, dangerous, disgusting work a person could do—transformative labor, from which a person emerges changed beyond recognition, barely human, an oddity, a *ghoul*, to be eyeballed by a live studio audience. The ghoul wanted out of *the life*. The ghoul was *trying to change*. But it was so hard. Nearly impossible. The daytime television host understood, frowning, nodding, as she moved through the live studio audience like a god, and with her wand-like microphone bestowed upon the reformed ghoul a school fund and a new car and a well-deserved vacation to a Caribbean Iberostar of her choosing. The live studio audience, and women like Dani from home, flung themselves from their seats, howled and shrieked, the god-host quieting them with her hands—*nothing to me, really, a small price to pay, a pittance really, in exchange for so much worship.* And the audience was insatiable for this astonishing generosity, so grateful to witness the ghoul's return to regulated labor and taxable income.

Dani didn't really watch shows like that anymore. Maybe they didn't even exist anymore. Nowadays, Dani discovered, if a person wanted to learn about sex work, they turned to the internet, articles and exposés and forums in which a woman posts: *I used to be a prostitute, ask me anything.* And the people in the forum clamor to inquire about the violence, the money, the johns: *What's the worst thing you ever did, what's the worst thing that ever happened to you.* This exchange of sex for money so alien to most people, despite the fact that it was the oldest job in the world. Someone piping in on the forum to add, rightfully, that the only reason the profession has been so grossly villainized is because it represents an avenue for true financial independence for women—not like multilevel marketing or pyramid schemes or *momfluencing.* Sex work was well-paid manual labor, like what men have easy access to on a jobsite, in which you're compensated fairly in exchange for gradual bodily attrition. Each joint, for example, has a finite number of flexions; a knee, for instance, might contain three million bends over the course of an average life span. It's your right to sell a few hundred thousand of those bends off, installing flooring or executing a fine blow job. It's your right to share a few of those bends too, for free, if you choose to, helping friends, blowing friends. Criminalizing sex work is not just a way of controlling women's bodies, but women's economic movement as well. And this forum poster, she is correct. She amasses many likes for her sound and interesting point. And then someone has the balls to reply with, *But it's so gross!* And gets just as many likes. And Dani felt sad that the original poster, the woman who'd decided so generously to share her story with the world, wouldn't be given an all-inclusive vacation to an Iberostar of her choosing for the trouble.

An offering, thought Dani. Maybe not a trip to a Caribbean Iberostar of her choosing, but she could at least bring Renata a coffee. Dani got out of the car, bought two Americanos from the intimidating little café; recalled, with a delighted gasp, the bag of mini donuts she had squirreled away in the car, procured that morning from the outrageously popular kiosk that'd opened in the mall. Its bustle seemed sick somehow. She'd had an instinct to cover Lotte's eyes from it but didn't know how that could be executed without a scene, so the child watched while salivating customers exsanguinated the little booth, a colony of vicious, sugar-mad ants, the clerks sweating, their arms spattered in small scabs from the roaring fryer.

Back in the car she put the coffees in the cupholders, the bag of donuts secured in between, then set her jaw, slivered her eyes, and scanned the street for Renata. The Temple was active tonight. So many lovely women. Maneuvering without friction. Mingling without ego. They were like another species, a nonhuman ecosystem. These women had transcended, moved beyond this earth. What Dani and the mom friends did over lunch felt like some arcane ritual to be studied, pitied, by these more evolved beings.

And then Renata emerged from the crowd, rings on her fingers, dark red lipstick, a cotton dress smooth against her musculature. She greeted her villagers with kisses and hugs and effortless touching, corrections to their appearance administered with the affectionate discipline of a gymnastics coach, tough but not unsympathetic to the mischief of the body and its vestments.

She spotted Dani right away.

Dani waved idiotically, lifted a coffee so Renata could see it through the windshield, which toppled the paper bag of donuts so they dumped and scattered across the console, into the passenger seat. Dani gasped, picked them up with her finger and thumb, careful to handle them as little as possible. Just as she returned the final donut to the bag, Renata appeared in the passenger-side window. Dani leaned over, batted sugar from the seat, then opened the door for her, the bag of donuts crushed in her other hand.

"What's that?" Renata asked, instantly curious about the bag.

"Oh, these are those donuts." She set the grease-splotched sack between them, opened it up and rolled down the sides. "From the mall."

"These are Glory Holes? Oh, wow, I've been dying to try them." She pulled one out, shoved the whole thing in her mouth. "My god"—muffled sugar clouds shooting out of her mouth— "these are incredible."

Renata insisted that Dani didn't owe her an apology, or donuts or coffee. Dani didn't owe her anything. "I'm just happy to see you again," she said, and pulled a cigarette from her pack.

Dani asked if they could smoke outside the car this time—"thirdhand smoke, it's a thing apparently." And Renata didn't do the thing that older women normally do, which was regale her with stories about smoke-filled movie theaters and no seat belts and everyone growing up *just fine*, which Dani always found such a strange thing to say being as no one in the world was doing *just fine*.

Instead Renata said, "Huh! That makes a lot of sense!" and they got out and leaned against the back of Dani's van. Dani set the bag of donuts on the small step that jutted out beneath the tailgate. Renata lit two cigarettes in her mouth and handed one to Dani, just as a slender gray cat swam past them without looking, sprang to a concrete windowsill on the vacant low-rise next to the car. Main-floor retail space. A large *For Lease* sign glued to the window. The cat flung its legs apart quick as a paper fan and buried its face in its crotch.

"I think I know that cat," said Dani, trailing off into her memory of Bunny's porch just a few days ago. "But that would be some trek."

"Oh, she can handle it," said Renata. "Look at her."

The cat resealed the fan of her legs and looked out onto Barton Street—the patio specifically, or so it seemed to Dani—turning her head slowly to watch the door, then gliding down again to the pavement, undulating to the curb, where she waited for several cars to pass before crossing. One of the villagers, a skyscraper blonde, bent over and lifted the cat beneath its armpits. The animal hung there for a moment, front legs stuck straight out, body stretched like goo, almost to its snapping point before the blonde scooped its bottom half with her other arm and cradled it like a child. Dani pondered its bizarre body, perhaps originally designed for a different environment, not earth or water but air: those big, gabled shoulder blades the vestigial roots of powerful wings.

"We leave food out," said Renata, her eyes still on the cat. "And water. Did you know most cats are actually allergic to milk?"

"Really?"

"Mmm-hmm," Renata hummed as she smoked.

"I should tell my mother. Why do we think they like it so much?"

Renata shrugged. "I mean, they do like it. It just makes them sick."

A strong wind blew Dani's hair into her face, and Renata reached over, brushed it away, the thrill of her fingers on Dani's skin. "Thank you," said Dani. Renata's touch an entitlement, a perk, a *benefit*, of working at The Temple. Dani flicked her cigarette. "Next you're going to tell me they don't eat perfectly preserved fish skeletons off metal trash can lids."

Renata laughed and her eyes widened. "Wow," she exhaled. "Metal trash cans. I can't believe you just mentioned metal trash cans." She pulled another cigarette from the pack, but Dani declined. Another cigarette would nudge the slight pulsing behind her eye into a full-blown headache, she was sure. Too much coffee. Sugar. The lie to Clark maybe affecting her in some subconscious way, like how faking a sick day from work used to take a small physical toll, involuntarily squaring up reality with the lie.

"Why's that?"

"It's just an incredible coincidence. I've been thinking about metal trash cans a lot lately. I want to put a few out here." She flapped unoccupied fingers at the patio. "You don't see them too often these days. Aesthetically speaking, the world really used to *look* a lot nicer, don't you think? Plastic is bad for a lot of reasons, but that's a big one for me. Think of the years of thoughtful design that went into the metal can. How nice and uniform they must have looked, standing at the curb on garbage night, reflecting streetlight, everything that much brighter. Nowadays everyone on a block could have a completely different bin. It's all just so cheap." And she wasn't gloomy now, but a bit pensive, rummaging through memories or scenes from television shows, one and the same anyway.

"I bet the cats are happy, though." Dani nodded at the gray cat, still cradled in the beauty's arms. "Bouncing between metal cans would be very noisy."

"Kept them leaner, though, I bet. Lighter. Practically *flying*." Renata smiled at her again. *Flying*. "Have you tried one of their affogatos yet?" She pointed her cup in the direction of the café.

"No, but I hear good things."

"Fucking delicious. Just super. Did you notice the big metal garbage cans they've got? Just next to the little cream-and-sugar station there."

Dani shook her head.

"Brand-new. Beautiful. I asked the girl behind the counter about them. She didn't know where they came from, but do you know what she said? She said *everybody* asks about them. Isn't that funny? Everyone prefers the metal cans. It's just amazing how we do so many things that everyone hates when we could really just . . ." She rotated her wrist so the cigarette smoke gathered there, dissipated quickly as she finished her thought. "We could really just not do those things anymore, you know?"

"People don't realize they have so much power."

"It's a scary thought. We'd rather off-load the power, for some reason. A defect of the human brain. Not unfixable, though. I used to be scared of my power too, but I'm not anymore."

"I don't know if I have any power."

Renata scoffed. "Of course you do."

"I don't think so." Dani's eyes still on the cat. "Because if I did, I don't think I'd be scared of it."

"What do you think scares you then?"

Dani thought for a moment—colon cancer, freak accidents. Lotte in Reebaks. "Not having any money," she said, finally. "And for some reason I've never done a single thing about it."

"But you are now. You're here. Sounds like you were just scared of your power too."

"How did you stop being scared?"

Renata smiled, flicked her cigarette. "Now that's a long story."

"That's okay," said Dani, scooting herself closer. *The human resources department are the stewards of company culture, working with leaders to turn vision into action. Strong company culture is a key driver for employee engagement, satisfaction, and productivity, and it starts with a compelling company history.* "I'd love to hear it."

Dani and Renata had begun in similar places really, with babies they needed to support. But it was a different time for Renata. A different place. There was no internet, more walking, so much fucking *walking*. She'd flirted with drugs, but never seriously. Shook off asshole boyfriends who always turned out to be wannabe pimps. She'd never had a pimp, herself. Never really needed one, she shrugged. She'd been surprised by how little violence she encountered on the stroll. There'd been some, of course. And friends of hers had some horror stories. And friends of friends always got it worst. But most of the men who solicited her were looking for pretty standard stuff. And over time Renata realized that it wasn't actually sex they wanted.

"But that, so, you don't—you *do* have sex with men here, though, don't you?"

Renata smiled. "We speak to them in their language."

"And that language is . . ."

"It depends. In the beginning, yes, it's more like what you're thinking, they don't realize that there are other ways to speak yet. They've never been taught."

"But you teach them."

"*We* teach them."

"Okay, but like . . . what does that *mean*?"

Renata's smile widened as she leaned forward, elbows on her spreading knees, smooth, subtle shape-shifting, an animal assuming the texture of its environment. "Imagine," she said, her voice lowering into a register that forced Dani to lean in closer too. "Imagine you're dropped into the ocean. Right into a reef full of sharks. Now you've got to pretend to be a shark. To survive. Your life depends on it. If these sharks find out you're not a shark, they're going to tear you to pieces. So you've gotta do what they do—you've gotta stalk prey, catch it and tear it apart with your teeth, you've gotta hold your *breath*. The whole time. But every once in a while you get a chance to sneak to the surface and breathe real air." Renata slid a fresh cigarette from the pack, held it, unlit, between her fingers. "You get to be *human* again. It's not *sex* that men are after, Dani. It's the fucking *break*." She lit the cigarette, took in the confusion on Dani's face, and laughed a plume of smoke between them. "When the involuntary systems required to ejaculate are engaged—the endocrine system, for example, releasing the necessary chemicals to prepare for orgasm—it's the only time that many men are able to experience vulnerability. Men have been trained, by fathers who want to make them strong, mothers who are scared to make them weak, to police themselves. Relentlessly. To bludgeon their feelings, their ability to really *connect* with other people. Their *humanity*."

Dani thought of Clark. Secreting his lavish little bowls of ice cream. That water balloon, the ghost of his humanity animating his body, those gentle kicks trying to lure Clark back to himself. Clark. A creature with pain. Inflicting pain on others. "Creatures with pain," said Dani. "I mean, I see what you're saying. I see it even with, you know, my friends, other mothers. There's a real fear of turning your son into a mama's boy, this fear of *ruining* him with affection or indulging his emotions."

"That's exactly right!" said Renata, pointing at Dani with her cigarette. "Exactly right. Imagine, starting that young, not giving your son the affection that you would give a daughter. Expecting him to toughen up, to take care of himself. Think of how *annoyed* people get at a whiny little boy, but little girls, it's sort of cute. The parents, they pass the policing down. The sons, they start to self-police. It's vicious, Dani. Absolutely brutal."

"That makes sense why they're so *obsessed* with sex too. It can't *all* be the biological imperative to spread seed."

"Wouldn't you eventually become obsessed with the surface? If you were that shark? Every moment you get to spend as a human again, as your true self. I've never believed that seed-spreading bullshit. It's one of those chicken-or-egg scenarios, scientists formulating conclusions based on data already twisted by our demented fucking world."

"But how do you undo all of that—that—"

"Brutalizing? We call it brutalizing, the process by which the humanity, the *crucial feminine*, is programmed out of young boys. We undo it by teaching them how to *extend* the break; how to decouple the release of control from the orgasm. With strategic sexual therapies, we help them learn how to be vulnerable not just in that moment but in their lives. And to see the release of control not as a weakness, not as something to be humiliated by, but something to cherish, as a gift from the body to the soul, the gateway to self-understanding, self-love, true *empathy*. Better people. *Better men.* Feeling better. Acting better. That is the only way we're going to make a better world. And *that's* the *cause*, that's—I know it's hard to believe. I know that. But we really *aren't* just getting these guys off," she said, flicking the mouth of her coffee cup, a languorous tempo, sleepy, persistent. "We're not just getting them off, even though to make someone orgasm, to deliver that moment of euphoria, is one of the most generous gifts a person can give. That's just a part of what we're doing here. We're *helping* them. We're *healing* them. I mean, look around you, Dani, men are in pain. And they're causing pain: hurting us, killing us, hurting the planet, destroying everything they touch. Obsessed with money. Power. To the detriment of all else, to the detriment of *life itself.* We've been living in a world where the most powerful group has systematically had the basic humanity, empathy, the *crucial feminine*, stamped out of them since birth. *Don't cry. Don't feel your feelings. No pain, no gain. Take it like a man.* No wonder everything is completely fucked. Our leaders can't *feel feelings*. Imagine how that must be, imagine the kind of monster—" And here she became emotional, as though she were talking about Romanian orphans silenced by neglect; elephants, poached and tuskless, leaking blood into dirt. "Imagine if men could enjoy tenderness, could *connect* with other people, the way they did when they were infants. Imagine the world this could be. Right now, a lot of men, not all men but a lot of them, when they indulge in tenderness, when they experience vulnerability, they become enraged, ashamed, humiliated. It makes them want to kill us, literally. Hurt people. But the men that come to The

Temple, the men we work with, they're changing. And they're changing each other. They're changing their brothers, their nephews. Their *sons*. We're making a difference here, Dani. Maybe even saving the fucking world."

Dani stared at her, speechless, accepted a cigarette from Renata's outstretched pack and lit it in a daze.

"You think I'm crazy, right?" Renata laughed, sniffed, her voice moist, curdled, from having been so close to tears.

"No," said Dani, breathing deeply. Her heart softened, *tenderized*. Creatures with *pain*. "I think you're amazing."

# 12

WHEN DANI WALKED into their bedroom that night, Clark was tucked in in front of his laptop, working. His glasses, blasted by the white light of his screen, flung a strange shadow mask over his face. A good man or a bad man, for the first time he was neither. He was just Clark, who loved her. Who provided for her. Who cared when she came home and announced that she'd be taking a night class. She thumbed toward Lotte's door.

"Not a peep," Clark whispered.

Dani smiled.

"How was class?"

Dani shrugged. "It was good. Talent acquisition. Apparently good people are hard to find."

"They are."

"You say that, but I know lots of good people looking for better jobs."

Clark shrugged. "It should be the *right* people. The *right* people are hard to find."

Dani tilted into the door frame, arms crossed, eyes narrowed. Studying Clark. The *right* people. He'd always been the *right* person. Tall, but not intimidatingly so. Effortlessly lean, but not gangly. He kept his dark hair short and unfussy. His facial hair, thick, relentless, like the rest of the hair on his body, had the effect of making his flesh seem like good, loamy soil.

Clark, neither good nor bad. Clark, a victim. A creature with pain: wretched, pitiable, forced by the world to obliterate a crucial part of his essential nature. The best part of his essential nature. Leaving behind this wreck of perfectly good, perfectly *right*, but miserable flesh. Dani thought of something she'd read back in school, another text she'd spent scads of money unpacking for her useless degree. The *Epic of Gilgamesh*, a poem dating back to ancient Mesopotamia, a section about a prostitute who spends a week fucking the humanity back into a warrior who's spilled so much blood he's gone feral.

Dani went to Clark's side of the bed and sat down, inching a bit of extra space from his thigh. He looked at her and she took off his glasses, folded them, and set them on the night table. She closed his computer with her palm and slid it next to his glasses. She kissed him with such unexpected lust that Clark, lips slack and eyebrows raised, needed a moment before he understood how to kiss her back, which he figured out quickly, hungrily.

Clark was never what you'd call a *natural* lover. He was relentless in his pursuit of bringing Dani to orgasm, and he wanted her to orgasm over and over again, maybe part of his fantasy, to have utter control over her body this way, her total loss of control in front of him a kind of smug victory, like how the only sober person at a party acts the next day at brunch. Or maybe it was all part of his intense worship, his dehumanizing devotion: Love was orchestrating a screaming, thrashing performance from the beloved; love was begrudgingly allowing the beloved to suffer only slightly for your pleasure too. Love was not enjoying it too much. Not experiencing pleasure in front of anyone. Ever. Not even the beloved. Dani faked her orgasms, not always but often. Too brutal to watch him fail at it.

She wouldn't fake it tonight. No matter what. Tonight he would know the truth of her body. She wrapped her arms around him, her legs, let the thought of his thickness fill her with a powerful, alien energy. His thick hair and the thick smell between his legs. The thickness of his dick and the thickness of his arms and the thickness of his gaze when he was about to come, or even when he was about to eat. Clark's whole family was thick and good. A density to their wholesomeness. Every layer she'd peeled back so far she found mostly kind people who'd led comfortable lives, but something drew her to keep peeling, something deep inside the family of two still married parents and three rambunctious boys, all of whom had strangled the crucial feminine within themselves and, in fact, lived the half lives of Normal Men. Fondling water balloons with their feet; hiding their love of sweet, creamy treats. Casually violent. Filled with shame. The poor things. A good man, deep down. Just doing his job. Supporting his family. Exactly what he was told to do, he was doing it, and yet still he wasn't happy. Wasn't he supposed to be happy now? Hadn't he done everything right? Dani stroked Clark's hair, let it gather between her fingers and pulled hard; she rubbed her palms into his chest, down his arms, and interlocked her fingers with his. She kissed him and looked into his eyes and felt a long-buried line from the *Epic of Gilgamesh* wriggle to the top of her mind:

> *she was not restrained, but took his energy*
> *she spread out her robe and he lay upon her*
> *she performed for the primitive the task of womankind*

# 13

ELLEN CHOSE the restaurant this week, a fancy pub that'd dedicated a whole month of Instagram posts to various money shots of its beer cheese—oozing off a soft pretzel, scooped by a celery stick. When Ellen said in the group chat that it was "the beer cheese place," everyone had heard of it and responded with *ooooooooooooh*.

The inside was meant to resemble, in an ironic way, the kind of chain restaurant where teenagers have first dates—plush, squeaky booths; butcher paper rolled out over the tables; mason jars of grubby crayons jammed into the condiment caddy. There were boardwalk caricatures of contemporary rappers, a wide watercolor of the season one cast of *Rock of Love* above a nonfunctioning fireplace, set with a nativity scene of fire-related Pokémon toys. At the counter, where you paid your bill, you could buy a whole pie or a Brittany Murphy bobblehead or a T-shirt that just said *Cheese*.

"Oh, this place is *fun*," Ellen declared as they were led to a bright, good-sized table by the front windows. Ellen kept commenting on the quality of the light, and Dawn indulged her by asking about her fancy camera, her Instagram account. Dani was distracted, thinking of something Renata had said, about the unnecessary pain that men inflict upon themselves—neglecting oral care, tuning out of important information about nutrition. *They just endure so much needless physical pain too, the discomfort of systematic neglect. Self-care requires vulnerability too; seeing a doctor regularly requires vulnerability.* Clark had had pain in both knees since she'd met him, lived for months with a broken tooth that eventually needed a three-part root canal.

Anya flipped through the menu, a sticky plastic folder, and complained that there were too many *varieties* of beer cheese. Ellen began talking about her application to Rewardfluence, a company that helped women like her monetize the digital spaces they were creating. She didn't have a ton of followers yet, and she was really only getting to know her extremely expensive camera, but she felt as though her page had that certain something, evident already.

"See?" She passed her phone around the table, starting with Anya, who smiled and passed it to Dani, who took in the photo of Ellen's cherubic three-year-old son crushing a fistful of blueberries with such glee, such freedom, that she had to agree was intoxicating. Something wild about him, in the absolute destruction of so much fruit at once, made her want to chug another cider, take her shirt off, dry-hump the patio cushion, because, fuck it, if it feels good, do it. She smiled, "Adorable," then passed the phone to Dawn, who, after putting in the obligatory coo and compliment, proceeded to batter Ellen with questions about Rewardfluence: How did it work exactly? What was the application process like? Did Ellen think they'd be interested in a *momfluencer* who was also very holistic? Raising her kids and her SCOBYs, all in the same house!

"There would also be an aspect of change too." Dawn rolled hand over hand. "Transformation." Spitballing to herself now about how she'd reformed her husband's eating habits, forced him to exercise, to practice good sleep hygiene, maintain friendships. Guidance he craved and loved and needed almost as much as he craved and loved and needed complaining about it, mostly to his friends, who also needed to be guided in this way, and the complaining almost became a hobby, a *club*, a way of connecting with one another, all of them enjoying more healthy happy years thanks to the bitch they married.

*Everything's a cult*—Dani recalled her conversation with Clark, chuckling.

"What's that?" asked Dawn.

Dani looked up. "Me? Oh, I didn't say anything."

"No, you laughed."

Dani shrugged. Dawn raised an eyebrow, more with concern than suspicion; then she turned and continued to Ellen: "Maybe that could even be my angle." She lit up, inspired. "A *wifefluencer* . . ."

Ellen let out a shriek of approval. "I love it!"

The way Dawn talked about her husband could be genuinely disturbing but also rang with such devastating truth. Dani recalled reading the findings of a major study—that married men live longer than unmarried men; married men are better protected from heart disease, dementia, depression, even experience more positive outcomes from cancer. And a widower was twice as likely to die within a year of his wife than a widow was.

Married women, on the other hand, had a decreased life

expectancy, decreased even further for those with children. Marriage and children, the two most powerful cultural currents for women, the two things they're trained from birth to desire more than anything else, were, in fact, destroying them.

When she'd brought the study up to the women a few brunches ago, all of them had laughed.

"But it isn't funny," Dani had whined, agitation amplified by the discomfort of having just consumed an entirely too acidic and unsatisfying green goddess salad. "It's actually horrifying," said Dani. "We're brainwashed into a life that's killing us."

"Well, of course it's horrifying!" Dawn had exclaimed. "But come on." Dawn, who was the type of woman who measured her own success as a human being on the happiness of her marriage, or at the very least its *perceived* happiness, insisted she was, despite what that study said, very, *very* happy with her choices.

"*If* you can even call them that," Dani had reminded her.

"Call them what?"

"*Choices.*"

Dawn had rolled her eyes, not unkindly.

Ellen had laid a hand on Dani's arm. "Dani," she said, "I have *chills.*"

And Anya had given Dani that look she'd seen a million times: *Oh, Dani, my poor, pitiful radical. My feral alien, no clue how things are done on this planet.*

And Dani had sulked. Excluded. Different from the Normal Women. Because maybe she *was* different from the Normal Women. A villager. A healer. How Clark had moaned last night, louder than he'd ever allowed her to hear before, how soundly he'd slept. *She performed for the primitive the task of womankind.*

The server startled her, arriving alongside their table with two massive, oozing platters of beer cheese in her outstretched arms. Dani and the mom friends gasped as though taking in the impressive wingspan of a mating bird.

It took the women a few minutes to come to terms with the platters on the table, reorganizing drinks, arranging the various cheese conduits—celery, carrots sticks, pretzels, tater tots, fries—so that everyone had easy access.

"You know, momfluencers are going to be represented by the Screen Actors Guild soon," Ellen continued, once the food was settled.

Anya snorted and immediately pulled out her phone to fact-check her. After a few seconds she raised her eyebrows, a wry, bested smile. "Well, I'll be damned," she said. "You're right, Ellen. It's called the Influencer Agreement."

Ellen extended her neck triumphantly. "I *told* you."

"Well, it makes sense," said Dawn. "It's a performance, isn't it?"

"*Performance* is a bit of a strong word," said Ellen, dismayed that her account might not be exuding the authenticity necessary for true success. "*Choreographed* is maybe better. *Curated.*"

"Come on, Ellen, no one's life really looks like that. All that *linen.*" Dawn placed disgusted emphasis on the word *linen.* Anya texted Dani beneath the table: *linen.* And Dani buried a laugh into her hand.

Dani thought there should be a union for the regular, non-influential mothers too, certain she'd developed a few repetitive strain injuries over the past twelve months, from her work with Lotte—the bouncing and the rocking and breastfeeding. At one point the only way Lotte would sleep was in a vibrating chair, perched on top of a yoga ball, a very specific bounce-rock combo over and over, hours and hours, Dani's wrists limp, arms weak and aching. The mothers in the forums had many remedies for motherhood's repetitive strain injuries: the sore, crooked backs (*Make sure you alternate hips when you hold him, hon!*), the bounce-worn knees (*Try to use your ankles a bit more, or if you can't, try to keep your knees in line with your second toe as you bounce, that helps*). There were special postpartum physical therapy packages, massages, fascia work.

And Renata should have a union too. A pension. Physical therapy coverage when too many hand jobs triggered a bout of tennis elbow. Though Dani was probably kidding herself that anyone would pay for something as tasteful and tidy as a hand job, even if it were part of the healing process. God, could Dani *really* do that? Could she really take a strange man's dick in her hands, the way a construction worker on a jobsite takes a nail and transforms it with his skill? *Decouple the release of control from the orgasm. The task of womankind.* Maybe she could. If that were the physical labor of changing the world, maybe, honestly, she could. *We're not just getting them off, Dani.* They were an empathy factory, manufacturing it from nothing. A type of alchemy, spinning beasts back into men.

"Have any of you heard of The Temple?" Dani blurted, bolstered by the cider, curious to see what the Normal Women might know.

"The Temple." Ellen furrowed her eyebrows, clipped the tip of her tongue to her upper lip. "What is it?"

"Oh, I don't know exactly." Dani took a big drink of her cider. "I guess it's a yoga studio? On North Barton up there, near the motel."

"Oh, *The Temple*, my god, of course I've heard of The Temple. Yeah, it's a yoga studio, I think, but also a little bit like a church, right? And maybe . . . am I crazy, or is there also something a bit sleazy about it? Maybe I'm thinking of something else . . ."

"Sleazy? What makes you say that?" asked Dani.

"Well, I think I must have heard something. Or just guilt by association, I guess. It's hard for anyone who grew up here not to see those places on North Barton as, you know, rub-and-tugs. Things like that. But honestly the neighborhood is changing. I'm seeing it every day."

"Half of our brunch spots are on Barton," said Dani.

"*South* Barton."

"So The Temple is new then?"

"Fairly new, right?" Ellen looked to Anya and Dawn.

"Is it new?" asked Anya. "I thought it'd been there for a while."

"Well, not that long. I think a yoga studio would have stood out a bit more on Barton Street five years ago, wouldn't it?"

"Oh, it's older than that," said Anya.

"Older than five years?"

"I've been seeing that place forever, I'm sure of it. Maybe it wasn't a yoga studio before, but it's been there forever."

"Well, of course the *building* has been there forever. It's practically rubble."

"No, but I mean *The Temple* itself. The sign. That sign has been there forever."

"The *neon* sign?"

"It's new," Dawn declared confidently, pulling a few structurally crucial fries from the haystack, babbling curses and apologies when a few fries were lost in the inevitable collapse. Dani would have happily eaten fries that touched the table, but not in front of Dawn, whose holistic aesthetic somehow lacked the grimier aspects of those Dani had encountered elsewhere. "And it's not a church, for god's sake. Or a yoga studio."

"Well, what is it then?" Dani asked.

"It's a *brothel*." Her voice hushed and husky, chin drawn to her chest.

"No, no," said Ellen. "I've heard it's sort of a church, isn't it? Buddhist stuff, Zen stuff, you can buy beads there? Crystals? I don't know."

"It's the shit they write on your leggings, Dawn, whatever religion that is," said Anya. "*Be where you are, not where you think you should be. Inhale your future, exhale your gas.* Stuff like that." Dani snorted. But Anya looked annoyed. Maybe just hungry. Dani nudged the pretzels closer to her, and Anya popped one into her mouth, flapped her eyelids in ecstasy.

Dani grabbed one too, loaded it with cheese. She'd always liked to watch Anya enjoy food, her reactions so animated. Ellen grabbed one too.

But Dawn just scoffed. "It's not *Buddhist stuff*, Ellen, they're fucking people there. It's a brothel."

"Oh, it is *not*," said Anya.

"It is! Why else would you open a yoga studio on *Barton Street*? How did your market research lead you to *that*? You open brothels on North Barton. Bars. Not a yoga studio. Plus, there are protesters there sometimes, haven't you seen them?"

Ellen loaded another pretzel with beer cheese, gestured with it as she spoke: "It's *affordable*, Dawn. It's up and coming. I think it's a good idea really, to have a yoga studio there. There's a café up on North Barton now. Have any of you been? It's honestly delicious. They make affogatos."

"That's with the ice cream and the espresso, right? Everyone keeps talking about these things," said Dani. Ellen pressed her lips together and nodded enthusiastically. "I took the boys." She shoved the pretzel into her mouth, clapped off the crumbs, and opened her Instagram page again. Dani acknowledged the picture of her whipped-cream-covered sons with a smile.

"It's a rub-and-tug," Dawn persisted, too loud, and Ellen

quickly closed her phone, as though to protect her cream-covered boys.

"Wait, the gelato place is a rub-and-tug? All right, Ellen, now I want to see that picture." Anya reached toward Ellen.

"No, *no*." Dawn, irritated, took a deep drink of her cider, peeled open the menu with a disturbing crack. "Do they not have, like, a vegetable here? This goddamn beer cheese is like eating lava."

"There's the carrot sticks . . ." said Ellen, beginning to chafe from the tension, and feeling personally attacked by Dawn's critique of her restaurant choice.

"It's a *yoga studio*," Anya repeated with finality. "And why the fuck are you asking about it anyway, Dani?" Anya turned on her, face blazed with irritation.

Only then did it occur to Dani that Bill might be a client. "I just—I saw it, and I was curious. I think it's a yoga studio too." Her mouth itched to ramble, panicked by Anya's rage. "I just, I was thinking about taking some classes, so I wanted to know if you guys had heard of it."

"I'd stay away, personally," said Dawn, and snapped a carrot stick in half with her teeth. She would now demonstrate her superiority by resisting all but the vegetables on the table.

"Okay, *why* is this such a trigger for you, Dawn?" asked Anya, knowing what she was doing, knowing that to identify another person's *trigger* was to press it, firmly. Fired. Blasted first by recoil, then by retaliation.

Dani twisted to look at the kitchen as though something there might save them.

"Why am *I* triggered?" Dawn's eyes, dangerously wide, hand flattened against her chest as though holding herself back.

"Guys, let's not—" Dani tried to intervene.

Dawn barreled over her. "I just don't like criminals hiding under the guise of religious freedoms. This is the kind of thing that makes us all look like quacks."

"*Us?*" Anya jutted her head forward, eyebrows raised. "Are you a sex worker too?"

"Fuck you, Anya. I'm talking about people who identify as spiritual, which I do."

"So they're fucking with your brand. Ellen, do you think Rewardfluencer is going to reject Dawn's application because of her potential association with The Temple?"

"I'm not associated with The Temple!"

"Well, you seem to know an awful lot about what goes on there."

"We should just get another round," Ellen interrupted. "Let's get another round." She waved her arm at the waitress, who was behind the bar tapping something into the touch screen. *Another round, please!* she mouthed. The waitress nodded, smiled, tapped it in.

"Oh, *I* get it." Dawn leaned back in her chair.

"What?" said Anya, daring her to say what Dani, and probably Ellen too, had already put together.

"Nothing, Anya," said Dawn.

"No, say it, Dawn. Say what you want to say."

"That's where Bill takes his classes, isn't it."

Anya's eyes widened, lit with fury. "Ha!" she yelled, sparking sideways glances from surrounding patrons. "You *would* think that. You *would* think that that's the only reason I would want to defend a small, probably female-owned business from the baseless rumor mill of this fucking town. Well, no, actually, Dawn, he takes his classes at the Y downtown."

"The gross Y?" Ellen whispered.

Anya spun on her. "Obviously not, Ellen!" Nearly screaming. "The good Y! With the new fucking pool!"

"Oh." Ellen looked relieved, mimed a swipe across her forehead. She turned to Dani quietly. "That's a very good Y."

Dani nodded, breath trapped in her throat, unable to speak.

"It's bullshit like that, the fucking yoga studio is a brothel, come on. You're just a snob, Dawn, trying to smother these parts of town that are finally getting revitalized, that are finally seeing some *real* growth. Just because it's affordable doesn't mean it's sleazy, all right? *That's* what I'm so annoyed by. You act like you're all Zen and welcoming and open-minded, but really, you're just a fucking asshole." Anya stood up. Her chair roared against the tile floor.

"Anya, please!" Dani grabbed her wrist, and in one smooth single axel, Anya flung off Dani's hand, swooped up her purse, and left the restaurant.

Ellen, Dawn, and Dani sat at the table in silence, all of them checking in with their own drunkenness now, trying to understand how things had escalated so quickly.

It was Dani's fault. She should have known better than to bring up The Temple to a table of born-and-raised Metcalfians, a breed well-known for having strong opinions on subjects they knew very little about.

There had been *opinions* about Dani's family too. The extravagant gifts the Garbage King bestowed upon the city of Metcalf, what he might be gaining from the city in return. His ruined queen, and their only daughter, the poor thing, Princess of Trash, poised to fulfill an as-yet-unknown hellish prophecy. When they were kids, Dani would spend nights at Anya's house, crying in her lap, *Everyone hates me, everyone thinks I'm weird*, Anya running her fingers through her best friend's hair, telling her that

they were all idiots. Losers. Dani was the special one. The princess. And Anya regularly made good on her promise to figura-
tively disembowel anyone she discovered gossiping about Dani,
to battle *the baseless rumor mill of this fucking town*. An old habit
that now, it seemed to Dani, was dying hard. Anya still defending
Dani in a way, after all these years.

The waitress, who'd obviously witnessed the whole scene from
a distance, approached the table with caution. "Did you all still
want that other round?" she asked.

"No," said Dawn. "Just the bill please."

The waitress returned with the bill in record speed. Dawn
snatched the billfold before anyone could object. "Let me get
this, please, for ruining everyone's lunch."

"Oh, no, Dawn," said Ellen sadly.

"You don't have to . . ."

"I insist," Dawn said. She pulled a card from her slim wallet,
tucked it into the billfold's little pocket, and set it hanging over
the side of the table. The three of them sat in a silence so palpa-
bly awkward that Ellen nearly stopped breathing, scanning the
room, the table, for anything at all to talk about.

"Oh!" She finally found it, straightened herself with a deep,
restorative breath, and pointed at Dawn's credit card. "Is that one
of those travel reward cards?"

Dawn leaned over, looked at it. "I have no idea. Is that what
you have?"

"Oh, I'm—I'm not really sure," she said, spine crumbling
again like an ancient column. "Points. I think. Some sort of . . .
points . . . system."

Dawn nodded, returned her attention to the waitress, track-
ing her movements, every agonizing task she saw fit to prioritize
before returning to their table with the machine.

Dani offered Ellen a supportive smile. The silence they now shared altered slightly, depressurized by their own private anxieties.

Dani wished she could tell them about Renata, how she'd looked last night, wrapped in a gauze of cigarette smoke. *This fucked-up world, it specifically undermines reproductive power.* Ellen, Dawn, Anya, Dani—Normal Women in a normal state: unemployed; policed and self-policing. *WE WEREN'T BUILT TO OUTSOURCE OUR BABIES*, shrieked legendary Normal Woman MUM2GABBY. *We're trapped in a system that privileges the inhumane. Monsters rise. Humans fall. The crucial feminine is decimated. Enslaved. By men, who are enslaved themselves. To bosses. To the system. There's a quote, I can't remember who said it, someone fucking smart, though, about how being the slave of a slave is the worst kind of slavery.*

Dani watched Dawn plug her PIN into the portable machine, the waitress tapping a combat boot with her arms crossed, looking away politely. The record of this transaction would be sent to Dawn's husband, Charlie. As Ellen's would have, to Travis. He might even have an alert on his phone, like Clark did. A quiet notification when there was any activity on the card. Normal Women. Punished for their power. Enslaved by monsters. Sometimes. Other times they'd married one of *the good ones*, a term used by elder slaves to describe men who didn't abuse their power, but simply perched comfortably, quietly, above the fray. Bringing home free Bellini powder. Letting their tired wives sleep in on the weekend. Not raping.

*We can fix them, Dani. We will fix them. We don't have a choice.*

# 14

DANI WAS ABLE to get a partial refund for her Intro to Human Resources course, in the form of credit, so Clark wouldn't see. She could apply it to another course or to the college bookstore, where she bought Lotte a Metcalf Community College sweatshirt. And when she spotted a little key chain of a metal garbage can hanging from a display at the cash register, she drew a brief gasp and bought that too. For Renata. Who she would be meeting every Monday night for the rest of the semester instead.

Renata hadn't invited Dani to come and work for her, waiting, Dani assumed, for Dani to broach the subject. And though Dani wanted to help, to be a part of the cause, she still wasn't sure if *healing* was something she could handle, or even, honestly, *do* very well. But she did love speaking with Renata, feeling included in what felt like such a *radical* and promising program. It was giving Dani a sort of strength. *Power.* The clarity to figure out what the fuck to do with herself. "I like you so much,

Dani," Renata had said, leaning over, brushing donut crumbs off of Dani's chest. "I'd love to keep seeing you."

Even conjuring this community college universe of lies for Clark felt good, the scope of it almost invigorating. Her fake teacher, Lorraine, an Amazonian divorcée who wore heels to every class, making up for decades of wearing flats so as not to humiliate her diminutive ex. And then there was the fake group of peers Dani'd been assigned to work with for the year, in touch almost daily over the school's unreliable chat software (in actuality, texting with Renata, of course). There was Willem, cagey with his contact information after having had his identity stolen last year; Deanna, who'd be moving in with her boyfriend soon, already working as a recruiter but eager to pivot into a more senior role with a nonprofit or something; Sean, who was a keener, taking control of their group chat, volunteering without opposition to be their representative to the professor; and finally Beth, who was clever, bookish, and proudly busty. She had a realistic and tasteful tattoo of her cat, Kid Kitty, on her shoulder.

Dani had texted Anya a few times, apologizing, asking if she was all right. She hadn't yet received a response, of course, but she hadn't been expecting one either. Not yet anyway. Anya's silent treatments were legendary, her endurance practically heroic.

Each week Dani brought something to Renata, an offering in exchange for her time. The little garbage can key chain. Coffees. A plastic tray of cinnamon pita chips from another kiosk in the mall. They leaned against the front of Dani's van, Renata's foot propped up on a pocked wooden phone pole just beneath an ad for personal salsa lessons.

Dani asked Renata about the legalities of The Temple, how they were able to operate so openly. "Openly! Ha! A pain in my

ass." Cigarette bouncing in her mouth. "You might have noticed
them—" She nodded toward a small group of six or so people
gathered on the corner between The Temple and the Pleasant
Stay Inn. Dani hadn't noticed them before, but she remembered
now that Dawn had mentioned them, during the fight: protesters. Proof enough to her that The Temple was a brothel. There
were four men and three women, all in white, holding handmade
signs, hastily drawn messages about The Temple's abuse of religious freedoms.

"They seem pretty quiet at least."

"For now." Renata shook her head. "Strictly speaking, our
healers don't accept money for their services. Our visitors pay
for their drinks, for yoga classes, and they can tip or donate,
handsomely if they'd like to, and the girls, if they're having a good
night, they can kick up to us if they want, but no one pays to
be healed. We've been able to register temporarily as a religious
organization, but these clowns are trying to get us shut down."

"But *aren't* you a religious organization?" asked Dani. "Just a
little bit?"

"For their purposes, sure. We use physical stimulation to
achieve an altered state of consciousness. Just as Indigenous religions might use peyote, or certain Christian religions might use
speaking in tongues. We're unconventional, sure. We make them
uncomfortable, yeah, but it *works*. It's working. The men who
come to us, they're *better* for it. Happier, more connected men.
And yeah, you could probably say the same for people who go to
church every Sunday."

Dani watched the protesters, the syncopated dance of their idle
bodies: fiddling with the various fastening and tightening hitches
of their clothes; examining and reexamining their signs, testing
the integrity of the corners with competent-looking thumbs.

Chatting a little, but mostly focused. Serious work. They'd left their homes tonight. They'd gone to a dollar store with this rage in their hearts, purchased stiff, colorful pieces of bristol board, the kind usually procured for science fair projects and lemonade stands; they'd brought markers, dug from their children's craft bins maybe, borrowed from their fellow protesters. They were going to *accomplish* something.

Dani wondered if they realized that protesting a brothel made them all look very bad at sex. She considered walking over, reefing a sign out of the arms of one of the weaker-looking ones, crossing out what they'd written and replacing it with *I AM BAD AT SEX* instead.

"They're just scared," said Renata. "They don't understand." Then waved at a woman with a fat, curly bun and oversized hoop earrings, striding toward the Pleasant Stay Inn.

"How does that work," asked Dani, "with the inn?"

"The owner, Aaron, he's a friend of The Temple. He donates a block of rooms to us that we can use whenever we want. Takes care of the cleaning and everything. A nice guy. You might have seen him actually, rides a recumbent bike up and down Barton, but honestly, he's a nice guy."

"Despite the bike."

"Despite the bike. The bike was actually my idea—he would have been too embarrassed before, to ride one of those things in public. But he loves to ride. Honestly, he needs the exercise."

And that reminded Dani of Dawn—the budding wife-fluencer. And Ellen, with her @mymonkeys account. She told Renata about the Influencer Agreement. "Good for them!" Renata cheered, a fist in the air. "We need more reproduction propaganda." Another necessary calling, she insisted, in a world where birth rates were plummeting, capitalism finally pricing people out of propagating the species. "Who can afford it? The cost of raising a child these days? It's eugenics in disguise," said Renata. "We'll end up with a controlled little population of smooth-skinned sociopaths, trying to squeeze a labor force out of themselves."

Dani laughed and shuddered and nodded at the same time. "We certainly couldn't have afforded it, I don't think, even just a few years ago. And if we were to have another one, I'd be at least thirty-six, and I'm nervous about that, of course. Birth defects and all that, but also, I'm just so *tired*. My back is killing me. There's a reason you're supposed to do this when you're young."

Renata laughed. She'd been sixteen when she had her child and she wouldn't recommend that either. Then they both laughed. Because kids were, in many ways, just an absolute living nightmare, but it was funny! Because they also agreed that it was the best thing that ever happened to them; that they both loved being mothers more than anything else in the entire world. It'd been different for Renata, though; her mother had done most of the early work of raising her daughter while Renata recovered from a difficult labor at a boarding school for problem teenagers. "Though I wouldn't call it a recovery," she said grimly, and Dani didn't pry.

"I secretly wished for my C-section," said Dani, a sacrilege on the mom forums.

"Pity it had to be a secret. The world just wants all of us pissing ourselves again. In this society it's acceptable to discredit people who piss themselves."

"Oh, haven't you heard? Just do your fucking Kegel exercises, you'll be right as rain."

"Well, it can't hurt, anyway."

"I know someone who sets a timer for her Kegel exercises. Like the men who pray seven times a day."

"A devout Kegeller."

Dani pressed her hands together and bowed. "Hy-*men*," she said, like *amen*.

Renata laughed. "It's too bad everything doesn't just bounce back overnight."

"Fixed by elves. The Keegler Elves. Remember those guys?"

"Keebler elves?"

"Keebler elves, that's it."

"Seems it should go against elf code to be making cookies for profit. What do elves need money for anyway?"

Dani shrugged. "Maybe they've started outsourcing their shoe repairs?"

Renata smiled, then leaned over and used her thumb to wipe coffee from Dani's lip, grazing the dull edge of Dani's teeth. Dani realized then how close their faces were, how far Renata was leaned over toward her. "You're a good mother, aren't you, Dani," she said, her gaze sleepy but unblinking.

Normally Dani would be writhing in the spotlight of such sincerity, chest and mouth bursting with deflections. But it was true. She was a good mother. "Yes," she said. "I am." The only role in her life in which she'd felt like an actual human resource, and not a drain.

"It's not nothing, you know, to be a good mother. In fact, it's everything. I can see it in you," said Renata, her palm now on Dani's cheek. "The crucial feminine. *Your* crucial feminine. It actually *glows*. Did you know that?"

Dani stared at her, breathing deeply, allowing this compliment to penetrate instead of immediately deflecting with self-deprecation. *Oh god, no, the glowing you see is from growing up too close to the uranium-processing plant on Highway 11.* It was dizzying, to let it in, shifting things inside her, drawing her gift out further: the crucial feminine. What made her such a wonderful mother to Lotte, why it felt as amazing as it had to nurture her, finally exercising her innate talent, what she'd been put on this earth to do.

"To share your crucial feminine."

She'd always *known* there'd been something.

"Lotte is a very lucky baby," Renata continued. "Clark too. The luckiest little family in the world."

# 15

ANYA FINALLY TEXTED Dani back and agreed to let her come over. Dani knocked on her door with a bottle of wine and a carefully worded yet heartfelt apology murmured to perfection on the walk.

Anya led her to the back porch. She'd just bought new patio cushions, cream, with lime-green stripes, and triangular accent pillows meant to look like sliced watermelon. "Adorable," said Dani, steadying her full wineglass as she sank into one of the low wicker chairs.

"I'm obsessed with these watermelons," Anya said, laying one over her lap.

A welcome breeze jostled the shady sugar maple above them, cicadas screaming for their lives. Dani squirmed, pulled a small plastic lion out from between the cushions. She set it on the table between their wineglasses. "Have you talked to Dawn yet?" she asked.

"No," said Anya. "I will. I know I overreacted. She just gets on my nerves sometimes. All of her judgmental health-food bullshit."

As if on cue, the whir of the blender from inside. Bill was making smoothies for the boys. Chia seeds and hemp hearts. He was trying to get less of his protein from meat. "This one too. Honestly, if his hair weren't so bad, I'd think he was gay."

Dani spat wine into her lap. "Fucking hell, Anya. All that work not to spill this ridiculous glass and now look." She rubbed the droplets off her bare thighs. "Look at my legs."

"Is there any on your shorts—BILL!" Anya reached back and pounded on the sliding glass door to the kitchen. "Can you bring out a Tide pen?"

Bill tilted his head, tapped his ear.

"TIDE PEN!" Anya bellowed, drawing out each word.

Bill nodded, disappeared, and within seconds reappeared on the porch. He wore a pair of loose running shorts, a gray T-shirt with a lotus flower unfurling across the chest. Bare feet. Clean hair. A creature with pain.

"Hi, Dani." He smiled.

"Hi, Bill."

He turned to Anya, extended a fist full of Tide pens into her face. "I'm not sure which one of these is the good one," he said. She took them, popped open each cap, and pressed their damp tips against her thumb. She handed one to Dani, passed the rest to Bill. "Garbage?" he asked. "Not quite," she said. He winked and went back inside.

But *was* Bill a creature with pain? Anya would know if he were. Dani had learned at one of their very first brunches, dim sum near the airport, that all of the Normal Women were a little bit psychologists, each having worked on their husbands for the past decade or so.

At that brunch Dawn revealed that she was fairly certain her husband had *intermittent explosive disorder*. "An impulse-control disorder," she'd explained. "Sudden episodes of unjustified anger."

"Oh, Jesus." Anya had shaken her head. "They've *all* got that."

Ellen's husband, Travis, was, of course, perfect, except she suspected he might masturbate too much. She'd caught him dozens of times, and no one else she knew had ever caught her husband, even once.

"The sneaky fucks," Anya said, chopsticks slipping at the clasp of a steamed dumpling. "Bill might not masturbate at all anymore for all I know. He certainly never pesters *me*, anyway. Which was nice at first, of course . . ." But because Anya, like all Normal Women, had been trained to understand male love as near constant sexual harassment, the battling of insistent, relentless paws, she couldn't shake the feeling, despite his many assurances, that he'd stopped loving her altogether. And not loving her, that definitely had to be a mental illness of some kind. *Oh, absolutely*, the women agreed. *No question.*

Then the Normal Women had fixed their eyes on Dani, the next phase of her acceptance, she now understood, conditional upon the release of some private detail about her married life.

"Well," Dani had begun, looking into the Normal Women's eyes, each of whom, she knew, had cherry-picked their vulnerabilities to optimize likability, maintain their egos, cultivate a benign and friendly envy in all who met them. How could she tell them that sometimes she couldn't believe how lucky she'd been, finding a person like Clark who loved her so much and took such good care of her and believed right by her side that she was destined to one day find her calling. And how he loved her in a way that other women were hardwired to envy. In a way that, at first, Dani experienced as a kind of jackpot—the gratuitous devotion of romance novels. Friends told her how lucky she was. Bunny told her too after their first and only visit before getting married. Just imagine, this whole time, Dani had been a person worthy of adoration. But adoration, dehumanizing worship, that wasn't love. They both thought it was, both tricked into believing they were almost supernaturally compatible. But it wasn't love. Not really. It kept Dani hobbled. Kept Clark a creature with pain. A bad man. Childish. Miserable. But secretly, only in front of her. His support as calculated as the golden retriever version of himself he presented to others. And this calculated support was designed to stoke her most pathetic, secret suspicion: that she was special. Important. The Trash Princess of Metcalf. And as long as he encouraged this delusion, she would remain unemployable, poor, trapped. Enslaved by him. Indebted to him. Paying him back in wretched, unconscious ways that made her feel ashamed and ugly and insecure (*blow jobs and braised meats!*), feeding a network of artificial veins he'd built between them, where money flowed instead of blood. She was a victim host, the warm-blooded life source he required to nourish the ancient, ugly evil inside him. Or maybe that was just how marriage felt sometimes. Maybe everything was *fine*. "Well . . ."

And then one of the servers nearly zipped right past them with Anya's favorite rice noodle roll. "STOP!" she roared, and requested three plates. Dawn asked the waitress if there would be more turnip cakes coming soon, and Anya, face mutilated by revulsion, spat, "*Turnip* cakes." And Dani had been spared.

When Bill poked his head again from the sliding door and asked them if they wanted any smoothie, Anya had made that same disgusted face. "Absolutely not, Bill," she said. "Absolutely *not*."

Dani offered an appreciative half smile. Good old Bill. A great dad, a wonderful provider. Bill was funny and sensitive and weird in all the right ways. He was the kind of person who naturally attracted a lot of nicknames. A good sport. Enthusiastic. Helpful. When Dani had first met him, he asked if she'd encountered a pull-and-peel seal yet, common now, on new ketchup and mustard bottles. "They've added a big flap, see, right across the top, and you pull up the seal that way, instead of digging around for those slippery little folds over the edges." He seemed so genuinely grateful, not just for this invention that would improve his life, but that the world could still surprise him so pleasantly. And Bill was handsome too, in a cozy way. Like a high-quality rug. A fine jacket. An anthropomorphized fox. That he'd happily taken up self-improvement when Anya was diagnosed with her sexual dysfunction was proof of his genuine superiority to other husbands. That he tolerated her accusations that he didn't love her anymore, despite the fact that *she* was the one who had stopped having sex with *him*, proved it even more. Bill wasn't a creature with pain. Maybe the only one who wasn't.

For now.

She was a few sessions in with Clark, or at least what she thought sessions at The Temple might look like, performing for the primitive the task of womankind. Letting him fail to please her, making him aware of the contours of his ego, that it was a thing that could be broken but also repaired. Forcing booming, unhinged noises from his throat. Rehumanizing one another. More and more Clark was the good person she'd thought he was when they first met. More and more she thought she could tell him about The Temple. Renata. *Clark, I think this is something I might want to do. My calling. Finally.*

By their third glass of wine, Anya was able to ease up on her *wronged party* performance. They started talking about high school—Emily Tate and her insane pubes. "Her mother wouldn't let her shave! How fucked is that?" Dani shrieked with laughter as Anya continued, reminding Dani of Jeremy Sizemore, who'd paid Emily Tate $40 to kick him in the balls. "And oh my god!" Anya was tipsy now. "Do you follow Rebecca Giorgio?"

Dani shook her head. Rebecca Giorgio, a memory from another lifetime. She and Anya had beefed over something, she was certain. "Here," said Anya, and spun her phone around for Dani to see. "Hit play." A short video of Rebecca, who looked almost exactly the same, getting a lemon meringue pie smashed into her face, then turning to the camera, creamed beyond recognition, radioactive yellow falling in gobs from her face as she batted her cervine lashes.

"What the fuck is this?"

"She sells the lashes. They're magnetic or something. The whole page is her getting things smashed into her face and the lashes stay on. There's one video—here, let me find it." She took her phone back from Dani, began to scroll. "There's one video of her being bitch-slapped by someone from an early season of *Big Brother*."

"*No!* Someone from around here was on *Big Brother*?"

"Davisville, I think. She sells the lashes too. They're *colleagues*." Anya kept scrolling.

"Did you hate Rebecca Giorgio?"

"I did, yes." Matter-of-factly, still absorbed by her search.

"Why?"

"Because for some reason, at one of Roddy's keggers, she told all the fucking guys she loved anal. Then every high school boy thought that shit was on the menu. And she didn't love anal, give me a break. High school girls do not love anal. Maybe you learn to love anal one day, but you're not coming out of the gate wanting a dick in your ass. Do you not remember the *turmoil* she caused for so many of us back then?"

Dani did remember now. It'd caused her grief too, this idea that if one of them was doing it, they all had to rise to this level or fall out of the competition completely. Dani, drunk now too, shook her head in disbelief, retraumatized by the pressure of a demand that had then seemed unthinkable. "God, why would she *say* that?"

Anya shrugged. "I was *this close* to letting that freak Eric from up north do it to me."

"*Old* Eric? From the cottage? Anya, no! He had a lizard!"

"I know! I know. She got to me, see? Fucking Rebecca Giorgio. Oh, here, here she is getting slapped." And Anya handed the phone back over to Dani, who watched the clip of Rebecca Giorgio being slapped an unseemly number of times.

"I have to stop," said Dani, passing it back. "It's too good."

"*Too* good," Anya laughed, slipped her phone back into her pocket. "I won't tell you how many times I've watched it. Oh! *Speaking* of local celebrities, you didn't tell me about Clark and the splash pad." A gentle slap on Dani's thigh. "The Metcalf moms are going to be so horny for him, Dani, you better watch it."

Dani's wineglass, pressed against her bottom lip. "What are you talking about?"

"Ellen told me Urban Visions is redoing the downtown splash pad for free. Great PR for them, honestly, was that Clark's idea?"

"They *are*? He didn't tell me that."

"Oh, maybe he doesn't know?"

"Of *course* he knows." Dani set her wineglass on the table with unnecessary force. "He's the *boss*, for Christ's sake." Instinctively, she pulled her phone out of her pocket, started to text Clark.

"Stop, Dani, why are you mad?" Anya set down her wineglass,

put her hand over Dani's phone. "Don't text him. Was I not supposed to say anything? Do *not* get me in trouble with Clark!"

Dani looked up from her phone. Let it fall to her lap. Furious.
But she couldn't explain to Anya. Anya would never understand.
"No, I'm, it's not a big deal at all. I'm just surprised. I hate when
he doesn't tell me things. It's a *thing*."

"Well, listen, maybe Ellen's wrong. She's an idiot, after all. Let's
get some food in you. Bill will make us popcorn." She stood up,
flung her watermelon-slice pillow on the couch, then knocked on
the sliding door and whispered to Bill through the crack.

# 16

DANI WALKED IN to find Clark, socked feet up on the coffee table, crossed at the ankles, watching one of the popular political satire shows that galvanized people like them for exactly thirty minutes at a time. One hand submerged to the wrist in a bag of chips leaned against his side, rustling around. Dani had to stifle the urge to cry out, *Shut up!*

As she approached the couch, he pulled in his legs to let her by. She sat down next to him, tapped his forearm to hurry his hand from the bag, then set it in her own lap and began to demonstrate how a person could gather a handful of chips from a bag without making the loudest, most annoying sound in the world.

"How was Anya?" he asked, smacking chip dust against his pants.

"Good," she said. "Bill made us popcorn with coconut oil."

Clark raised his eyebrows, impressed, as he tongued a wad of masticated chip from behind his molar.

Dani breathed through a few loudly munched chips before

speaking. "Clark, why didn't you tell me Urban Visions was fixing up the downtown splash pad?"

"Damn, who told you?"

"Anya, obviously."

"I wanted it to be a surprise. I was going to bring home a few designs and let Lotte choose."

"Oh," said Dani, nodding. "Well, that's nice of you," she said.

Even though they'd only had a few *sessions* so far, Dani had truly felt, foolishly perhaps, naively, as though she'd been making some progress. Restoring Clark to the person he was before he and his brothers pummeled the crucial feminine out of one another. But obviously she'd been wrong. Because he really didn't see it, no empathy still, not even for the woman he adored: Clark, the big new man at Urban Visions, creating jobs all over town, building an extravagant splash pad for all of Metcalf's children, taking up the open position her father had left behind, relegating her to the sidelines, just like Bunny. Anya her only ally. Her tireless defender. Anya her Wanda—Jesus Christ, even their names sounded the same. He should have drawn these easy connections. He knew about her *legacy*. *You could have asked me, Clark. You should have asked me.* But then again, why would he have seen it? He hadn't even noticed she'd been depressed, for god's sake. And why should she have expected him to? He was doing his job; she was more or less doing hers. Lotte was alive, wasn't she? She was happy. It was irrelevant to him then that his wife had been annihilated by their daughter's bottomless need, overdosing on the putrid bliss of disappearing without dying. Indulging it the way she had been, making herself sick, making Lotte sick too. A *healer*. Ha! What a fool she'd been.

"Yeah, well, I know you guys use it a lot. And it's a real dump."

"It is"—sarcastically, offended. "It is a real dump." *What do you fucking know about it, Clark. Metcalf is a dump. And you're an outsider.*

Confused by her sarcasm, proceeding with caution. "I just thought it might be a nice gesture too, to the town, you know, hopefully get some support for our projects when the time comes. Show them we're not the bad guys, why we're really here."

"And why is that?"

"To improve the city, obviously. To make it a better place."

"Oh, wow, dramatic percussion. Brass fanfare!" Killing the nice little joke they had, from when Lotte was first born. "Clark, come on. That's not why you're here."

"Oh, well, enlighten me then, Dani, you who know so much about my business."

Bastard. A bad, *bad* man. "You're here to make incredible sums of money. With absolutely no regard for what's best for this city or the people who live in it. You're one of the bad guys, Clark, do you honestly not know that?"

Clark sat up. Hurt. Showing *pain*. Perhaps their sessions hadn't been *completely* ineffective. "Jesus, Dani, that's honestly why you think I do what I do?"

"Of course it is, Clark, what are you even saying? You just have to make the Kool-Aid, you know, you don't actually have to drink it. But I guess it's more convincing, right? If you drink it too. Makes sense. You are nothing if not an excellent employee."

"What's that supposed to mean?"

"I mean there's no one here but us, Clark, you can drop the fucking act. A new splash pad is just going to make it easier for you to pillage this city and rape everyone who lives here."

He stood up. "Well, if I'm one of the bad guys, you are too. Every dollar I make goes to support this family."

"Not for long," Dani muttered.

"What?"

"Nothing."

"No, what did you say?"

"I said not for long."

"And why's that?"

"Because I'm going back to school, Clark, or have you forgotten already, that I actually have a life too."

One eye, winched tight to the corner of his mouth. Disgusted. Shaking his head. The face a person might make if they were trying to convince themselves and the world that they were better than they really were. "You're drunk," he said, trying to insult her, because for Normal Women there was nothing worse than being accused of drunkenness. Drunkenness was ugly. It was not chic. It implied hidden emotional pain. Domestic misery, failure at her job. Accuse a Normal Woman of racism, manipulation, vanity, anything in the world but drunkenness.

But Dani wasn't a Normal Woman. Dani didn't care.

"You're right," she said. "I am." And stared him down as he left the room.

She woke up into a throbbing skull. Lotte singing in her crib. Clark sleeping through it, roused only, almost miraculously, by nothing but the bleat of his alarm.

She unzipped Lotte from her sleep sack, pressed their warm bodies together, a deep, restorative breath of Lotte's skin. Down the stairs, she kept the lights low at first, helping Lotte's eyes acclimate to the day. Entering the dim kitchen, her and Lotte's distorted reflections rose like vapor in the polished chrome of a brand-new espresso machine. Styrofoam packaging pebbles flattened beneath her feet. She closed her eyes, exhaled a squall of rage, then set Lotte down and pinched pebbles into her palm until she was certain she got them all. *A choking hazard, Clark, you fucking fool.* The thick instruction booklet butterflied open against the counter. She lifted it, felt immediately overwhelmed, and commenced making breakfast as usual.

"Got it yesterday. Whaddya think?" asked Clark, propped in the kitchen door frame by his elbows like a giant insect.

"I think this is a big, stupid machine for assholes."

"Oh, okay. I'm glad you like it."

"I love it." The grind of her metal spoon against the pot, oatmeal bubbling, her teeth on edge.

"Hey," he whispered behind her, gently wrapping his arms around her waist, resting his chin on her shoulder. "I don't want to be in a fight. I'm sorry I didn't tell you about the splash pad, okay? I didn't think—I didn't realize it would be a big deal."

She stopped stirring, set down the spoon, hooked her hands to the counter by the heels of her palms, not wanting to be turned around. She could tell him exactly why it bothered her. *I don't want to be my mother, Clark, and you building this splash pad, you acting exactly like my father did, in the exact same town, I don't know if I can bear it. Not without some* real *exit hatch, some way to get off the path that Bunny took. I need to make money, Clark, my own money. I need a life.* "It was just . . ." But she knew what he would say: *You* do *have a life, Dani, you* are *going to make money, human resources management, it's a great idea, and it bears repeating, you will be* great *in human resources.* "It's just embarrassing, Clark, I felt stupid not knowing when everyone else did. It makes me feel like, I don't know, like you don't respect me. Go ahead and surprise Lotte if you want, but you don't have to surprise me too. I'm not your child. I'm your partner. I'm stuck in this fucking house all day. I want to *know* things."

"I understand. I know it's hard to be home with her all day. I'm sorry, Dani."

"I'm sorry too." She turned around. "I know I overreacted. I'm starting my period." A reset button, Dani knew, a thought-terminating cliché, *a semantic stop sign, intended to stop an argument from proceeding further and quell cognitive dissonance.* If Dani were on her period, then everything she'd said last night would be wiped from Clark's mind like a witch's spell.

He raised both hands, palms out. "I didn't say it." He smiled. She groaned and spun back around to her oatmeal.

And then Lotte raised her arms, demanding to be lifted by someone. Anyone. Clark bent over and raised her up over his head, delighted squeals, swinging her in circles.

"Careful." A mother's obligatory warning as she shuttled breakfast to the table. Clark fed Lotte, and Dani flipped through the espresso machine's instruction manual—her responsibility, they both understood, to get it up and running. And it would be her responsibility too, to make espresso each morning, like the tattooed beauty at the café on Barton Street. Her duties expanding once again, skilled operator of this big, intimidating machine. Clark would request an affogato one day. And Dani would disfigure his face with a tiny cup of boiling-hot espresso.

And to make matters worse, he kept distracting her from her newly assigned duty, talking about the splash pad, sourcing the fixtures, addressing drainage issues in the park. Her father had never made such a spectacle of his donations to the city—when the gross Y needed a trampoline, he simply bought it. Metcalfians had respected these quiet gestures, how DJ had made his wealth feel like a shared resource as opposed to something gifted upon them at his discretion. Clark was more like the showy god-host on daytime television, making a scene of his generosity, feeding on the worship of the masses. "We're going to call it the Edward Greene Memorial Splash Pad," he said proudly.

She looked up from the manual, the flutter of a flipped page settling. "Who's Edward Greene?"

"Eddie, you remember. Did I not tell you about our controller?" He scraped together a final spoonful of oatmeal. "He's in hospice now. Colon cancer. Super fast." He shook his head, a practiced pivot, clucking sadly at each end.

Hospice. In a matter of *weeks*. "Yes, Clark," Dani said. "You did tell me about that." Even if she'd been enrolled in a full course load, attending diligently all semester, she couldn't become legitimately employable fast enough for fucking colon cancer, apparently.

Clark checked his phone. "Well, another day," he said, shooting up from the table. He deposited his bowl next to the sink, took a moment to frown at the espresso machine as though this were all he needed to understand its inner workings, and went upstairs to shower and get ready for work.

When he kissed Dani goodbye, he smelled of soap and shaving cream, a cloud that would quickly assimilate into the smells of all the other clean people in his office, but here in the house, where Dani rarely showered and Lotte only with the gentlest of scent-free soaps, it terrorized the air like a frenzy of locust. A burp flapped between Clark's lips before he raised his arm goodbye, touched his stomach, then gently closed the front door behind him. Dani and Lotte sat for a moment in the excessive quiet that follows a closed front door. Breathing. Looking at one another. Until, without any warning at all, Lotte flipped her bowl and, with the full-body vigor of someone auditioning for a musical, smeared its former contents back and forth across the tray.

"Why?" Dani asked sincerely. Lotte grinned, so pleased with

the feeling of it, warm and sticky in her hands. Dani almost
choked up to think that soon she'd have to punish these pleasures out of Lotte, being rude and making messes. If Clark had
been here, he would have corrected Lotte; he would have furrowed his brow and said, *That's not nice, Lotte.* But he wasn't here,
was he. Lotte was all hers. So Dani didn't say anything. She let
Lotte enjoy this maniac joy for a while before going at her with
a warm, wet cloth, Lotte dodging and flailing and swatting Dani
away. Tonight she would ask Renata how many of the villagers at
The Temple had children. If they watched each other's children.
Loved each other's children.

That day they went to the park and the mall and a drive-thru
for ice cream. At night Dani made turkey chili for dinner, with
homemade biscuits. Lotte sat in her little chair on the counter,
licking butter from a rubber spatula, watching as Dani formed
the biscuits by pressing the mouth of a floured water glass into
the dough. She made a little ball with the excess dough and
handed it to Lotte, who smiled and pounded it flat against the
counter, then threw it across the room.

The biscuits rose and browned exactly as they were supposed
to in the oven. So perfect she even set some aside for Bunny. She
and Lotte would deliver them to her in the morning. They'd eat
them on the porch with Wanda's blackberry jam.

And she would be so kind to Bunny. How easy it was, she
now saw, to become her. *Not your fault, Bunny. It was never your
fault.* Dani would listen to her inane stories. She would laugh at
her jokes. When Bunny told the story *again* about Wanda and
her six bathrooms, Dani would actually *listen.* She would ask
more about it—who needs more bathrooms than bedrooms, and
how many was she having removed? Because you know what,
Dani *was* curious about the ridiculous number of bathrooms

in Wanda's new house. She *did* want to know more. And what harm could there be in making Bunny feel as though what she said mattered for a change?

Dani bathed Lotte, took a moment to be present with her perfect butt cheeks. She lifted her from the bathwater, held her over the tub, watched a few straggling suds slide down her legs. A little shake, which made Lotte laugh. Then, wrapping her in a soft, hooded towel, Dani brushed Lotte's fine hairs, her half henge of blunt teeth, kissed her nose, both cheeks. In the bedroom she plugged Lotte into snug footless pajamas, read her a book and sang her a song and placed her in her crib. Lotte rolled over, her breath catching its rhythm right away thanks to the horrible sleep-training.

She left the monitor with Clark, working at the dining room table, and left for The Temple. Parked in her usual spot, where Renata could see her, and waited, watching the patio, glancing up every once in a while at the Silver Waste Management Campus, just visible from her spot. A jagged bite out of the sky. Black onyx towers, smokestacks belching like a demented pipe organ, moonlight spiking off the mechanized glass walls, which regulated heat without using energy.

A million years ago she would sometimes accompany her father there for the day, dodging pinches from his shimmering secretaries, pocketing the single-serve French vanilla creamers meant for coffee from the staff kitchen, sipping them delicately, like hot espresso, as she punched stories into the whirring typewriters.

Then, a freshly inked story folded in her back pocket, she'd slip away down concrete halls, polished floors. Tongue hugging her teeth, elbows in either palm, protecting her shatterables. She knew every inch of the compound, every building, every door, blueprinted in her mind. People in hard hats and filthy overalls stopped noticing her eventually, a quirk of the building, like an unsettling draft. Sometimes a new employee would spot her, alarmed, tell her it was too dangerous, ask her where she came from, if she even had a hard hat. She would stare at them without saying a word, and within seconds a more seasoned employee would appear to guide the new employee away, whispering into their ear.

She pressed herself against the walls, rattled by the incinerator. Eyes closed. Throat vibrating. Each breath tumbling in her throat like a stone, filling her lungs with glittering prizes.

Outside again, gravel paths to all the different buildings: the big buildings fitted with seafoam paneling, mottled by decades of industrial digestion; the smaller buildings were brick cubes with massive, impenetrable doors, dead bolts in place of handles. The household hazardous waste depot, Dani's favorite, was a big building. The biggest, actually. With speckled laminate floors and chain link over the windows. Due to the toxicity of its contents, it was almost always empty, and it sometimes gave Dani the feeling that it was her own private planet. She built forts with half-empty paint cans, dipping her fingers into the ones she managed to pry open, caps of coral and turquoise and canary yellow dried hard enough to drum with on the lids she hadn't been able to crack. She ran up and down the hallways till her chest hurt, coughing up prizes from her lungs. She sprayed her typewritten story in fluorescent liquids. She lurked in corners, screamed at no one, found her way to the roof and summoned storms with her paint-capped fingers.

By the end of the day she was filthy, eyes wrung pink from the fumes, tips of her fingers burning, the caps popped off, safe in her pocket. And if Bunny didn't notice, which she often didn't, Dani would crawl right into bed that way too, seal her throbbing head and agitated eyes in the good sting of sleep, letting so much filth set on her skin. Burrow into her pores. *Change* her.

She'd thought about her days in the household hazardous waste depot while pregnant with Lotte, searching things like:

> *Chemical birth defects*
> *Cumulative chemical exposure*
> *Long-term health effects of cumulative chemical exposure*
> *Cumulative childhood chemical exposure and birth defects*

This indifferent kingdom, to which she'd once been filthy heir, her DNA rewritten by its almighty toxicity, about to accept Clark as its new king.

## 17

IT WAS AN UNCOMMONLY windy night. When Renata finally ducked into the car, her hair was full of warm air, necklaces tangled, swooped over her shoulders and down her back. Safe, finally, from the wind's assaults. She exhaled loudly, laughed without mirth, as though the weather were rude. Dani reached over and pulled one of Renata's silver charms, the letter *R*, away from the clasp of a matching cable chain, dragging the clasp back behind Renata's neck, beneath her hair, the knuckle of her thumb dragged against the back of Renata's neck, setting the pendant between her breasts. When Dani looked up at Renata's face, her dove eyes were glowing, only slightly, but without question. *Glowing.* Magic, but also common. Comforting. Like a bright light's residue behind sealed tight eyes.

Renata wrapped her hand around Dani's at her chest. "Do you want to go to my room?" she asked.

"Oh," said Dani. "At the inn?"

Renata nodded. "Not that I don't love the van."

Dani laughed. "Of course," she said. "The van is great. We love the van."

"It's just more comfortable. There's a bathroom. I don't have the pelvic floor of your young Kegel-enthusiast friends."

Dani smiled, distracted by the evasive source of her hesitancy. Nervous, probably, that someone might spot her here, in Renata's company. The Trash Princess of Metcalf ducking into some seedy Barton Street motel. A blemish on Clark's reputation. On his budding *legacy*. Fuck him. "Sure, yeah," she said. "Let's go to your room." And almost immediately Renata was out of the van, standing in Dani's window, opening the driver-side door. Dani stepped out, locked the van, and followed Renata down the sidewalk, tight to her heels, as though Renata were the nucleus of some powerful, protective force field. Across the Pleasant Stay Inn parking lot, up the perforated metal stairs to the second floor.

Besides the buzz of the fluorescent lights running above them, it was quiet up there, and squat pots of bright red geraniums between doors masked the smell of cigarettes and damp asphalt below. Renata slid a card into the bulky locking mechanism of room 217. "This is my regular room," she said to Dani. "We call them havens." She opened the door to a tidy and unremarkable corner unit—a queen-sized bed with a rectangular headboard, beveled edges. A worn comforter smoothed over the mattress. On a matching nightstand stood a heart-shaped Himalayan salt lamp, and a small dish for rings and change. Two different kinds of phone chargers snaked between. There was a blue velvet wing-back chair in the corner, next to the wide front window, a floral footstool tucked beneath. The bathroom door was open, chilled by the white blast of one of the outside fluorescents through a bare window. When Dani closed the door behind her, it was all that lit the room.

An air-conditioning unit revved to attention. The click of the Himalayan salt lamp. Renata sat on the bed in its glow. She patted the quilt next to her, and Dani, vibrating with something, fear, excitement, sat down. Renata inched closer, took Dani's hand. "Now," she said. "Tell me more about the First Family of Metcalf."

No one in Metcalf had ever suspected Daniel "DJ" Silver of one day doing great things. At least that's what Dani's grandmother always said, her mother's mother, a woman who thought sunscreen was a hoax and for many years secretly bullied a neighbor with fibromyalgia. She, along with most Metcalfians, had known DJ's family as a rough one: mother vanished, a rumor that his father was to blame, and a litter of loud, dusty boys, all of them put to work as soon as they were legally able.

DJ worked in the hospital, first in the kitchen washing dishes, and then eventually as an orderly, full-time in the summers. He mopped blood and rinsed bedpans and helped nurses hoist unconscious flesh from beds to chairs and back again. He thought he might try to be a nurse too, one day.

Twice he accidentally cut himself on improperly disposed instruments.

The first time a dirty scalpel, a slash across his palm, not deep, but not insignificant either. He filled with a panic so profound it took his breath away, clinging to a metal bed frame to keep from fainting. Then, as quickly as the panic had swept over him, it withdrew, like a tide. He stood up straight, wrapped his hand with a bit of clean cloth from his kit, and pretended it never happened. This wasn't standard procedure, of course; an injury from medical waste was to be reported right away. He was to be tested for every imaginable disease, go home, have a rest, speak to a social worker if need be. But ignoring it seemed to make all that trouble unnecessary. And wasn't all that trouble unnecessary? Did it really matter if he contracted something and died? Maybe it was even a bit nice to know that this was finally it, the brevity of his existence somehow imbuing the suffering it'd contained with meaning.

His wound healed by the book.

The second time it happened, just a few months later—a syringe this time, sprung from an ordinary wastebasket and wobbling in his thigh—he actually laughed. Because he knew the secret now, that you could forget a thing on purpose and everything would be fine. Like the fights his mother and father had had, leading up to her disappearance—loud, wild, violent affairs, percussive cutlery, cymbal smash of broken glass and a palm's flat blast across flesh, noises easily penetrating the fissures between DJ's fingers, tight over his ears, his little brothers curled against him in bed like kittens.

Anyway, DJ didn't *completely* forget about these injuries in quite the same way he forgot about those fights. In fact, he buried them only as deep as necessary to harvest inspiration, an idea for a special container for disposing of "sharps"—needles and lancets and scalpels. Leakproof, puncture-resistant, available in a variety of color-coded sizes with a special section for labeling. DJ had a few prototypes made, pitched them to Metcalf General Hospital, and from there triggered the start of his long, lucrative career as the Garbage King of Metcalf, and really the garbage king of the country, because every hospital from sea to shining sea had adopted his special containers, orderlies everywhere finally safe. And hospitals too, from costly settlements or, god forbid, *litigation*.

Dani had only learned they were rich when, on the way home from school one day, a classmate snatched her backpack and flung it off the overpass into the great, rushing currents of highway below. It was quickly destroyed by a honking rash of startled cars. And the classmate said, angrily, his father recently fired from the SWMC, that her daddy could buy her a new one.

"That must have been very alienating," said Renata.

Dani nodded, crying now, dragged the edge of her wrist beneath her nose. "It was."

"When did he die?"

When Dani was eighteen. Diagnosed with a swift and cruel disease of the heart, so he sold the SWMC, to a pair of merciless brothers, investors who immediately shipped almost every aspect of production and labor to factories overseas and put half the town out of a job. DJ's heart couldn't take it. He died shortly after. And though he'd set up a network of foolproof investments that should have carried Bunny and Dani and even Lotte well past retirement, they'd been quickly dismantled by a moronic businessman who Bunny fell madly in love with. Wanda would only refer to this former boyfriend as *the Devil*, when she deigned to speak of him at all. The Devil divided Bunny's assets into a rickety portfolio of failed enterprises, mostly his own; then, once she'd been bled dry, left Wanda to pick up the pieces. A good chunk of DJ's fortune was thankfully still protected from the Devil's whims by a substantial trust that leaked a fair monthly allowance into Bunny's accessible account, with plenty left over for a nursing home eventually. How well Dani's father had known his wife. And yet still he chose to destroy her with infidelity. No one in town knew that, though, and Bunny guarded his legacy with the care she should have shown his fortune. Wanda knew, of course, disgusted by how readily the town celebrated a rich man, villainized his silly widow for losing it all. "This," she declared often, "is why I prefer the dogs."

Dani still missed him, sometimes. When the sneaking suspicion that nothing in the world mattered crept like an airborne poison into her thoughts. And she missed him dearly the first time she brought Lotte to visit Bunny. When Dani laid her baby in the valley between Bunny's pressed-together thighs, Lotte still so small at that point that she clung to thumbs for fun, exhausted and starving even after ten minutes of focused thumb clinging. Bunny grazed Lotte's cheeks with the tips of her lacquered fingernails. Lotte moved her mouth toward them because anything could be a nipple and at that point nipples were how she survived.

Bunny had bit her lip, wincing, as though this love she felt were actual torture. Dani caught herself searching for her father's gaze then, longing to share an exaggerated eye roll. Because the way Bunny loved Dani, how Bunny would love Lotte too, was all talk. Hyperbole. When Dani was small, Bunny would spin luscious yarns about a mother's love while simultaneously forgetting to feed Dani lunch. It used to make Dani feel like vapor: visible but temporary. A specter. Witness to a world she had no effect on. A character in her mother's self-mythologizing. But also, she knew, capable of hurting her mother very badly if she wanted to, if she acted out or *needed* any more than her mother was capable of giving. She wouldn't be contending with a mother's mere disappointment or guilt, but rather the unraveling of her mother's *self*—if Dani deviated, Bunny would have to revise, and revision after revision after revision would leave her even more scrambled than the great revision of her father's affair.

It was a paralyzing kind of love. And maybe, Dani sometimes

thought, when the weight of personal accountability was too much for her to bear, her mother was the real reason she'd never done anything with her life.

Bunny had been very beautiful once. That's all that'd mattered ever since.

Dark, lustrous eyes, polished baubles that might catch the greedy attention of a poacher. Scooped from her skull. Set above a mantelpiece.

Dani's eyes were the same, bigger even, brighter, but that's where their similarities ended. Bunny's nose was small, sloped and delicate, set between high cheekbones that slanted into the swollen pout of an exhausted nursling—a word Dani learned from the mom forums, which made her feel all the powers of a witch. Dani's nose was durable and inconspicuous, like her father's, and she had his crooked, easygoing smile. It worked. Dani had always been happy with the way she looked. Not the otherworldly beauty of her mother, but the pleasant glow of good genes. And it was better this way. She wanted the same for Lotte.

Dani wasn't sure how it happened that her mother had never really worked, and then Dani herself went ahead and never really worked, because surely the brain wasn't supposed to deform that way. On television, in movies, the daughters of women who couldn't support themselves grew up to *lean in*—asserting themselves in the workplace, exhibiting confidence, poise, expertise, grit, *EDGE*. It was a very easy, clear, *understandable* narrative. Meanwhile Dani had watched her mother depend completely on her father, a significantly older, established businessman, for every manner of support. Watched her mother wither prematurely into a state of utter helplessness. Watched her whole life blow up when her father cheated. Secretly understanding, shamefully, *why* he'd done it.

Bunny's *job*, of course, *technically*, had been to produce and raise babies. But that didn't go as planned, and Dani wasn't sure her father had wanted a child anyway, let alone several. There had been six miscarriages before Dani. Six! The determination. The will! Dani thought that another woman might have given up sooner than her mother had, but Bunny told her that she knew, she just *knew*, that there was a living girl inside her somewhere and it was only a matter of time before the stars aligned and she was delivered to her. Dani thought about the haunted womb where she'd spent nine months, the babies, all girls, who'd died there before her in varying stages of development.

The womb she'd actually shared with a twin, who'd taken a single breath at the house, in her mother's bedroom, lined in plastic for the occasion, before her heart simply stopped beating. Her name would have been Haley, and sometimes at night, when the house was especially dark and quiet, Dani thought she could hear Haley crying from some faraway place, hungry and cold and needing their mother. "Oh, Dani." Renata slid the fingers of her other hand between Dani's, brought both hands into her lap. "Do you remember her?"

And Dani did remember. Not regular memories, but something in her body had known that connection, had mourned it before she even knew what it was to be sad. She couldn't sleep without her. She screamed all night. Bunny called it colic—the stories about Dani's colic, my god, her legendary despair at the discomfort of being alive, a drama queen, a *terror*—but Dani knew. She knew she wasn't hungry or gassy or cold. She missed her sister. A piece of her dead the moment she was born.

The ghost she sometimes even now caught staring back at her in the mirror.

Dani had found herself that first visit to Bunny's and more and more in the visits since, listening for Haley in the house. Eyes closed, head tilted, ears open, servile, not like other ears, tuned in to signals from the afterlife. And Lotte, just brand-new that first visit, had fallen asleep in Bunny's arms. Dani still helplessly yoked to the rhythm of her deep, sleeping breath, watching it draw in the familiar prickle of Bunny's sweater—staleness beaten into submission, suppressed further by a chemical warfare of false florals. Lotte would know this smell, as Dani did, wormed into the intricate weave of her early consciousness. And it made her feel closer to her child, to share these early patterns. More than her mother. More like the vampire who'd turned her.

Dani sobbed now as she spoke. Lying on the bed. Renata stroking her hair, helping her understand exactly how she'd put herself in the same vulnerable position her mother had. For the same reason it was the hands of mothers and grandmothers who'd break their baby girl's toes, fold them, bind them tightly in cotton bandages so they'd curl into paisley. Because it would help her, as it had helped them, to attract a man, extract his seed, propagate the genes, and live well.

"Helplessness worked for your mother," said Renata. "While your father was alive, she'd lived like a queen. And hasn't it worked for you too?"

It had. Of course it had. Look at her life. Look how *lucky* she was. Look at her sweet baby, who she could stay at home with and raise if she wanted to. A dream come true. Newborn Lotte. In Bunny's arms. Her little eyelashes, short and farm fair, a fluttering hush against her cheeks. Fists full of calm. Disarmed. And her brain. Manufacturing synapses at a pace it never would again.

"How easily I just handed her off," said Dani, throat tightening, breath scraping. "Tucked her right into those same arms. Into the same miserable legacy."

Renata lay next to Dani, wrapped her arms around her, whispered in her ear. "But Bunny had no idea. She thinks, has always thought, that she was doing what's best for you." Dani felt hot. Glued into her clothes. Sweating. Swallowing gobs of saliva to keep her throat open. Imagining her mother that day, rocking Lotte gently, stroking Lotte's marshmallow cheek with her nail. An image so perfectly, paralyzingly deceptive. "But Bunny isn't Lotte's mother, Dani," Renata continued. "You are. And you're a good mother. A better mother than Bunny. And that doesn't mean keeping Lotte *away* from Bunny, or hovering over the two of them, pulsating with stress. No. Being a good mother, a better mother than Bunny, means giving Bunny a second chance, and trusting that your own maternal strengths will insulate Lotte from Bunny's shortcomings, or maybe even *strengthen* her in the way that you see yourself as having failed to thrive."

"Lotte *will* thrive," Dani whispered, tears soaked cold into the pillowcase. "Lotte will *live*."

"Of course she will."

"I'd never hurt her."

"Of *course* you wouldn't."

And Dani told her. *Baby only sleeps when dead.* The most shameful, disgusting thing she'd ever thought in her life. *Baby only sleeps when dead.* "I would never have done it, of course, never ever, but it just, I've done it before, haven't I? No one was there but me and Haley. I survived, and she didn't. I must have done *some*-thing, consciously or not, I just wish I could know what might have happened if I wasn't in there too. Why did I have to be there too?"

Renata, still stroking Dani's hair as she wept. "I'm so glad you *were* there, Dani. That Haley didn't have to be alone. Some people spend their whole lives looking for a bond like that, and she had it, with you, in a perfect place. And I'm glad that you're here now, with me, with *us*. You are so good, Dani. You're so, so, *so good*. And *powerful*. And Haley is a part of that power. She's part of Lotte's power too. You see that now. You're going to change everything. You're not afraid of your power anymore."

"I'm not afraid of my power anymore." Dani stared into Renata's dark dove eyes, enamored with the self she saw reflected back. Her true self. Independent. Capable. A *radical*. Unlike what she saw in Bunny's eyes. Bunny's eyes absorbed Dani's light like obsidian. Absorbed Dani. Like Clark had. Devouring, dehumanizing love. Creatures with pain.

"Dani." Renata took Dani's face in her hands. "Do you want to be a healer?"

*Yes*, thought Dani. *Yes, yes, yes*. Dani bit her lips together. *More than anything*. But she couldn't respond. Not out loud. Because no. Could she? Could she *actually* become a *healer*?

"Listen," Renata continued, moving her hands to the back of Dani's neck without breaking eye contact. "There are so many people in the world that want to help people. That are *trained* to help people, in the traditional sense: therapists, counselors, things like that. Years of training in some cases. And they never do. Not *really*. Everyone is still fucked. Because helping people, *really* helping people, isn't—it's not something that can be taught. It's an instinct. Even that's too strong a word. It's an essence. An essence which is nearly impossible to nurture in this world. But by some miracle, you've managed it. You've *got it*, Dani. And it's *strong*. You—*you*—can really *help* people. You can help people *change*. You've always wondered why, right, why you don't fit in, why you can't just have a regular job like everyone else, just make money, be successful. Dani, you have a gift. And it defies monetization. It actively *rejects* it. It's . . . it's absolutely *pure*."

And then Renata slid her hands and arms and legs around Dani, somehow locking into the imprint Haley had left behind like a fossil, and held her in this way, the way Dani'd been searching for her whole life, a restless spirit restored at long last to her eroded remains. She felt Renata's heart, which beat strong and steady as a kick pedal against her own chest. "You are powerful, Dani." Hearts pounding now in unison. Booming through fluid. The first sound she'd ever heard. "And *that's* why you're here." Dani's eyes closed, seeping warm, salty, silent tears. "Dani," Renata whispered, her balmy breath meandering the curves of Dani's ear. "Will you come inside The Temple this weekend? Will you come, just to see what it's like?"

Dani opened her mouth to respond, but the words halted in her chest. She didn't need to speak. Renata knew, from the beating of their hearts together, that she would come. *Yes yes, yes yes, yes yes, yes yes.*

# 18

AS DANI STEPPED OUT of the shower, her chest felt warm and loose, like a just-worn T-shirt. She brushed her wet hair. An alarming number of strands clung desperately to her flicking fingers over the sink. Typical for a while, that's what Ellen and Anya and Dawn told her, to shed this way after giving birth. The forums corroborated, offered recipes for topical serums, algae shakes. *Has anyone tried spirulina? Think I'm getting some regrowth??? But also terrible gas!!!* One forum mother had even opted to try cortisol shots in her head because she just couldn't take it anymore, *the stretch marks, the extra weight, the decimated crotch, and now this?* Dani had followed the thread. The original poster updated. It hadn't worked. Dani rinsed the hairs from her fingers, watched them swirl down the drain, and decided she'd buy some spirulina from the health-food store next week when she and Lotte visited the mall.

Standing at the sink, a towel wrapped snuggly around her chest, she laid out the instruments of her makeup routine, which, despite it being incredibly simple, she implemented rarely. Tinted moisturizer, nearly expired now so she applied it more generously, a race against the date. Some concealer thumbed beneath her eyes and over any other *problem areas*, then blended with an egg-shaped sponge so ancient and filthy that Dani had lunged across the room once to stop Lotte from even touching it.

Mascara, of course. The least anyone could do. She liked to get very close to the mirror, pull the brush through slowly so she could catch a glimpse of the frailty beneath her eyelids: how veiny, how pink, how *shockingly* round an eyeball is, just resting there in its vascular pink pocket. It gave her a thrill every time. She couldn't believe how she used to handle her eyelids as a child, using her dirty fingers to fold them up and chase her mother around the house. *Haley liked it.* The thought speared into her mind. Was that why she'd done it? She could hear Haley laughing now as Bunny covered her eyes, shrieking, cowered in a corner, Dani howling with laughter too.

*Try to remember her, Dani. I'll help you. The more you have of her, the less angry you'll be.*

And Renata was right. Dani's body was full of memories, her template for every kind of touch—tender, aggressive, playful—grafted into her body by Haley.

Bunny's touch had been the first to fall short. Then Clark's. But by that time she was used to it. By that time she'd learned that women weren't entitled to be touched properly anyway.

Dani rubbed small firm circles into a tin of tinted lip balm she'd borrowed from an old coworker and apparently never returned. The small thefts between Normal Women—lip balms, tank tops, headbands, sandals, they all had too much *stuff* anyway, didn't they? She remembered how Anya used to shoplift, rampantly, slithering silently into a dozen layers in the change rooms, shedding them later like snakeskin on her bedroom floor, selling them to classmates for half price. She'd made a decent amount throughout school, careful about her spending so as not to tip her parents off. Dani had completely forgotten about this, and couldn't wait to remind Anya that she'd once been a hustler, had once been a momtrepreneur or a girl boss or whatever modifier might have been used back then to differentiate how she made money from how men did. She'd admired Anya's daring. Her fearlessness as she passed through the gray sentinels at the stores' wide, wall-to-wall openings, confident there were no hidden security tags, that even if there were, none of the employees would bother chasing her through the mall. Dani would chew on her fingernails in the food court, waiting for her contraband-thickened friend to waddle up and lead them to the car. Anya would always have something for Dani too, free of charge, once an expensive pink cami, skintight, with a leopard-print trim that would, Anya insisted, look *too hot* with Dani's comically wide-legged jeans and swollen sneakers. A ball gown fit, of sorts. *I'm getting it for you*, Anya had declared, firm against Dani's protestations. How she'd taken care of Dani. How she took care of Dani still, in her way, after all these years, welcoming her into her group of friends, dropping off boxes of clothes, sharing her calendula-oil diaper cream, sending her promo codes for fancy leggings and leakproof underwear and wireless bras, explaining to her about *the mesh*. Locked still in a tireless battle against the rumormongers of Metcalf.

In the mirror, Dani leaned back, rolled the planes of her face beneath the light, surveying her work. A glimmer of Haley twinkling through her expression, gone again as though behind a cloud.

She was ready to go to The Temple.

She heard Clark flick on the television downstairs, the gentle thud of his weight falling onto the couch. She entered the living room, found him there with a pillow slumped over next to him. "Oh, that's tonight?" he asked when he noticed her at the front door, pawing through her bag for her keys, her phone.

"Yeah." She'd already been with Renata once this week. Tonight was a special, extra lie. "God, fuck. Have you seen my wallet?" Ever since Lotte was born, Dani never knew where her wallet was, one of the many unexpected inconveniences that vex the mostly housebound. Clark got up from the couch, opened the drawer where he kept his measuring tape, his few good pens. Of course he'd noticed it sitting out somewhere, set it aside someplace safe. A good man sometimes, a very good man. He began to hand it to her, pulled it back when she reached for it. "You look nice," he said, and with his other hand pulled her to him by the waist.

"Thanks," she said. And she knew it was true. The lip stain and the tinted moisturizer. Tight, high-waisted jeans, an expensive crop top she bought at a fancy vintage store literally a decade ago and never wore. She looked like a villager. Clark, on the other hand, was all ready for bed, snug jogging pants, a plain gray T-shirt. Maybe from a package. Like Brandon's. Looser on Clark. A copy of Brandon's original. She flushed with guilt. With something else.

He pressed his nose into her hair, breathed in deeply. "Dang," he exhaled. "A shower too?"

Renata's words: *When men want to control a woman's body, they have to control her mind. If a woman wants to control a man's mind, she must first control his body.* If Dani decided to become a healer, could Clark ever understand? Could Renata show her how to *make* him understand? And if it came to it, would *any* of this possibly be worth blowing up her whole life? Which really wasn't *that* bad. She had friends. Prejudiced, manipulative assholes, sure, who she had nothing in common with. But they'd taken her in, hadn't they? And Clark. She put too much on Clark. It wasn't his fault she wasn't happy. He just wanted to love her, the way that men do: find the woman they can finally open up to, sink their teeth in, and drain the emotional life from. *They don't know any better, Dani, but we're working on it!* And Renata had winked, because she was the winking type. And damn it, Dani wanted to be the winking type too.

"I had to shower," Dani told Clark. "I don't need perfect strangers bearing witness to my private greases, thank you," she said, leaning back, still held at the waist, both arms dangling at her sides.

"No, only *I* get access to your private greases." He lowered his hands, laced his fingers between hers. Kissed her throat. "Who are you meeting again?"

"It's this group project for class. We're meeting with, I don't know what you call it, there's this nonprofit, we're helping them staff for a fundraiser."

"Oh, right. What's the nonprofit?"

"I forget what it's called. Something for homeless women, I think."

"Cool. You really do look great."

"Thanks. The woman who runs the nonprofit, she'll be grading us. We're supposed to, you know, dress to impress."

"Well, I"—he kissed her again—"am very impressed." Controlling his body and now his mind. Dani had always been shocked by how easy it was to lie to Clark. Like it was something he deserved. Like all men deserve to be lied to and all women deserve to lie.

# 19

STANDING IN FRONT of The Temple, the patio's crusty, hip-height gate, Dani could feel her nerves buzzing, straining to process this manic new energy. Deep breaths, *ujjayi breaths*, Bill's voice reminded her, in and out, in and out. The women on the patio close enough to *hear*. Their skin, their hair, and all its many shades and textures. There were long legs and bare legs and innocent bruises on arms. Pointy elbows. Smooth thighs. Nail polish. Thick eyebrows. There were big smiles: rumble strips of straight white teeth. There were small smiles: pressed and sweet and somehow calculated, hiding bad teeth or bad thoughts. She glimpsed the very bottoms of butts peeking from short skirts, and angry red lines across the backs of thighs where they'd leaned too long against a railing or the hard plastic arm of a patio chair. There was laughter and mumbling and gripes and gasps, the charming incoherence of early birds, rousing something in Dani that she'd never had before, not even in the womb—*independence*. Independent women. A melody from another patio, or maybe just her memory, rode the breeze to her ears. She shivered. A true radical, like Anya had always thought. The woman she was meant to be.

"Dani!" A thin arm waving vigorously from deep in the crowd, the waver standing in a ribbed cotton halter dress, white, no bra, breasts like the ends of elf shoes. Keegler Elves. They were perfect breasts, but also strange breasts, and Dani wondered if all breasts, no matter how strange, might seem perfect when wielded with this kind of casual indifference to their bouncing. She'd loved her breasts in the hospital, when the labor and delivery nurses handled them like spare parts, but somehow, somewhere, she'd lost that love. And maybe, she hoped, if her body was once again a tool of her trade, it would be returned to her.

"Dani!" the woman called again, despite the fact that they'd made eye contact, that Dani had, in fact, already waved back.

Dani felt embarrassed now, like a child shuffling head down toward the bench at her first piano recital, avoiding the excruciating beams of pride blasting on her from her parents in the front row like something from a UFO. She worked her way through the pointy elbows and bruises and coconut-scented waves of the village in this shuffling fashion, all the way to the table, which was set against the tall chain-link fence, dense with waxy ivy and running the length of the patio like a backdrop. The waving woman sat with Renata, who looked untouchable in a black tank top, a yoke of chunky gold and silver chains around her neck. Dani spotted the *R* pendant. And then the three shots of tequila, topped with lime wedges, huddled together in the center of the table.

Renata stood up abruptly. "First!" she bellowed, startling Dani. "A shot!" And pried one of the long, slender glasses from the huddle and handed it to Dani, another to the waver, and picked up the final one for herself. They looked at one another, then dumped them quickly into their mouths, faces temporarily repositioned from the shock.

"Ugh," the waver shuddered, her face still settling. She threw herself back into her seat, breasts registering the force of it like seismographs. "I fucking hate tequila, I really do."

"Margot," said Renata, "this is Dani. Dani, this is Margot. Dani, Margot is my little sister and she hates tequila. Margot, Dani is new in town. But also old in town. Her dad started the original Silver Waste Management Campus. Silver Waste Management Corporation back then, right, Dani?"

"Get out," said Margot, dropping low, forearms flat to the table. "You're the daughter of the great DJ Silver? Jesus, people here talk about that trampoline like it literally blasted them to the moon."

Dani raised her eyebrows. "That thing is still functional?"

"Probably not. But it's certainly still serving some function, like, the childhood totem for every millennial who grew up here. You're basically a celebrity."

Dani flushed.

"All right, take it easy, Margot," said Renata. "The Princess of Trash is off duty."

Breath caught in Dani's liquor-scorched throat, shame-flushed cheeks, her private title uttered out loud. "He doesn't—we don't own it anymore. Haven't for years," she said.

"Well, still. Very happy to meet you, Dani," Margot said, smiling, reaching over the table, snatching up Dani's hand for a quick squeeze. Very deliberately *not* a handshake Dani noticed, and she liked it.

Dani smiled. "Me too," she said, and squeaked back into the ancient folding patio chair, her elbow already soaked from a wet splotch on the arm, hopefully rain. To Renata, who was hyper-extending her lime wedge, arching the fruit from the peel, Dani said: "I didn't know you had a sister!"

"Surprise!" She smiled, then tore the fruit up with her teeth and chewed it without wincing. "You want to express shock at how much younger she is. Go ahead."

"What's the age difference?"

"*Sixteen years,*" said Margot. "Different dads. That's why I'm hotter."

Renata and Dani laughed.

"Oh, stop laughing, Renata." Margot nudged her sister with her shoulder. "I make that joke all the time. Anyway, speaking of dads, *Dani*, it strikes me as awfully, what's the word, significant, I guess, that you should have found us here at The Temple. Being as the SWMC is practically why we're in business."

"How's that?"

"Just, *booming* housing markets, as they call them, tend to bring in a high concentration of what we like to call passive sociopaths, people who descend on an unsuspecting town and displace everyone who'd been living there for decades. They're our bread and butter."

"Oh, yes, we're that too, my husband and I. Passive socio-paths. He's a real estate developer. We moved here from the city last year."

"A real estate developer! Well, he's just a regular sociopath then. No offense, hon, of course."

"Oh, none taken, not at all." Dani smiled and Renata did too.

"Where does he work?"

"It's new actually, well, new to Metcalf. Urban Visions? They focus on, I don't know, *holistic* developments, things that are good for communities."

"I know them," said Margot. "Redoing the splash pad. Great PR. Especially in a town like this. Razing villages is highly unfashionable to the average eco-yuppie working on campus, or campus adjacent."

"Doing good by doing *good*," Dani mocked.

Margot laughed. "Must be strange for *you* to be back here, though, being who you are."

"It was at first. I always felt too conspicuous in this town. Which probably sounds incredibly self-absorbed. And to be honest I still do feel that way, like everyone is looking at me. But, I don't know, since meeting Renata it feels, sort of, like the right place to be, I guess."

Renata smiled, slid her arm across the table and squeezed Dani's wrist. Margot noticed, tilted her head, and smiled too. "Another shot?" she asked, shooting up out of her chair, breasts bouncing, nipples landing awry like the cockeyes of a busted baby doll.

Renata and Dani both nodded appreciatively, and watched Margot slide through the village, nodding hellos, grabbing arms, smiling brilliantly, a well-loved villager, Dani could tell.

"Margot manages the place," said Renata, without taking her eyes off of her. "Day-to-day stuff. An absolute whiz with the admin side of things. She's the one who thought to set us up as a religious organization." And as if on cue, Margot lobbed a twisted lime wedge at the huddle of protesters on the corner. Renata shook her head. "We'd be lost without her. I hope you actually weren't offended by what she said about Clark."

"About him being a sociopath? *God*, no. I've said far worse about him," Dani croaked, her throat still a bit traumatized by the tequila. "And I felt the same misgivings about moving here," she admitted, "but then figured having been born here might absolve me of any bad karma."

"I think that's fair."

"Does Margot—does she—is she—"

"A healer? No, that's not really her thing. None of this is, really. She's not exactly—let's just say it's not easy for her to see men the way that I do. She just wants to help me, make sure I'm not getting myself into trouble or going bankrupt or anything. She's always been protective. Honestly, she'd prefer me to just sell the place and become her live-in nanny."

Dani's head and jaw dropped. "If those things breastfed an infant, I'll kill myself."

"No, no, not yet. But soon. She keeps talking about it. And she has a good track record of getting what she wants."

"Is she married?"

Renata shook her head. "Nope." And they both watched as Margot headed back toward them. Palm suctioned to the bottom of a drink tray, nipples adjusted.

"Who wants to die?" she asked, leaning into the table.

"Please!" exclaimed Renata, and plucked another shot from the tray. "I was just telling Dani what you do here."

"Oh, it's nothing." She smiled at Renata. "She brags."

Dani learned, from Renata, that Margot had an MBA: a competitive program at a very good school, from which she'd graduated near the top of her class. She somehow knew how much everyone had *paid* for everything, their clothes, their cars, their rent, and she shared the information freely, as though everyone should know. "And they should!" Renata interjected—that was her philosophy, anyway. Keeping quiet about money and wages and rent only protected CEOs and landlords. "Information sharing is one of our tools," she explained. "A weapon that all of us have to fight the system."

"Personally, I'm just nosy," said Margot, and leaned back, laughing. The tendons in her neck reminded Dani of the inside of a piano.

There were more tequila shots, and plenty of water too, because they were women after all. They knew about water. How it was a kind of medicine in outrageous enough quantities.

Margot and Renata told Dani more about the villagers, a few of them just like Dani—or, to put it more accurately, a few who'd experienced exactly what Dani feared: recently divorced, widowed, separated, capable but lost, excluded for one reason or another from tapping legitimately into the money that seemed to flow easily into and out of pockets all around them. It's not that they *couldn't* get a job; it was that the full-time jobs they qualified for buoyed them only just above the poverty line, gulping, thrashing, zero flexibility, poor benefits, little respect. They'd been warmly welcomed by the village, so thoroughly stirred by the cause that many of them now saw the tragedy that had displaced them as a great blessing.

But most of the women *weren't* there out of necessity, or by some great upheaval in their lives. The Temple simply presented a far more appealing alternative to *straight work*, as Margot put it. The money they made in just a few nights of donations was far more than they'd ever made as social service workers, communications specialists, social media coordinators, early-childhood educators, and it freed up so much time for their creative pursuits. There were writers here. Artists. Musicians. Special, intelligent women systematically undervalued by an inhumane workforce.

Dani, eyes wide, nodded fervently, involuntarily, the rapture of suddenly being *seen*. "And why should anyone participate in it?" Margot asked. "Why should anyone spend the only life they've got writhing beneath the thumb of a cruel and abusive boss? With their only escape being to become a cruel and abusive boss themselves!"

"And I couldn't become a cruel and abusive boss, even if I wanted to!" Dani blurted.

"That's a good thing, Dani," Renata assured her. "It means you're one of *us*."

Dani looked down at the table, tightly coiled cords of worthlessness loosening in her chest. Dissolving. *One of us. Me? How? Ridiculous. Absolutely fucking insane.* But also grateful. Too grateful. If she didn't change the subject, she might begin to weep. "So, how do people hear about you? Do you advertise?"

"Ah, the details. A fellow pragmatist, I see." Dani quietly accepted the gross mischaracterization as Margot pulled her phone from the gaping maw of a massive tote bag tucked beneath her chair. Dani spied a laptop in there, notebooks. She had to check a pang of jealousy for Margot and her satchel of important objects. Perfect breasts and all the paraphernalia of self-sufficiency. Margot certainly knew the type of credit card reward program in which she'd been enrolled. Could refer to herself confidently as a feminist, checking all the required boxes: a career, financial literacy, a *laptop*. The mom friends believed in equality, of course, but didn't like the label, *feminist*, or so they claimed. Dani knew that in fact it made them feel inadequate. Excluded. *Judged.*

Dani observed her jealousy. A physical substance in her mind, which she scraped into a little pile, then packed into a ball, then

kicked across the patio. There would be no jealousy here. Not at
The Temple. Not among the villagers.

Margot leaned forward and opened The Temple's Instagram
page. It was quite unassuming—images of the yoga studio filled
with sunlight. Dani looked at the brick building, surprised that
the tinted display window out front, the few squares of dark
glass punched into the crumbling side, swallowed such incredible
light. The Temple. A holy place. Set apart from the rest of the
world. Where gods dwell. Goddesses. The goddesses of Barton
Street.

Another picture: Barton Street bustling on a Saturday morning.

Products from other local businesses.

Endorsements.

One of the villagers sipping an affogato.

There were a few shots of the patio—the canopy of light bulbs,
the flowering lavender bursting from the necks of baby dolls, the
glowing neon sign. A grid of selfies against the ivy wall.

And of course photos of the women. And more photos of the
women.

Dani noticed the skyscraper blonde who'd handled the stray
cat last week, sectioning a cell with the strong angles of a perfect
warrior pose. Dani clicked on her handle.

"That's Serena," said Margot, watching Dani navigate the
page. "The women are sort of independent contractors, right? So
we feature them on the page, but they're the ones that bring in
clients. Are you on Instagram? Yeah? Follow yourself too, when
you're done."

Dani took in Serena's page. There were no lewd photos. Very
little skin. In fact, the photos were quite unpolished, amateur,
unintimidating, *trustworthy*, compared to, for example, Ellen's

@mymonkeys account, or any of the other momfluencer accounts that had slithered into Dani's algorithm twelve months ago.

Serena's photos were grainy and unfocused, depicting nice things, like her cactus, which had sprouted a small red flower. But also things that were a little bit sad, like a lonely photo taken from her apartment window, an empty street on a snowy night.

There were infographics about male loneliness and addiction.

A pictorial that said: *Men are three times more likely to die by suicide than women.*

Another with just a quote: *When culture is based on a dominator model, not only will it be violent, but it will frame all relationships as power struggles.—bell hooks*

Serena's effortless tree pose, the muscles of her back, rippling like water: *Attn: providers! Provide love, not money. Provide support, not money. Provide acceptance, not money. Provide an open heart, mind, and ear. NOT. MONEY. Today's mantra, say it with me now. Deep breath first, okay? You do not need money to be loved. You do not need money to be accepted. You do not need money to be wanted.*

A black-and-white photo of a little boy laughing, the caption: *I don't have to be brave.* And a link to an article called "The Truth About Bootstraps."

"Is this her son?" asked Dani.

Margot nodded. "Toby, yeah. Tobes. Serena's a star." Margot smiled. "Really committed to Renata's cause."

This wasn't just a *job* for Serena, abundantly clear from her page. This was her life. And Dani thought of something she'd read for one of her fake HR classes, about nonmonetary incentives: People *want* to identify with their work. They're tired of submitting to the fact of working to live, mustering soul-sucking, obligatory enthusiasm. People want their work to *mean* something. And this work did. Dani could see it in Serena's page. Authentic, enthusiastic *consent*.

She thought of the beautiful barista sitting in her job interview, performing this enthusiasm for delicious affogatos. *Affogatos make people happy, and happy people make other people happy, and happy people make the world a better place. I want to be making the world a better place too, one affogato at a time.* Offering her authentic, enthusiastic consent to be exchanging hours of her life on earth, making coffee for minimum wage.

And of course, for the barista, for most people, it was bullshit. Her managers at the café, they had her consent, but not enthusiastically. They weren't entitled to her enthusiasm.

But Serena, she *really* felt it. You could see it here, all over her page. Authentic, enthusiastic consent. For sex work. If Clark had been here, his eyes would have rolled back in his head, replaced with dollar signs, bouncing around the room like a pinball, cha-ching, cha-ching, cha-ching!

Margot could tell that Dani understood. "Doing good by doing *good*," she said, through a slowly spreading smile. "The congregation can't give us their money fast enough."

"Don't call them that, Margot, don't say *congregation*," Renata interrupted, an edge to her voice. It was clear she didn't like this side of things, Margot's relentless but necessary *pragmatism*. Dani wondered why Margot had chosen to share this with her, the *necessary pragmatism* that would surely undermine any healer's ability to do the job. Had Dani misunderstood? Was she not here tonight to accept or decline an invitation to become a healer? *You have the most powerful healing energy I've ever encountered in my life.* Maybe too powerful. Maybe, Dani bit her lip, they had bigger plans for her.

"Well, don't let anyone from city hall hear you say that," Margot snapped back at Renata. "As far as they're concerned, these men are our congregation and *that's* the only reason we haven't been shut down."

Renata lowered her gaze, a warning.

"Fine, *sorry*." Margot, elbows on the table, threw up her palms. "Whatever you want to call it. They're not clients. They're not *patients*. What are they?"

"They're just people, Margot."

"Creatures with pain?" Dani offered.

"Fine." Margot nodded animatedly. "The *creatures* love authenticity too." She reached over and Dani handed her back her phone. "The *creatures* need authenticity for any of this to work. Passive sociopaths are happy to evict families from their homes, but they don't want anyone suffering for their coffee beans, you catch my drift?"

"Why don't you take it easy on the shots, Margot." Renata raised her voice.

But before any awkwardness could settle and putrefy the mood, an older woman rushed to the table, her short gray bob and long cotton dress still settling as she placed three more tequilas down. She kissed Margot on the cheek, apologized for being so frantic, then spun back into the crowd.

There were just as many older women as there were younger women here at The Temple, because, as Dani learned, it's easier to age out of an office than a bedroom. Men are men. But Excel, Margot explained, it has *updates*.

"*Updates*," Renata repeated for effect, then shuddered dramatically before continuing. "Edie there"—she pointed at another older woman with short white hair and muscular arms—"she'd kept the books for the same glass-installation firm for decades. Actually decades. She got the job right out of high school. Then she was phased out, you know, and no one else wanted to hire her—too close to retirement, not up-to-date enough on all the new technology—but none of the men here look at Edie and think she can't . . . speak their language."

And then Edie, who'd noticed them looking at her, sidled up to the table with more tequila. She wore a white tank top against which the tan on her powerful arms seemed to radiate vigor. She had a session in a few minutes (a session!) but was *so* excited to meet Dani. "I've heard such great things about you," she said. And she told Dani that she had a daughter too, that they'd have to talk about raising girls in this fucked-up world, and Dani laughed and said, "Tell me about it!" or she thought she'd said that. Too much tequila at that point. *Could I get a water?* And Margot darted from her seat to fetch some. Dani blinked. Margot was so nimble, scooting through the packed village like a cartoon mouse, and suddenly Edie was taking the arm of a decent-looking man, closer to Dani's age, wearing combat boots and a smartwatch. "He's hot!" Dani blurted to Renata, who laughed because he was *standing right there*, and Dani shook her head, embarrassed, reached for Edie's hand to apologize, but she was already gone.

"Can I leave my car here?" Dani realized there was no chance she'd be driving it home tonight.

"Where did you park?"

"Up the street, in front of the café."

"Technically you can't leave your car on the street overnight without a permit. And the cops are real dicks about it. Give me your keys—Erin's teaching the early yin class tomorrow morning, so she won't be drinking. I'll get her to move your car to our spot behind the building."

Dani did her best to hide her unexpected reluctance, took a

moment digging around in her bag, pretending she couldn't find them. Was this a stupid decision? To give her car keys to Renata? For some reason, more than anything she'd already done—lying about HR classes, seriously considering sex work behind his back—*this* felt like the true betrayal to Clark.

But Renata had done nothing to make her believe she'd steal her *van*, for Christ's sake, rust-eaten, pollinated with crumbs, probably steeped now in thirdhand smoke. And even if none of that were true, even if it were some fancy car, whatever a fancy car was these days, Renata was her mother. Or not her mother, no, Bunny was her mother. Renata was The Temple mother, so sort of her mother. And she'd already trusted Renata with everything— her most shameful secrets, her darkest fears, the parts of herself that her real mother, her husband, her best friend, hadn't even seen. Her fingers connected with the keys; she pulled them out and handed them to Renata, who'd barely noticed her hesitation and slipped the keys into a pocket with one hand as she beckoned more women over with the other.

There was Shannon with the white-blond eyebrows. Georgette, whose father, a prominent lawyer, helped The Temple out of legal trouble from time to time, free of charge, a very happy client. *Ew, I know that sounds gross*, Georgette had shrieked, covering her face with her hands and shaking her head behind them like a shampoo ad, *but honestly he's never been happier! My mom knows about it too, it's all good!* Margot came back with another drink tray, full of glistening glasses of ice water. She was stopped by a woman with long straight hair parted down the middle like a Manson disciple. "May I?" asked the woman, whose name was Fawn, and she slipped her hand into Margot's dress and adjusted an errant nipple. "Thanks," said Margot, and set down the tray. Fawn had two sons and a swimming pool that Dani was welcome to use anytime—*please*, she begged, *it would make the bills worth it at least!*

Then there was Alice. She and her husband were undergoing fertility treatments, so she had to decline a shot, a cigarette, *but dear god, I want them! I didn't know cigarettes affected fertility*, Dani had said, a few more tequilas in. *Oh, who knows. I'm pretty sure my husband's the problem anyway. His one nut, it just, it doesn't look right, you know? It's too big and sort of, not grainy exactly, but it doesn't feel whole in there.* And Dani and Renata and Margot laughed, and Alice laughed too, but she shushed them all and said that we weren't allowed to laugh at her husband's nut without her around, which struck Dani as very fair and also very different from the way Dawn and Ellen gushed about their husbands, as though to prove to themselves they hadn't married dicks; to show everyone else that behind closed doors their lives were good and happy all because they hadn't married a dick.

This was a fair village filled with good women who took care of one another, who shared their flaws and failings and fixed each other's cockeyed nipples. These women had imperfect husbands and imperfect sons. They were beautiful but not jealous. They were intelligent but not critical. They were comfortable in their own skin, in their own minds. They were women with real *meaning* in their lives, Dani realized, that thing she'd had fleetingly when Lotte was first born. Losing potency every day like some radioactive material, ferocity degrading.

A memory then, of her first orgasm, something she hadn't thought about in years. In her room after school, beneath the covers, trying and achieving over and over again, based on instructions in a magazine. And though she wasn't unhappy with the pleasurable tremor it produced, she couldn't believe that *this was it*—what everyone was so obsessed with. Just a *feeling?* Just this *feeling* in your body? "That's all," Renata said, "sure, but it's so much *more* than that." Had Dani told her? Jesus Christ, she must have told her. About everything, though? About the magazine? About reaching under the covers, under her pajama pants, the worn elastic of her underwear, finding easily what the magazine had described, and doing exactly what the magazine had said. And yes, she'd done it a lot, all the time, every day after school like that and every night too for a while, but if she'd had a delicious cookie available to her every day after school and every night before bed, she's sure she would have sometimes indulged in that instead. "But there was no food!" she said to Renata. "Not ever!" She felt her cheek. A tear. Leaking. How could Bunny, a woman who'd lost six babies, be so flippant about the nutrition, health, safety, *whereabouts*, of her only living daughter? "It makes sense, Dani, for her to always be testing the resiliency of her only living daughter, making sure that no matter what, you couldn't be killed. And you couldn't be. Can't be. Two souls in one body. You can survive anything, at least once. Haley is part of your power. And you're not scared of your power anymore."

Renata handed Dani another shot, which she blasted to the back of her throat, a good, cleansing sting. Margot reached out, grabbed another shot. "To The Temple!" she shouted, and tossed it back. A raucous reply from the village. Renata didn't take her shot; she sat back and watched Dani wrap her arm around Margot.

"Are you mad at me?" Dani screamed. But Renata just tilted her head, and Dani forgot why she'd asked in the first place, and then she and Margot were speaking very seriously. One of them had been crying. Margot raised another shot of tequila, which seemed to keep respawning in the center of the table like a relentless weed. Which they plucked and drank, plucked and drank, plucked and drank. "We've gotta go bigger. Bigger than Metcalf. Bigger than the country. Bigger, *bigger*!"

"Yes! Yes! Bigger!" Dani screamed, and then briefly tuned in to another conversation, someone shouting, "Pigs! Pigs were the test, and we *failed*, man. We know they're smart and we still eat them. We're gonna *pay*. We *deserve* to pay."

And then someone new was in Dani's face, a woman with big, soft cheeks and dark purple lipstick. "Is *any* work actually *empowering*? Does work *have* to be *empowering*? Like, what the fuck does that even fucking *mean*?"

Dani plunged her hand into her bag, produced her phone, and just as she was about to read the definition of the word *empowering* to the woman in purple lipstick, Renata commanded the attention of the table. It was time to talk about Dani. *Dani!* Cheers and hugs and howls from the crowd Renata had drawn. Her life story. A Metcalf original, the daughter of DJ Silver—*oh my god, I bounced my brains out on that motherfucking trampoline!* Her mother, Bunny—*oh, I've heard of Bunny, I used to be a vet tech where Wanda takes her dogs.* And Haley, Dani's other half—*the most powerful healing energy I've ever encountered in my life.* Hands found Dani's arms, her head, her legs, squeezed her, stroked her, filled her with strength, with the power of touching, of hands, of fingers, to open something, to keep it open. Margot's hands on her now, stroking her forearm, back and forth in the pit of her elbow.

"We are going to heal her," said Renata. Thumbs beneath her eyes, catching tears. Edie crying. Fawn crying. Shannon. Margot. The woman with the purple lipstick.

*Baby only sleeps when dead.* Nausea bloomed in Dani's stomach like a mushroom cloud. Grabbed by someone, squeezed so tight. Forgiven for what she'd seen in those dark, wicked hours. *You're good, Dani. You're so, so good.*

"We are going to *teach* her."

Margot's fingers entwine with hers, spreading the webs between them with her own. "Come with me." She'd said it a few times, Dani realized; slid her warm hand up Dani's arm, squeezed her shoulder, her back, knots dissolving beneath her touch, from the alcohol, relief for a moment from her aching breastfeeder's spine. Lotte. They snaked through the women on the patio, smelling of coconut, hand lotion, cigarettes, vanilla, light beer, through the dark front doors of The Temple.

*We are going to teach her.*

*Teach me.*

Nausea bloomed again. Oozed between her legs. Somewhere private. *To teach me.* Dani understood that she was about to have sex with a professional. Sex with a fucking *professional.* Which everyone should do. Why wouldn't everyone do this? "This is fantastic," she said. "Just fantastic. Do you know what happens when you don't go to a professional?" She tried to tell Margot about Clark and his sloppy bricklaying, how she still tripped. How he'd only just made it *worse.* But the words weren't coming out right. Margot looked confused. "Clark?" Still walking, she turned her head, as though she couldn't quite hear.

"Clark!" Dani shouted. "My husband, he works for Urban Visions, he—" Dani stopped herself—had she said all this already? What time is it?

*Lotte.*

What *time* was it?

Inside The Temple.

Color fields of red and blue light. Every face smooth, borderless.

Exposed brick walls.

A vintage pull-down anatomy chart. Muscles combed tight, tied at the joints.

Women took aerial photos of themselves on a plush velvet couch.

A few couples hunched over square tables with short glasses of golden liquids, beer bottles, twisted citrus wedges on square napkins.

A wall of cubbies at the front. Jackets shoved in. Clothes. Old books.

There was a bar full of people, laughing and talking and every once in a while spinning from their stools into a long dark hallway or out the door. To the inn.

Dani felt the lacquered hardwood wince beneath her feet, making a sound she could feel without hearing it over the music, fuzzy lo-fi with a steady beat, songs blending into one another, blending in with the beat of her own heart, her blood.

A small white flake on her hand. She felt it land, somehow, despite being thoroughly tequila-numb. She actually *felt* it. Arm a glowing red tube, she dragged her finger along it, a pleasant, almost fluey sensitivity, pressed the pad of her finger against the white flake, lifted it before her eyes. A paint chip. She looked up. Tracks of exposed beams, tin ceiling tile once, and now chipping paint falling like snow on The Temple's gorgeous healers. On its beautiful congregation. Its *creatures*.

Somehow Margot had been standing next to her the whole time. She smiled, ran two fingers along the back of Dani's arm. Dani shivered. Nausea. Margot placed both hands on Dani's forearm, pulled her close, whispered right into her ear. "Let's go to the office," Margot exhaled. "There's a couch." She pulled Dani to the bar, reached over and dug half a bottle of tequila out from beneath. "Hurry," she said. "We don't want to run into Brandon." *Brandon*.

"Brandon?" The wind knocked out of her, Dani snapped at the air, trying to get it back.

"Brandon." Margot's warm breath. Her big, spirited breasts, attentive nipples sliding beneath the ribbed fabric of her dress. Heavy heat filled Dani's crotch, her skin dangerously attuned to it, so when Margot squeezed her wrist tighter, led her down the dark hallway, Dani had to bite her lip. *Brandon*. Down this dark hallway. *Brandon* in the dark. "Brandon is Renata's—I don't even know what you'd call it." Toned and toasted arm in the air, she swirled her hand, conjuring the words. "Her *Mona Lisa*, her white whale, whatever that is. She's obsessed with him."

"Brandon," Dani whispered to herself.

"He started coming here after he got back from Afghanistan, or so he says. Claims he was an engineer there, but I think it's all bullshit. Did you know that faking military service is actually a crime? It's called stolen valor, isn't that beautiful? Actually, you might have read about him, he's making those filters for the SWMC, the ones that reduce carbon emissions somehow? Anyway, he killed someone over there, allegedly. Told Renata he has PTSD. Every time he has an orgasm, it triggers rage, fear, all kinds of shit. He's scared about what he might do to a potential girlfriend one day, you know, that he might hurt her, so Renata, she's helping him get over it. He's a tough case, though, apparently, she's been working with him forever. And honestly he gives me the fucking creeps."

The vaguest recollection of an episode of *Oprah* Dani once saw, Glenn Close helping men with PTSD? Or were they incarcerated? Recently released, reformed, reintegrating into society and needing Glenn Close for some reason. Was she fucking them? Giving them dogs? Were they fucking the dogs?!

"Isn't she scared? That he's going to hurt her?"

Margot shrugged. "I think he *likes* to scare her. I think that's his kink. The PTSD thing, I don't believe a word of it."

"But how can he be lying, isn't Renata a human lie detector?"

Margot laughed. "You're sweet, Dani."

Dani smiled. Sweet. *Baby only sleeps when dead.* Pummeled by another wave of nausea, she had to stop and brace herself on the wall. Nerves. Guilt. *Brandon. Lotte.*

"Are you okay?" Margot stopped, reached for her. "Oh, Brandon, hi, hon!" A very different greeting than Dani had been expecting, considering what Margot had just said about him. But this was part of the job, wasn't it, to set aside your ego. It wasn't his fault. He was as much a victim of the patriarchy as they were.

"Hi, I, I'm a bit early"—a deep voice. Dani still bracing herself, elbow up, palm flat on the wall, hinged at the waist like a puppet taking her fifteen. That's how she noticed his shoes first, a sort of dress shoe/sneaker hybrid that made Dani think of slender ankles, vaulting down the grand concrete steps of a landmark building in a big city, playing basketball in a tie. Clark would own these shoes. Clark *did* own these shoes. Of course men would have designed and normalized a dress shoe for themselves that's even more comfortable than the regular kind, even easier to chase down and murder women disabled by high heels. His ankles were bare beneath short khakis, lean legs, a black polo shirt. Jesus fucking Christ, *was* this Clark? A bigger wave of nausea. No, not Clark. Brandon from the patio. His perfect torso. Big, messy smile. A broken soldier. A climate change hero. A dark past. A lonesome secret.

*Brandon.*

A tsunami of nausea this time.

"I need to sit down," Dani whispered.

Brandon reached for her arm, gently; she looked into his face, a large nose, somehow both gourd-like and handsome. Dark, expressive eyes, forehead tight with concern. Margot shot up beneath her other arm, releasing the seal of her palm from the wall. Together they helped Dani into the office. A small room with a couch and a desk. Cool and comfortable and smelling of fabric softener. Mouthwash.

Dani's mind raced with ways she could salvage her image at this point, for Brandon, for Margot, but just the thought of opening her mouth and formulating anything beyond a whimper brought on more violent nausea. She would just be obedient. She would do what they said. She would be a docile and helpful drunk and hope for the best.

"This is why I hate the stupid fucking tequila ritual. This is *not* how you do business." Then leaning over, looking into Dani's eyes: "Do you want to rest, sweetie? Or do you want us to call you a cab? Brandon, could you run and grab Renata, she's just at her table there, on the patio." Brandon gave Dani an awkward, sympathetic smile before ducking out the door.

Dani anchored herself to the couch with both fists, survived a perilous squall of wet belches, then, finally, was able to ask for a bit of water.

Margot was already pouring some from a tall bottle into a glass. "Here you go," she said.

Dani received it carefully, took a few sips. Better. She was feeling better. She leaned back. "Thanks," she whispered. The room was quiet. Cool. She could just lie down for a minute, a rest would do wonders.

*Lotte.*

"What time is it?" she asked abruptly, sitting up straight, battling her bag for her phone. The strap clung to her arm like a kraken. Margot reached over, freed Dani's arm from its clutches. "Thank you," said Dani, then illuminated her face with her lock screen. A picture of Lotte. One in the morning. Fuck. And five texts from Clark. Two missed calls. *Fuuuuuuuuck.* "Sorry, one sec." She hunched over her phone, elbows on her knees.

*Heeeeeeeeey sorry, I know you're out for school stuff but Lotte's awake.*

*I think she might be warm.*

*Yeah, she won't let me take her temp. Definitely warm tho. I think.*

*You coming home soon?*

*Hello?*

*Daaaaaaaaniiiiiiiiiiiiiiiiiiii.*

Warm Lotte, sweet baby. Guilt conspired with dark drunkenness to form another squall, this time in her chest. *Tears.* Dani gulped, frantic, patting herself down for something. "I've got to"—then footsteps down the hall. Renata entered the room like the sun, obliterating the dense, painful clouds in her chest. "I've got to get out of here," Dani said, *pleaded.*

Renata squatted into her line of sight, elbows on her thighs, hands hanging between them, limbered up and ready for their next task. "You want some food first? Some coffee?" Hands twitching to help.

And maybe it was the water, or looking into the eyes of her mother, the *village* mother, but suddenly Dani's strength was renewed. Or not renewed exactly; her strength had been there the whole time, but hidden from her, deliberately obscured by a fiend in her brain that insisted on *performing* helplessness, in front of Margot, in front of Brandon, drunk, of course, but also affecting it. To appear helpless. To be *taken care of*. By Clark. Because that's how *he* wanted it. Not her. And not Renata. Here now, in Renata's presence, the performance was eroding. She was able to embody the truth of herself. How she really *felt*. Drunk, sure. Able to drive? Definitely not. But not such a mess that she couldn't *walk*, for god's sake. She stood up. Formulated a few coherent goodbyes, a kiss for Renata. She was strong now. Because of Renata? Because of what Renata had done? Her darkest secrets exposed, *baby only sleeps when dead*, her ego melted. Which wasn't real anyway. Which didn't matter. Maybe her ego was the fiend in her brain, wounded now, from Renata's kill shot. Losing its grip. Dani's true self gaining. Her brain was too soft right now to turn this over properly. All that mattered was that Renata had freed her. No more performance. No more helplessness. No more *lies*. Outside, in front of The Temple, she flung an arm in the air and flagged down a cab, crouched into it without hitting her head, and waved goodbye to Renata from the open window. Renata waved back, smiling.

Dani's head wobbled in the backseat, erratic lights illuminating her face in the rearview as they drove. Dani couldn't stop staring at herself, thrilled by her own reflection every time Metcalf's lights gave it to her.

At the house she handed the cabdriver a little clamshell of cash, made it all the way to her front door, and slid her key into the lock before realizing she was about to puke. She skidded back down the front steps, tripped over the uneven goddamn driveway, and landed on her chest with an evacuating thud. Vomit sprayed across the brick. She got up on all fours, summoned two explosive gushes followed by what felt like an eternity of painful gags, wringing every morsel of food and liquid from her stomach, her chest. Afterward she felt light. Liberated. *Clean.* She stood up, returned to the house keys still dangling from the front door, and waved off the cabdriver, who unfortunately, having stayed to make sure she got in okay, had witnessed the whole thing. Finally she slipped gently into the mercifully silent, mercifully dark house. Lotte must have fallen back asleep. Clark asleep too.

She went to the kitchen, filled a glass with water, sat at the table to finish it off before making her way upstairs.

Restored by Renata's presence, she'd been able to text Clark back from the cab.

She opened her phone to review it:

*Lottrre girlk sge okk!! ok om om my waY.*

He'd left her, quite rightfully, on read.

# 20

THE NEXT MORNING, before opening her eyes, Dani flung her arm to the nightstand in search of water, her phone. She'd lost a bit of life to this hangover; there would be a marked dip in her long-term health, she was sure. She could only take in the phone's screen through squinting peripheral. The last thing she'd texted, gibberish to Clark. The last thing she'd looked up, the word *empowering*: *To give power, or authority to; to enable or permit.* Fucking embarrassing. And the *car*. She'd left the car at The Temple. She texted Renata, and when the three dots didn't appear immediately to indicate a reply, she began to panic. *I'm such a fucking idiot. I'm such a fucking fool. I've handed the keys to our car over to a complete fucking stranger and Clark is going to kill me, he's going to murder me, I don't make any money, I don't do anything important, I'm shirking more and more Lotte work onto him and now I've cost us a whole entire car. I am a drag on us, I'm a weight on anyone I touch. Please kill me, Clark, please god, kill me, I don't deserve to live. I want to die I want to die I want to die*

*I want to die I want to die.* And then the buzz of her phone, like a disarm code entered with one second left on the clock. Total destruction narrowly avoided. Everything fine now. Even a bit boring, *tee-hee!* Of course it was Renata.

*Morning sweetie, about to start a class, but I'll send someone over soon with your car.*

Renata's dove eyes focused. Strong hands in a downward dog, tendons raised, knuckles twitching.

Dani tried to sit up. Texted Renata back instead: *Thank you.*

The only thing strong enough to pull Dani from bed was her visceral need for Lotte. Her small, fat hands, the smell of her, that perfect weight in her lap, staring into her enormous eyes. Every day a little different, said the momfluencers. Time is what you don't get back, you see.

A memory, like a drop of ink, spread through her mind. An endless hallway with Margot. Brandon, the broken soldier, hoisting her the rest of the way like a casualty. Tall and strong, the press of his firm warmth along her side, beneath her palm. Handsome warrior gone feral with bloodlust, seeking to restore his crucial feminine, reclaim his humanity. Like the poem. A perfect man in the making, Renata's greatest work. The *Epic of Brandon.*

From downstairs Lotte let out a long squeal. Clark blasted a raspberry into her belly, both of them screamed with laughter. *I'm sorry, Clark.* She would just tell him she'd gotten carried away with her classmates. Didn't she deserve that? After all this time taking care of Lotte? Wasn't this—she pressed her lips tight against a hostile burp—wasn't this technically *self-care?* Clark went out with coworkers all the time, and it was *networking,* or whatever drinking on weeknights is called when you want to justify it. Now that he was the boss, in fact, she'd been getting the *don't wait up* text every other week. She'd been networking too, in a way, hadn't she? She pulled out her phone and looked up the word *networking*: *The exchange of information or ideas among people with a common interest, usually in an informal setting.* She nodded, cleared her tobacco-thickened throat. She'd most definitely been networking.

Oh, Clark. Sex with Clark. Honest sex with Clark. *No more lies. If you're going to join us, there can be no more lies.* Eventually, with enough time, enough sessions, real training from Renata, her healing honesty would infiltrate the atomic fissures of his fragile stoicism. Soften him. How quickly joy wants to root.

> *she was not restrained, but took his energy*
> *she spread out her robe and he lay upon her*
> *she performed for the primitive the task of womankind*

She would extend Clark's vulnerability. Decouple it from orgasm. Find out once and for all if he was very, very good or very, very bad.

Dani felt ashamed to go downstairs. She should be ashamed. She stood up. *Don't be ashamed of yourself, Dani,* speaking to herself, speaking as Renata. *You know, not even all* women *are in touch with their crucial feminine, not even all* mothers. Like MUM2GABBY. Dani had explained MUM2GABBY to Renata and Margot last night. They'd laughed. *Exactly! The patriarchy is so powerful that it's staunched the crucial feminine in so many women too: Nurturing, receptivity, creativity, compassion, intuition, sensuality, inclusion, mystery, renewal, and unconditional love, this world snuffs these qualities out of everyone, because they're not rewarded; it's hard to actually* survive *and nurture these qualities at the same time, hard to make money, to thrive in the world, when you're nur-*

*turing these precious things.* Dani had nodded hard—yes, my god, *yes*, it made sense! It made *so much sense.* Her gift, the thing she'd never been able to articulate, never been able to spin into money or a career or meaning in this world, it was her powerful and uniquely indestructible *feminine.* Her *crucial feminine. I could see it in you, Dani, I saw it in you that first night*, said Renata. And Margot, swooped breasts sitting on the table like a pair of gravy boats, grabbed her wrist, shook it as she spoke, *But you'll make money here, girl, my god. We've got it figured it out. You're going to make a fortune.*

*Really, though? Good money? I need to make money. I don't want to be afraid anymore.*

*Dani, Fawn paid for that massive pool with the money she made here. Alice was able to finance her fertility treatments. And Edie, she's putting her granddaughter through college. You think she could have done that working at the glass company?*

Dani stood at the sink and splashed water on her face.

*Don't be ashamed.*

*You're doing what you have to do.*

*This is for your family.*

*This is for Lotte, who needs a role model.*

*This is for Clark, whose glimmers of humanity might soon be lost forever if you don't keep helping him. If you don't learn how to save you both.*

*Trust me.*

*Trust me, Clark.*

And if he didn't trust her, if he didn't understand, she would make him understand. And if that didn't work then, well, she was too hungover to think about that.

She patted herself dry, rubbed moisturizer into the creases of her tequila-tortured face. Cleared her throat again, spit the hangover poison into a tissue, then tossed the revolting little dumpling into the trash. No more smoking, for god's sake.

She made it to the foot of the stairs before Clark noticed her, looked up from a spread of documents taking up most of the dining room table. Lotte sat in front of a little mountain of playdough, a few tools strewn about, a roller, a star-shaped stamp, a mold shaped like a car. Clark had made her a few, which she crushed in one hand and, with the other, waved at Dani.

"Good morning," said Clark. Clark, the good one. Dani, the bad one, her tail between her legs.

"I'm sorry," she said.

"I guess you had quite a night."

"It was—I'm sorry, I just, I haven't been out in a while like that. I like my HRM group. Then I saw a few old friends. I should have texted." *No more lies.*

"Lotte was warm."

"I know." Dani rushed over to Lotte, knelt next to the high chair, pushed her hair up off her forehead. "How are you, my sweet thing?" Lotte smiled and made a high-pitched squeal and handed her mother the car mold. So much of being a parent was simply accepting things that had been handed to you—a cloth for cleaning glasses, the coil binding from an old notebook, a small plastic cheeseburger with eyes, this playdough car, part of a foam gorilla with teeth marks in it—saying *thank you*, and finding a place to put it. By the end of each day almost every surface in the house rendered unusable with clutter, a curation of chaos so pure as to be, somehow, *moving*. Dani thought of photographing these lunatic sets, capturing the thrilling, preverbal *truth* they contained. On display at The Temple. An exhibition. My god, she *was* an artist. Just how much of her deepest, truest self had the tequila ritual excavated last night?

"I hope you didn't get too drunk in front of the woman."

Dani frowned. "Woman?"

"The nonprofit woman?"

"Oh, her! No, no, definitely not. This was after. She thought—" Dani gulped, feeling the lie now, how bad it was, like a slick of grime on her skin, sticky, inescapable. "She thought we were great." *No more lies.*

"Oh, good," said Clark. "I'm glad. And I am glad you got out too, for the record. I'm glad you saw some old friends. I just wish you would have called me. I was worried about you."

"I know, Clark. Fuck, I'm really sorry. And if it makes you feel any better, I feel like fucking dogshit." Dani sat in the chair next to Lotte, pressed a little ball of playdough into the car mold, and then another. *Old friends.* Clark should know that she didn't have any old friends. He should know that Anya was her only friend. Moms have friends. They build villages. They create *bonds.* Of course Clark thought Dani had old friends. Of course. Because he didn't know her. Had never known her. Had bought her a necklace last Christmas, of Lotte's birthstone, for fuck's sake. But he *would* know her. He'd know her soon enough. Her stomach growled audibly.

"Hungry?" Clark asked.

"Starving."

"Let me guess, you need something greasy?"

Dani looked down at her thighs, ashamed. "Yes."

Clark pulled out his phone to order egg sandwiches, hash browns, and Dani caught a glimpse of the papers he was looking over, a zoning map. Barton Street. The Temple circled lightly in pencil.

"What's that?" she asked.

Clark looked up from his phone, took off his glasses and

blinked a few times. "Well, I guess I can't jinx it now—we bought that motel at the end of Barton Street." He looked back down at his order. "Do you want sausage or bacon?"

"Really?" She raised her chin, eyes downcast, trying to get a better look at a bit of writing scribbled over the Pleasant Stay Inn. "For The Ellison?"

"No, no, this is for another project." He grinned mysteriously. "Sausage or bacon."

"But where will the truck drivers sleep?"

"Hell, I don't know. There aren't any other hotels in town? I'm getting you sausage."

"Yeah, sausage." She rolled another ball of playdough, against the table this time, made Lotte another car. "But, I don't know, that just seems like, they've got a good thing going there, don't they?" Renata's words, when Dani had inquired as to whether they healed anyone other than the passive sociopaths: *We try our best not to encroach on Barton Street's former arrangements. They've got a good thing going there. We don't need to mess with it.* And Dani had kept it to herself that it didn't look like anyone from Barton Street's former marketplace was still in business. Because what did she know about it? Suddenly she wanted a cigarette very badly; a deep breath dragged ragged through her lungs did nothing to squelch the craving.

Clark laughed. "I don't think it's going so good for the motel. The owner's nearly bankrupt."

"How do you know that?"

"Oh, we have our ways." He raised an eyebrow. A bad person. Then he said, "I think I'm going to get waffles," and bit his lips together in a kind of shameful glee, like someone currently getting away with farting in a crowd.

Lotte held a wad of playdough tightly in each fist, pounded

them flat into her tray, held the flattened wads out to Dani to make more balls. Dani accepted the playdough absently, rolled it between her palms, still confused. "But why is that spot circled"—she leaned over and tapped The Temple with her ball of playdough—"right there."

"Oh, just another business owner who might be open to an offer is all."

"Open to an offer." Dani kept rolling the playdough, putting together what this meant. "So, wait, she's broke too?"

"How do you know it's a woman?"

"No, I just, I mean, it's a yoga studio, isn't it? I assume it's a woman." Lotte snatched the playdough ball from Dani's hand, and Dani started on another one.

"Oh, right, yes, that makes sense. Yeah, she's about to lose the building."

And then, as though she could smell the breath of any word about her, Dani got a text from Renata: *Erin will be by soon with your car.*

Dani put down the playdough and held her thumbs over her phone:

*How could you be going fucking bankrupt, Renata? You told me I could make money, real money, you told me I could support Lotte! You told me I wouldn't have to be scared anymore! You told me everything would be okay! We can do good and do good, you said, make money and make the world better.* She took a deep breath, *ujjayi* breath, said Bill, dragged in and out, in and out, hard against her throat.

*Hey I'm just talking to Clark, I thought—*

No. She deleted and started again:

*Has anyone from Clark's company—*

No. Not that either. She couldn't tell her about Clark. She

couldn't sabotage his deal. He'd worked so hard. And she'd be sabotaging herself too. And Lotte. The fact was right now Clark was alive and well and the sole provider for this family. She couldn't keep food out of Lotte's mouth to save the world. She just couldn't. And she couldn't do this over text either. She furrowed her brow, thumbs dancing over the keyboard, then sent off a *sounds good*.


An hour after breakfast, Dani was still lying on the couch, heavy with sausage and hash browns, a hot beanbag over her eyes. She listened to the digitized bleat of one of Old MacDonald's sheep from a television program that sometimes held Lotte's attention for up to an hour. Just the classics—"Old MacDonald," "London Bridge," "Row, Row, Row Your Boat"—alongside sloppily rendered, brightly colored animations. Lotte was wedged, folded nearly in half, in fact, between Dani's torso and the couch, bouncing her heels off Dani's side.

The hush and shuffle of Clark's papers at the table. Working hard. On a weekend. A creature with pain. *I'm sorry, Clark. I'm so sorry. I'm sorry for everything.* And then she felt him lift Lotte. She let the beanbag fall from her face.

"I'm going to take Lotte to the pool and let you rest," said Clark.

"You're a good person," said Dani, moving only the muscles required to utter this compliment.

"Well, I *want* to go too."

"Exactly," said Dani, and then, still rationing energy like a marooned sailor, she stuck out her lips and Clark brought Lotte down to kiss her goodbye. He kissed her too. Then placed the warm beanbag back over her eyes, taking care to work it gently into the contours of her skull. Good old Clark.

He liked to have adventures with Lotte, when he could, on the weekends, and had always been particularly obsessed with teaching her to swim. As a child, he'd slipped silently into the deep end at a pool party and drifted, quite peacefully, to the bottom. Then suddenly he was awake, frantic shapes blotting out the brightest sun he'd ever seen in his life. His chest hurt. His lungs. But in a way like he'd never experienced pain before, which of course he had, being the youngest of three brothers; physical pain was a fact of daily life. It was a curse, he'd once told Dani, to know that death could be so nice. And sometimes, when he was feeling anxious, he regretted that that wasn't the way he'd gone. Dani wondered if he'd thought about it when he heard about Eddie and his colon cancer—what a nightmare that would be compared to simply absorbing warm, chlorinated water like a sponge, heavy, heavier, then asleep forever. And Dani felt guilty that she hadn't really considered how Clark might have felt about his coworker's untimely diagnosis. What a dick she'd been about Clark wanting to name the splash pad after him. "I'm a meanie," she whispered, her eyes filling with tears beneath the beanbag. One drew a cool line down the side of her face. Clark rubbed his thumb against it. Still standing there.

"You're not a meanie," he said.

More tears. "I love you, Clark."

"I love you too. Drink some water." Then she listened as he crammed Lotte's feet into her jangly sandals, hoisted her unnecessarily heavy diaper bag over his shoulder with a groan, remembered just as she heard the door close that he'd need the car seat, which was in the van, which was still at the fucking Temple. Any

second now Clark would come back into the house, irritated—
*Dani, come on, where the hell's the van?* Dani jumped from the
couch, opened the front door, just in time to see the van pulling
out, the reflection of tittering leaves crawling up the windshield.

She took out her phone: *Hey, thanks for getting the car back. Let
me know a good time to come by, okay? We should talk.*

Then she went to the kitchen, filled a glass of water at the
sink, and chugged it. Checked her phone. Another glass of water.
Checked her phone. The hollow sound of the empty glass against
the counter rattled painfully in her head.

She went upstairs, and with big, anguished gestures she peeled
off her clothes and got into the shower, let the warm water batter her face numb. The shampoo smelled too good for her. The
conditioner too creamy. Checked her phone. Clean underwear,
clean clothes. She didn't deserve them. Checked her phone.

Still no reply from Renata.

# 21

WHEN SHE DIDN'T HEAR from Renata the next day or the day after that, she texted her again: *Hello?*

No reply.

The next day: *Can we talk?*

No reply.

The next day: *Are you mad at me?*

Dani felt guilty. Confused. Embarrassed. Angry. Alone. Had something happened at The Temple? Had she made a fool of herself? Had she fought someone? Hurt somehow? Had she repeated some awful thing that the Normal Women said? There must have been *something*. Something bad enough to make Renata never want to speak to her again.

*Renata, what did I do wrong?*

The only thing that kept her from self-destructing was Lotte's sudden, strong preference for the color blue. The blue bird in her book: she tapped it. The blue bead on her abacus: she tried to eat it—another precious clue, at exactly the right time, about the little stranger Dani was obsessed with.

Dani made blue playdough out of flour and water and salt and food coloring. They made sugar cookies with blue icing. She cut everything blue out of the Sunday flyers, and she and Lotte glued them to paper plates, serving one another meals of blueberries, Concord grapes, Cool Ranch Doritos, and Chips Ahoy. Lotte, already understanding what it was to pretend, pinched up the foods and munched gleefully at her empty fingers. *Genius*, thought Dani. *An absolute genius.*

Dani showed Lotte how the paper plates could move air. They spent the whole afternoon fanning frail detritus off the stone porch this way, acorn caps and twigs and fallen oak leaves that had curled into the shape of small animal skulls. Dani was able to hang one like a trophy from a corroded hook, which had been screwed for mysterious reasons into the brick next to the front door.

*Please Renata. You have to tell me what I did wrong.*

*Please?*

*Listen, fine, you hate me now, I don't know why, but you do. Fine. But there's something I have to tell you. Something important. About The Temple, all right?*

One night Renata had asked Dani, "What makes you think Clark is so bad?"

And it was hard to explain. Maybe by Clark's design. How he imagined himself an ally to women, she could tell, when he mentioned that an actress had become too thin. How sometimes, in public, he treated Lotte like an accessory—*excuse me, hot dad coming through, make some room on the swing please.* That fucking birthstone necklace. And how he'd tricked Dani, with his intoxicating worship, into allowing herself to be transformed by it. Maybe not on purpose, maybe a victim himself, but *she* was the one who'd suffer the real consequences, one of the millions of older women living in poverty. Long, anxious, pathetic years in exchange for a few decades of absolute worship from a passive sociopath. A few decades of slavery, freed by his death into a cruel and punishing world.

*A creature with pain.*

How Clark had known about the promotion, moving to Metcalf, she was certain, *months* before he told her about it. He'd waited until her nesting instinct had flared like an illness so she could do nothing but agree. Because it was what was *best*, wasn't it? A house. Family nearby. And he was the one who always knew what was best.

Then, with nothing but air lobbed from her plate, Lotte stripped the fuzz from a dandelion, plucked the bare nub, and crawled to Dani, grinning proudly.

"Oh my god, Lotte! Great job!" Dani scooped her up and hugged her tight. "You are the most amazing baby, did you know that?" Lotte opened her mouth against Dani's cheek and left a trail of slime as she squirmed down, out of her arms, and wobbled toward a carpet of fluffy weeds she'd spotted cowering in a corner of the yard. She noticed too that the overstuffed yard-waste bag had finally split. She went to the garage, pried another bag from the pack, whacked it open, and set it down next to the old one. With a pair of gardening gloves she found in one of Lotte's buckets she began to scoop through almost twelve months of organic waste, rot strata, the deepest nearly liquid. She wiped sweat from her forehead with the bend of her wrist, raised her foot to Lotte when she toddled too close, yelled at her to keep away. Dani filled three yard-waste bags with what came from that first one. Then, using the new Silver Waste Management Campus app, she figured out how to properly dispose of it. Now that was done. She'd done it. The most disgusting job in the house. So, there was no way in fuck she was *also* going to learn how to use that fucking espresso machine.

Back inside, Lotte deep into her nap, Dani opened her text conversation with Renata again.

*I'm serious, Renata. I have to talk to you. It's about Clark.*


After a full week passed with no response, she couldn't take it anymore. She told Clark there was some end-of-semester stuff she wanted to take care of, a few library books she had to return, meeting up with one of her professors to secure a "teamwork" badge she could add to her online résumé. A teamwork badge! Clark thought that was cool. Dani knew he would. The way he lauded her soft skills. She felt like a child presenting a glue-damp macaroni portrait to her father, starting to become suspicious of his effervescent praise.

She parked on Barton. Two coffees in the console cupholders collected beads of steam on their lids. She lifted one, rubbed the dew from its mouth with her thumb, then took a careful sip, eyeballing the waxy brown bag she'd brought containing two dozen rock-hard and curiously aromatic peanut butter cookies.

She watched a couple women link arms and enter The Temple. A few assembling on the patios the way they always did. A beautiful blond woman sat at a table with a tall glass of water, reading on her phone. She wore dark lipstick, black denim shorts, sneakers, and a stylishly bedraggled T-shirt. A few others had grabbed gelato from one of the new spots on the south end of the street, a bit of a hike but worth it for the gelato, according to Ellen. The villagers stood in a circle, carving into slabs of gelato with the curiously flat utensils that always accompany fancy ice cream, something more elegant about scraping soft sweets off into your mouth.

But they were enjoying themselves, it seemed. As always. Chatting, sharing small bites.

Usually she would have spotted Renata by now. Especially on such a nice night.

She checked her phone. Fifteen minutes had passed, which felt like a long time in the van.

And then another fifteen minutes. Dani peered into the dense crowd on the patio, thinking once that she'd spotted her, but it was someone else. Someone she'd met that night. Krista? Kayla? And then fifteen more minutes passed. And fifteen more. Dani finished her coffee. Three peanut butter cookies. A whole hour gone by with no trace of Renata. Dani, in the middle of tapping and licking crumbs from her own shirt like a lonely, long-nippled primate, jumped when the door of The Temple opened abruptly. She held her breath as Margot stuck half her body out the door. Another tight dress. Black. Braless. Some of Renata's chains from the other night. Dani nearly jumped out of the van, waving, screaming her name, but something about Margot's expression, frustration edged with concern, stopped her. Margot peeked in and out of the front door like that a couple more times before retiring. And Dani, unnerved by her expression, by Renata's absence, quickly drove home, where she tossed and turned until she heard birds.

## 22

IN THE MORNING Dani tried to settle into a normal day with Lotte but couldn't. Distracted through breakfast. She could take Lotte to Bunny's. She could take her to the Metcalf Community Pool. Be with other mothers. Mom friends. Couldn't she make a village of the swimming mothers? She remembered her own mother taking her to the exact same pool, a blinding oasis of bright turquoise across the street from the only synagogue in town. Bunny with, but not *a part of*, the other mothers, submerged to the waist, chatting, bobbing. Dani swimming beneath the surface with the rest of the children, winding through their mothers' legs, which dangled like long sprouts from the big, patterned tubers of their bodies, making contact with a clammy thigh. Horror, humiliation. Soft, wet, *ancient* skin against hers. At the end of the day Bunny would roll Dani's wet bathing suit into a rope around her ankles. Sun-sleepy. Tight skin. More chatter, Bunny mostly excluded from it now, echoey in the change room.

Dani got them both dressed. She strapped Lotte into her car seat with a drinkable yogurt and drove to Barton Street again.

A few women she recognized, drinking smoothies in tight shorts on the patio, doing much the same as they did at night, scrolling through their phones, enjoying one another's company, flushed and breathless from what must have been a strenuous class. Renata had mentioned the importance of physical exercise: *As healers, it can feel like you've relinquished your body to the cause, as I know it feels sometimes with Lotte too. But you haven't. Not really. After Lotte you realized that it's still your body, you'd just used it to grow your baby, feed your baby, raise your baby, populate the world, improve the world. Physical exercise, yoga especially,* breathing, *helps remind you that your body is still yours. You know what I mean? No one owns your body but you. And you're making it stronger. You're making it better. You're improving your focus, rewarding it with endorphins. It's just also your tool now. And you should take care of your tools.*

Lotte's babble began to develop its signature edge—tired or hungry or just ready to not be strapped into a chair anymore.

Dani parked, pulled Lotte from the seat, fastened her to her hip. She would walk to that café, finally get one of those goddamn affogatos. A chocolate milk for Lotte.

And that's when she spotted her.

Renata.

Her face broad and smiling, a pin through her forehead, stabbed into a spongy telephone pole, textured with stapled triangles of torn paper, lifted like feathers by the wind. The word *MISSING* in large black print above Renata's face.

Dani stared at it.

*Baby only sleeps when dead.*

Renata's face smiling at her from the missing person poster. *Baby only sleeps when dead.*

Dani blinked. She blinked again. Tried to make Renata's face disappear from the poster, how those words had disappeared from her search bar. *Baby only sleeps when dead*—blink—*when held.* Blink—*when held.* But it was still Renata. Still Renata. Still missing. The blinking hadn't worked. *Baby only sleeps when dead. Baby only sleeps when dead.* Anxiety's dark fiction creating a memory now, in which she'd been seconds from obeying the search bar, from really doing it, from smothering Lotte with a pillow just so she could get some goddamn sleep. Closer than she'd allowed herself to realize. Because it happens to women, some of them kill their babies, their brains are so fucked from the hormones and the lack of sleep and they see their babies, these little loaves of perfection, and they know that they can't do it, they're not good enough for this little loaf. This little loaf deserves better, but there's no option for that now, a little loaf put up for adoption won't have a better life. A little loaf separated from its mother is doomed. The only thing to do is destroy the little loaf, slice it into tiny pieces. And get some sleep. If the little loaf were dead, then it wouldn't matter if Clark got colon cancer. It wouldn't matter that she was only capable of menial, low-paid labor because she would have only herself to look after. She wouldn't need a village. She could just be all alone. Arms glued to her sides, slid into a test tube. Set in a rack and put away in a drawer, where she could wait to expire peacefully.

"Dani?"

She spun around. Lotte tightened around her waist, pressed her head against Dani's shoulder.

"Brandon! Oh my god!" And without thinking she hugged him—Lotte leaned back, keeping her distance. He smelled like fresh air. As though he'd hiked through the Swiss Alps to this very spot right behind her on Barton Street. "*What* is going on right now?" she said, looking again at the poster, an expression like someone had just cued the *Twilight Zone* theme.

He shook his head. "I can't believe it. We were supposed to hang out a couple nights ago. She just never showed up. I was actually kind of, you know"—he lowered his voice to a whisper—"*pissed.*" A client. Wanting what he'd paid for.

"Right, yeah." Dani was distractingly aware of her unwashed hair, the oily tracks of a hasty combing; her neglected eyebrows, shapeless and unruly; the barbs of black hairs shooting from her thighs like the defense mechanism of some homely cephalopod. Dani was covered, head to toe, in the durable foliage of a common houseplant. A common houseplant. And Brandon was rare and lovely. A sensitive soldier, as brutal as he was vulnerable. He needed careful pruning. Cold, clean water. Regular care. And Renata had been providing that for him. But maybe, Dani suddenly realized, her skin rippling with goose bumps, it'd gone too far one night. Maybe his last climax had triggered the murderous blow she'd been trying to heal out of his system.

She noticed now a stack of white papers pressed between his forearm and chest. "Are those . . ." she began.

He nodded, turned them around, and presented her once again with Renata's face.

"Oh. I assumed Margot had put these up." She recalled one of the procedurals she'd watched when Lotte was a newborn, about a killer who got off on the idea of aiding the investigation. Dani took a step back. Held Lotte tighter.

"No." Brandon shook his head, looked down, flapped the stack in front of him like a child being punished. "She actually . . . she told me to fuck off."

"She *did*?"

He tucked the papers back under his arm. "She said reacting this way, being so scared that someone had hurt her, was a product of my misogyny. Women can go missing without being murdered. Which, I don't know, maybe she's right."

"When is the last time you saw her?"

"With you, that night . . ." The way he trailed off, he was hoping, Dani could tell, that he hadn't embarrassed her by mentioning it.

"Oh," she said. "I was a mess that night, I'm sorry, I hope I didn't—"

"Oh god, no, you don't have to apologize, honestly. I've seen much worse. I've *been* much worse. I was hoping, though, that you weren't scared off by me. By what you might have heard. I wanted to see you again."

"You did?"

He nodded. "This is just, honestly it's really fu—" An apologetic frown at Lotte. "*Messing* me up. Are you—you're not taking clients yet, are you?"

Dani sipped a cold shot of air, a tremor rattled her core, the possibility of that freedom again, what she'd felt just after Lotte was born and everyone handled her body like a machine. Brandon was seeking to replace his old equipment as quickly as possible, her body, disconnected, serving its profound function. She glanced at Lotte.

"Oh, I'm sorry," he said. "That was gross of me. Who's this?" He smiled broadly at Lotte, who pulled her chin in sheepishly, smiled back, and released a big, happy yelp.

"This is"—she felt reluctant for some reason to share Lotte's real name—"Haley." Lotte waved. Brandon waved. "My daughter."

"She's adorable," he said. "Listen, sorry about that, I just, I'm desperate."

"Oh, thanks."

"Fuck, no, oh—" He covered his mouth. "Sorry, I mean, no, not like that, just, that this happened to Renata, something maybe violent, it's, it's really *messing* with my head, I can't . . . can I tell you something?"

Dani winced for some reason. "Sure."

"One of my, my, my intrusive thoughts, that's what they call it, is the way that, when a person is about to die, they say *please*. That's real, not just in the movies. People beg you, *Please, please, please, please, please*, because—" He bit his lips together, eyes glazing quickly; he caught a tear with the heel of his hand, just before it fell. Dani reached out and squeezed his wrist, transferring strength so he could continue. *Healing.* He sniffed loudly. "Because people, when they're about to die, they think that *manners* might work, you know what I mean? Because it's what their, their *moms* taught them, you know? Then, then they call for their mom, because *please* didn't work and, and she always said it would and, and . . ." He gave his head a brutal shake, and like the image from an Etch A Sketch, the sorrow was gone. "I just can't stop hearing Renata's voice." Calm now, steady. "Saying that word, *please please please please please*, and I just, I need someone. Some help. I—"

"I understand," said Dani. And she did understand. Here he was, *a creature with pain*, a person who needed healing. "I'm not sure what the protocol is here in terms of your, your *care*, but listen, I'll call you, all right? I promise I will. We'll get this sorted." *We'll get this sorted.* As though she worked at a call center and he'd phoned to report unusual activity on his credit card.

But the tone was right. With a hand over his chest, the slightest bow, he thanked her. Then pulled a business card from his back pocket and handed it to her.

"*Engineering consultant,*" she read from the card. "Margot told me that you're making a filter or something?"

"Something like that, yeah." He looked down, ground the ball of his foot into the concrete, embarrassed. "I really do appreciate it, Dani. There's just, I don't know, as soon as I met you, I just, I knew that you could help me. I felt it. Did you feel it?"

And she had to admit that she had, the sharp ricochet of a violin bow against tight strings, friction, heat, commanding clarity, her attention, tequila-battered focus. On Brandon. On his face. "Yes, I did," she said, and slipped the card into the pocket of her denim cutoffs, rubbed her legs together, the barbs. Disgusting. But not to Brandon, who could see the glow of her crucial feminine, an energy paralleled only by Renata's, or maybe, she thought guiltily, *surpassing* Renata's. Brandon was more attuned to these things because of what he'd experienced overseas, the things he'd had to do as a warrior, the pain he'd endured. *She performed for the primitive the task of womankind.*

*Please.*

*Please, please, please, please, please.*

Already sharing with her the source of his trauma. A death he was responsible for, Dani assumed. Or maybe he only *thinks* he's responsible. In the movies he wouldn't actually be responsible, not directly, but his masculine sense of duty, of accountability, a force as big and powerful as gravity, had pulled the responsibility deep into his core.

Dani's crucial feminine. Brandon's masculine force. Could these powerful essences bring about the hellish prophecy Lotte had tried to warn her about in utero, when she still had access to all the mysteries of the universe? How she'd thrashed inside her the night before their move to Metcalf. Dani had assumed it was panic, that the Princess of Trash should never return, but perhaps it was actually excitement. In Metcalf the Princess of Trash will collide with the Broken Soldier, and together they will fix the world!

She could see now why Renata had been obsessed with Brandon, how his healing would represent to her *proof*, once and for all, that her methods really *worked*. How his interest in another healer might have threatened her, caused her to push the new healer away . . .

"I knew you felt it too." He smiled. His watch lit up, and he checked it. "Oh, I've got to run," he said, and reached out to hug her again, and even though he might be a murderer, Dani didn't flinch. She hugged him back; Lotte put an arm around him too, patted his back. They both laughed. And Dani and Lotte watched him, the living curves of his calf muscles, like the anatomy poster hanging in The Temple. The shape of his back beneath his white button-down shirt, dappled in sweat, a print, where Dani had pressed her hand down against his back. Where Lotte had patted him. He turned a corner and Dani exhaled. Lotte wiggled to be put down. Dani had to sit, catch her breath. Renata missing. Renata *gone*.

# 23

BUNNY HADN'T HEARD anything about a missing woman. Neither had Wanda, who'd phoned while Dani and Lotte had been visiting. A warm, rainy afternoon, the three of them in the kitchen. Lotte sliding two small bee figurines along the linoleum floor's busy pattern; Dani standing at the sink, letting the tap run cold enough to fill Lotte's water bottle, flooding a crusty topography of stacked dishes. Cutlery, displaced by rising water, clanked against dishes, attracting a side glance from Bunny as she yakked with Wanda on the landline, phone clamped between her jaw and her shoulder, handling the extra long coil like a gymnast's ribbon as she paced the room. There were issues with a couple of Wanda's dogs, agitated by all the bathroom drama—*workers in and out of the house, and the* drilling, *my* god, *you can't even see straight.* One of them, Teddy, a ten-pound mop with leaky eyes and a discernible wheeze, had been staying with Bunny for a few days while things settled down over there.

"That wheeze is really something," Dani said after Bunny hung up the phone.

"They've all got it." Bunny shook her head. "Poor things. Wanda and her cigarillos." Teddy, who'd been sleeping on the couch, lifted his head at the mention of Wanda's name. Lotte was surprisingly uninterested in Teddy, and Dani was irrationally bothered by it. She brought Lotte over to Teddy, her voice tight as she explained to Lotte that the dog was sweet, a good boy, enjoyed nice, gentle pets. Bunny noticed that Dani was upset, and she came to Dani's side, put an arm on her shoulder, and rolled her into a hug, where Dani melted a little, and Lotte squeezed in too.

The mom friends hadn't heard about a missing woman either.

"How did you find out? Was it in the paper?" Anya asked.

Anya was interested but distracted. She'd ordered a salad and wore the regret on her face like a cream pie. She stabbed at her tall plate of yard waste, which dodged her fork playfully. Obnoxiously. Dani offered her some fries, which she accepted gratefully.

"I don't think so. Not that I saw." Dani rotated her plate so that Anya could access the aioli.

"I would have known if it were in the paper," said Ellen, who sometimes liked to play the part of the *informed* mother, keeping everyone up to date on the latest social media controversies, the dramas of her fellow momfluencers.

"So, how did you hear about it?" asked Anya.

"Oh." For some reason Dani hadn't been anticipating this question, though it was an obvious one. "Clark is doing a deal over there. I think he was going to see about buying her out, maybe? Something like that." She'd been waiting actually for Clark to mention it. Surely at some point he'd notice that the

woman he was potentially doing business with had gone missing. And wouldn't that be something you'd share with your wife?
Like updates on Eddie's colon cancer. Last she'd heard, he was
in hospice; then Clark never mentioned him again. A bad man.
Unsettlingly stoic. As he'd been when they were sleep-training
Lotte. As Lotte was in the presence of an adorable, fluffy little
dog, for fuck's sake. What the fuck was *wrong* with them.

In fairness, she and Clark hadn't been speaking about much of
anything lately, engaged in a quiet war over the espresso machine.
Neither of them would learn how to use it. To Clark, though he
wouldn't dare utter this out loud, the espresso machine fell firmly
within Dani's jurisdiction. The home. The kitchen, no less. Not
that he was that kind of husband, but the labor of life, of having a family, had to be divided *some*-how, didn't it? That was just
good management. Why should Clark go to work all day, put in
extra time at night, on weekends, only to *also* make the espresso
every morning?

And sure, thought Dani, maybe that *was* reasonable, but why
did they have to have *espresso* every morning? Why should Dani,
who'd been perfectly content with the old machine, grains and
all, have this completely unnecessary luxury tacked to her daily
responsibilities for no good reason? She would continue to make
coffee using the old machine. That coffee was part of her contract. Espresso was above and beyond.

Now in the mornings Clark conspicuously sucked the grounds
from his teeth, left his mostly full cup on the table. In the kitchen,
reflected in the chrome, he'd shake his head at the shame of it.
The *waste*.

"Really!" Ellen perked up. "A deal on *North* Barton? *That's*
interesting." Since the official launch of her @mymonkeys
account, Ellen had been acting like she was now in the position

to *do* something with information like this. Move some money around. *Invest.* Behind her back Anya had been referring to her as Warren Buffett.

Dani caught Anya's subtle eye roll, and she hid a smile behind her hand. Incredible how strong the bond was between two people who hate the same things, even stronger sometimes than between two people who love the same things, like co-parenting exes; if only they hated their children together, then maybe there could be more peace, or maybe they wouldn't even have gotten divorced at all. Something that Dani had thought about when she was especially certain that Clark was the worst person in the world, what a nightmare it would be to have to share Lotte that way. She simply wouldn't. She'd just kill him.

"Was she married?" asked Anya. "It's always the husband."

And Ellen nodded, knowingly, as though she knew a few women, friends of friends, who'd been murdered by their husbands. "It is, though," she said, still nodding. "It's always the husband."

"Oh, please, she couldn't have been married," said Dawn.

"Why not?" asked Dani.

"Honestly, am I the only one around here with any common sense? You can guess why not. Probably no one has contacted the police yet either," said Dawn. "It's a shame, of course, but that kind of thing happens all the time with, you know, *that* kind of business." Her eyes flashed up at Anya, deferentially, all due respect, hoping she wouldn't be punished for this comment, which might, had Anya been less antagonized by her salad, have been perceived as fanning the embers of their previous disagreement.

Dani recalled the conversation she'd had with Margot the day she'd discovered the poster. Home again, Lotte finally settled into her nap. She'd immediately called Margot—the number Brandon had put on the poster—who sounded exasperated when she answered the phone.

"Margot, sorry, is this a bad time? It's Dani."

"Oh, Dani, hi, no, just that fucking idiot Brandon put my phone number on these—but I guess that's where you got it from, isn't it," she said, her mouth moving away from the phone periodically as though she were carrying on another conversation at the same time. The distinct muffle of palm over speaker. A man's voice? Dani could tell that Margot was telling someone who it was on the phone.

"I did, I, I'm shocked, I—"

More mumbling. As though she were receiving instructions. She returned to the conversation with her script. "Sorry. Listen, don't worry. I mean, I don't know where she is at this exact moment, no, but she does this kind of thing a lot."

"She does?"

"Yeah."

"So you're not worried at all? Brandon said her phone is going right to voicemail—"

"Dani, you stay away from that fucking idiot." Someone spoke again in the background, Margot turned her head, palm roughed over microphone, then returned. "He's got a fucking hero complex. It's all bullshit. Everything is fine. I've got to go all right, I'll call you soon."

"But I—" Margot had hung up before Dani could finish. She'd looked at the dark screen on her phone and closed her eyes. *Baby only sleeps when dead.* Impotent. Useless. A woman she'd loved was gone. She should have been there, at The Temple, pounding the pavement the way they do on television, interviewing and re-interviewing every person in the area. Someone must have seen something. Someone had always seen *something*. A dark thought had crossed her mind. That she'd somehow caused this. That blackout night at The Temple. The hellish prophecy. In returning to Metcalf she'd actually *destroyed* humanity's last hope for peace.

At the table now with the Normal Women, Dawn still shaking her head at the sad realities of *that* kind of business, Dani was filled again with the excruciating helplessness she'd felt on the phone with Margot. She wanted to stand up and scream in Dawn's face: *Fuck you, Dawn, of course someone has contacted the police, you fucking asshole. ME! I'm going to contact the police, what do you think of that?* And why couldn't she? A concerned citizen. A *mother* in the community! A missing woman is no joke. A missing woman is *serious*, Dani would remind them all.

She thought again of the procedurals she'd watched endlessly when Lotte was a newborn and all she could do was sleep and eat and sleep and eat, so all Dani did was eat and watch the procedurals and chug prune juice and try to take shits and let water run over her incision in the shower and gently peel the Steri-Strips from her frantic-looking pubes, stretched painfully straight before finally letting go, the worst part of the whole surgery, honestly. And she counted Lotte's wet diapers and dirty diapers and mopped spit-up from every surface and stared into her eyes and chewed on her squishy appendages, and in the background two detectives in trench coats investigated murders and rapes and discussed rectal swabs and people of interest and pieced together a victim's last day.

Instead of standing up and screaming in Dawn's face, Dani excused herself. "Ah, shit," she announced, too loud. "I forgot." She fingered a few bills from her wallet and tossed them on the table, shaking her head. "I have an appointment." She hurriedly shoved her wallet back in her bag, slung it over her shoulder.

"What? What are you talking about?"

"I forgot I have an appointment today."

"On a Saturday?"

"Yeah, it's, the—"

"Oh, is it the physio?" asked Anya. "Are they going to look at your diastasis recti?"

For a moment Dani had no idea what Anya was talking about. Anya's eyes flicked down to Dani's stomach. "Oh, yes! The ab separation, yes, yes." When Dani had complained of lower back pain, weakness in her core, Anya had given her the name of what ailed her, *diastasis recti*, when the rectus abdominis muscles separate during pregnancy and don't fuse back together again, as well as the name of a physical therapist. Anya always had things like that—the names of good doctors, the exact ratios for making cleaning products out of things you find in your cupboard. Anya had even brought her to her first prenatal yoga class, all of the women lying on the floor, moving in unison, piles of leaves agitated by the yoga instructor's whispered commands.

"Good, good," said Anya. "And tell her you know me, all right? You never know."

Dani had never been comfortable with the kind of name-dropping Anya did, but also she admired the kind of name-dropping Anya did. The things that Normal Women did to save bits of money here and there, things they had to tune into—flyers and coupons and sales. Things they had to do—tip reasonably, for example, separate checks, something that even when she used to waitress Dani never begrudged—in order to make up for earning less money, for falling behind in financial literacy, for having to bankroll more years on earth. The other waitresses would roll their eyes when a group of women walked in, cross their fingers that they wouldn't sit in their section, but Dani had preferred it, grateful for whatever they could spare.

Dani finished her water, dropped her crumpled napkin onto her plate, and Ellen and Dawn chimed in with their own tales of postpartum ab separation, sharing exercises, bragging about the severity. Dawn's ab separation had been three fingers wide, and Ellen's? *Four.* As Dani walked away, all of them, at the mention of these crucial interior muscles, were Kegelling unconsciously, frantically, quietly, like a colony of pulsing coral.

# 24

DANI SAT ON HOLD with the Metcalf Police Department until the endlessly repeating digitized version of "I Will Always Love You" became, to Dani's ear, its own language. Dani had actually been singing out loud when a detective from the missing persons unit finally answered.

"Detective Pete Gracy, how can I help you?"

"Oh, hi, hello," Dani warbled, voice almost too limber now for regular speech. "My friend has gone missing, or at least, I haven't been able to get ahold of her for days. I want to file a report, I think."

"All right. Name please."

"My name or—"

"We'll get to you. Name of the missing person."

"Renata Dean."

"When and where did you last see the missing person?"

"Saturday. So about a week. I texted with her the next day as well."

"What did you do on Saturday?"

"We were at, we went to a bar."

"Just the two of you?"

"No, her sister was with us as well."

"And why wouldn't her sister be filing this report?"

"I, well, she's not worried, but I—"

"Does the missing person have any mental health problems, developmental delays, or any other medical reason that you should be concerned about her safety or well-being?"

"No."

"Was she acting erratically when you last saw her? Confused? Agitated?"

"No, she—"

"And is there anything about her lifestyle that causes you concern about her safety or well-being? Substance abuse problems, for example?"

"Her lifestyle?"

"Does she go out a lot? Party? Make a lot of enemies? What's her line of work? That kind of thing."

"Her line of work is . . . she's a business owner."

"What type of business?"

"A yoga studio."

"What's the name of the yoga studio?"

"The Temple."

Detective Pete Gracy paused and Dani knew he recognized the name. "Right." Dani heard papers shuffling, the click of a pen. "Listen, what you're telling me is that the missing person is an adult woman who's not endangered in any way." He needed, desperately, to clear his throat. Dani's eyes fluttered in disgust. She cleared her own throat, a hint, she hoped, triggering his subconscious to follow suit. "And that her own sister isn't concerned about her whereabouts. I appreciate that you're worried about your friend, but at this point, in the absence of any evidence that a crime has been committed, there's not much we can do."

"So, you need evidence of a crime," said Dani, jotting down the words *evidence of a crime* into a small blue notebook dug from a box of first-year-university-era rubble she'd lugged over several moves. She tucked a juice-stiff hank of hair behind her ear and glanced up at Lotte, who was still chewing happily on a mesh bag of frozen mango. A goatee of that sticky juice just met the collar of her shirt. Dani moved to wipe it with a rag. Lotte squirmed from her reach.

"That's right," said the detective. "Kind of important."

"Evidence of a crime is like—like a body?"

"That would certainly qualify."

"What else?"

Detective Gracy finally, mercifully, cleared his throat. She heard him pause to sip what she assumed was an acrid cup of cold black coffee but could actually be anything. Vitamin water. Kombucha tea. One of Dawn's untested liquid therapies. An *affogato*. "What did you say your name was?" he said.

Dani hesitated for no good reason, really, being of a demographic historically well protected by the police. "I didn't, I—"

"It doesn't matter. Listen, I'm sorry about your friend. But people have the right to go missing, do you know what that means?"

"Not really."

"A person has the right to disappear. And it might hurt your feelings and it might be difficult for you to process, but it's not up to me, or us, or anyone, to drag them out of hiding just because we want to, you understand?"

"Do you know Renata?"

"No."

"Never heard of The Temple?"

"We'll let you know if we hear anything."

"But you don't even know my name—"

The slam of the receiver, something she hadn't heard in a long time, everyone with cell phones having to gently thumb the end button even when enraged. And the slam of this artifact, like the snap of a hypnotist's fingers, made her certain she was on to something. Her heart quickened. She bit her lip. *Excited* all of a sudden. The *intuition* of her crucial feminine *awakened*.

She looked at her notebook, the only thing she'd scribbled from the conversation: *evidence of a crime.* "Well, duh," she said out loud, and propped her forehead onto her fingers. Lotte blew a raspberry. Droplets of cold mango juice pierced Dani's arms. She looked up. "Your mother is an idiot," she said, and smiled, nodding. "Yes, she is! Yes, she is!" Tickling Lotte's ribs so she squirmed and screamed and squealed and rubbed her mango face all over the carpet.

Dani opened her laptop and typed *Detective Pete Gracy + Metcalf* into the search engine, for no other reason than to see what he looked like, how he dressed, and thereby determine what he might actually have been drinking during their call. The page populated with a couple of articles in which the detective, then a constable, provided statements on basically insignificant regional matters. One paraphrased quote about a dangerous intersection: *Gracy said police received a 9-1-1 call around 8:41 p.m., their sixth regarding the intersection since the beginning of the month.* Another statement about road closures during the Christmas parade, this time a direct quote: *"I always say, get your shopping done early, because the week before Christmas you'll have to contend not just with other procrastinators, but the parade as well."* Dani, a chronic procrastinator, sneered. *You probably don't even do the Christmas shopping,* she thought to herself. *Your wife does it all. Just like she does everything else.* She found him on social media. Based on his profile picture, she would put him in his early forties. His wife, a pretty woman with light hair and a cowl neck for every occasion, reminded her of the *mom friends.* In fact, she could have shown up to one of their lunches without Dani even noticing, some sort of mythical mom friend changeling, a supernatural interloper, swooping in to consume the feast of confusion and chaos and terror when the check came divided by five instead of four.

Detective Pete Gracy had two preteen daughters who both, thankfully, took after their mother, lean and small, in startling opposition to his bulk, firm but fatty, like something a person could request sliced from a deli. And there was a baby, held high by its mother, little more than a patch of squalling red flesh peeking from a long, blindingly white baptismal shroud. All of them smiling. So proud they were to have protected this baby from purgatory. Dani thought of Haley, of course. Poor, wandering Haley. How that single breath on earth had damned her.

Dani secretly hoped the children weren't his. That his wife had been cheating on him with some floppy-haired tennis instructor, pinched off at every end with a sweatband. She wanted Detective Pete Gracy to find out only when his doctor ordered a few routine tests that revealed somehow that he was, in fact, sterile.

Because Detective Pete Gracy definitely hadn't been drinking coffee or kombucha tea. He'd been drinking some lurid bullet of liquid energy, the kind that neutralizes sperm, and sponsors first-person-shooter tournaments, and introduces murmurs to ambitious young hearts like Clark's. His buzzed blond hair sparkled boyishly in his picture. A short-sleeved, button-up shirt, pastel plaid. A springtime type of picnic-blanket plaid. Echoing the colors in his wife's dress. She would have picked it all out, of course, photos like this, Dani now knew from the mom friends, serving as a sort of achievement badge for women like her. Maybe even a momfluencer herself. Dani wrote her name in the note-book: *Jacqueline Gracy.* One of the mom friends might know her. She clicked on her name. Her profile photo was an aerial shot of her face, neck torqued to force angles from postpartum fleshiness. It made Dani think of her old neighbor's bunny hatch, how all the bunnies had caught what her father called *wry neck,* what was medically referred to as *torticollis,* a parasitic infection that eroded the creatures' central nervous systems, caused their necks to twist till their heads were upside down. The neighbor wouldn't treat or euthanize them, and her father grumbled about it, increasingly agitated, for weeks: *What is she waiting for? Their necks to snap clean off?*

When she heard the neighbor scream one Sunday morning, the news traveling through town that someone had poisoned her babies, Dani knew it was her father who'd done it, rat poison in their pellets maybe or something more sophisticated. No one would have ever suspected the great Garbage King of having carried out this mass bunnycide, and when DJ listened to the neighbor cry, his face bloated with concern, his mouth dripping with thoughtful sympathies, Dani felt as proud of him as she was terrified.

She screenshotted Jacqueline Gracy's profile picture and texted it to Anya: *Do we know her?*

Back to the search engine results. Mostly annual reports through the past decade. Detective Pete Gracy seemed to regularly receive Awards of Merit along with about three hundred other Metcalf police officers, which, Dani confirmed with another search, was over half the sworn force. So not a terribly impressive distinction. In the most recent annual report, however, Detective Pete Gracy received an Award of Excellence, shared with just a few other officers, whose names Dani jotted down in her book. Constable Katie Patience, who had an Instagram account dedicated to workplace wellness—mindfulness routines, breathing exercises, yoga poses—a worthy pursuit if she didn't also look like a person who would pull her gun out on a rude hostess. Detective Brad Phillips, whose results looked almost identical to Pete Gracy's, though with fewer Awards of Merit and a couple placements in local marathons. He'd also made several comments on the corporate page of a protein powder product, inquiring vaguely about certain side effects mentioned by a few of his *customers*, which is the word people in pyramid schemes use for *family*. Finally there was Constable Bogden Borza, whose unusual name and relatively small digital footprint surfaced an extremely interesting document in which all three of the other officers had been named as coauthors: *The Nicolas Project: An Action Plan for Eliminating Sex Trafficking in Metcalf and Revitalizing the Barton Strip*.

Though it was a public document, it was inaccessible online. According to the City of Metcalf site, Dani would have to make a formal Freedom of Information request to the appropriate division in order to see it in full. For now she could only see the title page, which included a Project Overview:

> *For the past three years the Metcalf Police Department has convened with the country's foremost experts, commissioning top-tier research in order to build a comprehensive and powerful plan to combat human trafficking*

*in Metcalf. Among many urgent findings, this research has revealed unequivocally that the demand for sexual exploitation in this city far outpaces the supply, that is, the number of mentally sound and willing participants in the sex industry. This dangerous imbalance calls for the need to substantially increase the scope and scale of interventions, as well as seek novel approaches to this disturbing problem. The Nicolas Project is just such an approach. The following report outlines a solid game plan for revitalizing the Barton Street Strip. Piggybacking onto the area's growing economic significance (due in large part to its proximity to the Silver Waste Management Campus), we will work with local businesses and developers to turn the area into a thriving hub, and alongside social workers and border patrol, perform the outreach and long-term support necessary to restore these exploited workers to their family, friends, and, most importantly, themselves.*

And a quote:

> *It is a happy day indeed when our moral imperatives support our economic growth.*
> —FORMER MAYOR FREDDY FRANCIS

Mayor Freddy Francis. *Former* Mayor Freddy Francis. He'd been a friend of Dani's father. Personal recipient of many of his gifts. Another man who knew the value of making garbage disappear. Or what he believed to be garbage. All the things they used to just incinerate when her father ran the SWMC that now they rinsed and recycled or turned into fuel, fertilizer, energy, *tote bags.*

One of the procedurals she watched when Lotte was just fresh was based on the real case of the Grim Sleeper—a man who stalked women in South Central for twenty-two years before the LAPD informed the community there was a threat. The LAPD's internal documents revealed that they used an acronym for the types of women the Grim Sleeper targeted—drug addicts, sex workers, women of color who were neither—*NHI*: no humans involved.

How would Renata be categorized in official documentation— a human, surely, by their standards of property ownership, whiteness. But also, she was something else. Beyond human. Transformed by her creatures, but into *what?*

Dani jumped when her phone lit up. A reply from Anya.

Anya: *omg you don't remember Jacqueline? Her last name used to be Rivard. In grade school she told everyone she tried to kill herself by eating a pot of English ivy? She's super religious now. I just saw her dressed in a sheet, protesting Dawn's horny yoga studio. But more importantly . . . you missed some drama when you left brunch.*

Dani: *Oh no, what happened?*

Anya: *Well, Warren Buffett's application to Rewardfluencer was denied.*

Dani: *Oh, that's shitty.*

Anya: *Even shittier though, Dawn applied too. And she got accepted. Check out the world's first wifefluencer.*

Dani clicked the link that followed, @mightygoodman.

A photo of Dawn's husband, Charlie, on the floor with baby Vic, now a burly four-month-old, wielding a big foam puzzle piece, part of a floor mat of stylish geometric shapes. A wooden train set toppled between them.

*Would you believe I didn't trust him with our*
*baby? Would you believe I didn't trust his judgment, his*
*ability to be a parent, his ability to keep our baby safe?*
*And can you imagine how my mistrust undermined*
*his own sense of self-worth? What that must have*
*been like to hold your baby and feel as though none of*
*your instincts were right? Wifeys it's important to be*
*aware of all the ways in which you—yes YOU—are*
*contributing to your husband's incompetence at home.*
*It's a vicious cycle, but you can end it.*

There were photos of Charlie about twenty pounds heavier, links to dubious research linking BMI to life expectancy.

Dawn and Charlie both in chunky cardigans: Charlie's making him look bigger, bulkier in a good way; Dawn's making her look small, like a sick bird he was nursing back to health. She pressed a swath of its collar against her cheek. Smiling. Matching sunglasses. Promo codes. Bright blue sky and shredded clouds behind them.

There were photos of just Dawn, splashed with activewear, bladelike bob threatening her bare shoulders. A hero's triangular silhouette, waxing poetic in the caption and comments about a woman's obligation, not just to her own body, but to the bodies of those she loves as well.

*For better or for worse, the health of your family falls*
*on your shoulders—you are stocking the cupboards, you*
*are modeling healthy habits. You are the first architect*
*of your children's bodies. You are the gatherer who*
*must remind her hunter husband that he's no longer in*
*danger of being slaughtered by a saber-toothed tiger, so*

*there's no need to live and eat as though it's his last day on earth.*

Dani opened her texts with Anya.

Dani: *I guess I didn't realize that . . . Dawn is actually insane?*

Anya: *I told you so!!*

# 25

DANI FOUND CLARK carving corpuscular wedges from half a grapefruit at the dining room table, holding steady the bowl and dodging pink acid. "Where's the espresso machine?" she asked.

"I took it back," he said. "It was too much work."

Dani nodded, restrained, allowing nothing that could be perceived as gloating infiltrate her expression. The war was over. She'd won. She would be very mature about it. There was no reason not to be. Because she'd been absolutely right: They didn't need an espresso machine, and if Clark wanted one, it should be his responsibility to learn about it. She had to put her foot down sometime, this contract of hers; it couldn't be revised forever.

"Were you able to get a refund?"

"Huh?" Elbow up, his wrist corkscrewing into the rind. "This is a lot of work," he complained. "Like, it's a lot of work for the amount of energy you actually get, you know? It's a wonder grapefruits have made it this far. The numbers, calorically speaking, don't add up."

"Calorically speaking."

"Yeah, it's not worth it." He gave up on the disemboweled rind, turned to his toast instead.

*It's always the husband.*

"A *refund*. Were you able to get a refund? Or store credit. If you got store credit, I was thinking we could just buy a new drip coffee machine." A compromise. The epitome of maturity. Even though she'd defeated him, they were still a team, after all.

"Oh, that's a good idea. Sure, let's do that."

"Where did you get it? Lotte and I can go this afternoon."

"Oh, just get one wherever, I actually sold ours to a colleague."

"Oh. Then why did you say you returned it?"

Clark shrugged. "I don't know, seemed like too much to explain. Has she tried almond butter yet?" He held his toast out to Lotte.

*It's always the husband.*

"Yeah." She stared at him. "Loves it."

"Such a good little eater." He booped her nose.

She wasn't actually. Not according to the mom forums. But this morning Dani was finding it difficult to speak to Clark. About anything. Grapefruits, almond butter. A woman he'd been looking to do a deal with had gone missing, and he still hadn't mentioned a word. A missing woman in their city, a missing woman who worked ten minutes from their house, vanished. And here he was talking about how taxing it is to eat a grapefruit. Reminding her that she didn't really need to know the details about the purchasing and reselling of expensive home appliances.

*It's always the husband.*

"You okay?" he asked.

She nodded again, cleared her throat. "Yes, just tired. I didn't sleep well last night."

"You want the rest of this grapefruit?"

"I don't think I can spare the energy."

He chuckled. Stood up and wiped his hands on Lotte's cloth, then tossed it back on the table instead of using it to wipe his spot, which was sticky with grapefruit juice, scattered in toast crumbs.

"Well, I'm off," he said, a nearly full cup of grainy coffee abandoned on the table. "I'll be a bit late tonight."

"That's fine," she said.

When he finally left, she realized she'd been holding her breath. *It's always the husband.*


Dani and Lotte lay on the floor in the living room. Lotte, recently wiped down from breakfast, crawled over and laid her cool, cloth-clammy hands on Dani's bare stomach. Dani yelped, shocked by the cold, pulsated Lotte's hands in hers to warm them. Lotte yanked her hands out and touched Dani again, giggling as Dani mimed excruciating pain, screaming, slithering away. Lotte kept after her, crawled farther up Dani's body, opened her nubby little mouth and latched to Dani's face, first her cheek, then her chin, which she wrapped her whole mouth around and released a long, low moan, delighted by the succession of quick silences produced when Dani bounced her jaw.

Then they lay on the floor in the kitchen, where Lotte crawled over and yanked a flouncing tail of hair from Dani's head. Dani grabbed her scalp. "Lotte!" she shrieked, and Lotte laughed. So they both laughed. "Bad baby." Dani pinched her nose.

Then they lay on the floor of the dining room, where Lotte somehow managed to scratch the inside of Dani's mouth. Her gums, just above her canines.

Then they lay on Lotte's bedroom floor, where Lotte rested her head on Dani's neck, listening, smiling, at the tap of Dani's pulse against her ear. She knew this sound. The first sound she'd ever heard. Before she even knew what a sound was. Dani pulled out her phone, looked up the word *sound*: *A vibration that propagates as an acoustic wave; in human physiology and psychology, sound is the reception of such waves and their perception by the brain.* Lotte hadn't realized that something else had to exist to produce the waves, hadn't realized that Dani's beating heart wasn't simply part of the texture of the environment. The texture of her own body. As Haley had been to Dani. Part of her body. And then Dani began to breathe the way that Renata had shown her in her motel room—her haven—deep through the nose, hot, heavy spill from the mouth, over and over again, picturing her steady, sturdy heart up against a typhoon of blood, processing, processing, beating faster, faster, just like Renata's had; Dani was doing it, just like Renata—*this is how you can control your whole body, your mind, your reign starts with the lungs*—and Lotte squealed, grinning, drool leaking from the side of her mouth, warm, then cool down Dani's neck, and Dani felt dizzy; she laughed, slowing down, and Lotte laughed and slapped her chest to indicate that she wanted Dani to do it again.

But Dani had laundry to fold. And Lotte had wadded-up socks to shove in her mouth, a massive dump to take, a plastic horse to slam against the floor repeatedly.

Dani stood for a moment beneath a fresh sheet like a ghost, inhaling dryer-warm detergent, wondering about the actual possibility of a massive conspiracy, perpetrated by the city of Metcalf, to take down a woman whose establishment, though barely profitable and murky in its legitimacy, was preventing the economic boom the city had so desperately needed. And maybe not even because it was sort of a brothel, but because it was sort of a church—both blights on the bottom line.

It couldn't be true, could it? Conspiracies weren't uncovered this easily. By a nobody like Dani, conducting a very basic internet search. Or maybe that was the exact kind of *logical fallacy* that helped to conceal them. *Faulty reasoning.* Terms from her useless philosophy degree.

And besides, The Temple was hardly preventing Barton Street from booming. It was by far the most popular patio on the street. But of course the facts didn't matter when it came to policing a *social evil.* Or even an *actual* evil, like sex trafficking, which the Nicolas Project claimed was rampant on Barton Street. A crime so notoriously difficult to track and prove, it struck Dani as a heinous veil beneath which, obscured from scrutiny, the Nicolas Project could keep money and power out of the hands of women—the sole proprietors of the most coveted resource in the world. *Separate the workers from the means of production.* Another nugget of wisdom from her degree, the ingenious way in which the law could separate a woman from her own body.

A massive conspiracy.

Or just Clark.

A warrior.

Taking out an obstacle. A woman. Who couldn't be moved by money. Devoted only to her purpose. Clark, equally devoted to his own nefarious cause. A bad man. A very bad man.

A creature filled with pain.

Dani bit her index finger, slivered her eyes, then pulled the sheet off of herself in a crackling whoosh of static, her hair on end. "Hey, Lotte," she said. Lotte looked up, a sock hanging from her mouth. "Look at my hair." Lotte, so full of silent under-standing, took in the rays sprouting from Dani's scalp, then said, "Ooooh," and returned to her chewing.

Did Brandon know about the Nicolas Project?

Did *Margot* know?

Dani brought the corners of the sheet together again and again, ironed the edges with bladed hand. "Gorgeous," she whispered. Lotte clapped her hands. Too thrilled by the sight of this perfectly folded sheet. Dani placed it in the laundry basket. She beat the next sheet against the air, sent a few aggressively crayoned papers, wax-sodden, sailing across the floor. She imagined telling Margot about the Nicolas Project, watching her breasts rise to attention, nipples glowing red like an alarm in a submarine. *Finally* some concern. Maybe not *evidence of a crime*, exactly, but concern. And together she and Margot could *investigate*. They would *find* evidence of a crime. Figure out what happened to Renata.

They *had* to.

Renata was trying to change the world. Make it better. Her methods were unorthodox. Frightening, even. With the potential to shift a certain amount of power and economic freedom into the hands of women. And wasn't that exactly the kind of thing that people were murdered for?

And would figuring this out, publicly whistle-blowing the whole Metcalf police force, the whole *government*, be enough to save Lotte from the same miserable fate as Dani? *Look at my mother. The Princess of Trash. Defender of what's right. Destroyer of what's not. Smart, you see? Special. Just like she's always known. That's my mother, right there. That's my mother.*

# 26

THE SIDEWALKS OF BARTON STREET were too narrow to be described as stroller-friendly, cluttered with chained bikes, bins of used books and records, racks of vintage sweaters, patio chairs outside the café, and the gelato spot. But Dani, and some of the other mothers she spotted, knew how to navigate these things. No place was *really* stroller-friendly. *Stroller-tolerant* was probably the better term for it. Lotte faced outward, kicking her legs, gripping a little tray with a cupholder and a section for snacks, which Dani had filled with animal crackers.

Dani wore a sage-green sundress, slippery against her freshly shaved thighs. She wouldn't come prickly to Barton Street again, not since she ran into Brandon with his posters, which she noticed now had all been torn down, replaced by a black-and-white photo of a missing cat, the word *ORANGE* in bold beneath it. *Friendly. Answers to Bubba.*

Dani approached The Temple. For the first time the patio was completely empty. Massive. Its decay obvious now, in the absence of Renata's magic. As though her enchantment on the property had been broken by her disappearance. And this transformation, The Temple's palpable return to decrepitude, felt so much like *evidence of a crime* that Dani had to bite her lips to keep from sobbing, absolutely certain, for the first time, that Renata was dead.

She cleared her throat. Shook her head. No. They were going to find her. Margot and Dani were going to find her. Dani hoisted the stroller over The Temple's front step, reached across the length of the stroller to turn the door handle, pushed it open. It was too bright outside, too dark inside, so she couldn't quite tell who'd rushed from within The Temple to help her out, heart leaping hopefully for a split second that it might be Renata.

"Oh, thanks," she said squinting, flustered, "thank you." She heaved Lotte in, eyes still adjusting. The person closed the door behind them.

"Did you call?" It was Margot. "I didn't get a call." Dani turned around.

"Oh, hi, no, I didn't call, sorry."

Margot wore a loose white T-shirt tucked into black jeans, perforated leather oxfords. Her hair was up in a ponytail and it bounced with disarming playfulness.

"Oh my god, is this Lotte?" Margot squatted down and smiled. Lotte, who'd never been shy, began to talk, mostly gibberish, but lately Dani had been able to discern a few words: *Mama! Uppy!*

"This is Lotte." Dani smiled, a reflex, sparked by pride. "Is this—are you closed today?"

"Just this morning. Erin canceled her yin class and I have a meeting anyway."

Dani recognized what she'd seen in pictures as their yoga studio, nighttime's chairs and tables squirreled away. The cubbies along the back wall more visible now, populated with books and succulents potted in antique teacups. A few left bare for patrons to store bags and sneakers. A big, sunny Rothko reproduction. A Victorian portrait of a troll doll. Snake plants. Yoga mats packed into wicker baskets. A pyramid of purple foam blocks. And behind the long bar, a brand-new espresso machine, the box open, packaging disheveled across the counter. Styrofoam pebbles. Dani's chest tightened. No. Not possible. Theirs had been different, shinier, bigger, right? Hadn't theirs been huge? Or had it just seemed huge, devouring half the counter space in their cozy Corkton kitchen.

Margot's face lit up at Lotte. "Do you want out?" she exclaimed, the fiendish tone of an amusement park employee. Lotte smiled, clapping. Margot looked up at Dani. "May I?" she asked, then deftly lifted the snack tray, unlocked the stroller harness, and propped Lotte on her hip. "Let's go to the office," she said. "Renata kept a few crayons back there."

*Kept.*

Dani fought an urge to snatch Lotte back and run. But to where? To who? Clark was involved, possibly. And the police didn't care. She followed Margot and Lotte with the empty stroller, which she left in the hall just outside the office door. She heaved Lotte's diaper bag from the bottom and watched as Margot shook out a blanket that had been folded neatly over the arm of a long black couch. The couch Dani had sat on that night, drunk out of her mind.

Margot laid out the blanket, set Lotte on top of it with a brick of printer paper and a scrubby bucket of broken crayons.

"She's adorable, Dani. What a sweetheart." Margot went around behind the desk, interlocked her fingers, and leaned forward so she could still see Lotte.

"Thanks, yeah, she's definitely not shy," said Dani, and sat on the couch. For a moment they both watched Lotte in contented silence, like a pair of stone sentries. Soothing to them both, to watch what flowed across the paper from the arm of this pudgy, perfect thing.

"Have you heard from her?" asked Dani.

Margot sighed, losing something to the animated exhale. Patience. Irritated now. "Not yet."

"Me neither," said Dani.

"Dani." Margot frowned kindly. "I promise you she's *fine*." *Kept.*

"All right." She glanced at the door. *I sold it to a colleague.* A coincidence. Not the same one. Espresso machines were everywhere now. Just as blenders and bread machines and pressure cookers had once been. It made sense to have an espresso machine in a yoga studio. In a bar. At The Temple, especially. Espresso martinis. Passive sociopaths *loved* an espresso martini. And *passive sociopaths are our bread and butter!* Dani shook away whatever was taking shape in her mind. Stuck to the facts. "I think I might have some information. I don't know. Maybe it's nothing." Dani rubbed her palms against her bare knees. She regretted wearing this sundress now. It'd been too breezy outside, she'd been preoccupied with keeping it in place, and now she was sitting on this couch, preoccupied again with the idea of the bottom flaps of her ass cheeks somehow gobbling up germs. "I called the police and spoke with a detective."

Margot's eyes widened; she brought her hands to either side of her head. "Da-*ni*," she moaned. "Come on. You didn't do that, did you?"

"I—I did, Margot, I don't understand how you're not *worried* about her."

"Because I *know* her, Dani, all right? We had a little fight, she's cooling off, the end. This is what she does, what she's always done. You and fucking Brandon, I swear to god, you're killing me, with his fucking *flyers*." She nudged something with her foot, a small can with a stack of flyers curved inside. "You didn't have anything to do with that, did you?"

"No, no." Dani shook her head. "Nothing."

Margot pulled a small, sensitive smile into one of her cheeks. "Listen, she'll be back. And she'll be full of apologies. And the next time she takes off, it won't be quite so traumatic, all right? This is how it works."

"What did you two fight about?"

Margot shifted, took a deep breath, and held it for a moment. "Nothing," she exhaled.

"Nothing?"

And Margot's expression chilled, the secret frozen inside. "Nothing," she repeated, with alarming finality.

Dani recoiled, struck almost physically by the shift in Margot's tone. "I'm sorry," she said, releasing damp fistfuls of her dress, smoothing it over her thighs.

"No, don't be sorry," said Margot. Had Dani imagined that shift in her tone? "It's really just a lot to explain. You know how it is with sisters." She said it absently, a thing that everyone understood whether they had a sister or not. But hadn't Renata told her about Haley that night? Hadn't she told everyone? "Anyway, that doesn't matter," she continued. "Go on. Tell me what the cops said."

*You tell me what you fought about.* "I know I should have asked you first. I just, I thought it couldn't hurt to let them know. What's the harm in just letting them *know*? I mean, the reality is, no one has *heard* from her. And that's *strange*, isn't it? Not to you, but to anyone who"—Dani gulped, pained to admit—"who *doesn't* know her, it's alarming."

"I understand that," said Margot, her voice excessively calm, making Dani feel once again feral, the way the Normal Women sometimes made her feel. Silly. Stupid. Unaccustomed to how the world really works. "I honestly do understand, Dani. She's special to you, you haven't heard from her. It makes sense. Now, what did the cops say?"

"Well, nothing really, just that a person has the right to go missing if they want to, and unless we have any reason to suspect she might be in trouble, there's not much we can do."

Margot nodded sympathetically, but not without an *I told you so* frown.

"But then I looked him up—Detective Pete Gracy."

Margot put both hands down on the table, shifted in her seat. "Yeah," she said.

"And I learned that he and a few other detectives have a sort of *task* force in place to 'clean up' Barton Street."

"Clean it up?"

"Get rid of sex workers."

Margot raised an eyebrow, tilted her head. "So you think that Renata was, what, murdered by the police?"

"I didn't say murdered."

"Oh, okay, so, what, they sent her to Disney World?"

"All right, so none of that interests you then."

"I mean, as far as it having anything to do with Renata acting the way she always does when we get into an argument, it seems like a reach."

"There's money in this town now, Margot. Real money. People get killed over real money, or hurt anyway. There's this doctor in Brazil, he—"

Dani was cut off by a sound from the main room, the front door opening. Dani spun to look, startled. "Ah, fuck, oh, sorry."

Margot winced at Lotte, who was absorbed still by the crayons. "That's my—I've got my meeting—would you excuse me a moment?" Margot got up from the chair. Dani heard her squeeze past the stroller, blocking the hallway.

"Oh! Sorry!" Dani squeaked. Pathetic. The walking, talking embodiment of her flappy, germy butt cheeks beneath her embarrassingly short dress.

Margot mumbled something back at her, then more mumbling, farther away, in the front room. Men's voices, Margot's voice. Dani couldn't make anything out. She ran her hand along the black couch, the coarse, sturdy fabric delivering a memory of her night here, Renata squatting in front of her, dissolving Dani's performative helplessness. Dani pulled a canvas pillow onto her lap. Waited. Then stood up, which Lotte clocked but ignored, too absorbed still by her coloring. Dani hoped she wouldn't put up a fuss when it was time to leave. The walls of the office were light brown, detailed white paneling halfway up. Two gray filing cabinets. A few framed photographs on the wall. One large photograph of a pink roadside motel. Another of Renata and Margot hugging tight, cheeks together, oversized smiles, in front of a Big Boy restaurant, somewhere sunny. The desk was tidy. A laptop. A phone charger. A chipped enamel mug filled with bobby pins, earring backs, broken clasps and chains—hardware a clever woman might smelt and sell after the apocalypse. The garbage can key chain Dani had bought for Renata from the community college bookstore, it was in there too, half-buried. Dani hooked her finger around its shiny ring, the tinkle of light metals resettling. She pressed it between her palms. Closed her eyes. *Please be okay. Please be okay. Please be okay.* As she set it back in the mug she noticed the name of Clark's company written across a pale yellow file folder, *Urban Visions*, wide, tidy font and simple logo. Her heart began to pound. She bit her lip. Glanced at Lotte. At the door. Then pulled the folder over. Opened it up. Clark's handwriting hit her with unexpected force. A telephone number. Dani hurried to the couch to dig her phone from the diaper bag. Margot's voice down the hall: "I've just got to wrap up . . ." Dani fumbled her password, snapped several blurry pictures of the number, then closed the folder, slid it back where she found it, laid a hand over her chest, heart hammering into every tender pulse point in her body. More mumbling from the front room, Margot's voice louder, her footsteps closer, coming down the hall. Her head in the doorway.

"Hi, I guess my meeting is starting a bit early." She stepped closer to Dani. "I'm really sorry if I'm—if I seem insensitive." She reached out, asking with her body if Dani would be open to a hug. Dani stepped into it, and as Margot held her, she said, "I know you're worried. I'll have her call you, all right? She'll be back in a few days, I'm sure of it."

"Thanks, Margot." Dani stepped out of the hug, smiled.

Lotte relinquished the nub of a blue crayon to Margot with an ease she certainly wouldn't have shown Dani. Just disarmed by this stranger, Dani assured herself. Margot lifted the picture that Lotte had been working on. "Beautiful," she said, then tore a square of tape from a ceramic dispenser on the desk and stuck it to the wall. Lotte smiled and pointed. Dani lifted her up, exited the office, and as she tucked Lotte back into her stroller, Margot hurried past them, led the way down the hall, reefed open the front door quickly so the bright light it let in nearly obscured the two men in suits admiring the espresso machine behind the bar. But not quite. Not quite.

Dani could tell, in that split second of visibility, that one of the men was Detective Pete Gracy, sipping an affogato, a glint of cream lodged in the bow of his boyish lip.

## 27

DETECTIVE PETE GRACY, appointed leader of a government initiative to cleanse Barton Street of sex workers, to facilitate the economic boom the city was otherwise primed for, was having a meeting with Margot at The Temple. A meeting. And Margot had opened the door so quickly, on purpose. Blasting away their identities with a blinding light, but she hadn't been fast enough. Dani had seen him. Had even seen the fucking ice cream on his stupid fucking face.

And what was almost *more* unbelievable was that Dani, in the wake of what felt now like absolutely undeniable evidence of a government conspiracy, one in which Margot and possibly even *Clark* were both involved, was still just heading over to Bunny's house as planned. Because it was lunchtime. And Lotte had to eat.

Wanda's dog Teddy greeted them at the front door, wheezing noisily, huffing out little barks. Lotte ignored Dani's exuberant reaction to the little dog, reaching instead for Bunny, who hugged her, then hooked her to her hip exactly as Margot had. "Leave it open, Wanda's on her way with potato salad. We're ordering sandwiches."

Dani obeyed, followed Bunny to the kitchen, where the little round table had been cleared of debris. The small square TV was on, mumbling something about Cape Cod being overrun with seals, images of them in thick, layered pods, oozing over hot rocks, flippers placed suggestively over their flaccid lengths. It was no wonder that pirates, blind drunk, desperate and delirious, used to mistake them for mermaids. Dani wondered if any pirate had tried to have sex with one and, after being mauled violently, complained to his friends about that bitch on the rocks who couldn't take a compliment. The program shifted gears to different aquatic invaders, clams and other gyrating mollusks propagating out of control. Why, Dani wondered, did you basically have to be a genital to survive underwater? She got up and turned the channel to something more wholesome, an infomercial for a blender, just as Wanda knocked on the storm door. "Hello?" The smoke of a just-flicked cigarillo crawling up her face.

"Come in!" shouted Bunny, Lotte still fixed to her; they all met Wanda at the door. Dani unburdened Wanda of her potato salad so she could brace herself against the wall, lift each foot, rip open her Velcro sandals. She knelt immediately into Teddy's face, agitated his gooey cheeks with her hands, kissed his head, the tips of his ears. "I don't like when you're far away," she whispered. And for a split second Dani felt love for her. *You see, Lotte? You see how you're supposed to worship a sweet, stupid thing?*

In the kitchen Wanda immediately flipped the channel back to the lewd sea creatures, protecting Bunny, Dani realized, from the relentless pressure of the infomercial, which roused her royal impulse to fill the house with garbage. She then sat at the table, pulled up the sandwich menu on her phone, and she and Bunny commenced bickering. Bunny wanted egg salad, had been talking about egg salad since the moment Dani had walked in, but Wanda wanted roast beef. And being as they were both women of a certain age, they'd begun to split every meal they ordered.

"Egg *salad*," said Wanda, sitting at the kitchen table, snipping chives into her potato salad. "I can *make* you egg *salad*. I can make you the best egg salad you've ever *had*. Let's get roast beef, Bun, we never eat roast beef."

Dani sat at the table too, eyes watering from Wanda's chives, Lotte straddling her thigh. Dani was breaking a banana into chunks, pressing her thumb into its sticky weave, destroyed immediately, too fine for the heat of her hand. The banana dissolved into sugary sludge. Sludge. Scraped in coils from beneath Renata's blue fingernails, packed with the DNA of whoever had taken her. *If* someone had taken her. But someone *must* have taken her. Had to have taken her. *You don't* know *her, Dani.*

But Margot did. Margot was her sister and business partner and closest confidante. Dani nothing but a groupie. A parasite. One of many parasites now severed from Renata's powerful energy source, wandering loose and desperate, soon to be eradicated by Detective Pete Gracy, a big, sterile fuckhead with an idiot face.

Dani felt as though she might cry. Bunny and Wanda didn't notice, still squabbling over their sandwich. But Lotte didn't notice either. And weren't babies supposed to be intuitive about these things? About other people's pain? But no, they weren't, were they. You had to teach them about empathy. Nothing more than animals that can learn. Had Dani ever really learned empathy? Could someone like her ever really teach it to someone else? An aimless mother, a sociopathic father. Lotte was fucked. She probably wouldn't end up a serial killer—women don't really do that—but whatever women become instead of murderers. Horrors they inflict on the world that no one even knows about. Because women are always flying under the radar: their bodies and minds unstudied. Mysteries. *I am petals unfurling, I am huge, I am opening wide as a cave, exactly as I should, for my baby to spill out painlessly.* Their gender an implicitly trustworthy disguise. She remembered lying in bed at night as a child, thinking about what she'd do if she was ever lost, ever in trouble. She would find a woman. Any woman. A woman will help you. A woman cares.

"Dani!" From the tone of her voice Dani guessed that Bunny had already said her name a few times. Lotte too had grown impatient, reaching both arms out toward the bowl of chunked banana.

"Sorry," said Dani. "What?" She brought the bowl closer to Lotte.

"Can *you* get the egg salad?" Bunny begged. "Please? I just, I just want a little bite. I just want to *try* it."

"Yeah, sure," said Dani, watching Lotte fill her cheeks with banana chunks.

"What a waste," Wanda muttered, and with a single index finger she carefully pressed their selections into her phone.


Lotte ate a good lunch. She tried a bit of roast beef, some egg salad, a whole pear. Nothing gave Dani a deeper sense of calm than knowing Lotte's body was pruning nutrients from a well-rounded meal. Bunny had, of course, preferred Dani's egg salad to her roast beef, so Dani offered to trade. Wanda tried a bite of the egg salad too. "It's good," she confessed, "but not as good as mine." And though Dani and Bunny exchanged a look, they also had to admit that Wanda's potato salad was absolutely delicious. Simple but decadent, and full of flavor. Maybe the best potato salad that Dani had ever had. Wanda accepted the compliment with a knowing nod, unsurprised. As though the recipe were an enchantment, spun into her spirit by the devil himself.

Dani had planned this visit strategically, of course, Lotte's nap serving as their nonnegotiable exit. They said their goodbyes, and Lotte, already drowsy in the car, went down even easier than usual. Dani sat at the dining room table and pieced together the telephone number Clark had scribbled out for Margot from the blurry, frenzied pictures on her phone.

Two brittle rings, then the nasal drone of a bored receptionist announced that Dani had reached the Metcalf East End Medical Center. Dani apologized and hung up.

Wrong number perhaps. Dani double-checked her pictures. Or maybe not a telephone number at all. Possibly the offer he'd made on The Temple? But no one would pay that much for The Temple, would they? Or maybe they would. What did Dani know? *Incapable of functioning in the straight world.*

A serial number maybe. But to what? And what exactly *was* a serial number? Dani typed into her search bar: *What is a serial number?*

*A number showing the position of an item in a series. Especially relevant to paper currency or manufactured articles, for the purposes of identification.*

She chewed her bottom lip. Maybe she should show the number to Brandon. He was smart. An engineer. He would know about serial numbers. But also he might be the one who hurt Renata, his sights set on Dani next. Plus, Margot would be *so* annoyed with her if she roped him back in. Dani should have just *asked* Margot about the number. That's what Anya would have done. Anya would have positioned herself as the wronged party: *Why the fuck do you have this file from my husband's office? Why the fuck is he writing down numbers for you? Where the fuck did you get that espresso machine?* She would have put Margot on the defensive, and Margot would have felt obliged to spill— Clark made an offer on The Temple, the espresso machine a little peace offering. Renata told him and his stupid espresso machine to fuck off. Margot, though, she knew, tried to *explain* to Renata what Clark had already figured out: that they were broke; that they were operating in a murky legal swamp that was about to be drained at any second; that, essentially, they didn't have a *choice*. And neither did Clark—the hot young developer whose *life depended* on Metcalf's economic transformation. *The town is really changing, Dani.*

Would Clark, could he—a bad person, sometimes a very bad person—could he have taken matters into his own hands? Disposed of the woman who stood in the way of his success? No. Of course not. Clark wasn't a murderer. He was annoying. He was selfish. He was entitled. He was tragically disconnected from the crucial feminine, like all men, cut off from his vulnerability, an automaton of untapped rage. Like all men. All men. But not *all* men were capable of murder, were they?

Or *were they*.

Perhaps that was the point, had always been the point, of destroying their crucial feminine—all men *should*, at the very least, be *capable* of murder, just in case. Warriors, all of them, at their core. Always the potential to be called to the battlefield. And what was the battlefield now? She pictured Clark the way he was last night, pursing his lips at the rim of a hot tea, poring over files. His *work*. Work was his battlefield. And deep down Dani knew that he would kill for it. For them. His silly little dependents.

*It's always the husband.*

# 28

CLARK PHONED to say he'd be stuck at work for a while. He was frustrated, dealing with pushback from city officials on his plans for the Edward Greene Memorial Splash Pad. Wasn't that a bit grim, the city officials had wondered? For the kids? Splash pads aren't generally memorialized. And, no offense, but was Eddie even *from* here? They suggested a bench instead, right near the splash pad. Free of charge. A nice bench for Eddie, who, they also had to point out, though Clark could tell it pained them to speak so indelicately, wasn't actually *dead* yet.

After Lotte had been fed and put down for the night, Dani poured herself a comically sized glass of wine, sat down at the dining room table, and prepared herself to phone Brandon. Possibly a murderer, but also possibly the only person she could trust.

He drew a quick breath when he heard her voice, which somehow seemed to pull directly from Dani's lungs. She bit her lips together, tamping the smile from her voice, and he relaxed into the practiced modulation of someone who spends a good deal of time on the phone. Not once did he speak at the same time as she did, or interrupt, and the soft silences between subjects never developed awkward edges, instead morphing naturally to whatever the next topic might be.

Dani told him what she'd discovered, when she looked up the detective, seasoning the tale with self-deprecating jabs about watching too many detective shows, about being paranoid, about how she wasn't the type of person to uncover grand conspiracies. "But grand conspiracies *do* happen, don't they? They're not *never* true. Police murder people all the time." *And so do husbands.*

Brandon had thought he wanted to be a cop once. He'd joined the army in the hopes of transitioning to the force one day. Or becoming a firefighter, maybe. He just wanted to *help* people, or so he thought. Renata had made him understand that what he really craved was brotherhood; she seduced memories to the surface, his father making him competitive, cagey around other men. He cried in her arms, for the loss of his boyhood friends, the ones he'd pushed away all the way back in first grade.

Then they talked about their mothers: Bunny, the tragic villain; Brandon's mother, detached, unavailable, terrified of making him soft. "They always mean well, don't they?" Brandon laughed, not expecting a response. Then he said: "Can I confess something to you?"

"Of course." *I am your healer*, thought Dani. "You can tell me anything."

"Even though, even though I'm worried about her, and obviously I hope she's okay, a part of me is glad Renata is gone."

Dani's stomach wobbled on its perch; she clutched her gut. *Stay away from him, Dani.*

"Why's that?"

"Because now it means that I can have you."

"Yes," she whispered, and could almost hear the smile curl into his lovely face. Did *you do it, Brandon? Are you the one who hurt her? You really do need the healing, don't you, you're a very pained creature.* But no. That's not what her *intuition* was telling her. Not Brandon. The husband. *It's always the husband.*

Then Dani heard the click of the front door unlocking, opening. Clark's smell. His sounds. Shoes worked off, the clunk of his bag on the floor. Startled, she elbowed her glass of wine, toppling it over, spilling across Clark's papers. "Fuck!" she hissed.

"Is everything okay?" Brandon asked.

"I've got to go. I'll text you." She hung up, bashed a wad of paper towels from the roll. Clark came in and found her pressing them uselessly into the mess, displacing the sea of red wine over the edge of the table. "I'm sorry, I'm sorry, I'm so, so, so, so, so sorry."

"Da-*ni*, no!" He rushed over, lifted his papers, dripping, over to the kitchen sink.

"I said I was sorry, Clark, I'm sorry, okay? I'll help you rinse them off, it's just a few that really got it."

"Why were you even at the table," he asked, running water into more paper towels, wiping his documents down against the counter. As though the table were some sort of altar, reserved only for his biblically important work.

"I was doing some *home*-work," she said. She felt like a child. She *sounded* like a child. And the two of them cleaned the mess together in silence. Dani on her hands and knees, wiping wine that had dripped over the sides of the table to the floor, and Clark fretting over his *documents*. A word for *important papers*. Which could have very easily just been thrown in the garbage and reprinted, in Dani's opinion. But she didn't say anything. Just cleaned quietly. He might be a murderer, after all.

# 29

DANI STOOD ON THE CORNER where Barton Street met the Pleasant Stay Inn parking lot, watching The Temple from across the road. Someone, Margot perhaps, had strung more bulbs over the patio. Too many, thought Dani. The glittering, *gaudy* excess of raindrops on a spider web. Her opinion, unpopular with the Normal Women, was that Mother Nature could actually be a bit *much*. Anya, Ellen, and Dawn hadn't been able to fathom why she'd been so relieved to be unceremoniously sliced open, so happy to avoid the great *spectacle* of childbirth. She imagined herself in conversation with them now, saying the things she really thought instead of pretending as though she too had been disappointed to have her vagina spared: *I'm sorry, but the other way, it's just, it's a bit dramatic, isn't it?*

The new lights did provide a nice view of the patio's nighttime bustle, though. For the religious protesters as well, who'd doubled since the last time Dani was there. A menacing density to them now, the agitated particles of an airborne toxin. One woman peeled back the packaging from a granola bar, ate it in sticky gobs that she worked off with her fingers. Another woman walked celery sticks up from a small plastic bag, chewed them eternally, miserably. Dani thought she might have seen the detective's wife, but it was hard to tell, everyone all in white, faces scrubbed, hair tied back. Dani was always unnerved by how similar people looked when stripped of their purchasables. Jacqueline Gracy. Almost lost to us. Suicide by English ivy. She felt a tap on her shoulder. Finally. Spun around quickly, hoping the smell of her freshly washed hair would waft into Brandon's face.

Anya. Sucking cream from her top lip, the sweet, fragrant steam of her coffee filling the air between them.

"Um, *hi*," she said, both eyebrows raised. She wore a pair of gray camo leggings, a white T-shirt that fell stylishly off her shoulders, a neon green belt bag. "You thinking of joining or something?"

"What? I—how—" Dani swallowed a nugget of air that sat uncomfortably in her chest until she burped—"Sorry"—and realized that Anya meant the religious protesters, not The Temple.

"Jesus, relax, would you? You want some?" She offered Dani her cup. "It's decaf."

Dani took it and, with her lips perched at the edge of the rim, asked what it was.

"An affogato."

Dani's eyes widened; she took a sip. "Wow." Another sip. "Pretty fucking good, actually."

"I know, right? Bill's at karate with the boys. I thought I might come out and get one of these things. Ellen literally doesn't shut up about them." Anya nodded at the cup Dani was still holding. She took a third drink before handing it back. "Why do you look so nice?"

Dani didn't know what to say. She opened her mouth, then closed it again. Brandon would be arriving any minute. *No more lies.* "I'm . . . I'm meeting someone."

"You're *what*?" Anya dropped her head forward, jaw practically dislodged.

"Not like *that*."

"Yeah fucking right. How long have I known you, Dani. You're wearing mascara, for fuck's sake."

Dani scanned frantically behind her, the patio, the street, dreading the sight of him. "No, Anya, I'm not—"

"Listen, I don't want to cockblock you, but I do need to know everything, I—" Dani's phone buzzed; they locked eyes just before Dani pulled it out of her bag.

*I just talked to Margot. Why didn't you tell me???*

She could imagine her face, illuminated by the phone, warped with confusion.

"What is it?" asked Anya.

Dani wasn't able to respond, couldn't take her eyes off the text.

*Tell you what?*

"Dani, what is it?" Anya pressed.

*Ah fuck, do you not know yet? I'm a fucking idiot. Forget I said anything. I'll see you in a few weeks, all right? Raincheck!*

*Brandon, what the fuck are you talking about? You're not coming?*

Reply bubbles animated, then stopped. Animated, then stopped. And she realized he wouldn't be responding.

"*Fuck* him," Anya said, ducking between Dani and her phone. "I'm free for the night. You've obviously got some kind of excuse going with Clark. Let's hang out."

Dani looked up from her phone. "A few weeks." Her eyes tracked nothing, her mind a blank. "What the fuck is he talking about?" Where was he going for two weeks?

Where was *she* going?

"What's a few weeks?"

"What?"

"You said 'a few weeks,' what's a few weeks?"

"Oh, he's, apparently he's going away for a few weeks."

"Right now?"

"Unexpectedly, yes."

"All right, put this away then." She grabbed Dani's phone, shoved it into her bag. "Let's go drink."

"No, Anya." She pulled it back out. "This is . . . I'm not . . . all right, remember I was telling you about a woman who went missing here?"

"Yeah." Anya reached for Dani's wrist, led her gently from the trajectory of a gaggle of buzzed hotties. "You asked if we'd heard about it."

"Right. Well, she was my friend."

"The prostitute?"

"She wasn't really a prostitute."

"Didn't you say that she was a prostitute?"

"Well, I guess she was, technically. Sort of. In that she exchanged sex for money, but not like what you're thinking."

"I mean—okay, I'll leave that for now. How did you know her?"

"We just . . ." Dani pressed the heels of her palms into both of her eyes and rubbed till something came to her. "We just got to talking one day, after a yoga class."

"See, now, this is what I mean, if you wore mascara more often, you'd know not to rub your eyes like that." Anya removed Dani's hands from her eye sockets, rubbed the flecks of mascara away with both her thumbs. "So who's the guy then who stood you up?"

"Just another friend. We were going to, I don't know, it's stupid, we were going to try to ask around about her, try to piece together her last day."

"Like, have you tried cardio? It's also a good way to pass the time."

"Shut up, Anya, I'm fucking bummed, all right? She was my friend and no one seems to give a shit that she's gone. Not even the police."

"Well, I'll help you," said Anya, taking up both of Dani's hands in one of hers. "I'll help you find her." Dani was startled by this tenderness from Anya. This generosity. Just as she opened her mouth to thank her, she spotted Margot bending into her sleek silver car parked in an hourglass of shadow between streetlights at the edge of the Pleasant Stay Inn lot. Her hair combed back into a smooth bun. She wore a tight skirt. A fitted blazer. The straps of her black heels brutalized with silver studs.

"Margot," she hissed, pulling Anya toward the van. "I've got to follow her. Come on."

Anya followed without question, hopped in, buckled up. She sniffed twice. "Have you been *smoking* in here?" She popped the glove compartment in the hope it would launch a pack into her lap. "Damn," she said.

"My friend," said Dani. "She smoked."

"Dani, have you considered the possibility that your new friend was perhaps a bad influence?"

Dani shot her a withering look and started the car.

It was harder to tail Margot than Dani thought it would be, keeping enough distance without losing her, especially after she turned east off Barton, onto Queen, one of Metcalf's main thoroughfares, busy, with lots of lights and people turning off and merging on. Every imaginable fast-food establishment appeared on Queen Street. Every different grocery store too. There were two libraries. The new community center. The gross Y. The good Y. They passed through the Polish village, where Dani's father had bought their stew beef and shish kebabs and a stick of pepperoni for Dani to munch on the drive home. They passed through the Italian neighborhood too, with the hourly pool halls and the fancy restaurants tucked in tight together, where DJ and Bunny would go on dates some Friday nights, toward the end especially, when DJ was trying to make things right again, for Dani's sake, she knew. And Dani couldn't wait for the leftovers they'd bring home—finally some food in the house! Oily clamshell containers reeking of garlic. Secretly, guiltily pleased that there was no sister she'd have to share with.

The homes grew and shrank like sound waves as they moved across town. And Dani explained, in dramatic detail, who Margot was: Renata's sister and business partner, completely unconcerned with her sister's whereabouts and in cahoots, it would seem, with a cop tasked with ridding Barton Street of sex workers. And Clark was involved too somehow.

*"Clark?"*

"When I went to her . . . office, I saw a folder from Urban Visions there, with a number written in Clark's handwriting."

Anya screamed and pretended to faint. "He was trying to buy them, obviously. But Christ, Dani, that doesn't mean they *killed* her. This is Clark we're talking about here. And her *sister*, for god's sake. She was broke, right? Maybe they just convinced her to step aside. Maybe she's bummed about it. Or pissed at her sister. Maybe she needed to get away for a bit. Does she have kids? People who don't have kids can do that, escape their lives for a while if they need to. The lucky fucks."

"But vanished? Into thin air? Without saying anything to anyone?"

"Well, without saying anything to *you*. Or this other friend. Seems like the sister isn't worried. Probably she's talked to the sister."

Dani shrugged. It wasn't such an illogical theory. Precisely the theory she'd come to at first too. Difficult to swallow, of course, because it meant admitting that she and Renata weren't close after all. That Dani might just have been another client. A mark. Turned out by an especially diabolical pimp. *A woman will help you. A woman cares.* Easier, better, more comforting to Dani to imagine that she'd died. Death the only thing that would keep Renata away from her. "I guess," said Dani. "Probably."

An abrupt stretch of industrial desolation silenced them both—crumbling factories, plastic bags caught by curls of barbed wire topping the tallest fences either of them had ever seen. An abandoned construction site. "I've read about this," said Anya. "Very scandalous. There was a cover-up, some developer doctored the environmental report and broke ground on these condos, sold half the units, but the soil is still super toxic. The old paint factory, remember? Just imagine if they'd finished. Imagine if *kids* had moved in."

Dani shook her head. "Metcalf might finally get its own signature birth defect," she said.

Anya bit her lip, wagged crossed fingers next to her head. "Maybe next year."

"It's hard to adjust, isn't it?" said Dani. "To Metcalf not being a shithole anymore."

"Oh god, not you too."

And they chuckled themselves back to comfortable silence.

Drove eastward, eastward, eastward. Deep into the eastest east end, until finally Margot turned off of Queen Street, into a residential neighborhood where all the houses had flattened into bungalows. Sprawling yards protected by noisy doodles. At a stop sign a group of jabbering teenagers passed on bikes, spikes of laughter, gliding and darting around each other like water bugs. A man on a ladder drilled a large star over his garage door and waved at them. Dani mentioned she thought it was an odd chore to do at night, and Anya said she'd read something about outdoor star decor being a signal to swingers. Dani raised her eyebrows, wrinkled her chin, and nodded in awe of the secret worlds that bloomed beyond her scope.

Margot turned another corner, slowed down, arriving, it would seem, at her destination. Anya fanned her hands excitedly. Dani shushed her, turned the wheel, hand over shaking hand, into the parking lot of a large medical center.

The same medical center Dani had phoned a few nights ago. The number written in Clark's handwriting on that paper in Margot's office. Not a serial number, not an offer, but a phone number after all. Clark had sent Margot to this medical center. But why?

"Jesus, Anya, this is the number, in Clark's handwriting, it was the phone number to this place."

Then it struck Dani with almost slapstick force. Comical. An abortion. Margot was pregnant with Clark's baby and he'd sent her here to have an abortion. They weren't in business together. He'd been using The Temple, hit it off with Margot. They'd have so much in common, wouldn't they? Two people who knew how to use the word *fiscal*. Who showered regularly. Who had laptops. Just a regular, run-of-the-mill affair. Like DJ had done to Bunny. The normal problems of Normal Women. And the espresso machine, a gift for his mistress. Renata had found out, felt guilty, didn't know how to look Dani in the eyes anymore. Dani held a deep breath in her lungs, the last breath she'd taken before realizing that life as she knew it was over. The last breath, a treasure from her former life that she would hold on to till she asphyxiated. If only she'd known, if only she'd *known*, that Clark's enduring, unshakable, excruciating love had actually been everything to her. If only she'd known that she would rather die than live without it. This might as well be colon cancer. She couldn't stay with him after this. But she couldn't leave him either. Poor. Worthless. Unemployable. The only person in the world who knew about her gift and could help her turn it into a career had vanished without a trace. Most likely dead. And now Clark would know, it'd be right out in the open, that he could do anything he wanted to her. That she was, literally, his slave.

Her lungs began to burn, eyes tingling. She closed them and finally exhaled the precious breath. She opened her eyes again. Margot had turned off her car and pulled down her mirror. She reapplied a dark brown lipstick, cutting into the edges with her thumbs. She rubbed her middle fingers beneath her eyes an almost ritualistic number of times. Then she stepped out carefully, hobbled by her tight skirt, and looked around. Was she embarrassed? Was she scared? Dani went from wanting to kill Margot to very suddenly wanting to hug her. Lay her hand low on her belly, where Lotte's sibling was forming, and tell her that it was okay; that she wasn't angry; that they could be sisters now. Renata and Haley gone. She could share Clark. She could. A healer now, in her heart, if not in practice. A better person. The pleasant clouds of false consciousness rolling in, another term from her worthless degree: *The systematic misperception of the dominant social relations that create my oppression. But I am not*

*being exploited. I merely choose to hold values and beliefs that benefit*
*the ruling class, Clark. Margot can be my sister-wife. It's all good!*

"Awfully late for a doctor's appointment," said Anya, slunk
low in her seat, fiddling her lower lip with her index and middle
finger, eyeballing Margot over her knuckles.

Head tilted, sudden clarity, false consciousness rolling out.
"That's *true*, isn't it," Dani said. It *was* awfully late for a doctor's appointment. And it was a strange way to be dressed for
an invasive medical procedure, wasn't it? The blazer, the Saran
wrap skirt. The lipstick and eye makeup. The slick bun. And why
would she need Clark to tell her where to get an abortion? Surely
she'd know better than he where to go. Dani was surprised by
how silly and paranoid she'd been just a moment ago; disgusted
by how close to the edge of complete subjugation she was at all
times.

"It almost looks like she's dressed for a job interview," Anya
observed, leaned forward, squinting against the dirty windshield.
Her seat belt growled and locked. She released an agitated huff
and unbuckled it, leaned further forward. "Wow, she's quite
beautiful isn't she."

"Yes," said Dani. "And she's smart as hell too."

Anya pulled out her phone and searched the medical center's
directory. She handed it to Dani. "Anything ring a bell?" she
asked.

Dani scrolled through. A podiatrist, a naturopath, a dermatologist. There was an X-ray clinic, several psychiatrists, a phys-
iotherapist, and a few GPs. A pharmacy on the ground floor.
Dani realized she'd actually been here before, an X-ray in middle
school when she'd fallen down the metal fire escape that ran along
the side of the household hazardous waste depot. And another
time too, when her family doctor had recommended a specialist

take a look at an unusual mole on her left shoulder—*the mark of the beast*, her mother had joked, and because Dani had been a teenager, subconsciously plagued by guilt over the murder of her own twin in utero, she'd taken the remark very badly. Bunny apologized. The doctor decided to remove her mole, and Dani, fascinated by her first real *wound*, took impeccable care of the tender warp of stitches, no small feat in their filthy home. She wished the doctor could have known what she'd been up against, so hungry she'd been for his approval, so terrified by the possibility of his disappointment if she failed to properly heal. All summer she obsessed over the fragile injury in readiness for her final follow-up appointment in the fall. Anya had been away since early June, as usual. Her family had a cabin on one of the big lakes up north. She had another set of friends up there. A whole other life. Apparently she'd even almost tried anal with that freak Eric, an oily, long-armed pothead who kept lizards and loved *The Crow.* When she returned at the end of August, hair lightened, skin baked brown and peeling, Dani would sniff at her the way a mother bunny sniffs one of her babies—suspicious, aloof, unsure whether to eat her or love her again.

Anya was Dani's only friend, and they both knew it. Dani had been too alienated by the facts of her birth: her father's position in the town, the strange way she was raised, a twin sister snatched straight from her heart. It was no wonder Dani assumed she was destined for something bigger, that there should be some *purpose* to her primal loneliness.

Dani shook her head. "Nothing," she said. "I went here a couple times as a kid, but that's it. You know anything about this place?"

"Sorry, hon," said Anya. "I don't think I've even been to this part of town before."

"Except for that swinger party."

"Yes, except that." Anya, distracted, glanced at the time on her phone. Dani knew she'd be antsy to get home. Karate ended half an hour ago, and she liked to put the boys to bed. She hadn't said anything, of course, because she was a good friend.

For all her terrible, unforgivable qualities, she really was, at the very least, a good, good friend. A whole village, Dani realized then, in the cozy dark of the parked van, in one Normal Woman. Anya had given Dani a community. She'd given her swaddling blankets and baby clothes and unsolicited but helpful advice. She was generous with her food and wine and skin creams and healthcare providers. What more could Dani even need?

Dani reached over and squeezed Anya's arm. "Thanks for coming," she said, then turned the ignition and headed back across town.

## 30

THE NEXT MORNING Dani watched Clark cut up a cantaloupe. Its juices spilled over the edges and beneath the cutting board. The thatch-hacked plastic slipped side to side as he applied pressure to the rind.

"Clark, this is the most stressful thing I've ever witnessed in my life," said Dani from the dining room table. Lotte was opening and closing her hand, an appendage recently transformed by the jam she'd squeezed out of the hollows of her toast—sticky now, creases grimed in red. Opening and closing. Different speeds, flexions, and extensions. At least she would be adequately distracted when Clark lopped his finger off. "Clark, seriously, the juice is all under the cutting board, it keeps slipping."

He nodded without listening, sucked juice from his thumb, and continued his treacherous project. Dani slivered her eyes. Could this idiot have actually murdered someone?

She let her mouth fill with the questions she couldn't ask yet:

*Clark, you idiot, did you murder Renata?*

*How do you know Margot?*

*Why did you send Margot to the Metcalf East End Medical Center?*

*Why did you give her that goddamn espresso machine?*

Because he would lie to her. As he often did. Little lies. For her own good. To ease her into what he knew was best for her, his silly little dependent. It would actually be worse for him to tell her the truth now. *Yes, I killed Renata. Yes, I'm being healed. By Margot. Her only client. And I sent her to the Metcalf East End Medical Center because we're going to have a baby together and what are you gonna do about it?* And what *would* she do about it? Leave him? Find a shit job, rent a sad basement apartment, where Lotte would stay every other week, both their lungs beleaguered by subterranean spores? Of course not. She would obviously stay with him. Because she had no other choice. Become a sister-wife to Margot; an accomplice to his crimes. Which she already was in a way, choosing not to pay attention to the fact that he destroyed communities for a living, tore families apart, squeezed money out of real people's pockets to drop into the bottomless bucket of his company's wealth. It's not as though she'd been perfectly honest with him either, of course. Human resources management. The Temple. *Brandon.* But what *choice* did she have? Freedom costs money. Just look at what Clark could do without consequence.

Abruptly Dani stood up. Lotte and Clark looked at her. It took her a moment to formulate an excuse. "Oh." A few forgetful taps against her forehead. "Shoot, I just remembered, I've got to run to Anya's."

"Now?" With the knife he slid cantaloupe chunks from the cutting board into a bowl.

"I won't be long. She has something for me. For Lotte, actually. I told her I'd come by this morning to get it."

Clark nudged Dani away from the chair she'd been sitting in, the bowl of cantaloupe in his hands. He sat down in front of Lotte and poked a finger into her sticky palm. "Aren't you just disgusting," he said, and Lotte smiled, opened and closed her magnificently filthy hand for him, in his face. He opened his mouth and cheered her on.

Dani darted from the dining room, up the stairs, hastily assembled an outfit, and shouted a goodbye halfway out the door, striding, just short of a run, toward nowhere in particular. She plugged her headphones into her ears, readied the medical center's directory on her phone, then dialed the first number.

The same nasal voice, the same bored tone. It gave Dani the sense that the receptionist hadn't moved since the last time Dani called, that she sat in the same position all day and all night, moving nothing but her lips against the foam of an ancient headset, a single manicured finger tapping along the directory speed dial. "Metcalf East End Medical Center, how can I direct your call?"

"Hello, can I be directed to Dr. Ivan Sionov, please?"

"Just a moment."

A quick and crunchy bar of classical music, followed by another woman's voice. "Good morning, you've reached Dr. Sionov's office."

"Oh, hi! This is Margot Dean, *D-E-A-N*, I'm just calling because I actually have to cancel my upcoming appointment."

"All right, let's see . . . Dean, Dean, Dean, hmm, when was your appointment? We don't seem to have you in our system. Are you sure you've got the right office?"

Dani quickly hung up and called back. She didn't bother to

change her voice for the receptionist. The woman would either not notice or not care that the same person was calling back.

*Hi, can I be directed to Dr. Nanson, please?*

*Hello, you've reached Dr. Nanson's office.*

*Yes, this is Margot Dean, I've got to cancel my upcoming appointment.*

*Can you spell that please?*

*Dean, D-E-A-N.*

*Hmm, Dean. Sorry, we don't have you down for any appointments. Would you like to book something now?*

*Hi, can I be directed to Dr. Rathod, please?*

*Dr. McLeod please.*

*Dr. Lev?*

*Dr. Beaune?*

*Dr. Olajide?*

*Dr. Marcon?*

*Yes, Dean, D as in* dragon, E *as in* Eisenhower, A *as in* apple, N *as in* napalm.

*I'm sorry, Miss Dean.*

*Sorry, Miss Dean, I don't seem to have you in our system.*

*Can you—would it be listed under a different name perhaps? Margot?*

*Still nothing. Sorry.*

*Sorry, Miss Dean.*

*Hi, can I be directed to Dr. Sven Hart please?*

"Hello, you've reached Dr. Sven Hart, how can I help you?"

"Oh, hello." Dani was taken aback to be speaking to the doctor right away and not another receptionist. "Are you, did you say this *is* Dr. Sven Hart?"

"Yes, how can I help you?"

"Hi, Dr. Hart, it's Margot Dean calling, I—"

"Margot, hello! I didn't recognize your voice. I'm so glad you've called. I was going to send over some of the documents you requested last night, but I realized I don't have your email address. I can send to Clark, of course, and he can send along to you, but I'd rather have a dialogue going between all three of us, if that makes sense, I—"

Dani hung up on him. A shock reflex. She stared at her phone, focused on the reflection bouncing off the dark screen: wide sky, quivering leaves, slashed by telephone wire. A shiver crawled up her spine, across her shoulders. Should she scream? No. She opened the directory again. Dr. Sven Hart, PhD. Psychologist.

Why the fuck would Clark have this man's number? Why the fuck would this man need to be *in dialogue* with Clark and Margot?

*Documents.*

Important papers.

Clark had wanted Renata's property. She knew that for a fact. He'd told her that himself. Circled The Temple on his little map, *just another business owner who might be open to an offer.* All of them warriors. All of them capable of murder, if need be. And Margot, a successful MBA, a woman with a laptop in her bag, tired of watching Renata bury herself in debt, fighting for a *cause* that could never possibly catch on, not in this world, where it was certainly illegal, already under scrutiny, protested by men and women in white, the police mobilizing right this second to shut her down. And here comes Clark with the answer to all their problems, an offer that Margot wanted but Renata rejected. The cops were happy to have Renata out of the way, a sex trafficker in their mind, holding back the community; happy to have Clark and Margot tag-teaming exciting new developments. The Nicolas Project. *The economic revitalization of Barton Street.* Clark a part of it. Always a part of it. Passive sociopath. *Our bread and butter!* Dani winced, clutched a whorl of nausea low in her gut. But who was this *doctor*? What did he have to do with anything? She needed some water. She needed to sit down. She looked up, almost at the edge of Corkton, close to Anya's house. Her village.

Dani forgot that there would be meddlers in her village this morning. Anya had mentioned it last night, invited her over. Dawn sat with Vic at her feet, sleeping in his car seat, cool beneath the shade of a gauzy muslin. Ellen and all three of her mesh monsters, screaming with Anya's children, terrorizing an enormous play set, swinging from thick knotted rope, crawling up the slide, one of them bashing sticks to smithereens against a metal ladder.

Anya was just setting a tray of soda waters and snack-size rice cakes on the table between the three of them when Dani poked her head over the fence. "Hey!" said Anya, surprised but happy to see her. Dawn and Ellen waved from their chairs. Dawn in the oversized hat and sunglasses of a celebrity. She'd taken her sandals off, tucked her recently pedicured feet beneath her chair.

Ellen, who'd just emptied a handful of mini rice cakes into her mouth, waved animatedly, apologizing with her hands for her full mouth. Feet crossed at the ankles beneath a long linen sundress.

Anya, in unflattering but trendy bubble shorts and a loose gray tank top dappled in sweat, groaned into an Adirondack chair. "Come in." She gestured with a rice cake. "Don't forget to latch the gate."

Dani did as she was told, pulled up a chair, and sat. She smiled at Ellen and Dawn before grabbing a handful of rice cakes and letting one wilt in her mouth.

Just as Dawn was about to say something, Ellen spotted one of her sons perched like a gargoyle on top of the tube slide. "Merrick!" she screamed, slapping the arm of the chair. "Get down from there!" And he quickly crawled inside the tube, slid to the bottom, emerged flushed and full of static. Ellen held scowling eye contact with him until he slinked, chastened, somewhere beneath the structure.

"Sorry, Dawn," she said. "You were going to say something?"

"Oh, I was just going to ask Dani how she's doing! I feel like we haven't seen you for a minute."

"I'm okay," said Dani. Dawn's eyes widened. "I mean, I'm good!" she corrected. "I'm good, just, I was out for a walk." She lifted her earphones for proof. Vic squeaked from beneath the muslin, and Dawn's eyes shrank to shards, spearing him with a spell of silence.

"So, Dawn," Dani continued, hushed by Vic's tenuous slumber, "Anya told me about your Rewardfluence application! Congratulations, that's so exciting."

"Oh," said Dawn, looking sideways at Ellen. "I'm not, it's not such a big deal. I barely have an account yet, they just liked the concept."

Ellen shifted in her chair, crossed her legs the other way beneath her linen. "It's fine, Dawn, we can talk about it. It's a good idea."

"The world's first *wife*-fluencer." Anya grinned, arms open toward Dawn. "Right here, in my backyard."

Dawn blushed. "Oh, stop," she said, pulling Vic's muslin tighter over the seat. "It's just—the amount of work we, women, put into a marriage, shouldn't that be documented somewhere? Shouldn't that be made visible? And more importantly, made visible by *us*. By wives. Finally in control of the narrative. Finally getting a *choice* in how we're represented."

"If you can call it that," said Anya.

"What?"

"A choice."

"Oh, right, the whole *did we choose to be wives and mothers or were we coerced by society into roles that are killing us* thing, right?"

"No, I just mean, you're not beholden to *nothing*, Dawn, now that you're part of Rewardfluence. You're going to have to generate money with this page, aren't you? Isn't that the whole point? Your content is going to be guided by the aspirational bullshit that makes people feel like shit and spend money."

"*My* page isn't aspirational," Ellen interjected. "That's not what @mymonkeys is about. My page is *for* normal women, by normal women. I'm certain that's why my application was denied."

"Ellen," said Anya. "You rented an Irish setter."

"Normal women don't have Irish setters?"

"They don't rent them! And they don't straighten the Irish setter's bangs either."

"You don't know what normal women do with their setters," Ellen grumbled.

"Do Irish setters *have* bangs?" Dani hadn't meant to ask this out loud.

Anya rolled her eyes. "I'm just saying, there's nothing wrong with what you two are trying to do, but don't go thinking you're out there doing the lord's work, all right? Like, whatever happened to just doing something for money? What was so bad about that?"

"Anya, this is going to save men's *lives*."

Anya scoffed with such force it shot her eyebrows to the middle of her forehead. "Come again?"

"Women are taught about nutrition. From friends, family, the media. Nutrition is an important part of a healthy lifestyle, and we're groomed early on to incorporate vegetables, fruits, healthy fats into our diets—"

"Yeah, programming disordered eating into our brains nice and early."

"Men, on the other hand, don't get that messaging. They're told that men, *real* men, eat the kind of food that puts you in an early grave. Fatty meats, processed carbohydrates, fast food, and snacks that are high in fat, sodium, and calories. Men aren't getting the breadth of nutrition they *need*. They're not getting exercise. They're drinking too much. They're not going outside or maintaining relationships. They're getting *fatter*, Anya."

"Okay, but technically," Ellen piped in, "being fat isn't actually dangerous. There are a lot of complicated factors to—"

"Oh, Ellen, stop. That's just—that's just wokeness gone *mad*."

"It's *science*, Dawn," said Anya. "And what does Charlie think of all this?"

"He thinks it's *great*. He thinks we're going to change the world."

Dani inhaled rice cake dust, coughed until her eyes watered and plump divining rods throbbed visibly in her neck. Anya hovered in front of her face with a soda water, offering it to her over and over again. "What the hell is the matter with you?" Anya's voice finally broke through.

"Can I, I need some regular water, I'm just going to—"

"Here." Anya took her by the arm and led her through the

sliding door into the kitchen. At the sink she whispered, "What's wrong?"

Dani filled a water glass and chugged it.

Anya looked at her. "What's *wrong*?"

"I think Clark and that woman, Margot, might have murdered Renata."

"Dani, come on."

"Anya, I'm serious. They've got a motive. They're both very . . . *driven*. Renata is dead. I know she is. I just, I feel it in my gut." She clutched her stomach. Warmth. *Glowing.* "She's dead. And they both have too much to gain. Clark wants the building. Margot doesn't want to be cleaning up her sister's messes anymore. It's obvious because it's always obvious. In real life things are simple. In real life you're never *shocked* by the killer, are you? It's the husband. It's always the husband. It's always the—"

"DANI!" Anya erupted. "Enough. You sound insane. You're not a detective, all right? You're not going to call the cops on your fucking husband, based on, what, our little stakeout last night? Give me a break."

"No, not just the stakeout, Anya, come on." Dani averted her eyes. Because Anya would find the real reason even more preposterous. Her *intuition* had guided her to this truth. A gift of her crucial feminine. Renata was dead. Margot and Clark were working together. Hiding something. These were facts. "Clark's not as good as you think he is, sometimes he's—"

"He's what, Dani? He's a human being? He doesn't have to be good or bad. He's the father of your child. You're not going to send him to jail over a missing prostitute, even if he did kill her."

"Anya, *Jesus*."

"Just get it out of your head, all right? He loves you, he supports you. You have a good life, Dani, you're just too spoiled to see it. You want a divorce? Get a divorce. You want a job? Get a fucking job. You want a *vocation*, then go back to school, start volunteering. Don't blow up your life because you don't know how to be satisfied with what everyone else has."

"I'm *not* spoiled."

"Danielle Silver. Not spoiled. *Please.* Dani, spare me, all right? Spare *me*, of all people. I know you. I know what you think. You've always been destined for bigger things, right? You've never been the same as everyone else. But it looks like you are. Exactly like us. And you just can't take it."

"Fuck *you*, Anya, I'm not—you just—you don't fucking understand, it's not *about* that anymore. It's not about *me*. She *meant* something to me."

"Really?" A cruel, sarcastic pout. "She *meant* something to you? Your hooker mommy?"

The air evaporated from Dani's lungs, misting her vision, so it was without really being able to see that she pulled back both arms, connected her palms to Anya's chest, and launched her into the fridge. A box of cereal wobbled and fell over, bouncing off of Anya's head and scattering its contents across the floor. Special K with dehydrated berries. Dani, coursing with adrenaline, with shame, immediately crouched to clean it up, guided the mess back into the box with the side of her hand along the floor, while Anya, bewildered, chest heaving, watched her.

Finally Dani stood up. Handed the box to Anya, who swiped it from her. "Thanks for ruining my whole box of Special K with floor germs, you fucking idiot."

"I—Anya, I'm sorry."

"You need help, Dani. You're not well."

"I know." Dani shook her head, heart pounding in her ears. "And she was going to help me too."

Anya looked confused. Dani didn't know how to explain. She turned around, heaved open the sliding door, Ellen and Dawn sitting up straight at the edge of their chairs, yapping about the commotion. They'd woken Vic, who was poking at his muslin.

"What's going on in there?" Ellen. A hand on her chest.

And Dani didn't know how to explain that either. So she said nothing and left through the gate, making sure to latch it behind her.

She walked slowly at first, hands trembling with the memory of Anya's chest, her skin, how smooth it was, warm beneath the pads of Dani's fingers, yielding to the heels of her palms.

Clark. A bad, bad man.

And her legs gave out, she landed on all fours, concrete biting into her knees, her hands. Clark, a murderer. Lotte's father, a murderer. Lotte at home, alone, with a murderer. She hurled herself up and into a sprint, breath jagged in her chest, screaming with every exhale till she blew through her front door, gasping. Lotte and Clark on the living room rug making ice-cream cones out of her magnetized blocks and pretending to eat them.

"What the hell?" said Clark; he stood up and let his ice cream fall with a crack to the floor. Lotte crawled over and pretended to lick it.

"Sorry, I, I decided to run." Dani slid into a kneel next to Lotte, rubbed her head, her back.

"You decided to *run*?" Clark sat down again.

"Yeah, sorry," she said, breathless.

"Why are you apologizing?"

"I don't know." She held Lotte's face between her finger and thumb till Lotte pulled away and offered her an ice-cream cone instead, which Dani accepted and pretended to eat, dread held painfully in her chest.

"Dani." Clark stepped toward her. "Your knees." She looked down at them, pebbled with sidewalk rubble. Small bits of blood. She rubbed them off, pinched the flecks of dirt from the rug into her cupped hand. And then Clark's phone, on the floor next to the pile of magnetized shapes, lit up. He picked it up. "Ah, shit." He shook his head. "I've got to do a dinner thing tonight."

"Oh, okay," she said, not looking at him.

Clark, still scanning his phone, got up, made his way up the stairs. "I'm going to shower," he hollered from the hallway.

"Sure," she yelled back.

Lotte indicated that she was done with the blocks by climbing up onto the couch and pointing at the television.

"You want your show, honey?" Dani grabbed the remote and Lotte's water, which she drew a long, satisfying pull from before handing it over to her. Lotte gave her a dirty look as she accepted it. Dani turned on the television show, the one with the songs and the poorly rendered computer animation. She sat down next to Lotte and texted Bunny.

*Would you be able to come by tonight and watch Lotte? It shouldn't be very long. And she'll be asleep the whole time.*

Bunny responded within seconds. *I would love to! Can Wanda come?*

Dani pressed the bridge of her nose. *Yeah. Tell her to stay away from our bathrooms.*

*Ha ha ha!*

Then she opened her photo roll and scrolled back to the day Lotte was born. The first picture of her, held by a doctor over Dani's gaping incision. Lotte was bloody, swollen, screaming, still connected by the long, rubbery umbilical cord. When this photo was taken, Dani had still only just heard her. Clark stood up to snap the picture. Dani did this often, gazed at pictures of Lotte as though she weren't sitting right next to her.

The next hundred pictures were all of Lotte: Squished and swaddled in Dani's arms. Dani's eyes full of tears, her lips pressed against Lotte's cheek. Pictures of her in Clark's arms. Lying on a blanket on the hospital bed. Naked in her clear plastic hospital bassinet, a pink label above her head: *Hello, world, I'm a girl!*

## 31

CLARK LEFT THE HOUSE in a white button-down shirt, slim blue shorts, and the same tidy dress sneakers that Brandon had worn the first time she'd met him. She'd tried texting Brandon a few more times since they were supposed to meet up, but he'd never responded, waiting, apparently, based on whatever Margot had told him. *I'll see you in a few weeks.*

From the front window, Dani and Lotte watched Clark duck into a cab; then Dani swung Lotte into the air, once, twice, then carried her to the kitchen. With one arm Dani made cauliflower and cheesy macaroni and apple slices. Lotte ate a few bites, then indicated by opening and closing her fists that she was ready for a bag of her iron-fortified pear puree. Dani tried to force a few more florets past her lips, but Lotte clamped shut, turned her head, opened and closed her fists with more force. *Louder,* somehow. "Oh, fine," Dani sighed. She got up, grabbed the bag, and finished off Lotte's macaroni and cauliflower herself. They had a quiet bath together. Dani spelled Lotte's name with foam letters. Lotte chewed on the *O* and left two tiny teeth marks in it, which delighted Dani. As gently as possible, careful not to disrupt Lotte's little marks, Dani dragged her own teeth against them. They read three books, Dani sang Lotte her special song, and she was asleep almost as soon as she lay down.

Bunny entered the home in a reverent hush—a sleeping baby upstairs, her daughter's trust finally within reach. Wanda followed, burdened, mule-like, with a small wrapped housewarming gift, a backgammon board, half a bottle of wine, and some snacks.

Bunny gave her a hug, a kiss on the cheek, whispered, "Everything will be just fine!" which filled Dani with the urge to shove her right back out the front door. While working her sandals off with her feet, Wanda accidentally dropped the backgammon board, which unlatched and scattered across the floor. Both of their faces contorted with abject horror, Bunny fell to her knees, picking up the coffee-colored counters. Wanda mouthed *I'm sorry I'm sorry I'm sorry* to everyone and everything.

"That's okay, it's fine." Dani on her knees too, walking counters from the floor into her palm. "She sleeps through anything."

The housewarming gift was a candle, accompanied by a story about the woman who made them—Wanda's new neighbor, Joan, who never got her period. She named each candle after a child she might have had. Mason, who Dani held in her hands now, was made of pale yellow beeswax and smelled of cinnamon. Wanda also, finally, gave her the details about her bathroom drama, and yet somehow, as soon as she was done speaking, Dani realized that she once again hadn't absorbed a single word.

She left them settled at the dining room table, each with a full glass of wine, a plate of snacks between them, the backgammon board laid out, pieces assembled. Dani showed Bunny how the monitor worked. Instructed her that if Lotte made any noise at all, to just leave her, for at least ten minutes. If she wasn't down again after ten minutes, Bunny was permitted to check on her, but *not* to lift her from the crib.

"You can rub her back, then leave. Quickly. In and out in under two minutes. That should work. And if it doesn't, you *call me*, do you understand? I won't be mad if you call me, but I'll be furious if you don't, all right?"

Bunny and Wanda nodded like fervent familiars, then whispered "Have fun!" accidentally in unison. They were still chuckling about it, repeating *Have fun! Have fun!* when Dani closed the front door.

On the drive Dani had to tamp down distressing images of Wanda and Bunny lighting her curtains on fire, inviting a serial killer into the house, dancing like fools to the bleat of the carbon monoxide detector.

Dani parked in a spot just across the street from The Temple and shut off the car. She spotted an eddy of cats, three of them, swirling around one another on the corner in front of the building. Stray cats. The last living traces of Barton Street's previous form, soon to be eradicated, she was sure, by newcomers who called animal control and secured their garbage cans and reduced the soft, flat surfaces the cats loved with landscaping. There was a mobile spay-and-neuter clinic she'd read about, targeting low-income neighborhoods, offering free sterilization to prevent overpopulation. These cats would be pulled into a retro silver Airstream trailer, drugged, snipped, and released, until, over time, there were almost none left.

There was another cat, on the patio now. Dani had seen her

once before, scooped and cradled by Serena. At that point, though, Dani hadn't yet met Serena. At that point Serena was just another gorgeous villager, soaring tall, showing uncommon kindness to something feral. Tonight the cat wound mostly unnoticed between bare legs, stopping to dip a paw into a minor puddle forming in the rubble of a cracked patio stone, bringing her soaked pads to her mouth and licking between her toes. Head low between those big gabled shoulder blades. *The vestigial roots of powerful wings.* How different things might be if only she still had them. Wings. Had any species in history had something so precious and useful eradicated from their bodies? It seemed impossible, but proximity to humans could do that to a creature. Proximity to people is dangerous.

Maybe not all people.

Just the *right* people.

Clark had called it *growing pains*, to wring a neighborhood of its *undesirables*.

And Renata hadn't called it anything. But regardless of what her intentions had been, she'd met the evolving market with everything it wanted: the illusion of a cruelty-free product; the promise of authenticity, of enthusiastic consent. The potential for a better world. And in the process she'd displaced Barton Street's original community, wrung them out, just like Clark did. Had they been pushed into another part of town? Or into their homes, negotiating digital marketplaces, rife with the same dreaded *software updates* that had nudged Edie from her long-term position with the glass company. *Whatever happened to just doing something for money?* Anya had asked, and she was right. What was wrong with acknowledging, proudly, that you did your work to collect a paycheck? Why did it have to be equivalent to some moral failure?

The cat brought all four feet together, a quick charge, before bounding off to join the whorl of cats gaining momentum on the sidewalk. Four of them now, possessed by their own mysterious agendas.

Then Clark rounded the corner on foot, blasting the cats in all different directions.

Dani sat up, jaw slack. Shocked. Even though she'd been expecting this. Even though this was the whole reason she'd come tonight, to catch him here, actually *seeing* him here, on Barton Street, *her* Barton Street, at The Temple, *her* Temple, in Metcalf, *her fucking Metcalf*, being *right* about him, a bad, bad man all along, her intuition infallible, it took her breath away. *I figured it out, Clark. I knew it was you.* Clark and Margot, working together, doing whatever it took. He waved at a few of the villagers. Knew them by name. The fucking asshole. Dani's body fizzed with rage, face frozen in a sneer as he ducked casually into The Temple's front door. She got out of the car, darted across the street; a car squealed to a stop, ground into the horn. Dani stifled the urge to roar at the driver.

With her fist wrapped around The Temple's door handle, she took a deep breath, tried to imagine herself as Renata saw her: Gifted. A radical. A person who *believed* in something.

The Temple devoured her as it had that first night, every sense engaged: Murky ponds of red and blue light. Pulsating music. Rumbling conversation.

"Dani!"

A face she recognized, Edie, behind the bar, one lean arm waving in the air. Dani approached her, smiling. "Hi," she said.

"So nice to see you again," said Edie. "Can I get you a drink?"

Dani shook her head. "Actually"—she cleared her throat— "have you seen Clark?"

And Edie nodded, without flinching, not a moment's pause, nothing to suggest that she was or had been asked to hide anything. "Just saw him. He's in the office, I think." Clark was just another regular face around The Temple. Maybe she even knew that he was Dani's husband. That first night, meeting everyone, maybe they'd all known everything and she'd known nothing.

"Thanks, Edie."

But Edie's attention was already diverted, flagged for a beer by a short, bearded man with nostalgic tattoos on his legs, the things he'd loved once when he was still human. Worshipped now. Enshrined in his flesh. A creature with pain.

Dani slipped down the hall toward Margot's office. The door was closed. She couldn't hear anything over the music. She made a fist, considered knocking, but then decided against it. Why should she? Anya certainly wouldn't. With a deep breath, she braced herself for what she might find on the other side of the door and swung it open.

"Dani!" Margot sat stunned at her desk: chin forward, eyes wide. She looked up at Clark, who was stooped over her shoulder, propped on one arm over a spread of glossy catalogues and samples. Paint. Fixtures. Tile. Flooring. He'd just been taking a swig from a water bottle. He wiped a dribble from his chin with the back of his hand.

"Oh, hi!" Dani shouted, heart pounding in her ears. "Is anyone going to tell me what the fuck is going on here, or what?"

"Daniiiiii." Clark was annoyed with her. *Annoyed* with her! He set the water bottle down and stepped around to the front of the desk. "We're nowhere near ready for you yet."

"Ready for me." Heat crawled up her neck, into her cheeks. "Clark, what the fuck is going on here?"

He stopped, looked back at Margot, then at Dani again.

"*Dani*, for god's sake, it's nothing like *that*. We're in business together."

"All right, so you did buy The Temple."

"Yes, sort of. We're in business *together*. The Temple, the Pleasant Stay Inn, the building across the street, this whole dead end here, it's *ours*. Yours too." Dani's face warped with stunned, irritated confusion. "Here." Clark gestured at the couch. "Sit down."

Dani tightened her fists. "No."

"What are you gaining by not sitting down?"

Dani couldn't answer that. Her knee buckled slightly. She hadn't breathed in a while. She inflated herself loudly, dizzily, and sat down.

"First of all, I'm the one who should be mad at you," said Clark, walking toward her.

"At *me*, what did I do?"

"Well, first, I assume you left Lotte with your mother, which you told me you wouldn't do without checking in with me first."

"She's fine, Clark, she's sound asleep. Plus, Wanda's there."

"Oh, great, well, if Lotte gets heartworm, we know she'll be okay."

Dani didn't laugh.

"Second, and this is a big one, you've been lying to me. For months. You were never taking HR classes, you were thinking about working at The Temple without telling me."

"I—" There was no excuse for this. She looked down into her lap. "Yes, that's true. That's a bad one. I was going to tell you. Eventually. But then—"

"But then Renata disappeared."

She looked up at him quickly, trying to catch the flash of guilt in his face, or whatever it was that might alter the expression of a murderer uttering his victim's name.

"Hi, hon." Dani spun at the sound of Renata's voice. She stood in the doorway in a crisp button-up shirtdress, blue suede ankle boots, scuffed, with a wide buckle. Chains hidden beneath her collar. Hair tucked up in a flattering mess at her crown.

Dani's heart overheated; steam shot through her arms and legs. She stood up. Dizzy. Sat down again. Clark stepped aside and made room for Renata to sit down next to Dani. Dani shook her head, then launched at her, a long, tight squeeze, whispering, halted by tears, into Renata's hair, "I was so worried about you."

"I know." Renata rubbed her back. "I'm sorry."

"Where did you go?"

Renata sat back, held both of Dani's hands. "Nowhere, really."

"*Why* did you go? Why didn't you answer me?"

"Well . . ." Renata shifted uneasily, looked at Margot. "Here." She squeezed Dani's hand, used the other to summon Margot toward the couch. "Why don't you let these two explain first, okay?"

Margot stood up, led by a glossy trifold in an outstretched hand. Dani took it, cautiously, a deep breath with her eyes closed before looking down at it.

Soft neutral colors, an italicized quote floating by on the front:

> *There is no greater cure for the woes of the mind than the pleasures of the body.*
>
> —DR. SVEN HART, RENOWNED PSYCHOLOGIST,
> SEXOLOGIST, AND AUTHOR OF THE INSTANT
> BESTSELLER *The Pleasure Index*

"The doctor," Dani whispered.

"You've heard of him?" asked Renata.

"Not exactly. I found his number here in the office and phoned."

"Ahh." Margot wagged a finger. "I wondered about that. He called me back. I had no idea what he was talking about." She and Clark laughed, a casual chuckle between colleagues. As though Dani weren't sitting here with her skull cracked open, viscous fluids leaking warm over her face, into her lap, where she held a bizarre, excessively glossy trifold, sitting next to a woman she'd presumed dead. Not just dead. Murdered.

"Sven is one of our key experts," said Clark. "This is all, I just, we really had a great presentation planned, it would have made this much less conf—"

"Your *key experts*?"

"Just open the pamphlet," said Renata. "It's really very good."

Margot lowered her head appreciatively.

Dani opened the pamphlet. A sweeping mock-up of a massive spa. The same faceless ciphers who lived at The Ellison were here wearing robes, dipping in and out of warm pools, some lying on their backs, some up on all fours, worked on by different ciphers, stretched and slender as Martians, wearing white coats. There were shelves of faceless product. Classrooms with vague charts, whiteboards. Plants in corners. On desks. In picture frames. Canopies of healing greenery.

"*The Danielle Silver Wellness Center,*" Dani read.

"The *revolutionary* Danielle Silver Wellness Center," said Clark.

"Groundbreaking," Margot added. "Innovative. Miraculous."

"*Radical,*" whispered Renata.

And then Margot spoke, arms and legs in motion, making a stage of the room: "Renata had this great idea, right? She really did. Her philosophy about speaking to people in their own language, as she put it, her gift for harnessing the chemicals in a person's own brain, controlling dopamine through sexual stimulation, these things work. They really work. What she's come up with, it was, it *is*, a miracle. But what good is a miracle, buried from sight in Metcalf, you know what I mean? What good is a miracle until it's scaled?"

"That's when I came in," Clark picked up. "I was just interested in the building at first. It's a great location—didn't I tell you Barton Street would surprise you?" He grinned. Dani trapped her fists beneath her thighs. "But then Margot explained to me what they did here. She showed me the numbers. This philosophy Renata invented, this method. It's real science. There are doctors who've conducted actual peer-reviewed research about how orgasms can retrain the brain, in essence *fix* the brain, relieve trauma, heal pain. It's a kind of magic, Dani. An actual real live cure-all. Dr. Sven Hart, he's a hugely respected PhD. And there are others too, psychiatrists, neuroscientists, chemists, who are helping us to successfully make the case for legitimate sexual healing, with real practitioners who we certify ourselves, under the most rigorous standards, right here at the center. You can see it there on the pamphlet, see? The classroom there, do you see it?"

"But what about—isn't this, I mean, technically sex work is still illegal, is it not?"

"Technically, yes, unfortunately." Margot again. "Though we're protected by our designation as a religious organization for now. And local government, the police, they're our biggest supporters. Which is what a truly transformational idea *needs*, right? I mean, if Renata had continued on the way she was, without any real money or meaningful support, The Temple would have been shut down. With a difficult precedent standing in the way of us trying to re-create it."

"Things are only illegal until the *right* people want to change it," said Clark. The *right* people. The *right* people are hard to find.

"You mean the rich people," said Dani.

Clark shrugged.

"You're not—are you part of the Nicolas Project?"

"Well, not me personally. Urban Visions had a hand in its development, though. Donated quite a bit of money for the privilege, let me tell you. The revitalization of Barton Street, right? What do you think a massive, revolutionary wellness center like this, a wellness district, an attraction, filled with real practitioners of a science-backed cure, will do for the town? These newcomers, all the eco-yuppies working for the Silver Waste Management Campus, trying to fix climate change, fix the world, fix themselves, you think they won't be interested in a product like this? It's like that doctor, Dani, from Brazil, his healing, it brought the whole area back to life, and that's what we're going to do too. Doing good and doing *good*."

Dani looked at Margot, who averted her eyes. Then at Renata, who was already staring at her.

"Renata. This isn't what you want. You told me that my gifts *defy* monetization. That they're absolutely pure."

"They do—they *are*. But that's because I just couldn't see, I don't have the—the skill set that these two have. You can be gentle about these things. Compassionate. Dani, what Margot and Clark have put together here, it's more than I could have ever accomplished on my own. This is it. This is our chance to fix the whole world. We couldn't, at the rate we were going, working on a small group of men in Metcalf, we weren't going anywhere. We were spinning our wheels. Liable to get shut down before we could even really get going. Dani, this, this is *major*."

There was some truth to this, of course. Without the support of the government, the police, The Temple wasn't long for this world. And what good was it then, to anyone? Why shouldn't

Renata have this chance to grow her magic, distribute it to the world? "Will it be the same, though? This way?" Dani passed her the glossy trifold.

Renata took it, held it horizontally with both hands against her lap. "Yes, Dani. Because *we'll* still be there. Right at the top. Me, Margot. And you. Front and center. The face of the Danielle Silver Wellness Center. Its namesake."

Dani shook her head. "But why me? Honestly now. Don't lie."

"Dani," Renata said solemnly, her dark dove eyes vibrating with sincerity. "I meant everything I said to you. You *are* special. A born healer. I wouldn't even consider taking this, this delicate thing we've built here, and trying to bring it to the masses, without the power of your crucial feminine right there beside me. Our guiding light."

"Dani, you're the daughter of a legend. Of the man who *built* this town." Margot stepped closer, knelt in front of them. "Ushering it into the next phase of its development." Her eyes wide. Hopeful. "With you at the helm, we believe we have a good shot at being accepted by the town, by the various religious organizations giving us a hard time right now. People trust you, Dani. They trusted your dad. And for good reason. He was a great, *great* man. And you, you're a great, great woman. This is your chance to realize that, Dani, this is your chance to be who you were meant to be. Your birthright."

Clark leaned in close now too, grabbed her other hand. "This is it, Dani." He tucked a lock of hair behind her other ear. "*This* is what you were meant to do."

The Princess of Trash, finally returned. Revitalizing the town, exactly like her father had. And Clark, just her husband, fixing splash pads, sure, erecting his little condo buildings, but Dani, she was changing the *world*.

Except Renata had abandoned her. *You don't know her, Dani.* And she didn't. Not really. "No," said Dani. "Something's not right here. Why did you just leave, Renata, why didn't you *talk* to me?"

Renata's lips tightened, tucked into her cheek. She turned to Margot and Clark.

"We didn't exactly see eye to eye at first," Clark piped in.

Margot threw her head back. "Ha! That's an understatement. Dani, I told you already, we got in a fight. About this. Renata always disappears when she's upset."

"I needed some time," said Renata. "Just some space to process all of *this*." She lifted the pamphlet, blew a noisy sigh through loose lips. "It's a lot."

Dani took her hand, held it over her heart, breathed the way Renata had shown her, in and out, deeply. "*Why* are you doing this?"

Renata looked down into her lap, concealing her dove eyes, then glanced back up at Margot, who gave a nervous little shrug and returned to her desk, almost protecting herself with it. Wringing her fingers, biting her lip.

Renata turned back to Dani. "All right, I do believe that this is a good idea. I know it seems, in some ways, antithetical to the cause, but it's not. Not really. Frankly it's the only way for us to keep going. It's also just, this *is* how you impact the world. Going bigger. Becoming more accessible. It's not a good world, right?" She laughed nervously, cleared her throat. "But you're right to smell a rat, Dani. *No more lies.* Margot isn't my sister."

Dani turned to look at Margot, a stranger now. Both lips, trapped by her teeth, made a thin line beneath wide, anxious eyes.

"She's my daughter."

Dani began to stammer.

"We don't really talk about it much because she wasn't raised that way. By me, as my daughter. She was raised as my sister. I was only sixteen. But Dani, I owe her this. I *want* to give her this chance, to take, to take my *business*, and grow it the way she wants to. An inheritance, I guess. And it really *is* a great idea. It really is going to change so many people's lives this way." She held Dani's hand. "Please. Join us, Dani."

In Renata's dark, dove eyes, Dani had seen her true self. Her true self born in that inky black, reflected back at her. She saw her there again now.

*Hello, world, I'm a girl!*

The face of a new frontier. For Metcalf. For humanity. A cure. The cure. For the plague of toxic masculinity. The root of all known evil.

And Renata smiled, reading her mind, wrapping Dani up in her arms. "Yes," she said. "Yes, yes, yes. Welcome home, honey."

## 32

IN THE MORNING Dani woke up wanting to bite Lotte. Wanting to press her face against Lotte's delicious skin. Lotte's ear sealed against Dani's chest, her heartbeat, her deep breaths. Smelling Lotte. Kissing every part of Lotte. Rotating her wrists, her fingers, her legs, and her toes. Cleaning her constantly. Slathering her in lotion. How Dani would let Lotte scratch her and slap her, pull her hair and bite. Getting to know Lotte so well this way first. They had spoken to one another through their skin, stimulating the same chemicals listed in Clark's pamphlet—oxytocin; dopamine, *the motivation chemical*, according to Dr. Sven Hart:

> Dopamine levels signal how good a certain situation is, as it pertains to the value of its reward. If we can control, through strategic sexual stimulation, dopamine, for example, and the group of neural structures responsible for the brain's reward system, we

can create the same motivation for peace, health, happiness that a person has for food, sex, water. If executed correctly, under the careful supervision of properly trained and certified professionals, this could cure—cure—depression, addiction, PTSD. The positive outcomes would be immeasurable, unparalleled. *Miraculous.*

Just from the touch of Dani's hand.

The secret language of skin.

Anya, dermatology enthusiast that she was, had told Dani all about the different kinds of skin when she was pitching her calendula-oil diaper cream treatment. There was hairy skin, which covers most of the human body, even when hair isn't present. And *glabrous* skin, of the palms and lips, innervated by special nerves that help us comprehend subtle tactile details. Dani ran her fingertips along her cheeks. That calendula diaper cream Anya gave her was also a miracle. Miracles do happen. They happen right here on earth. She picked up her phone, thumb hovering over Anya's name. Her whole village in one Normal Woman. She opened their text thread. *I miss you*, she wrote. And hit send.

Since that night at The Temple, Clark had been engaging Dani in one long, barely broken conversation about the wellness center—services and pricing and the certification processes—over dinner, before bed, as they tidied up together during Lotte's nap. Speaking with her as though she were a colleague, no longer his employee.

"And what about the work, Clark, you're actually fine if I get *certified*?" Whispering—Lotte had just gone down for her nap—as she gently placed plastic blocks in a bag.

Clark cleared crayons and paper from the couch. "If you *want* to be doing it, then, honestly yes. It's actually kind of a turn-on."

Dani's mouth bent skeptically. "Oh, it is not."

"It is, I swear, I don't know why. Maybe it's the idea of everyone wanting you." He sat down on the freshly cleared couch and reached for her, pulled her toward him.

"No." She sat down next to him. "You're more disgusting than that."

"What do you mean?"

"If I'm having sex with other men, then physiologically, you're going to want to compete with their sperm. It's evolutionary, you wanting this, it's beyond your control. You're an animal."

Clark laughed, "Yeah, maybe, sure."

"Also, you think it's going to make you a lot of money. And that's what really gets you hot."

Clark pried open her legs. "Yes." He brought them to either side of his body. "It's definitely that too."

"Because you're fucked, Clark."

He smiled. "But aren't you fucked too?"

And then Dani's brain de-emulsified. Another layer of false consciousness separated from the rest, the one that had obscured her aimless and unimpressive professional history, her almost pathological fear of authority, money, power, which allowed her to be lulled, led, easily, to subjugation—the keeper of Clark's house; the extractor of Clark's seed, for disposal and procreation; the mother of Clark's child. His slave. She could feel it dissolving. A *resource* now. The sole proprietor of Clark's most coveted resource. She *was* the Princess of Trash. Daughter of the legend who built this town. The key to Clark's biggest payday yet. He was speaking to her like a colleague, but actually, technically, she was now his boss.

An overwhelming smile seized her face. Which made Clark smile. He kissed her knee. Her thigh. Activated an unexpected charge between her legs: their contract dissolving, warm particles trickling over her body. Enthusiastic consent. The truth of her body.

Her phone buzzed. She disentangled herself from Clark. "I have to check this," she said. *Please be Anya, please be Anya.*

Anya: *You can come tonight. Bring wine.*

She pressed the phone to her chest. Somehow the smile grew even bigger. *Yay! I'll be there after I put Lotte down.*

And then back to the couch. To Clark. Where she performed for the primitive the task of womankind.

Anya opened the door in an enormous kaftan she'd ordered with a promo code from a reality TV star. An amount of fabric that wasn't *worn* so much as *haunted* by a human body. "Don't," said Anya. "Don't even." Dani took in all the colors, the long, irregular train that wrought havoc along the floor behind her, catching on a stray nail head in the hardwood, overturning one of Bill's boots. "I know."

"How much?"

"I can't talk about that." Anya snatched the bottle of cold white wine by the neck and turned around. Dani followed her, shut the door behind them. Anya put the bottle on the kitchen counter. Shook her arm free of a sleeve before digging around in a drawer for the bottle opener and handing it to Dani.

"It's quiet," Dani remarked as she drilled the opener into the cork, elbow up, gritting her teeth.

"Everyone's in the basement watching *The Karate Kid*."

"That's nice."

"Should we sit on the back porch?" She clanked two wine-glasses from the cupboard, set them on the counter. "Oh, I've got a box of clothes for you too, don't let me forget. And a belly binder, for the diastasis recti." Anya reached for the wine bottle, then snatched the gaping maw of her kaftan sleeve from being soaked by its dew.

"Thank you, Anya," said Dani.

Anya clasped the crossed stems in one hand, the wine bottle in the other, and led the way to the back porch. Dani followed, careful to avoid the kaftan's fussy train. Anya set their glasses on a small wooden table, hoofprints of dried red muddying its surface, twelve months of sloppily filled glasses. Twelve months of teetering home after brunch.

Dani sat down, brought a watermelon pillow into her lap. Anya needed a minute to adjust her idiotic parachute, mumbling, irritated.

"At least you look really cool," said Dani.

Anya laughed, sipped her wine. "Fuck off."

"Anya," said Dani, rubbing her thumb against the pillow's pink zipper, "I am so, so sorry about what I did. I'm so sorry for pushing you, that was, that was completely crazy and out of line, and I'm just really sorry."

"I know. I'm sorry too. I wasn't being sensitive at all. I just, I was trying to help, I guess, by being blunt, but I was an asshole. I'm always an asshole, I don't realize half the time. Or I do actually, but I don't care. Which is a big part of what makes me an asshole."

Dani reached over the table, squeezed Anya's hand, then lifted her wineglass for a toast.

"To the last twelve months," said Dani. "Here in Metcalf, being a mom with you."

Anya smiled, clinked her glass against Dani's, and they both sipped, followed up with loud, satisfied exhales. "It's good. It's good. It'sgood, it'sgood, it'sgood. Tsssgood, tsssgood," hissed Anya. "Tsssssgooooooooooood. Goooooooooood. Good, good, good, good, good, cood, cood, cood, cood, cood, coot, coot, coot, coot, coot, coot, coot . . ." Anya whispered sibilant appreciation for the wine until her words came undone, and Dani chimed in too, more sizzle than speech, "Coooooooooot, coot, coot, coot, coot, coot, coot . . ." repeating it together until everything unraveled into laughter.

"Anya, I have to ask you something," said Dani.

Anya, leaning back, using her kaftan to blot a tear from her eye. "Hmmm?"

"Well, I have to tell you something, and then I have to ask you something."

Anya sat up, looked at her seriously. "Okay, shoot."

Dani started with the colon cancer, which felt like a lifetime ago. How it had twisted her inside out: visions of cleaning Lotte's hair in a bus station bathroom, of watching her open acceptance letters to schools Dani couldn't afford to send her to, her future incinerating before Dani's very eyes. And then how the idea of prostitution had *calmed* her, and not just the irrational anxiety triggered by the colon cancer, but calmed her deeply, in a way she hadn't felt since Lotte was first born. Her calling, finally realized. A balm. Cool. Soothing. The whole world finally making *sense*. That's how she'd ended up on Barton Street in the first place, just to check it out, really, "I didn't even know what I was doing." But then Renata spotted her. She'd made her feel so sane. And capable. "It was like I finally saw who it was I was meant to be, in her eyes. Like she was a mirror reflecting who I *really am*. I've always felt different, Anya, you know that. And with Renata it was like, I just felt completely normal. So I was going to do it, I was going to work there."

"Oh, Dani," Anya sighed. "I have to confess something to you too."

"What?"

"That night I saw you on Barton Street, I wasn't just out for a decaf affogato."

Dani sat up, staring at her. Anya's head bobbed in a pond of fabric, her gaze aimed at her wineglass, which she spun between her thumb and forefinger. Then she looked up at Dani with big, worried eyes. "Bill and I, we were leaving The Temple."

"You *weren't*."

Anya sipped her wine. "We were just grabbing some ice cream to bring home for the boys when I saw you. I was so curious, I told Bill I'd just meet him at home."

"So you know about it. You know about the healing."

"It's really been helping me. Since the boys, I'm just so, I've lost touch with myself. And our healer, Diane, maybe you've met her? She's been helping me with that. She said that mostly my sexual dysfunction is in my head. I mean, it's definitely in my crotch too. I've got to do those fucking Kegels more. But mostly it's my head. And she's right."

"Anya, that's wonderful, honestly. I'm so happy for you that you're doing that, and that it's working. You know, I thought there was something different about you, I really did, you just seem so much more, I don't know, *calm*. Happy. The Temple. Of course. Of *course* that's where Bill takes his fucking yoga classes."

"*Ob*-viously," she laughed, then cleared her throat, batted at an invisible ambush of insects. "But I'd never met Margot. Or your friend. Did you find her?"

Dani nodded. She explained about the wellness center, about what they wanted her to do.

"And so the thing you want to ask me is if I think you should do it?"

"Yes," said Dani.

"Well, I think you should."

"But Anya, it's sex work. Very public sex work. It's going to be a battle. With the whole town. And we might not win it."

"Sex work? Please. Not when the marketing department is done with it. And Dani, as we've already established, I'm the biggest asshole *in* this town. And I think The Temple is a goddamn miracle."

"I'm going to be in *commercials*, Anya. On the website. Doing interviews. They want to call it the Danielle Silver Wellness Center, for Christ's sake. My face will be all over this thing. And Lotte's going to have to live with this too. What if we fail? What if we embarrass her? What if she hates us?"

"You're not going to fail. And I think she'll find it hard to hate being filthy fucking rich. That's yet another thing the two of you will do better than DJ and Bunny. Listen, none of that even matters, all right? Do you *want* to do it?"

Dani nodded. "Yes," she whispered. "More than anything."

"Then that's your answer." Anya punctuated this by flinging the arm of her kaftan, then leaned back in her chair with her wineglass set in her fingertips like a crystal ball. "There will be times, maybe, that it'll be hard for Lotte. There's no getting around that. But one day she'll realize just how special it is to have a mother who followed her dreams. *Self-care isn't just for you, mama, it's for the little people watching too.* That's from Warren Buffe—*Ellen's* Instagram, god help me, but it's true. Imagine how different things would have been for you, Christ, for *her*, if

Bunny'd had some independence." She pressed her glass against her bottom lip and stared out into the yard. A warm wind passed. The swing set creaked gently. The kaftan fluttered at the hem like a pinned moth. "I don't know, Dani. The world is changing. It seems to me sometimes that people have gotten tired of being hypocrites."

"That's an awfully positive thing to say."

Anya blinked. Looked at her. "Well, that's Diane for you. She's a miracle worker."

"I'll bet she is." Dani smiled.

Anya leaned forward and set down her wine, which for her was a gesture that commanded attention. "Dani, what if this is it? What if this is the thing you've been waiting for? Because this thing, honestly, it's going to be huge. This thing, I'm telling you, it's going to change the world."

Dani grinned, lowered her chin. "What's wrong with just doing something for money?"

Anya smiled. Winked. The winking type. "Good question," she said, and leaned back into her colorful puddle of fabric, took a sip of wine, and closed her eyes. "Good question. Good good good cood cood coot coot coot coot coot . . ."

"Coot, coot, coot, coot, coot, coot, coot, coot, coot, coot."

# 33

DANI, IN HAIR AND MAKEUP since six a.m. this morning, resembles an angel. The shimmer along her cheekbones, the dew they've used on her lips. She barely recognizes herself.

She finishes off an affogato. Carves cream from the corners of her mouth. Someone swoops in to dispose of the cup and reapply her gloss. She steps out onto the set. Margot and Clark are chatting with the creative director who insisted, and they'd all agreed, that the website should have video. A lot of *video*.

*People are going to need help visualizing this*, he said. *It's just nothing like anyone has ever seen before. Truly radical.*

A woman dripping with cords, a headset, a backward baseball cap, leads Dani by the shoulders to her mark, grins as she departs, a wad of pink gum crushed between her molars.

Bright lights suck all the energy from the room. Hot in its beams, cold everywhere else.

Dani closes her eyes.

A director barks instruction, and then, with much less ceremony than Dani had been expecting, they start rolling.

Dani opens her eyes.

*Hello. I'm Danielle Silver. If you're seeing this video, then you've made the decision to come to the Danielle Silver Wellness Center. Congratulations. You've just made the best decision of your life.*

## Acknowledgments

Absolutely none of this is possible without my first line of radiant geniuses, who work so hard behind the scenes: Rach Crawford, wise and wonderful agent; Caitlin Landuyt, brilliant and hilarious editor. Thank you so much for continuing to be such a dream to work with.

Thank you to James Roxburgh and Kirsty Doole; to Annie Locke and Mark Abrams; to Jordan Ginsberg, Tonia Addison, and Sam Chater; to Kate Johnson and Hannah Vaughn, for making this book either better and/or shinier.

And eternal thanks, of course, to my shrimps and my fella, for being so darn supportive.

Thank you, thank you, thank you all.

Ainslie Hogarth is the author of *Motherthing*, *The Boy Meets Girl Massacre (Annotated)*, and *The Lonely*. She lives in Canada with her husband, kids, and little dog.

ainsliehogarth.com